Praise for FEAR NOTHING:

'This is a moral fable for the turn of the millennium, an engagingly written, hugely entertaining parable for our times. Just what I expected' *The Times*

'Fast and furious – like a hospital trolley on a toboggan run' *Mail on Sunday*

'Readers will be riveted to the narrative' *Publishers Weekly*

'Plausibly chilling . . . Koontz at his best' *Express on Sunday*

'Scary. Koontz can really spook, and his dialogue and pacing rival the best' *New York Post*

'The sheer terror of [Koontz's] other books leaves readers afraid to turn out the lights. This book does, too, but for different reasons. Its gentle humor, spirit of camaraderie and conversational first-person tone heighten the fear of what our future could hold' *Associated Press*

'An adrenaline-pumping new adventure. FEAR NOTHING demonstrates a master of darkness's continuing power to scare the daylights out of us' *People*

Praise for Dean Koontz:

'Tumbling, hallucinogenic prose . . . "Serious" writers might do well to examine his technique' *New York Times*

'Koontz has bridged the commercial gap between the occultism of Stephen King and the scientism of Michael Crichton' *Publishers Weekly*

'Masterfully styled, serious entertainment. These are Koontz's great years' *Kirkus Reviews*

'Koontz keeps up a breakneck pace, and provides spectacular set-pieces' *Locus*

Also by Dean Koontz from Headline

Fear Nothing

Dean Koontz

headline

First published in Great Britain in 1997 by
HEADLINE BOOK PUBLISHING

First published in paperback in 1998
by HEADLINE BOOK PUBLISHING

This edition published in paperback in 2005 by
HEADLINE BOOK PUBLISHING

18

ISBN 978 0 7472 5832 2

Typeset by Palimpsest Book Production Limited,
Polmont, Stirlingshire

Printed and bound in the UK by
CPI Group (UK) Ltd, Croydon, CR0 4YY

Headline's policy is to use papers that are natural,
renewable and recyclable products and made from wood grown
in sustainable forests. The logging and manufacturing
processes are expected to conform to the environmental
regulations of the country of origin.

HEADLINE BOOK PUBLISHING
A division of Hodder Headline
338 Euston Road
London NW1 3BH

www.headline.co.uk
www.hodderheadline.com

To Robert Gottlieb
for whose vision, genius, dedication,
and friendship I am daily grateful.

We have a weight to carry
and a distance we must go.
We have a weight to carry,
a destination we can't know.
We have a weight to carry
and can put it down nowhere.
We *are* the weight we carry
from there to here to there.

—*The Book of Counted Sorrows*

One

TWILIGHT TIME

1

On the desk in my candlelit study, the telephone rang, and I knew that a terrible change was coming.

I am not psychic. I do not see signs and portents in the sky. To my eye, the lines in my palm reveal nothing about my future, and I don't have a Gypsy's ability to discern the patterns of fate in wet tea leaves.

My father had been dying for days, however, and after spending the previous night at his bedside, blotting the sweat from his brow and listening to his labored breathing, I knew that he couldn't hold on much longer. I dreaded losing him and being, for the first time in my twenty-eight years, alone.

I am an only son, an only child, and my mother passed away two years ago. Her death had been a shock, but at least she had not been forced to endure a lingering illness.

Last night just before dawn, exhausted, I had returned home to sleep. But I had not slept much or well.

Now I leaned forward in my chair and willed the phone to fall silent, but it would not.

The dog also knew what the ringing meant. He padded out of the shadows into the candleglow, and stared sorrowfully at me.

Unlike others of his kind, he will hold any man's

or woman's gaze as long as he is interested. Animals usually stare directly at us only briefly – then look away as though unnerved by something that they see in human eyes. Perhaps Orson sees what other dogs see, and perhaps he, too, is disturbed by it, but he is not intimidated.

He is a strange dog. But he is my dog, my steadfast friend, and I love him.

On the seventh ring, I surrendered to the inevitable and answered the phone.

The caller was a nurse at Mercy Hospital. I spoke to her without looking away from Orson.

My father was quickly fading. The nurse suggested that I come to his bedside without delay.

As I put down the phone, Orson approached my chair and rested his burly black head in my lap. He whimpered softly and nuzzled my hand. He did not wag his tail.

For a moment I was numb, unable to think or act. The silence of the house, as deep as water in an oceanic abyss, was a crushing, immobilizing pressure. Then I phoned Sasha Goodall to ask her to drive me to the hospital.

Usually she slept from noon until eight o'clock. She spun music in the dark, from midnight until six o'clock in the morning, on KBAY, the only radio station in Moonlight Bay. At a few minutes past five on this March evening, she was most likely sleeping, and I regretted the need to wake her.

Like sad-eyed Orson, however, Sasha was my friend, to whom I could always turn. And she was a far better driver than the dog.

She answered on the second ring, with no trace of sleepiness in her voice. Before I could tell her what had happened, she said, 'Chris, I'm so sorry,' as though she had been waiting for this call and as if in the ringing of her phone she had heard the same ominous note that Orson and I had heard in mine.

I bit my lip and refused to consider what was coming. As long as Dad was alive, hope remained that his doctors were wrong. Even at the eleventh hour, the cancer might go into remission.

I believe in the possibility of miracles.

After all, in spite of my condition, I have lived more than twenty-eight years, which is a miracle of sorts – although some other people, seeing my life from outside, might think it a curse.

I believe in the possibility of miracles, but more to the point, I believe in our *need* for them.

'I'll be there in five minutes,' Sasha promised.

At night I could walk to the hospital, but at this hour I would be too much of a spectacle and in too great a danger if I tried to make the trip on foot.

'No,' I said. 'Drive carefully. I'll probably take ten minutes or more to get ready.'

'Love you, Snowman.'

'Love you,' I replied.

I replaced the cap on the pen with which I had been writing when the call had come from the hospital, and I put it aside with the yellow legal-size tablet.

Using a long-handled brass snuffer, I extinguished the three fat candles. Thin, sinuous ghosts of smoke writhed in the shadows.

Now, an hour before twilight, the sun was low in the sky but still dangerous. It glimmered threateningly at the edges of the pleated shades that covered all the windows.

Anticipating my intentions, as usual, Orson was

already out of the room, padding across the upstairs hall.

He is a ninety-pound Labrador mix, as black as a witch's cat. Through the layered shadows of our house, he roams all but invisibly, his presence betrayed only by the thump of his big paws on the area rugs and by the click of his claws on the hardwood floors.

In my bedroom, across the hall from the study, I didn't bother to switch on the dimmer-controlled, frosted-glass ceiling fixture. Even the indirect, sour-yellow light of the westering sun, pressing at the edges of the window shades, was sufficient for me.

My eyes are better adapted to gloom than are those of most people. Although I am, figuratively speaking, a brother to the owl, I don't have a special gift of nocturnal sight, nothing as romantic or as thrilling as a paranormal talent. Simply this: Lifelong habituation to darkness has sharpened my night vision.

Orson leaped onto the footstool and then curled on the armchair to watch me as I girded myself for the sunlit world.

From a pullman drawer in the adjoining bathroom, I withdrew a squeeze bottle of lotion that included a sunscreen with a rating of fifty. I applied it generously to my face, ears, and neck.

The lotion had a faint coconut scent, an aroma that I associate with palm trees in sunshine, tropical skies, ocean vistas spangled with noontime light, and other things that will be forever beyond my experience. This, for me, is the fragrance of desire and denial and hopeless yearning, the succulent perfume of the unattainable.

Sometimes I dream that I am walking on a Caribbean beach in a rain of sunshine, and the white sand under my feet seems to be a cushion of pure radiance. The warmth of the sun on my skin is more erotic than a lover's touch. In the dream, I am not merely bathed in the light but pierced by it. When I wake, I am bereft.

Now the lotion, although smelling of the tropical sun, was cool on my face and neck. I also worked it into my hands and wrists.

The bathroom featured a single window at which the shade was currently raised, but the space remained meagerly illuminated because the glass was frosted and because the incoming sunlight was filtered through the graceful limbs of a metrosideros. The silhouettes of leaves fluttered on the pane.

In the mirror above the sink, my reflection was little more than a shadow. Even if I switched on the light, I would not have had a clear look at myself, because the single bulb in the overhead fixture was of low wattage and had a peach tint.

Only rarely have I seen my face in full light.

Sasha says that I remind her of James Dean, icon of the fifties, more as he was in *East of Eden* than in *Rebel Without a Cause*.

I myself don't perceive the resemblance. The hair is the same, yes, and the pale blue eyes. But he looked so wounded, and I do not see myself that way.

I am not James Dean. I am no one but me, Christopher Snow, and I can live with that.

Finished with the lotion, I returned to the bedroom. Orson raised his head from the armchair to savor the coconut scent.

I was already wearing athletic socks, Nikes, blue jeans, and a black T-shirt. I quickly pulled on a black denim shirt with long sleeves and buttoned it at the neck.

Orson trailed me downstairs to the foyer. Because the porch was deep with a low ceiling, and because two massive California live oaks stood in the yard, no direct sun could reach the sidelights flanking the front door; consequently, they were not covered with curtains or blinds. The leaded panes – geometric mosaics of clear, green, red, and amber glass – glowed softly like jewels.

I took a zippered, black leather jacket from the coat closet. I would be out after dark, and even following a mild March day, the central coast of California can turn chilly when the sun goes down.

From the closet shelf, I snatched a navy-blue, billed cap and pulled it on, tugging it low on my head. Across the front, above the visor, in ruby-red embroidered letters were the words *Mystery Train*.

One night during the previous autumn, I had found the cap in Fort Wyvern, the abandoned military base inland from Moonlight Bay. It had been the only object in a cool, dry, concrete-walled room three stories underground.

Although I had no idea to what the embroidered words might refer, I had kept the cap because it intrigued me.

As I turned toward the front door, Orson whined beseechingly.

I stooped and petted him. 'I'm sure Dad would like to see you one last time, fella. I know he would. But there's no place for you in a hospital.'

His direct, coal-black eyes glimmered. I could have sworn that his gaze brimmed with grief and sympathy. Maybe that was because I was looking at him through repressed tears of my own.

My friend, Bobby Halloway, says that I tend to

anthropomorphize animals, to ascribe human attributes and attitudes to them which they do not, in fact, possess.

Perhaps this is because animals, unlike some people, have always accepted me for what I am. The four-legged citizens of Moonlight Bay seem to possess a more complex understanding of life – as well as more human kindness – than at least some of my neighbors.

Bobby tells me that anthropomorphizing animals, regardless of my experiences with them, is a sign of immaturity. I tell Bobby to go copulate with him-self.

I comforted Orson, stroking his glossy coat and scratching behind his ears. He was curiously tense. Twice he cocked his head to listen intently to sounds that I could not hear – as if he sensed a threat looming, something even worse than the loss of my father.

At that time, I had not yet seen anything suspicious about Dad's impending death. Cancer was only fate, not murder – unless you wanted to try bringing crimi-nal charges against God.

That I had lost both parents within two years, that my mother had died when she was only fifty-two, that my father was only fifty-six as he lay on his deathbed . . . Well, all this just seemed to be my poor luck – which had been with me, literally, since my conception.

Later, I would have reason to recall Orson's tension – and good reason to wonder if he had sensed the tidal wave of trouble washing toward us.

Bobby Halloway would surely sneer at this and say that I am doing worse than anthropomorphizing the mutt, that now I am ascribing *super*human attributes to him. I would have to agree – and then tell Bobby to go copulate *vigorously* with himself.

Anyway, I petted and scratched and generally comforted Orson until a horn sounded in the street and then, almost at once, sounded again in the driveway.

Sasha had arrived.

In spite of the sunscreen on my neck, I turned up the collar of my jacket for additional protection.

From the Stickley-style foyer table under a print of Maxfield Parrish's *Daybreak*, I grabbed a pair of wraparound sunglasses.

With my hand on the hammered-copper doorknob, I turned to Orson once more. 'We'll be all right.'

In fact, I didn't know quite how we could go on without my father. He was our link to the world of light and to the people of the day.

More than that, he loved me as no one left on earth could love me, as only a parent could love a damaged child. He understood me as perhaps no one would ever understand me again.

'We'll be all right,' I repeated.

The dog regarded me solemnly and chuffed once, almost pityingly, as if he knew that I was lying.

I opened the front door, and as I went outside, I put on the wraparound sunglasses. The special lenses were totally UV-proof.

My eyes are my point of greatest vulnerability. I can take no risk whatsoever with them.

Sasha's green Ford Explorer was in the driveway, with the engine running, and she was behind the wheel.

I closed the house door and locked it. Orson had made no attempt to slip out at my heels.

A breeze had sprung up from the west: an onshore flow with the faint, astringent scent of the sea. The leaves of the oaks whispered as if transmitting secrets branch to branch.

My chest grew so tight that my lungs felt constricted, as was always the case when I was required to venture outside in daylight. This symptom was entirely psychological but nonetheless affecting.

Going down the porch steps and along the flagstone walk to the driveway, I felt weighed down. Perhaps this was how a deep-sea diver might feel in a pressure suit with a kingdom of water overhead.

2

When I got into the Explorer, Sasha Goodall said quietly, 'Hey, Snowman.'

'Hey.'

I buckled my safety harness as Sasha shifted into reverse.

From under the bill of my cap, I peered at the house as we backed away from it, wondering how it would appear to me when next I saw it. I felt that when my father left this world, all of the things that had belonged to him would look shabbier and diminished because they would no longer be touched by his spirit.

It is a Craftsman-period structure, in the Greene and Greene tradition: ledger stone set with a minimum of mortar, cedar siding silvered by weather and time, entirely modern in its lines but not in the least artificial or insubstantial, fully of the earth and formidable. After the recent winter rains, the crisp lines of the slate roof were softened by a green coverlet of lichen.

As we reversed into the street, I thought that I saw the shade nudged aside at one of the living-room windows, at the back of the deep porch, and Orson's face at the pane, his paws on the sill.

As she drove away from the house, Sasha said, 'How long since you've been out in this?'

'Daylight? A little over nine years.'

'A novena to the darkness.'

She was also a songwriter.

I said, 'Damn it, Goodall, don't wax poetic on me.'

'What happened nine years ago?'

'Appendicitis.'

'Ah. That time when you almost died.'

'Only death brings me out in daylight.'

She said, 'At least you got a sexy scar from it.'

'You think so?'

'I like to kiss it, don't I?'

'I've wondered about that.'

'Actually, it scares me, that scar,' she said. 'You might have died.'

'Didn't.'

'I kiss it like I'm saying a little prayer of thanks. That you're here with me.'

'Or maybe you're sexually aroused by deformity.'

'Asshole.'

'Your mother never taught you language like that.'

'It was the nuns in parochial school.'

I said, 'You know what I like?'

'We've been together almost two years. Yeah, I think I know what you like.'

'I like that you never cut me any slack.'

'Why should I?' she asked.

'Exactly.'

Even in my armor of cloth and lotion, behind the shades that shielded my sensitive eyes from ultraviolet rays, I was unnerved by the day around and above me. I felt egg-shell fragile in its vise grip.

Sasha was aware of my uneasiness but pretended not to notice. To take my mind off both the threat and the boundless beauty of the sunlit world, she did what she does so well – which is be Sasha.

'Where will you be later?' she asked. 'When it's over.'

'*If* it's over. They could be wrong.'

'Where will you be when I'm on the air?'

'After midnight . . . probably Bobby's place.'

'Make sure he turns on his radio.'

'Are you taking requests on tonight's show?' I asked.

'You don't have to call in. I'll know what you need.'

At the next corner, she swung the Explorer right, onto Ocean Avenue. She drove uphill, away from the sea.

Fronting the shops and restaurants beyond the deep sidewalks, eighty-foot stone pines spread wings of branches across the street. The pavement was feathered with shadow and sunshine.

Moonlight Bay, home to twelve thousand people, rises from the harbor and flatlands into gentle serried hills. In most California travel guides, our town is called *The Jewel of the Central Coast*, partly because the chamber of commerce schemes relentlessly to have this sobriquet widely used.

The town has earned the name, however, for many reasons, not least of all because of our wealth of trees. Majestic oaks with hundred-year crowns. Pines, cedars, phoenix palms. Deep eucalyptus groves. My favorites are the clusters of lacy *Melaleuca luminaria* draped with stoles of ermine blossoms in the spring.

As a result of our relationship, Sasha had applied protective film to the Explorer windows. Nevertheless, the view was shockingly brighter than that to which I was accustomed.

I slid my glasses down my nose and peered over the frames.

The pine needles stitched an elaborate dark embroidery on a wondrous purple-blue, late-afternoon sky bright with mystery, and a reflection of this pattern flickered across the windshield.

I quickly pushed my glasses back in place not merely to protect my eyes but because suddenly I was ashamed for taking such delight in this rare daytime journey even as my father lay dying.

Judiciously speeding, never braking to a full stop at those intersections without traffic, Sasha said, 'I'll go in with you.'

'That's not necessary.'

Sasha's intense dislike of doctors and nurses and all things medical bordered on a phobia. Most of the time she was convinced that she would live forever; she had great faith in the power of vitamins, minerals, antioxidants, positive thinking, and mind-body healing techniques. A visit to any hospital, however, temporarily shook her conviction that she would avoid the fate of all flesh.

'Really,' she said, 'I should be with you. I love your dad.'

Her outer calm was belied by a quiver in her voice, and I was touched by her willingness to go, just for me, where she most loathed to go.

I said, 'I want to be alone with him, this little time we have.'

'Truly?'

'Truly. Listen, I forgot to leave dinner out for Orson. Could you go back to the house and take care of that?'

'Yeah,' she said, relieved to have a task. 'Poor Orson. He and your dad were real buddies.'

'I swear he knows.'

'Sure. Animals know things.'

'Especially Orson.'

From Ocean Avenue, she turned left onto Pacific View. Mercy Hospital was two blocks away.

She said, 'He'll be okay.'

'He doesn't show it much, but he's already grieving in his way.'

'I'll give him lots of hugs and cuddles.'

'Dad was his link to the day.'

'I'll be his link now,' she promised.

'He can't live exclusively in the dark.'

'He's got me, and I'm never going anywhere.'

'Aren't you?' I asked.

'He'll be okay.'

We weren't really talking about the dog anymore.

The hospital is a three-story California Mediterranean structure built in another age when that term did not bring to mind uninspired tract-house architecture and cheap construction. The deeply set windows feature patinaed bronze frames. Ground-floor rooms are shaded by loggias with arches and limestone columns.

Some of the columns are entwined by the woody vines of ancient bougainvillea that blankets the loggia roofs. This day, even with spring a couple of weeks away, cascades of crimson and radiant purple bracts overhung the eaves.

For a daring few seconds, I pulled my sunglasses down my nose and marveled at the sun-splashed celebration of color.

Sasha stopped at a side entrance.

As I freed myself from the safety harness, she put one hand on my arm and squeezed lightly. 'Call my cellular number when you want me to come back.'

'It'll be after sunset by the time I leave. I'll walk.'

'If that's what you want.'

'I do.'

Again I drew the glasses down my nose, this time to see Sasha Goodall as I had never seen her. In candlelight, her gray eyes are deep but clear – as they are here in the day world, too. Her thick mahogany hair, in candlelight, is as lustrous as wine in crystal – but markedly more lustrous under the stroking hand of the sun. Her creamy, rose-petal skin is flecked with faint freckles, the patterns of which I know as well as I know the constellations in every quadrant of the night sky, season by season.

With one finger, Sasha pushed my sunglasses back into place. 'Don't be foolish.'

I'm human. Foolish is what we *are*.

If I were to go blind, however, her face would be a sight to sustain me in the lasting blackness.

I leaned across the console and kissed her.

'You smell like coconut,' she said.

'I try.'

I kissed her again.

'You shouldn't be out in this any longer,' she said firmly.

The sun, half an hour above the sea, was orange and intense, a perpetual thermonuclear holocaust ninety-three million miles removed. In places, the Pacific was molten copper.

'Go, coconut boy. Away with you.'

Shrouded like the Elephant Man, I got out of the Explorer and hurried to the hospital, tucking my hands in the pockets of my leather jacket.

I glanced back once. Sasha was watching. She gave me a thumbs-up sign.

3

When I stepped into the hospital, Angela Ferryman was waiting in the corridor. She was a third-floor nurse on the evening shift, and she had come downstairs to greet me.

Angela was a sweet-tempered, pretty woman in her late forties: painfully thin and curiously pale-eyed, as though her dedication to nursing was so ferocious that, by the harsh terms of a devilish bargain, she must give the very substance of herself to ensure her patients' recoveries. Her wrists seemed too fragile for the work she did, and she moved so lightly and quickly that it was possible to believe that her bones were as hollow as those of birds.

She switched off the overhead fluorescent panels in the corridor ceiling. Then she hugged me.

When I had suffered the illnesses of childhood and adolescence – mumps, flu, chickenpox – but couldn't be safely treated outside our house, Angela had been the visiting nurse who stopped in daily to check on me. Her fierce, bony hugs were as essential to the conduct of her work as were tongue depressors, thermometers, and syringes.

Nevertheless, this hug frightened more than comforted me, and I said, 'Is he?'

'It's all right, Chris. He's still holding on. Holding on just for you, I think.'

I went to the emergency stairs nearby. As the stairwell door eased shut behind me, I was aware of Angela switching on the ground-floor corridor lights once more.

The stairwell was not dangerously well lighted. Even so, I climbed quickly and didn't remove my sunglasses.

At the head of the stairs, in the third-floor corridor, Seth Cleveland was waiting. He is my father's doctor, and one of mine. Although tall, with shoulders that seem round and massive enough to wedge in one of the hospital loggia arches, he manages never to be looming over you. He moves with the grace of a much smaller man, and his voice is that of a gentle fairy-tale bear.

'We're medicating him for pain,' Dr. Cleveland said, turning off the fluorescent panels overhead, 'so he's drifting in and out. But each time he comes around, he asks for you.'

Removing my glasses at last and tucking them in my shirt pocket, I hurried along the wide corridor, past rooms where patients with all manner of maladies, in all stages of illness, either lay insensate or sat before bed trays that held their dinners. Those who saw the corridor lights go off were aware of the reason, and they paused in their eating to stare at me as I passed their open doors.

In Moonlight Bay, I am a reluctant celebrity. Of the twelve thousand full-time residents and the nearly three thousand students at Ashdon College, a private liberal-arts institution that sits on the highest land in town, I am perhaps the only one whose name is known to all. Because of my nocturnal life, however, not every one of my fellow townspeople has seen me.

As I moved along the hall, most of the nurses and nurses' aides spoke my name or reached out to touch me.

I think they felt close to me not because there was anything especially winning about my personality, not because they loved my father – as, indeed, everyone who knew him loved him – but because they were devoted healers and because I was the ultimate object of their heartfelt desire to nurture and make well. I have been in need of healing all of my life, but I am beyond their – or anyone's – power to cure.

My father was in a semiprivate room. At the moment no patient occupied the second bed.

I hesitated on the threshold. Then with a deep breath that did not fortify me, I went inside, closing the door behind me.

The slats of the venetian blinds were tightly shut. At the periphery of each blind, the glossy white window casings glowed orange with the distilled sunlight of the day's last half hour.

On the bed nearest the entrance, my father was a shadowy shape. I heard his shallow breathing. When I spoke, he didn't answer.

He was monitored solely by an electrocardiograph. In order not to disturb him, the audio signal had been silenced; his heartbeat was traced only by a spiking green line of light on a cathode-ray tube.

His pulse was rapid and weak. As I watched, it went through a brief period of arrhythmia, alarming me, before stabilizing again.

In the lower of the two drawers in his nightstand

were a butane lighter and a pair of three-inch-diameter bayberry candles in glass cups. The medical staff pretended to be unaware of the presence of these items.

I put the candles on the nightstand.

Because of my limitations, I am granted this dispensation from hospital rules. Otherwise, I would have to sit in utter darkness.

In violation of fire laws, I thumbed the lighter and touched the flame to one wick. Then to the other.

Perhaps my strange celebrity wins me license also. You cannot overestimate the power of celebrity in modern America.

In the flutter of soothing light, my father's face resolved out of the darkness. His eyes were closed. He was breathing through his open mouth.

At his direction, no heroic efforts were being made to sustain his life. His breathing was not even assisted by an inhalator.

I took off my jacket and the Mystery Train cap, putting them on a chair provided for visitors.

Standing at his bed, on the side most distant from the candles, I took one of his hands in one of mine. His skin was cool, as thin as parchment. Bony hands. His fingernails were yellow, cracked, as they had never been before.

His name was Steven Snow, and he was a great man. He had never won a war, never made a law, never composed a symphony, never written a famous novel as in his youth he had hoped to do, but he was greater than any general, politician, composer, or prize-winning novelist who had ever lived.

He was great because he was kind. He was great because he was humble, gentle, full of laughter. He was married to my mother for thirty years, until her death two years previous to his, and during that long span of temptation, he had remained faithful to her. His love for her had been so luminous that our house, by necessity dimly lighted in most rooms, was bright in all of the ways that mattered. A professor of literature at Ashdon – where Mom had been a professor in the science department – Dad was so beloved by his students that many remained in touch with him decades after leaving his classroom.

Although my affliction had severely circumscribed his life virtually from the day that I was born, when he himself was twenty-eight, he had never once made me feel that he regretted fathering me or that I was anything less than an unmitigated joy and a source of undiluted pride to him. He lived with dignity and without complaint, and he never failed to celebrate what was *right* with the world.

Once he had been robust and handsome. Now his body was shrunken and his face was haggard, gray. He looked much older than his fifty-six years. The cancer had spread from his liver to his lymphatic system, then to other organs, until he was riddled with it. In the struggle to survive, he had lost much of his thick white hair.

On the cardiac monitor, the green line began to spike and trough erratically. I watched it with dread.

Dad's hand closed weakly on mine.

When I looked at him again, his sapphire-blue eyes were open and focused on me, as riveting as ever.

'Water?' I asked, because he was always thirsty lately, parched.

'No, I'm all right,' he replied, although he sounded dry. His voice was barely louder than a whisper.

I could think of nothing to say.

All of my life, our house was filled with conversation. My dad and mom and I talked about novels, old movies, the follies of politicians, poetry, owls and deer mice and raccoons and bats and fiddler crabs and other creatures that shared the night with me, music, history, science, religion, art. Our discourse ranged from serious colloquies about the human condition to frothy gossip about neighbors. In the Snow family, no program of physical exercise, regardless of how strenuous, was considered to be adequate if it didn't include a daily workout of the tongue.

Yet now, when I most desperately needed to open my heart to my father, I was speechless.

He smiled as if he understood my plight and appreciated the irony of it.

Then his smile faded. His drawn and sallow face grew even more gaunt. He was worn so thin, in fact, that when a draft guttered the candle flames, his face appeared to be hardly more substantial than a reflection floating on the surface of a pond.

As the flickery light stabilized, I thought that Dad seemed to be in agony, but when he spoke, his voice revealed sorrow and regret rather than pain: 'I'm sorry, Chris. So damn sorry.'

'You've nothing to be sorry about,' I assured him, wondering if he was lucid or speaking through a haze of fever and drugs.

'Sorry about the inheritance, son.'

'I'll be okay. I can take care of myself.'

'Not money. There'll be enough of that,' he said, his whispery voice fading further. His words slipped from his pale lips almost as silently as the liquid of an egg from a cracked shell. 'The other inheritance . . . from your mother and me. The XP.'

'Dad, no. You couldn't have known.'

His eyes closed again. Words as thin and transparent as raw egg white: 'I'm so sorry . . .'

'You gave me *life*,' I said.

His hand had gone limp in mine.

For an instant I thought that he was dead. My heart fell stone-through-water in my chest.

But the beat traced in green light by the electro-cardiograph showed that he had merely lost consciousness again.

'Dad, you gave me life,' I repeated, distraught that he couldn't hear me.

≈ ≈ ≈

My dad and mom had each unknowingly carried a recessive gene that appears in only one in two hundred thousand people. The odds against two such people meeting, falling in love, and having children are millions to one. Even then, both must pass the gene to their offspring for calamity to strike, and there is only one chance in four that they will do so.

With me, my folks hit the jackpot. I have xeroderma pigmentosum – XP for short – a rare and frequently fatal genetic disorder.

XP victims are acutely vulnerable to cancers of the skin and eyes. Even brief exposure to sun – indeed, to any ultraviolet rays, including those from incandescent and fluorescent lights – could be disastrous for me.

All human beings incur sunlight damage to the DNA – the genetic material – in their cells, inviting melanoma and other malignancies. Healthy people possess a natural repair system: enzymes that strip out the damaged segments of the nucleotide strands and replace them with undamaged DNA.

In those with XP, however, the enzymes don't function; the repair is not made. Ultraviolet-induced cancers develop easily, quickly – and metastasize unchecked.

The United States, with a population exceeding two hundred and seventy million, is home to more than eighty thousand dwarfs. Ninety thousand of our countrymen stand over seven feet tall. Our nation boasts four million millionaires, and ten thousand more will achieve that happy status during the current year. In any twelve months, perhaps a thousand of our citizens will be struck by lightning.

Fewer than a thousand Americans have XP, and fewer than a hundred are born with it each year.

The number is small in part because the affliction is so rare. The size of this XP population is also limited by the fact that many of us do not live long.

Most physicians familiar with xeroderma pigmentosum would have expected me to die in childhood. Few would have bet that I could survive adolescence. None would have risked serious money on the proposition that I would still be thriving at twenty-eight.

A handful of XPers (my word for us) are older than me, a few significantly older, though most if not all of them have suffered progressive neurological problems associated with their disorder. Tremors of the head or the hands. Hearing loss. Slurred speech. Even mental impairment.

Except for my need to guard against the light, I am as normal and whole as anyone. I am not an albino. My eyes have color. My skin is pigmented. Although certainly I am far paler than a California beach boy, I'm not ghost white. In the candlelit rooms and the night world that I inhabit, I can even appear, curiously, to have a dusky complexion.

Every day that I remain in my current condition is a precious gift, and I believe that I use my time as well and as fully as it can be used. I relish life. I find delight where anyone would expect it – but also where few would think to look.

In 23 B.C., the poet Horace said, 'Seize the day, put no trust in the morrow!'

I seize the *night* and ride it as though it were a great black stallion.

Most of my friends say that I am the happiest person they know. Happiness was mine to choose or reject, and I embraced it.

Without my particular parents, however, I might not have been granted this choice. My mother and father radically altered their lives to shield me aggressively from damaging light, and until I was old enough to understand my predicament, they were required to be relentlessly, exhaustingly vigilant. Their selfless diligence contributed incalculably to my survival. Furthermore, they gave me the love – and the love of life – that made it impossible for me to choose depression, despair, and a reclusive existence.

My mother died suddenly. Although I know that she understood the profound depth of my feeling for her, I wish that I had been able to express it to her adequately on that last day of her life.

Sometimes, out in the night, on the dark beach, when the sky is clear and the vault of stars makes me feel simultaneously mortal and invincible, when the wind is still and even the sea is hushed as it breaks upon the shore, I tell my mother what she meant to me. But I don't know that she hears.

Now my father – still with me, if only tenuously – did not hear me when I said, 'You gave me life.' And I was afraid that he would take his leave before I could tell him all the things that I'd been given no last chance to tell my mother.

His hand remained cool and limp. I held it anyway, as if to anchor him to this world until I could say good-bye properly.

≈ ≈ ≈

At the edges of the venetian blinds, the window frames and casings smoldered from orange to fiery red as the sun met the sea.

There is only one circumstance under which I will ever view a sunset directly. If I should develop cancer of the eyes, then before I succumb to it or go blind, I will one late afternoon go down to the sea and stand facing those distant Asian empires where I will never walk. On the brink of dusk, I'll remove my sunglasses and watch the dying of the light.

I'll have to squint. Bright light pains my eyes. Its effect is so total and swift that I can virtually feel the developing burn.

As the blood-red light at the periphery of the blinds deepened to purple, my father's hand tightened on mine.

I looked down, saw that his eyes were open, and tried to tell him all that was in my heart.

'I know,' he whispered.

When I was unable to stop saying what didn't need to be said, Dad found an unexpected reserve of strength and squeezed my hand so hard that I halted in my speech.

Into my shaky silence, he said, 'Remember . . .'

I could barely hear him. I leaned over the bed railing to put my left ear close to his lips.

Faintly, yet projecting a resolve that resonated with anger and defiance, he gave me his final words of guidance: 'Fear nothing, Chris. Fear nothing.'

Then he was gone. The luminous tracery on the electrocardiogram skipped, skipped again, and went flatline.

The only moving lights were the candle flames, dancing on the black wicks.

I could not immediately let go of his slack hand. I kissed his forehead, his rough cheek.

No light any longer leaked past the edges of the blinds. The world had rotated into the darkness that welcomed me.

The door opened. Again, they had extinguished the nearest banks of fluorescent panels, and the only light in the corridor came from other rooms along its length.

Nearly as tall as the doorway, Dr. Cleveland entered the room and came gravely to the foot of the bed.

With sandpiper-quick steps, Angela Ferryman followed him, one sharp-knuckled fist held to her breast. Her shoulders were hunched, her posture defensive, as if her patient's death were a physical blow.

The ECG machine beside the bed was equipped with a telemetry device that sent Dad's heartbeat to a monitor at the nurses' station down the hall. They had known the moment that he slipped away.

They didn't come with syringes full of epinephrine or with a portable defibrillator to shock his heart back into action. As Dad had wanted, there would be no heroic measures.

Dr. Cleveland's features were not designed for solemn occasions. He resembled a beardless Santa Claus with merry eyes and plump rosy cheeks. He strove for a dour expression of grief and sympathy, but he managed only to look puzzled.

His feelings were evident, however, in his soft voice. 'Are you okay, Chris?'

'Hanging in there,' I said.

4

From the hospital room, I telephoned Sandy Kirk at Kirk's Funeral Home, with whom my father himself had made arrangements weeks ago. According to Dad's wishes, he was to be cremated.

Two orderlies, young men with chopped hair and feeble mustaches, arrived to move the body to a cold-holding room in the basement.

They asked if I wanted to wait down there with it until the mortician's van arrived. I said that I didn't.

This was not my father, only his body. My father had gone elsewhere.

I opted not to pull the sheet back for one last look at Dad's sallow face. This wasn't how I wanted to remember him.

The orderlies moved the body onto a gurney. They seemed awkward in the conduct of their business, at which they ought to have been practiced, and they glanced at me surreptitiously while they worked, as if they felt inexplicably guilty about what they were doing.

Maybe those who transport the dead never become entirely easy with their work. How reassuring it would be to believe as much, for such awkwardness might mean that people are not as indifferent to the fate of others as they sometimes seem to be.

More likely, these two were merely curious, sneaking glances at me. I am, after all, the only citizen of Moonlight Bay to have been featured in a major article in *Time* magazine.

And I am the one who lives by night and shrinks from the sight of the sun. Vampire! Ghoul! Filthy whacko pervert! Hide your children!

To be fair, the vast majority of people are understanding and kind. A poisonous minority, however, are rumormongers who believe anything about me that they hear – and who embellish all gossip with the self-righteousness of spectators at a Salem witch trial.

If these two young men were of the latter type, they must have been disappointed to see that I looked remarkably normal. No grave-pale face. No blood-red eyes. No fangs. I wasn't even having a snack of spiders and worms. How boring of me.

The wheels on the gurney creaked as the orderlies departed with the body. Even after the door swung shut, I could hear the receding *squeak-squeak-squeak*.

Alone in the room, by candlelight, I took Dad's overnight bag from the narrow closet. It held only the clothes that he had been wearing when he'd checked into the hospital for the last time.

The top nightstand drawer contained his watch, his wallet, and four paperback books. I put them in the suitcase.

I pocketed the butane lighter but left the candles behind. I never wanted to smell bayberry again. The scent now had intolerable associations for me.

Because I gathered up Dad's few belongings with such efficiency, I felt that I was admirably in control of myself.

In fact, the loss of him had left me numb. Snuffing

the candles by pinching the flames between thumb and forefinger, I didn't feel the heat or smell the charred wicks.

When I stepped into the corridor with the suitcase, a nurse switched off the overhead fluorescents once more. I walked directly to the stairs that I had climbed earlier.

Elevators were of no use to me because their ceiling lights couldn't be turned off independently of their lift mechanisms. During the brief ride down from the third floor, my sunscreen lotion would be sufficient protection; however, I wasn't prepared to risk getting stuck between floors for an extended period.

Without remembering to put on my sunglasses, I quickly descended the dimly lighted concrete stairs – and to my surprise, I didn't stop at the ground floor. Driven by a compulsion that I didn't immediately understand, moving faster than before, the suitcase thumping against my leg, I continued to the basement where they had taken my father.

The numbness in my heart became a chill. Spiraling outward from that icy throb, a series of shudders worked through me.

Abruptly I was overcome by the conviction that I'd relinquished my father's body without fulfilling some solemn duty, although I was not able to think what it was that I ought to have done.

My heart was pounding so hard that I could hear it – like the drumbeat of an approaching funeral cortege but in double time. My throat swelled half shut, and I could swallow my suddenly sour saliva only with effort.

At the bottom of the stairwell was a steel fire door under a red emergency-exit sign. In some confusion, I halted and hesitated with one hand on the push bar.

Then I remembered the obligation that I had almost failed to meet. Ever the romantic, Dad had wanted to be cremated with his favorite photograph of my mother, and he had charged me with making sure that it was sent with him to the mortuary.

The photo was in his wallet. The wallet was in the suitcase that I carried.

Impulsively I pushed open the door and stepped into a basement hallway. The concrete walls were painted glossy white. From silvery parabolic diffusers overhead, torrents of fluorescent light splashed the corridor.

I should have reeled backward across the threshold or, at least, searched for the light switch. Instead, I hurried recklessly forward, letting the heavy door sigh shut behind me, keeping my head down, counting on the sunscreen and my cap visor to protect my face.

I jammed my left hand into a jacket pocket. My right hand was clenched around the handle of the suitcase, exposed.

The amount of light bombarding me during a race along a hundred-foot corridor would not be sufficient, in itself, to trigger a raging skin cancer or tumors of the eyes. I was acutely aware, however, that the damage sustained by the DNA in my skin cells was cumulative because my body could not repair it. A measured minute of exposure each day for two months would have the same catastrophic effect as a one-hour burn sustained in a suicidal session of sun worship.

My parents had impressed upon me, from a young age, that the consequences of a single irresponsible act might appear negligible or even nonexistent but that inevitable horrors would ensue from *habitual* irresponsibility.

Even with my head tucked down and my cap visor

blocking a direct view of the egg-crate fluorescent panels, I had to squint against the glare that ricocheted off the white walls. I should have put on my sunglasses, but I was only seconds from the end of the hallway.

The gray-and-red-marbled vinyl flooring looked like day-old raw meat. A mild dizziness overcame me, inspired by the vileness of the pattern in the tile and by the fearsome glare.

I passed storage and machinery rooms.

The basement appeared to be deserted.

The door at the farther end of the corridor became the door at the nearer end. I stepped into a small subterranean garage.

This was not the public parking lot, which lay above ground. Nearby were only a panel truck with the hospital name on the side and a paramedics' van.

More distant was a black Cadillac hearse from Kirk's Funeral Home. I was relieved that Sandy Kirk had not already collected the body and departed. I still had time to put the photo of my mother between Dad's folded hands.

Parked beside the gleaming hearse was a Ford van similar to the paramedics' vehicle except that it was not fitted with the standard emergency beacons. Both the hearse and the van were facing away from me, just inside the big roll-up door, which was open to the night.

Otherwise, the space was empty, so delivery trucks could pull inside to off-load food, linens, and medical supplies to the freight elevator. At the moment, no deliveries were being made.

The concrete walls were not painted here, and the fluorescent fixtures overhead were fewer and farther apart than in the corridor that I had just left. Nevertheless, this was still not a safe place for me, and I moved quickly toward the hearse and the white van.

The corner of the basement immediately to the left of the roll-up garage door and past those two waiting vehicles was occupied by a room that I knew well. It was the cold-holding chamber where the dead were kept until they could be transported to mortuaries.

One terrible January night two years ago, by candle-light, my father and I had waited miserably in cold-holding more than half an hour with the body of my mother. We could not bear to leave her there alone.

Dad would have followed her from the hospital to the mortuary and into the crematorium furnace that night – if not for his inability to abandon me. A poet and a scientist, but such similar souls.

She had been brought from the scene of the accident by ambulance and rushed from the emergency room to surgery. She died three minutes after reaching the operating table, without regaining consciousness, even before the full extent of her injuries could be determined.

Now the insulated door to the cold-holding chamber stood open, and as I approached it, I heard men arguing inside. In spite of their anger, they kept their voices low; an emotional note of strenuous disagreement was matched by a tone of urgency and secrecy.

Their circumspection rather than their anger brought me to a stop just before I reached the doorway. In spite of the deadly fluorescent light, I stood for a moment in indecision.

From beyond the door came a voice I recognized. Sandy Kirk said, 'So who is this guy I'll be cremating?'

Another man said, 'Nobody. Just a vagrant.'

'You should have brought him to my place, not here,' Sandy complained. 'And what happens when he's missed?'

A third man spoke, and I recognized his voice as that of one of the two orderlies who had collected my father's body from the room upstairs: 'Can we for God's sake just move this along?'

Suddenly certain that it was dangerous to be encumbered, I set the suitcase against the wall, freeing both hands.

A man appeared in the doorway, but he didn't see me because he was backing across the threshold, pulling a gurney.

The hearse was eight feet away. Before I was spotted, I slipped to it, crouching by the rear door through which cadavers were loaded.

Peering around the fender, I could still see the entrance to the cold-holding chamber. The man backing out of that room was a stranger: late twenties, six feet, massively built, with a thick neck and a shaved head. He was wearing work shoes, blue jeans, a red-plaid flannel shirt – and one pearl earring.

After he drew the gurney completely across the threshold, he swung it around toward the hearse, ready to push instead of pull.

On the gurney was a corpse in an opaque, zippered vinyl bag. In the cold-holding chamber two years ago, my mother was transferred into a similar bag before being released to the mortician.

Following the stone-bald stranger into the garage, Sandy Kirk gripped the gurney with one hand. Blocking a wheel with his left foot, he asked again, 'What happens when he's missed?'

The bald man frowned and cocked his head. The

pearl in his ear lobe was luminous. 'I told you, he was a vagrant. Everything he owned is in his backpack.'

'So?'

'He disappears – who's to notice or care?'

Sandy was thirty-two and so good-looking that even his grisly occupation gave no pause to the women who pursued him. Although he was charming and less self-consciously dignified than others in his profession, he made me uneasy. His handsome features seemed to be a mask behind which was not another face but an emptiness – not as though he were a different and less morally motivated man than he pretended to be, but as though he were no man at all.

Sandy said, 'What about his hospital records?'

'He didn't die here,' the bald man said. 'I picked him up earlier, out on the state highway. He was hitchhiking.'

I had never voiced my troubling perception of Sandy Kirk to anyone: not to my parents, not to Bobby Halloway, not to Sasha, not even to Orson. So many thoughtless people have made unkind assumptions about me, based on my appearance and my affinity for the night, that I am reluctant to join the club of cruelty and speak ill of anyone without ample reason.

Sandy's father, Frank, had been a fine and well-liked man, and Sandy had never done anything to indicate that he was less admirable than his dad. Until now.

To the man with the gurney, Sandy said, 'I'm taking a big risk.'

'You're untouchable.'

'I wonder.'

'Wonder on your own time,' said the bald man, and he rolled the gurney over Sandy's blocking foot.

Sandy cursed and scuttled out of the way, and the

man with the gurney came directly toward me. The wheels squeaked – as had the wheels of the gurney on which they had taken away my father.

Still crouching, I slipped around the back of the hearse, between it and the white Ford van. A quick glance revealed that no company or institution name adorned the side of the van.

The squeaking gurney was rapidly drawing nearer.

Instinctively, I knew that I was in considerable jeopardy. I had caught them in some scheme that I didn't understand but that clearly involved illegalities. They would especially want to keep it secret from me, of all people.

I dropped facedown on the floor and slid under the hearse, out of sight and also out of the fluorescent glare, into shadows as cool and smooth as silk. My hiding place was barely spacious enough to accommodate me, and when I hunched my back, it pressed against the drive train.

I was facing the rear of the vehicle. The gurney rolled past the hearse and continued to the van.

When I turned my head to the right, I saw the threshold of the cold-holding chamber only eight feet beyond the Cadillac. I had an even closer view of Sandy's highly polished black shoes and the cuffs of his navy-blue suit pants as he stood looking after the bald man with the gurney.

Behind Sandy, against the wall, was my father's small suitcase. There had been nowhere nearby to conceal it, and if I had kept it with me, I wouldn't have been able to move quickly enough or slip noiselessly under the hearse.

Apparently no one had noticed the suitcase yet. Maybe they would continue to overlook it.

The two orderlies – whom I could identify by their white shoes and white pants – rolled a second gurney out of the holding room. The wheels on this one did not squeak.

The first gurney reached the back of the white van. I heard the bald man open the rear cargo doors on that vehicle.

One of the orderlies said to the other, 'I better get upstairs before someone starts wondering what's taking me so long.' He walked away, toward the far end of the garage.

The collapsible legs on the first gurney folded up with a hard clatter as the bald man shoved it into the back of his van.

Sandy opened the rear door on the hearse as the remaining orderly arrived with the second gurney. On this one, evidently, was another opaque vinyl bag containing the body of the nameless vagrant.

A sense of unreality overcame me – that I should find myself in these strange circumstances. I could almost believe that I had somehow fallen into a dream without first falling into sleep.

The cargo-hold doors on the van slammed shut. Turning my head to the left, I watched the bald man's shoes as he approached the driver's door.

The orderly would wait here to close the big roll-up after the two vehicles departed. If I stayed under the hearse, I would be discovered when Sandy drove away.

I didn't know which of the two orderlies had remained behind, but it didn't matter. I was relatively confident that I could get the better of either of the young men who had wheeled my father away from his deathbed.

If Sandy Kirk glanced at his rear-view mirror as he drove out of the garage, however, he might see me. Then I would have to contend with both him and the orderly.

The engine of the van turned over.

As Sandy and the orderly shoved the gurney into the back of the hearse, I eeled out from under that vehicle. My cap was knocked off. I snatched it up and, without daring to glance toward the rear of the hearse, crabbed eight feet to the open door of the cold-holding chamber.

Inside this bleak room, I scrambled to my feet and hid behind the door, pressing my back to the concrete wall.

No one in the garage cried out in alarm. Evidently I had not been seen.

I realized that I was holding my breath. I let it out with a long hiss between clenched teeth.

My light-stung eyes were watering. I blotted them on the backs of my hands.

Two walls were occupied by over-and-under rows of stainless-steel morgue drawers in which the air was even colder than in the holding chamber itself, where the temperature was low enough to make me shiver. Two cushionless wooden chairs stood to one side. The flooring was white porcelain tile with tight grout joints for easy cleaning if a body bag sprang a leak.

Again, there were overhead fluorescent tubes, too many of them, and I tugged my Mystery Train cap far down on my brow. Surprisingly, the sunglasses in my shirt pocket had not been broken. I shielded my eyes.

A percentage of ultraviolet radiation penetrates even a highly rated sunscreen. I had sustained more exposure to hard light in the past hour than during the entire previous year. Like the hoofbeats of a fearsome black horse, the perils of cumulative exposure thundered through my mind.

From beyond the open door, the van's engine roared. The roar swiftly receded, fading to a grumble, and the grumble became a dying murmur.

The Cadillac hearse followed the van into the night. The big motorized garage door rolled down and met the sill with a solid blow that echoed through the hospital's subterranean realms, and in its wake, the echo shook a trembling silence out of the concrete walls.

I tensed, balling my hands into fists.

Although he was surely still in the garage, the orderly made no sound. I imagined him, head cocked with curiosity, staring at my father's suitcase.

A minute ago I had been sure that I could overpower this man. Now my confidence ebbed. Physically, I was more than his equal – but he might possess a ruthlessness that I did not.

I didn't hear him approaching. He was on the other side of the open door, inches from me, and I became aware of him only because the rubber soles of his shoes squeaked on the porcelain tile when he crossed the threshold.

If he came all the way inside, a confrontation was inevitable. My nerves were coiled as tight as clockwork mainsprings.

After a disconcertingly long hesitation, the orderly switched off the lights. He pulled the door shut as he backed out of the room.

I heard him insert a key in the lock. The deadbolt snapped into place with a sound like the hammer of a heavy-caliber revolver driving the firing pin into an empty chamber.

I doubted that any corpses occupied the chilled

morgue drawers. Mercy Hospital – in quiet Moonlight Bay – doesn't crank out the dead at the frenetic pace with which the big institutions process them in the violence-ridden cities.

Even if breathless sleepers were nestled in all these stainless-steel bunks, however, I wasn't nervous about being with them. I will one day be as dead as any resident of a graveyard – no doubt sooner than will other men of my age. The dead are merely the countrymen of my future.

I *did* dread the light, and now the perfect darkness of this cool windowless room was, to me, like quenching water to a man dying of thirst. For a minute or longer I relished the absolute blackness that bathed my skin, my eyes.

Reluctant to move, I remained beside the door, my back against the wall. I half expected the orderly to return at any moment.

Finally I took off my sunglasses and slipped them into my shirt pocket again.

Although I stood in blackness, through my mind spun bright pinwheels of anxious speculation.

My father's body was in the white van. Bound for a destination that I could not guess. In the custody of people whose motivations were utterly incomprehensible to me.

I couldn't imagine any logical reason for this bizarre corpse swap – except that the cause of Dad's death must not have been as straightforward as cancer. Yet if my father's poor dead bones could somehow incriminate someone, why wouldn't the guilty party let Sandy Kirk's crematorium destroy the evidence?

Apparently they needed his body.

For what?

A cold dew had formed inside my clenched fists, and the back of my neck was damp.

The more I thought about the scene that I had witnessed in the garage, the less comfortable I felt in this lightless way station for the dead. These peculiar events stirred primitive fears so deep in my mind that I could not even discern their shape as they swam and circled in the murk.

A murdered hitchhiker evidently would be cremated in my father's place. But why kill a harmless vagrant for this purpose? Sandy could have filled the bronze memorial urn with ordinary wood ashes, and I would have been convinced that they were human. Besides, it was unlikely in the extreme that I would ever pry open the sealed urn once I received it – unlikelier still that I would submit the powdery contents for laboratory testing to determine their composition and true source.

My thoughts seemed tangled in a tightly woven mesh. I couldn't thrash loose.

Shakily, I withdrew the lighter from my pocket. I hesitated, listening for furtive sounds on the far side of the locked door, and then I struck a flame.

I would not have been surprised to see an alabaster corpse silently risen from its steel sarcophagus, standing before me, face greasy with death and glimmering in the butane lambency, eyes wide but blind, mouth working to impart secrets but producing not even a whisper. No cadaver confronted me, but serpents of light and shadow slipped from the fluttering flame and purled across the steel panels, imparting an illusion of movement to the drawers, so that each receptacle appeared to be inching outward.

Turning to the door, I discovered that to prevent anyone from being accidentally locked in the cold-holding room, the deadbolt could be disengaged from within. On this side, no key was required; the lock could be operated with a simple thumbturn.

I eased the deadbolt out of the striker plate as quietly as possible. The doorknob creaked softly.

The silent garage was apparently deserted, but I remained alert. Someone could be concealed behind one of the supporting columns, the paramedics' van, or the panel truck.

Squinting against the dry rain of fluorescent light, I saw to my dismay that my father's suitcase was gone. The orderly must have taken it.

I did not want to cross the hospital basement to the stairs by which I had descended. The risk of encountering one or both of the orderlies was too great.

Until they opened the suitcase and examined the contents, they might not realize whose property it was. When they found my father's wallet with his ID, they would know I had been here, and they would be concerned about what, if anything, I might have heard and seen.

They had killed a hitchhiker not because he had known anything about their activities, not because he could incriminate them, but merely because they needed a body to cremate for reasons that still escaped me. With those who posed a genuine threat to them, they would be merciless.

I pressed the button that operated the wide roll-up. The motor hummed, the chain drive jerked taut overhead, and that big segmented door ascended with a frightful clatter. I glanced nervously around the garage, expecting to see an assailant break from cover and rush toward me.

When the door was more than halfway open, I

stopped it with a second tap of the button and then brought it down again with a third. As it descended, I slipped under the door and into the night.

Tall pole lamps shed a brass-cold, muddy yellow light on the driveway that sloped up from the subterranean garage. At the top of the drive, the parking lot was also cast in this sullen radiance, which was like the frigid glow that might illuminate an anteroom to a precinct of Hell where punishment involved an eternity of ice rather than fire.

As much as possible, I moved through landscape zones, in the nightshade of camphor trees and pines.

I fled across the narrow street into a residential neighborhood of quaint Spanish bungalows. Into an alleyway without streetlamps. Past the backs of houses bright with windows. Beyond the windows were rooms where strange lives, full of infinite possibility and blissful ordinariness, were lived beyond my reach and almost beyond my comprehension.

Frequently, I feel weightless in the night, and this was one of those times. I ran as silently as the owl flies, gliding on shadows.

This sunless world had welcomed and nurtured me for twenty-eight years, had been always a place of peace and comfort to me. But now for the first time in my life, I was plagued by the feeling that some predatory creature was pursuing me through the darkness.

Resisting the urge to look over my shoulder, I picked up my pace and sprinted-raced-streaked-*flew* through the narrow back streets and darkways of Moonlight Bay.

Two

THE EVENING

5

I have seen photographs of California pepper trees in sunlight. When brightly limned, they are lacy, graceful, green dreams of trees.

At night, the pepper acquires a different character from the one that it reveals in daylight. It appears to hang its head, letting its long branches droop to conceal a face drawn with care or grief.

These trees flanked the long driveway to Kirk's Funeral Home, which stood on a three-acre knoll at the northeast edge of town, inland of Highway 1 and reached by an overpass. They waited like lines of mourners, paying their respects.

As I climbed the private lane, on which low mushroom-shaped landscape lamps cast rings of light, the trees stirred in a breeze. The friction between wind and leaves was a whispery lamentation.

No cars were parked along the mortuary approach, which meant that no viewings were in progress.

I myself travel through Moonlight Bay only on foot or on my bicycle. There is no point in learning to drive a car. I couldn't use it by day, and by night I would have to wear sunglasses to spare myself the sting of oncoming headlights. Cops tend to frown on night driving with shades, no matter how cool you look.

The full moon had risen.

I like the moon. It illuminates without scorching. It burnishes what is beautiful and grants concealment to what is not.

At the broad crown of the hill, the blacktop looped back on itself to form a spacious turnaround with a small grassy circle at its center. In the circle was a cast-concrete reproduction of Michelangelo's *Pietà*.

The body of the dead Christ, cradled on His mother's lap, was luminous with reflected moonlight. The Virgin also glowed faintly. In sunshine, this crude replica must surely look unspeakably tacky.

Faced with terrible loss, however, most mourners find comfort in assurances of universal design and meaning, even when as clumsily expressed as in this reproduction. One thing I love about people is their ability to be lifted so high by the smallest drafts of hope.

I stopped under the portico of the funeral home, hesitating because I couldn't assess the danger into which I was about to leap.

The massive two-story Georgian house – red brick with white wood trim – would have been the loveliest house in town, were the town not Moonlight Bay. A spaceship from another galaxy, perched here, would have looked no more alien to our coastline than did Kirk's handsome pile. This house needed elms, not pepper trees, drear heavens rather than the clear skies of California, and periodic lashings with rains far colder than those that would drench it here.

The second floor, where Sandy lived, was dark.

The viewing rooms were on the ground floor. Through

beveled, leaded panes that flanked the front door, I saw a weak light at the back of the house.

I rang the bell.

A man entered the far end of the hallway and approached the door. Although he was only a silhouette, I recognized Sandy Kirk by his easy walk. He moved with a grace that enhanced his good looks.

He reached the foyer and switched on both the interior lights and the porch lights. When he opened the door, he seemed surprised to see me squinting at him from under the bill of my cap.

'Christopher?'

'Evening, Mr. Kirk.'

'I'm so very sorry about your father. He was a wonderful man.'

'Yes. Yes, he was.'

'We've already collected him from the hospital. We're treating him just like family, Christopher, with the utmost respect – you can be sure of that. I took his course in twentieth-century poetry at Ashdon. Did you know that?'

'Yes, of course.'

'From him I learned to love Eliot and Pound. Auden and Plath. Beckett and Ashbery. Robert Bly. Yeats. All of them. Couldn't tolerate poetry when I started the course – couldn't live without it by the end.'

'Wallace Stevens. Donald Justice. Louise Glück. They were his personal favorites.'

Sandy smiled and nodded. Then: 'Oh, excuse me, I forgot.'

Out of consideration for my condition, he extinguished both the foyer and porch lights.

Standing on the dark threshold, he said, 'This must

be terrible for you, but at least he isn't suffering any-more.'

Sandy's eyes were green, but in the pale land-scape lighting, they looked as smooth-black as certain beetles' shells.

Studying his eyes, I said, 'Could I see him?'

'What – your father?'

'I didn't turn the sheet back from his face before they took him out of his room. Didn't have the heart for it, didn't think I needed to. Now . . . I'd really like just one last look.'

Sandy Kirk's eyes were like a placid night sea. Below the unremarkable surface were great teeming depths.

His voice remained that of a compassionate courtier to the bereaved. 'Oh, Christopher . . . I'm sorry, but the process has begun.'

'You've already put him in the furnace?'

Having grown up in a business conducted with a richness of euphemisms, Sandy winced at the bluntness with which I'd phrased the question. 'The deceased is in the cremator, yes.'

'Wasn't that terribly quick?'

'In our work, there's no wisdom in delay. If only I'd known you were coming . . .'

I wondered if his beetle-shell eyes would be able to meet mine so boldly if there had been enough light for me to see their true green color.

Into my silence, he said, 'Christopher, I'm so dis-tressed by this, seeing you in this pain, knowing I could have helped.'

In my odd life, I have had much experience of some things and little of others. Although I am a foreigner to the day, I know the night as no one else can know it. Although I have been the object on which ignorant fools have sometimes spent their cruelty, most of my understanding of the human heart comes from my relationships with my parents and with those good friends who, like me, live primarily between sunset and dawn; consequently, I have seldom encountered hurtful deception.

I was embarrassed by Sandy's deceit, as though it shamed not merely him but also me, and I couldn't meet his obsidian stare any longer. I lowered my head and gazed at the porch floor.

Mistaking my embarrassment for tongue-binding grief, he stepped onto the porch and put one hand on my shoulder.

I managed not to recoil.

'My business is comforting folks, Christopher, and I'm good at it. But truthfully – I have no words that make sense of death or make it easier to bear.'

I wanted to kick his ass.

'I'll be okay,' I said, realizing that I had to get away from him before I did something rash.

'What I hear myself saying to most folks is all the platitudes you'd never find in the poetry your dad loved, so I'm not going to repeat them to you, not to you of all people.'

Keeping my head down, nodding, I eased backward, out from under his hand. 'Thanks, Mr. Kirk. I'm sorry to've bothered you.'

'You didn't bother me. Of course you didn't. I only wish you'd called ahead. I'd have been able to . . . delay.'

'Not your fault. It's all right. Really.'

Having backed off the stepless brick porch onto the blacktop under the portico, I turned away from Sandy.

Retreating once more to that doorway between two darknesses, he said, 'Have you given any thought to the service – when you want to hold it, how you want it conducted?'

'No. No, not yet. I'll let you know tomorrow.'

As I walked away, Sandy said, 'Christopher, are you all right?'

Facing him from a little distance this time, I spoke in a numb, inflectionless voice that was only half calculated: 'Yeah. I'm all right. I'll be okay. Thanks, Mr. Kirk.'

'I wish you had called ahead.'

Shrugging, I jammed my hands in my jacket pockets, turned from the house once more, and walked past the *Pietà*.

Flecks of mica were in the mix from which the replica had been poured, and the big moon glimmered in those tiny chips, so that tears appeared to shimmer on the cheeks of Our Lady of Cast Concrete.

I resisted the urge to glance back at the undertaker. I was certain he was still watching me.

I continued down the lane between the forlorn, whispering trees. The temperature had fallen only into the low sixties. The onshore breeze was pure after its journey across thousands of miles of ocean, bearing nothing but the faintest whiff of brine.

Long after the slope of the driveway had taken me out of Sandy's line of sight, I looked back. I could see just the steeply pitched roof and chimneys, somber forms against the star-salted sky.

I moved off the blacktop onto grass, and I headed uphill again, this time in the sheltering shadows of foliage. The pepper trees braided the moon in their long tresses.

6

The funeral-home turnaround came into sight again. The *Pietà*. The portico.

Sandy had gone inside. The front door was closed.

Staying on the lawn, using trees and shrubs for cover, I circled to the back of the house. A deep porch stepped down to a seventy-foot lap pool, an enormous brick patio, and formal rose gardens – none of which could be seen from the public rooms of the funeral home.

A town the size of ours welcomes nearly two hundred newborns each year while losing a hundred citizens to death. There were only two funeral homes, and Kirk's probably received over seventy percent of this business. Death was a good living for Sandy.

The view from the patio must have been breathtaking in daylight: unpopulated hills rising in gentle folds as far to the east as the eye could see, graced by scattered oaks with gnarled black trunks. Now the shrouded hills lay like sleeping giants under pale sheets.

When I saw no one at the lighted rear windows, I quickly crossed the patio. The moon, white as a rose petal, floated on the inky waters of the swimming pool.

The house adjoined a spacious L-shaped garage, which embraced a motor court that could be entered only from the front. The garage accommodated two hearses and Sandy's personal vehicles – but also, at the end of the wing farthest from the residence, the crematorium.

I slipped around the corner of the garage, along the back of the second arm of the L, where immense eucalyptus trees blocked most of the moonlight. The air was redolent of their medicinal fragrance, and a carpet of dead leaves crunched underfoot.

No corner of Moonlight Bay is unknown to me – especially not this one. Most of my nights have been spent in the exploration of our special town, which has resulted in some macabre discoveries.

Ahead, on my left, frosty light marked the crematorium window. I approached it with the conviction – correct, as it turned out – that I was about to see something stranger and far worse than what Bobby Halloway and I had seen on an October night when we were thirteen . . .

~ ~ ~

A decade and a half ago, I'd had as morbid a streak as any boy my age, was as fascinated as all boys are by the mystery and lurid glamor of death. Bobby Halloway and I, friends even then, thought it was daring to prowl the undertaker's property in search of the repulsive, the ghoulish, the shocking.

I can't recall what we expected – or hoped – to find. A collection of human skulls? A porch swing made of bones? A secret laboratory where the deceptively normal-looking Frank Kirk and his deceptively normal-looking son Sandy called down lightning bolts from storm clouds to reanimate our dead neighbors and use them as slaves to do the cooking and house-cleaning?

Perhaps we expected to stumble upon a shrine to the evil gods Cthulhu and Yog-Sothoth in some sinister bramble-festooned end of the rose garden. Bobby and I were reading a lot of H. P. Lovecraft in those days.

Bobby says we were a couple of weird kids. I say we were weird, for sure, but neither more nor less weird than other boys.

Bobby says maybe so, but the other boys gradually grew out of their weirdness while we've grown further into ours.

I don't agree with Bobby on this one. I don't believe that I'm any more weird than anyone else I've ever met. In fact I'm a damn sight less weird than some.

Which is true of Bobby, too. But because he treasures his weirdness, he wants me to believe in and treasure mine.

He *insists* on his weirdness. He says that by acknowledging and embracing our weirdness, we are in greater harmony with nature – because nature is deeply weird.

Anyway, one October night, behind the funeral-home garage, Bobby Halloway and I found the crematorium window. We were attracted to it by an eldritch light that throbbed against the glass.

Because the window was set high, we were not tall enough to peer inside. With the stealth of commandos scouting an enemy encampment, we snatched a teak bench from the patio and carried it behind the garage, where we positioned it under the glimmering window.

Side by side on the bench, we were able to reconnoiter the scene together. The interior of the window was covered by a Levelor blind; but someone had forgotten to close the slats, giving us a clear view of Frank Kirk and an assistant at work.

One remove from the room, the light was not bright enough to cause me harm. At least that was what I told myself as I pressed my nose to the pane.

Even though I had learned to be a singularly cautious boy, I was nonetheless a boy and, therefore, in love with adventure and camaraderie, so I might knowingly have risked blindness to share that moment with Bobby Halloway.

On a stainless-steel gurney near the window was the body of an elderly man. It was cloaked in a sheet, with only the ravaged face exposed. His yellow-white hair, matted and tangled, made him look as though he had died in a high wind. Judging by his waxy gray skin, sunken cheeks, and severely cracked lips, however, he had succumbed not to a storm but to a prolonged illness.

If Bobby and I had been acquainted with the man in life, we didn't recognize him in this ashen and emaciated condition. If he'd been someone we knew even casually, he would have been no less grisly but perhaps less an object of boyish fascination and dark delight.

To us, because we were just thirteen and proud of it, the most compelling and remarkable and wonderful thing about the cadaver was also, of course, the grossest thing about it. One eye was closed, but the other was wide open and staring, occluded by a bright red starburst hemorrhage.

How that eye mesmerized us.

As death-blind as the painted eye of a doll, it nevertheless saw through us to the core.

Sometimes in a silent rapture of dread and sometimes whispering urgently to each other like a pair of deranged sportscasters doing color commentary, we watched as Frank and his assistant readied the cremator in one corner of the chamber. The room must have been warm, for the men slipped off their ties and rolled up their shirt sleeves, and tiny drops of perspiration wove beaded veils on their faces.

Outside, the October night was mild. Yet Bobby and I shivered and compared gooseflesh and wondered that our breath didn't plume from us in white wintry clouds.

The morticians folded the sheet back from the cadaver, and we boys gasped at the horrors of advanced age and murderous disease. But we gasped with the same sweet thrill of terror that we had felt while gleefully watching videos like *Night of the Living Dead*.

As the corpse was moved into a cardboard case and eased into the blue flames of the cremator, I clutched Bobby's arm, and he clamped one damp hand to the back of my neck, and we held fast to each other, as though a supernatural magnetic power might pull us inexorably forward, shattering the window, and sweep us into the room, into the fire with the dead man.

Frank Kirk shut the cremator.

Even through the closed window, the clank of the furnace door was loud enough, final enough, to echo in the hollows of our bones.

Later, after we had returned the teak bench to the patio and had fled the undertaker's property, we repaired to the bleachers at the football field behind the high school. With no game in progress, that place was unlighted and safe for me. We guzzled Cokes and munched potato chips that Bobby had gotten en route at a 7-Eleven.

'That was cool, that was so cool,' Bobby declared excitedly.

'It was the coolest thing ever,' I agreed.

'Cooler than Ned's cards.'

Ned was a friend who had moved to San Francisco with his parents just that previous August. He had obtained a deck of playing cards – how, he would never reveal – that featured color photographs of really hot-looking nude women, fifty-two different beauties.

'Definitely cooler than the cards,' I agreed. 'Cooler than when that humongous tanker truck overturned and blew up out on the highway.'

'Jeez, yeah, megadegrees cooler than that. Cooler than when Zach Blenheim got chewed up by that pit bull and had to have twenty-eight stitches in his arm.'

'Unquestionably quantum arctics cooler than that,' I confirmed.

'His eye!' Bobby said, remembering the starburst hemorrhage.

'Oh, God, his *eye*!'

'Gag-o-rama!'

We swilled down Cokes and talked and laughed more than we had ever laughed before in one night.

What amazing creatures we are when we're thirteen.

There on the athletic-field bleachers, I knew that this macabre adventure had tied a knot in our friendship that nothing and no one would ever loosen. By then we had been friends for two years; but during this night, our friendship became stronger, more complex than it had been at the start of the evening. We had shared a powerfully formative experience – and we sensed that this event was more profound than it seemed to be on the surface, more profound than boys our age could grasp. In my eyes, Bobby had acquired a new mystique, as I had acquired in his eyes, because we had done this daring thing.

Subsequently, I would discover that this moment was merely prelude. Our *real* bonding came the second week of December – when we saw something infinitely more disturbing than the corpse with the blood-red eye.

$$\approx \quad \approx \quad \approx$$

Now, fifteen years later, I would have thought that I was too old for these adventures and too ridden by conscience to prowl other people's property as casually as thirteen-year-old boys seem able to do. Yet here I was, treading cautiously on layers of dead eucalyptus leaves, putting my face to the fateful window one more time.

The Levelor blind, though yellowed with age, appeared to be the same one through which Bobby and I had peered so long ago. The slats were adjusted at an angle, but the gaps between them were wide enough to allow a view of the entire crematorium – into which I was tall enough to see without the aid of a patio bench.

Sandy Kirk and an assistant were at work near the Power Pak II Cremation System. They wore surgeon's masks, latex gloves, and disposable plastic aprons.

On the gurney near the window was one of the opaque vinyl body bags, unzipped, split like a ripe pod, with a dead man nestled inside. Evidently this was the hitchhiker who would be cremated in my father's name.

He was about five ten, a hundred sixty pounds. Because of the beating that he had taken, I could not estimate his age. His face was grotesquely battered.

At first I thought that his eyes were hidden by black crusts of blood. Then I realized that both eyes were gone. I was staring into empty sockets.

I thought of the old man with the starburst hemorrhage and how fearsome he had seemed to Bobby and me. That was nothing compared to this. That had been only nature's impersonal work, while this was human viciousness.

≈ ≈ ≈

During that long-ago October and November, Bobby Halloway and I periodically returned to the crematorium window. Creeping through the darkness, trying not to trip in the ground ivy, we saturated our lungs with air redolent of the surrounding eucalyptuses, a scent that to this day I identify with death.

During those two months, Frank Kirk conducted fourteen funerals, but only three of those deceased were cremated. The others were embalmed for traditional burials.

Bobby and I lamented that the embalming room offered no windows for our use. That sanctum sanctorum – 'where they do the wet work,' as Bobby put it – was in the basement, secure against ghoulish spies like us.

Secretly, I was relieved that our snooping would be restricted to Frank Kirk's dry work. I believe that

Bobby was relieved as well, although he pretended to be sorely disappointed.

On the positive side, I suppose, Frank performed most embalmings during the day while restricting cremations to the night hours. This made it possible for me to be in attendance.

Although the hulking cremator – cruder than the Power Pak II that Sandy used these days – disposed of human remains at a very high temperature and featured emission-control devices, thin smoke escaped the chimney. Frank conducted only nocturnal cremations out of respect for bereaved family members or friends who might, in daylight, glance at the hilltop mortuary from lower in town and see the last of their loved ones slipping skyward in wispy gray curls.

Conveniently for us, Bobby's father, Anson, was the editor-in-chief of the *Moonlight Bay Gazette*. Bobby used his connections and his familiarity with the newspaper offices to get us the most current information about deaths by accident and by natural causes.

We always knew when Frank Kirk had a fresh one, but we couldn't be sure whether he was going to embalm it or cremate it. Immediately after sunset, we would ride our bikes to the vicinity of the mortuary and then creep onto the property, waiting at the crematorium window either until the action began or until we had to admit at last that this one was not going to be a burning.

Mr. Garth, the sixty-year-old president of the First National Bank, died of a heart attack in late October. We watched him go into the fire.

In November, a carpenter named Henry Aimes fell off a roof and broke his neck. Although Aimes was cremated, Bobby and I saw nothing of the process, because Frank Kirk or his assistant had remembered to close the slats on the Levelor blind.

The blinds were open the second week in December, however, when we returned for the cremation of Rebecca Acquilain. She was married to Tom Acquilain, a math teacher at the junior high school at which Bobby attended classes but at which I did not. Mrs. Acquilain, the town librarian, was only thirty, the mother of a five-year-old boy named Devlin.

Lying on the gurney, swathed in a sheet from the neck down, Mrs. Acquilain was so beautiful that her face was not merely a vision upon our eyes but a weight upon our chests. We could not breathe.

We had realized, I suppose, that she was a pretty woman, but we had never mooned over her. She was the librarian, after all, and someone's mother, while we were thirteen and inclined not to notice beauty that was as quiet as starlight dropping from the sky and as clear as rainwater. The kind of woman who appeared nude on playing cards had the flash that drew our eyes. Until now, we had often looked at Mrs. Acquilain but had never *seen* her.

Death had not ravaged her, for she had died quickly. A flaw in a cerebral artery wall, no doubt with her from birth but never suspected, swelled and burst in the course of one afternoon. She was gone in hours.

As she lay on the mortuary gurney, her eyes were closed. Her features were relaxed. She seemed to be sleeping; in fact, her mouth was curved slightly, as though she were having a pleasant dream.

When the two morticians removed the sheet to convey Mrs. Acquilain into the cardboard case and then into the cremator, Bobby and I saw that she was slim, exquisitely proportioned, lovely beyond the power of words to describe. This was a beauty exceeding mere eroticism, and we didn't look at her with morbid desire but with awe.

She looked so young.

She looked immortal.

The morticians conveyed her to the furnace with what seemed to be unusual gentleness and respect. When the door was closed behind the dead woman, Frank Kirk stripped off his latex gloves and blotted the back of one hand against his left eye and then his right. It was not perspiration that he wiped away.

During other cremations, Frank and his assistant had chatted almost continuously, though we could not quite hear what they said. This night, they spoke hardly at all.

Bobby and I were silent, too.

We returned the bench to the patio. We crept off Frank Kirk's property.

After retrieving our bicycles, we rode through Moonlight Bay by way of its darkest streets.

We went to the beach.

At this hour, in this season, the broad strand was deserted. Behind us, as gorgeous as phoenix feathers, nesting on the hills and fluttering through a wealth of trees, were the town lights. In front of us lay the inky wash of the vast Pacific.

The surf was gentle. Widely spaced, low breakers slid to shore, lazily spilling their phosphorescent crests, which peeled from right to left like a white rind off the dark meat of the sea.

Sitting in the sand, watching the surf, I kept thinking how near we were to Christmas. Two weeks away. I didn't want to think about Christmas, but it twinkled and jingled through my mind.

I don't know what Bobby was thinking. I didn't ask. I didn't want to talk. Neither did he.

I brooded about what Christmas would be like for little Devlin Acquilain without his mother. Maybe he was too young to understand what death meant.

Tom Acquilain, her husband, knew what death meant, sure enough. Nevertheless, he would probably put up a Christmas tree for Devlin.

How would he find the strength to hang the tinsel on the boughs?

Speaking for the first time since we had seen the sheet unfolded from the woman's body, Bobby said simply, 'Let's go swimming.'

Although the day had been mild, this was December, and it wasn't a year when El Niño – the warm current out of the southern hemisphere – ran close to shore. The water temperature was inhospitable, and the air was slightly chilly.

As Bobby undressed, he folded his clothes and, to keep the sand out of them, neatly piled them on a tangled blanket of kelp that had washed ashore earlier in the day and been dried by the sun. I folded my clothes beside his.

Naked, we waded into the black water and then swam out against the tide. We went too far from shore.

We turned north and swam parallel to the coast. Easy strokes. Minimal kicking. Expertly riding the ebb and flow of the waves. We swam a dangerous distance.

We were both superb swimmers – though reckless now.

Usually a swimmer finds cold water less discomfiting after being in it a while; as the body temperature drops, the difference between skin and water temperatures becomes much less perceptible. Furthermore, exertion creates the impression of heat. A reassuring but false sense of warmth can arise, which is perilous.

This water, however, grew colder as fast as our body temperatures dropped. We reached no comfort point, false or otherwise.

Having swum too far north, we should have made for shore. If we'd had any common sense, we would have walked back to the mound of dry kelp where we'd left our clothes.

Instead, we merely paused, treading water, sucking in deep shuddery breaths cold enough to sluice the precious heat out of our throats. Then as one, without a word, we turned south to swim back the way we had come, still too far from shore.

My limbs grew heavy. Faint but frightening cramps twisted through my stomach. The pounding of my riptide heart seemed hard enough to push me deep under the surface.

Although the incoming swells were as gentle as they had been when we first entered the water, they felt meaner. They bit with teeth of white foam, and crystals of icy venom formed a brittle glaze in blood and marrow.

We swam side by side, careful not to lose sight of each other. The winter sky offered no comfort, the lights of town were as distant as stars, and the sea was hostile. All we had was our friendship, but we knew that in a crisis, either of us would die trying to save the other.

When we returned to our starting point, we barely had strength to walk out of the surf. Exhausted, nauseated, paler than the sand, shivering violently, we spat out the astringent taste of the sea.

We were so bitterly cold that we could no longer imagine the heat of the crematorium furnace. Even after we had dressed, we were still freezing, and that was good.

We walked our bicycles off the sand, across the grassy park that bordered the beach, to the nearest street.

As he climbed on his bike, Bobby said, 'Shit.'

'Yeah,' I said.

We cycled to our separate homes.

We went straight to bed as though ill. We slept. We dreamed. Life went on.

We never returned to the crematorium window.

We never spoke again of Mrs. Acquilain.

All these years later, either Bobby or I would still give his life to save the other – and without hesitation.

How strange this world is: Those things that we can so readily touch, those things so real to the senses – the sweet architecture of a woman's body, one's own flesh and bone, the cold sea and the gleam of stars – are far less real than things we cannot touch or taste or smell or see. Bicycles and the boys who ride them are less real than what we feel in our minds and hearts, less substantial than friendship and love and loneliness, all of which long outlast the world.

On this March night far down the time stream from boyhood, the crematorium window and the scene beyond it were more real than I would have wished. Someone had brutally beaten the hitchhiker to death – and then had cut out his eyes.

Even if the murder and the substitution of this corpse

for the body of my father made sense when all of the facts were known, why take the eyes? Could there possibly be a logical reason for sending this pitiable man eyeless into the all-consuming fire of the cremator?

Or had someone disfigured the hitchhiker sheerly for the deep, dirty thrill of it?

I thought of the hulking man with the shaved head and the single pearl earring. His broad blunt face. His huntsman's eyes, black and steady. His cold-iron voice with its rusty rasp.

It was possible to imagine such a man taking pleasure from the pain of another, carving flesh in the carefree manner of any country gentleman lazily whittling a twig.

Indeed, in the strange new world that had come into existence during my experience in the hospital basement, it was easy to imagine that even Sandy Kirk had disfigured the body: Sandy, as good-looking and slick as any *GQ* model; Sandy, whose dear father had wept at the burning of Rebecca Acquilain. Perhaps the eyes had been offered up at the base of the shrine in the far and thorny corner of the rose garden that Bobby and I had never been able to find.

In the crematorium, as Sandy and his assistant rolled the gurney toward the furnace, the telephone rang.

Guiltily, I flinched from the window as though I had triggered an alarm.

When I leaned close to the glass again, I saw Sandy pull down his surgical mask and lift the handset from the wall phone. The tone of his voice indicated confusion, then alarm, then anger, but through the dual-pane window, I was not able to hear what he was saying.

Sandy racked the telephone handset almost hard

enough to knock the box off the wall. Whoever had been on the other end of the line had gotten a good ear cleaning.

As he stripped out of his latex gloves, Sandy spoke urgently to his assistant. I thought that I heard him speak my name – and not with either admiration or affection.

The assistant, Jesse Pinn, was a lean-faced whippet of a man with red hair and russet eyes and a thin mouth that seemed pinched in anticipation of the taste of a chased-down rabbit. Pinn started to zip the body bag shut over the corpse of the hitchhiker.

Sandy's suit jacket was hung on one of a series of wall pegs to the right of the door. When he lifted it off the peg, I was astonished to see that under the coat hung a shoulder holster sagging with the weight of a handgun.

Seeing Pinn fumbling with the body bag, Sandy spoke sharply to him – and gestured at the window.

As Pinn hurried directly toward me, I jerked back from the pane. He closed the half-open slats on the blind.

I doubted that I had been seen.

On the other hand, keeping in mind that I am an optimist on such a deep level that it's a subatomic condition with me, I decided that on this one occasion, I would be wise to listen to a more pessimistic instinct and not linger. I hurried between the garage wall and the eucalyptus grove, through the death-scented air, toward the backyard.

The drifted leaves crunched as hard as snail shells underfoot. Fortunately, I was given cover by the soughing of the breeze through the branches overhead.

The wind was full of the hollow susurrant sound of the sea over which it had so long traveled, and it masked my movements.

It would also cloak the footsteps of anyone stalking me.

I was certain that the telephone call had been from one of the orderlies at the hospital. They had examined the contents of the suitcase, found my father's wallet, and deduced that I must have been in the garage to witness the body swap.

With this information, Sandy had realized that my appearance at his front door had not been as innocent as it had seemed. He and Jesse Pinn would come outside to see if I was still lurking on the property.

I reached the backyard. The manicured lawn looked broader and more open than I remembered it.

The full moon was no brighter than it had been minutes earlier, but every hard surface, which had previously absorbed that languid light, now reflected and amplified it. An eerie silver radiance suffused the night, denying concealment to me.

I dared not attempt to cross the broad brick patio. In fact I decided to stay well clear of the house and the driveway. Leaving via the same route by which I had arrived would be too risky.

I raced across the lawn to the acre of rose gardens at the back of the property. Before me lay descending terraces with extensive rows of trellises standing at angles to one another, numerous tunnel-like arbors, and a maze of meandering pathways.

Spring along our mellow coast doesn't delay its debut to match the date celebrating it on the calendar, and already the roses were blooming. The red and other darkly colored flowers appeared to be black in the moonlight, roses for a sinister altar, but there were enormous white blooms, too, as big as babies' heads, nodding to the lullaby of the breeze.

Men's voices arose behind me. They were worn thin and tattered by the worrying wind.

Crouching behind a tall trellis, I looked back through the open squares between the white lattice crossings. Gingerly I pushed aside looping trailers with wicked thorns.

Near the garage, two flashlight beams chased shadows out of shrubbery, sent phantoms leaping up through tree limbs, dazzled across windows.

Sandy Kirk was behind one of the flashlights and was no doubt toting the handgun that I had glimpsed. Jesse Pinn might also have a weapon.

There was once a time when morticians and their assistants didn't pack heat. Until this evening I had assumed I was still living in that era.

I was startled to see a third flashlight beam appear at the far corner of the house. Then a fourth. Then a fifth.

A sixth.

I had no clue as to who these new searchers might be or where they could have come from so quickly. They spread out to form a line and advanced purposefully across the yard, across the patio, past the swimming pool, toward the rose garden, probing with the flashlights, menacing figures as featureless as demons in a dream.

7

The faceless pursuers and the thwarting mazes that trouble us in sleep were now reality.

The gardens stepped in five broad terraces down a hillside. In spite of these plateaus and the gentleness of the slopes between them, I was gathering too much speed as I descended, and I was afraid that I would stumble, fall, and break a leg.

Rising on all sides, the arbors and fanciful trellises began to resemble gutted ruins. In the lower levels, they were overgrown with thorny trailers that clawed the lattice and seemed to writhe with animal life as I fled past them.

The night had fallen into a waking nightmare.

My heart pounded so fiercely that the stars reeled.

I felt as though the vault of the sky were sliding toward me, gaining momentum like an avalanche.

Plunging to the end of the gardens, I sensed as much as saw the looming wrought-iron fence: seven feet high, its glossy black paint glimmering with moonlight. I dug my heels into the soft earth and braked, jarring against the sturdy pickets but not hard enough to hurt myself.

I hadn't made much noise, either. The spear-point verticals were solidly welded to the horizontal rails;

instead of clattering from my impact, the fence briefly thrummed.

I sagged against the ironwork.

A bitter taste plagued me. My mouth was so dry that I couldn't spit.

My right temple stung. I raised a hand to my face. Three thorns prickled my skin. I plucked them out.

During my flight downhill, I must have been lashed by a trailing rose brier, although I didn't recall encountering it.

Maybe because I was breathing harder and faster, the sweet fragrance of roses became too sweet, sharpened into a half-rotten stench. I could smell my sunscreen again, too, almost as strongly as when it had been freshly applied – but with a sour taint now – because my perspiration had revitalized the scent of the lotion.

I was overcome by the absurd yet unshakable conviction that the six searchers could sniff me out, as though they were hounds. I was safe for the moment only because I was downwind of them.

Clutching the fence, out of which the thrumming had passed into my hands and bones, I glanced uphill. The search party was moving from the highest terrace to the second.

Six scythes of light slashed through the roses. Portions of the lattice structures, when briefly backlit and distorted by those bright sweeping swords, loomed like the bones of slain dragons.

The gardens presented the searchers with more possible hiding places to probe than did the open lawn above. Yet they were moving faster than before.

I scaled the fence and swung over the top, wary of snaring my jacket or a leg of my jeans on the spear-point pickets. Beyond lay open land: shadowed vales, steadily rising ranks of moonlit hills, widely scattered and barely discernible black oaks.

The wild grass, lush from the recent winter rains, was knee-high when I dropped into it from the fence. I could smell the green juice bursting from the blades crushed beneath my shoes.

Certain that Sandy and his associates would survey the entire perimeter of the property, I hurried away from the funeral home, bounding downhill. I was eager to get beyond the reach of their flashlights before they arrived at the fence.

I was heading farther from town, which wasn't good. I wouldn't find help in the wilderness. Every step eastward was a step into isolation, and in isolation I was as vulnerable as anyone, more vulnerable than most.

Some luck was with me because of the season. If the searing heat of summer had already been upon us, the high grass would have been as golden as wheat and as dry as paper. My progress would have been marked by a swath of trampled stalks.

I was hopeful that the still-verdant meadow would be resilient enough to spring shut behind me, for the most part concealing the fact that I had passed this way. Nevertheless, an observant searcher would most likely be able to track me.

Approximately two hundred feet beyond the fence, at the bottom of the slope, the meadow gave way to denser brush. A barrier of tough, five-foot-high prairie cordgrass was mixed with what might have been goat's beard and massive clumps of aureola.

I hurriedly pushed through this growth into a ten-foot-wide, natural drainage swale. Little grew here because an epoch of storm runoff had exposed a spine of bedrock under the hills. With no rain in over two weeks, this rocky course was dry.

I paused to catch my breath. Leaning back into the brush, I parted the tall cordgrass to see how far down into the rose gardens the searchers had descended.

Four of them were already climbing the fence. Their flashlight beams slashed at the sky, stuttered across the pickets, and stabbed randomly at the ground as they clambered up and over the iron.

They were unnervingly quick and agile.

Were all of them, like Sandy Kirk, carrying weapons?

Considering their animal-keen instinct, speed, and persistence, perhaps they wouldn't need weapons. If they caught me, maybe they would tear me apart with their hands.

I wondered if they would take my eyes.

The drainage channel – and the wider declivity in which it lay – ran uphill to the northeast and downhill to the southwest. As I was already at the extreme north-east end of town, I could find no help if I went uphill.

I headed southwest, following the brush-flanked swale, intending to return to well-populated territory as quickly as possible.

In the shallowly cupped channel ahead of me, the moon-burnished bedrock glowed softly like the milky ice on a winter pond, dwindling into obscurity. The embracing curtains of high, silvery cordgrass appeared to be stiff with frost.

Suppressing all fear of falling on loose stones and of snapping an ankle in a natural borehole, I gave myself to the night, allowing the darkness to push me as wind pushes a sailing ship. I sprinted down the gradual slope with no sensation of feet striking ground, as though I actually were *skating* across the frozen rock.

Within two hundred yards, I came to a place where hills folded into one another, resulting in a branching of the hollow. With barely any decrease in speed, I chose the right-hand course because it would lead more directly back into Moonlight Bay.

I had gone only a short distance past that intersection when I saw lights approaching. A hundred yards ahead, the hollow turned out of sight to the left, around a sweeping curve of grassy hillside. The source of the questing beams lay beyond that bend, but I could see that they must be flashlights.

None of the men from the funeral home could have gotten out of the rose gardens and ahead of me so quickly. These were additional searchers.

They were attempting to trap me in a pincer maneuver. I felt as though I were being pursued by an army, by platoons that had sprung sorcerously from the ground itself.

I came to a complete halt.

I considered stepping off the bare rock, into concealment behind the man-high prairie grass and other dense brush that still bracketed the drainage swale. No matter how little I disturbed this vegetation, however, I was nearly certain to leave signs of my passage that would be obvious to these trackers. They would burst through the brush and capture me or gun me down as I scrambled up the open hillside.

At the bend ahead, the flashlight beams swelled brighter. Sprays of tall prairie grass flared like beautifully chased forms on a sterling platter.

I retreated to the Y in the hollow and took the left-hand branch that I'd forgone a minute earlier.

Within six or seven hundred feet, I came to another Y, wanted to go to the right – toward town – was afraid I'd be playing into their assumptions, and took the left-hand branch instead, although it would lead me deeper into the unpopulated hills.

From somewhere above and off to the west arose the grumble of an engine, distant at first but then suddenly nearer. The engine noise was so powerful that I thought it came from an aircraft making a low pass. This wasn't the stuttering clatter of a helicopter, but more like the roar of a fixed-wing plane.

Then a dazzling light swept the hilltops that rose to the left and right of me, passing directly across the hollow, sixty to eighty feet over my head. The beam was so bright, so intense, that it seemed to have weight and texture, like a white-hot gush of some molten substance.

A high-powered searchlight. It arced away and reflected off distant ridges to the east and north.

Where did they get this sophisticated ordnance on such short notice?

Was Sandy Kirk the grand kleagle of an anti-government militia headquartered in secret bunkers jammed with weapons and ammo, deep under the funeral home? No, that didn't ring true. Such things were merely the stuff of real life these days, the current events of a society in freefall – while this felt *uncanny*. This was territory through which the wild rushing river of the evening news had not yet swept.

I had to know what was happening up there on higher ground. If I didn't reconnoiter, I would be no better than a dumb rat in a laboratory maze.

I thrashed through the brush to the right of the

swale, crossed the sloping floor of the hollow, and then climbed the long hillside, because the search-light seemed to have originated in that direction. As I ascended, the beam seared the land above again – indeed, blazing in from the northwest as I'd thought – and then scorched past a third time, brightly illumin-ating the brow of the hill toward which I was making my way.

After crawling the penultimate ten yards on my hands and knees, I wriggled the final ten on my belly. At the crest, I coiled into an outcropping of weather-scored rocks that provided a measure of cover, and I cautiously raised my head.

A black Hummer – or maybe a Humvee, the original military version of that vehicle before it had been gentrified for sale to civilians – stood one hilltop away from mine, immediately leeward of a giant oak. Even poorly revealed by the backwash of its own lights, the Hummer presented an unmistakable profile: a boxy, hulking, four-wheel-drive wagon perched on giant tires, capable of crossing virtually any terrain.

I now saw two searchlights: Both were hand-held, one by the driver and one by his front-seat passenger, and each had a lens the size of a salad plate. Consider-ing their candlepower, they could have been operated only off the Hummer engine.

The driver extinguished his light and put the Hum-mer in gear. The big wagon sped out from under the spreading limbs of the oak and shot across the high meadow as though it were cruising a freeway, putting its tailgate toward me. It vanished over the far edge, soon reappeared out of a hollow, and rapidly ascended a more distant slope, effortlessly conquering these coastal hills.

The men on foot, with flashlights and perhaps hand-guns, were keeping to the hollows. In an attempt to prevent me from using the high ground, to force me down where the searchers might find me, the Hummer was patrolling the hilltops.

'Who *are* you people?' I muttered.

Searchlights slashed out from the Hummer, raking farther hills, illuminating a sea of grass in the indecisive breeze that ebbed and flowed. Wave after wave broke across the rising land and lapped against the trunks of the island oaks.

Then the big wagon was on the move again, rollicking over less hospitable terrain. Headlights bobbling, one searchlight swinging wildly, along a crest, into a hollow and out again, it motored east and south to another vantage point.

I wondered how visible this activity might be from the streets of Moonlight Bay on the lower hills and the flatlands, closer to the ocean. Possibly only a few townspeople happened to be outside and looking up at an angle that revealed enough commotion to engage their curiosity.

Those who glimpsed the searchlights might assume that teenagers or college boys in an ordinary 4X4 were spotting coastal elk or deer: an illegal but bloodless sport of which most people are tolerant.

Soon the Hummer would arc back toward me. Judging by the pattern of its search, it might arrive on this very hill in two more moves.

I retreated down the slope, into the hollow from which I had climbed: exactly where they wanted me. I had no better choice.

Heretofore, I had been confident that I would escape. Now my confidence was ebbing.

8

I pushed through the prairie grass into the drainage swale and continued in the direction that I had been headed before the searchlights had drawn me uphill. After only a few steps, I halted, startled by something with radiant green eyes that waited on the trail in front of me.

Coyote.

Wolflike but smaller, with a narrower muzzle than that of a wolf, these rangy creatures could nonetheless be dangerous. As civilization encroached on them, they were quite literally murder on family pets even in the supposedly safe backyards of residential neighborhoods near the open hills. In fact, from time to time, you heard of a coyote savaging and dragging off a child if the prey was young and small enough. Although they attacked adult humans only rarely, I wouldn't care to rely on their restraint or on my superior size if I were to encounter a pack – or even a pair – of them on their home ground.

My night vision was still recovering from the dazzle of the searchlights, and a tense moment passed before I perceived that these hot green eyes were too closely set to be those of a coyote. Furthermore, unless this beast was in a full pounce posture with its chest pressed to the ground, its baleful stare was directed at me from too low a position to be that of a coyote.

As my vision readjusted to nightshade and moonlight, I saw that nothing more threatening than a cat stood before me. Not a cougar, which would have been far worse than a coyote and reason for genuine terror, but a mere house cat: pale gray or light beige, impossible to tell which in this gloom.

Most cats are not stupid. Even in the obsessive pursuit of field mice or little desert lizards, they will not venture deeply into coyote country.

Indeed, as I got a clearer view of it, the particular creature before me seemed more than usually quick and alert. It sat erect, head cocked quizzically, ears pricked, studying me intensely.

As I took a step toward it, the cat rose onto all fours. When I advanced another step, the cat spun away from me and dashed along the moon-silvered path, vanishing into the darkness.

Elsewhere in the night, the Hummer was on the move again. Its shriek and snarl rapidly grew louder.

I picked up my pace.

By the time I had gone a hundred yards, the Hummer was no longer roaring but idling somewhere nearby, its engine noise like a slow deep panting. Overhead, the predatory gaze of the lights swept the night for prey.

Upon reaching the next branching of the hollow, I discovered the cat waiting for me. It sat at the point of division, committed to neither trail.

When I moved toward the left-hand path, the cat scurried to the right. It halted after several steps – and turned its lantern eyes on me.

The cat must have been acutely aware of the searchers all around us, not just of the noisy Hummer but of the men on foot. With its sharp senses, it might even perceive pheromones of aggression streaming from them, violence pending. It would want to avoid these people as much as I did. Given the chance, I would be better off choosing an escape route according to the animal's instincts rather than according to my own.

The idling engine of the Hummer suddenly thundered. The hard peals echoed back and forth through the hollows, so that the vehicle seemed to be simultaneously approaching and racing away. With this storm of sound, indecision flooded me, and for a moment I floundered in it.

Then I decided to go the way of the cat.

As I turned from the left-hand trail, the Hummer roared over the hilltop on the eastern flank of the hollow into which I had almost proceeded. For an instant it hung, suspended, as though weightless in a clock-stopped gap in time, headlights like twin wires leading a circus tightrope walker into midair, one searchlight stabbing straight up at the black tent of the sky. Time snapped across that empty synapse and flowed again: The Hummer tipped forward, and the front wheels crashed onto the hillside, and the rear wheels crossed the crest, and gouts of earth and grass spewed out from under its tires as it charged downhill.

A man whooped with delight, and another laughed. They were reveling in the hunt.

As the big wagon descended only fifty yards ahead of me, the hand-held searchlight swept the hollow.

I threw myself to the ground and rolled for cover. The rocky swale was hell on bones, and I felt my sunglasses crack apart in my shirt pocket.

As I scrambled to my feet, a beam as bright as an

oak-cleaving thunderbolt sizzled across the ground on which I had been standing. Wincing at the glare, squinting, I saw the searchlight quiver and then sweep away to the south. The Hummer was not coming up the hollow toward me.

I might have stayed where I was, at the intersection of the trails, with the narrower point of the hill at my back, until the Hummer moved out of the vicinity, rather than risk encountering it in the next hollow. When four flashlights winked far back on the trail that I had followed to this point, however, I ceased to have the luxury of hesitation. I was beyond the reach of these men's lights, but they were approaching at a trot, and I was in imminent danger of discovery.

When I rounded the point of the hill and entered the hollow to the west of it, the cat was still there, as though waiting for me. Putting its tail to me, it scampered away, though not so fast that I lost sight of it.

I was grateful for the stone under me, in which I could not leave betraying footprints – and then I realized that only fragments of my broken sunglasses remained in my shirt pocket. As I ran, I fingered my pocket and felt one bent stem and a jagged piece of one lens. The rest must be scattered on the ground where I had fallen, at the fork in the trail.

The four searchers were sure to spot the broken frames. They would divide their forces, two men to each hollow, and they would come after me harder and faster than ever, energized by this evidence that they were closing on their quarry.

On the far side of this hill, out of the vale where I had barely escaped the searchlight, the Hummer began to climb again. The shriek of its engine rose in pitch, swelled in volume.

If the driver paused on this grassy hilltop to survey the night once more, I would run undetected beneath him and away. If instead he raced across the hill and into this new hollow, I might be caught in his headlights or pinned by a searchlight beam.

The cat ran, and I ran.

As it sloped down between dark hills, the hollow grew wider than any that I had traveled previously, and the rocky swale in the center widened, too. Along the verge of the stone path, the tall cordgrass and the other brush bristled thicker than elsewhere, evidently watered by a greater volume of storm runoff, but the vegetation was too far to either side to cast even a faint dappling of moonshadows over me, and I felt dangerously exposed. Furthermore, this broad declivity, unlike those before it, ran as straight as a city street, with no bends to shield me from those who might enter it in my wake.

On the highlands, the Hummer seemed to have come to a halt once more. Its grumble drained away in the sluicing breeze, and the only engine sounds were mine: the rasp and wheeze of breathing, heartbeat like a pounding piston.

The cat was potentially fleeter than I, wind on four feet; it could have vanished in seconds. For a couple of minutes, however, it paced me, staying a constant fifteen feet ahead, pale gray or pale beige, a mere ghost of a cat in the moonglow, occasionally glancing back with eyes as eerie as seance candles.

Just when I began to think that this creature was purposefully leading me out of harm's way, just as I began to indulge in one of those orgies of anthropomorphizing that make Bobby Halloway's brain itch, the cat sped away from me. If that dry rocky wash had been filled with a storm gush, the tumbling water could not have outrun this feline, and in two seconds, three at most, it disappeared into the night ahead.

A minute later, I found the cat at the terminus of the channel. We were in the dead end of a blind hollow, with exposed grassy hills rising steeply on three sides. They were so steep, in fact, that I could not scale them quickly enough to elude the two searchers who were surely pursuing me on foot. Boxed in. Trapped.

Driftwood, tangled balls of dead weeds and grass, and silt were mounded at the end of the wash. I half expected the cat to give me an evil Cheshire grin, white teeth gleaming in the gloom. Instead, it scampered to the pile of debris and slinked-wriggled into one of many small gaps, disappearing again.

This *was* a wash. Therefore the runoff had to go somewhere when it reached this point.

Hastily I climbed the nine-foot-long, three-foot-high slope of packed debris, which sagged and rattled and crunched but held beneath me. It was all drifted against a grid of steel bars, which served as a vertical grate across the mouth of a culvert set into the side of the hill.

Beyond the grate was a six-foot-diameter concrete drain between anchoring concrete buttresses. It was apparently part of a flood-control project that carried storm water out of the hills, under the Pacific Coast Highway, into drains beneath the streets of Moonlight Bay, and finally to the sea.

A couple of times each winter, maintenance crews would clear the trash away from the grate to prevent water flow from being completely impeded. Clearly, they had not been here recently.

Inside the culvert, the cat meowed. Magnified, its

voice echoed with a new sepulchral tone along the concrete tunnel.

The openings in the steel-bar grid were four-inch squares, wide enough to admit the supple cat but not wide enough for me. The grate extended the width of the opening, from buttress to buttress, but it didn't reach all the way to the top.

I swung legs-first and backward through the two-foot-high gap between the top of the grate and the curved ceiling of the drain. I was grateful that the grid had a headrail, for otherwise I would have been poked and gouged painfully by the exposed tops of the vertical bars.

Leaving the stars and the moon behind, I stood with my back to the grate, peering into absolute blackness. I had to hunch only slightly to keep from bumping my head against the ceiling.

The smell of damp concrete and moldering grass, not entirely unpleasant, wafted from below.

I eased forward, sliding my feet. The smooth floor of the culvert had only a slight pitch. After just a few yards, I stopped, afraid that I would blunder into a sudden drop-off and wind up dead or broken-backed at the bottom.

I withdrew the butane lighter from a pocket of my jeans, but I was reluctant to strike a flame. The light flickering along the curved walls of the culvert would be visible from outside.

The cat called again, and its radiant eyes were all that I could see ahead. Guessing at the distance between us, judging by the angle at which I looked down upon the animal, I deduced that the floor of the huge culvert continued at an increased – but not drastic – slope.

I proceeded cautiously toward the lambent eyes.

When I drew close to the creature, it turned away, and I halted at the loss of its twin beacons.

Seconds later it spoke again. Its green gaze reappeared and fixed unblinking on me.

Edging forward once more, I marveled at this odd experience. All that I had witnessed since sundown – the theft of my father's body, the battered and eyeless corpse in the crematorium, the pursuit from the mortuary – was incredible, to say the least, but for sheer strangeness, nothing equaled the behavior of this small descendant of tigers.

Or maybe I was making a lot more of the moment than it deserved, attributing to this simple house cat an awareness of my plight that it didn't actually possess.

Maybe.

Blindly, I came to another mound of debris smaller than the first. Unlike the previous heap, this one was damp. The flotsam squished beneath my shoes, and a sharper stench rose from it.

I clambered forward, cautiously groping at the darkness in front of me, and I discovered that the debris was packed against another steel-bar grate. Whatever trash managed to wash over the top of the first grate was caught here.

After climbing this barrier and crossing safely to the other side, I risked using the lighter. I cupped my hand around the flame to contain and direct the glow as much as possible.

The cat's eyes blazed bright: gold flecked with green now. We stared at each other for a long moment, and then my guide – if that's what it was – whipped around and sprinted out of sight, down into the drain.

Using the lighter to find my way, keeping the flame low to conserve butane, I descended through the heart of the coastal hills, passing smaller tributary culverts that opened into this main line. I arrived at a spillway of wide concrete steps on which were puddles of stagnant water and a thin carpet of hardy gray-black fungus that probably thrived only during the four-month rainy season. The scummy steps were treacherously slippery, but for the safety of maintenance crews, a steel handrail was bolted to one wall, hung now with a drab tinsel of dead grass deposited by the most recent flood.

As I descended, I listened for the sounds of pursuit, voices in the tunnel behind me, but all I heard were my own stealthy noises. Either the searchers had decided that I hadn't escaped by way of the culvert – or they had hesitated so long before following me into the drain that I had gotten well ahead of them.

At the bottom of the spillway, on the last two broad steps, I almost plunged into what I thought at first were the pale, rounded caps of large mushrooms, clusters of vile-looking fungi growing here in the lightless damp, no doubt poisonous in the extreme.

Clutching the railing, I eased past sprouting forms on the slippery concrete, reluctant to touch them even with one of my shoes. Standing in the next length of sloping tunnel, I turned to examine this peculiar find.

When I cranked up the flame on the lighter, I discovered that before me lay not mushrooms but a collection of skulls. The fragile skulls of birds. The elongated skulls of lizards. The larger skulls of what might have been cats, dogs, raccoons, porcupines, rabbits, squirrels . . .

Not a scrap of flesh adhered to any of these death's-heads, as if they had been boiled clean: white and yellow-white in the butane light, scores of them, perhaps a hundred. No leg bones, no rib cages, just skulls.

They were arranged neatly side by side in three rows – two on the bottom step and one on the second from the bottom – facing out, as though, even with their empty eye sockets, they were here to bear witness to something.

I had no idea what to make of this. I saw no satanic markings on the culvert walls, no indications of macabre ceremonies of any kind, yet the display had an undeniably symbolic purpose. The extent of the collection indicated obsession, and the cruelty implicit in so much killing and decapitation was chilling.

Recalling the fascination with death that had gripped me and Bobby Halloway when we were thirteen, I wondered if some kid, far weirder than we ever were, had done this grisly work. Criminologists claim that by the age of three or four, most serial killers begin torturing and killing insects, progressing to small animals during childhood and adolescence – and finally graduating to people. Maybe in these catacombs, a particularly vicious young murderer was practicing for his life's work.

In the middle of the third and highest row of these bony visages rested a gleaming skull that was markedly different from all of the others. It appeared to be human. Small but human. Like the skull of an infant.

'Dear God.'

My voice whispered back to me along the concrete walls.

More than ever, I felt as though I were in a dreamscape, where even such things as concrete and bone were no more solid than smoke. Nevertheless, I did not reach out to touch the small human skull – or any of the others, for that matter. However unreal they might seem, I knew that they would be cold, slick, and too solid to the touch.

Anxious to avoid encountering whoever had acquired this grim collection, I continued downward through the drain.

I expected the cat to reappear, bearing its enigmatic eyes, pale paws meeting concrete with feather-on-feather silence, but either it remained out of sight ahead of me or it had detoured into one of the tributary lines.

Sections of sloped concrete pipe alternated with more spillways, and just as I was beginning to worry that the lighter didn't contain enough fuel to see me to safety, a circle of dim gray light appeared and gradually brightened ahead. I hurried toward it and found that no grate barred the lower end of the tunnel, which led into an open drainage channel of mortar-set river rock.

I was in familiar territory at last, in the northern flats of town. A couple of blocks from the sea. Half a block from the high school.

After the dank culvert, the night air smelled not merely fresh but sweet. The high points of the polished sky glittered diamond-white.

9

According to the digital light board on the Wells Fargo Bank building, the time was 7:56 p.m., which meant that my father had been dead less than three hours, though days seemed to have passed since I'd lost him. The same sign set the temperature at sixty degrees, but the night seemed colder to me.

Around the corner from the bank and down the block, the Tidy Time Laundromat was flooded with fluorescent light. Currently no customers were doing their laundry.

With the dollar bill ready in my hand, with my eyes squinted to slits, I went inside, into the flowery fragrance of soap powders and the chemical keenness of bleach, my head lowered to maximize the protection provided by the bill of my cap. I ran straight to the change machine, fed it, snatched up the four quarters that it spat into the tray, and fled.

Two blocks away, outside the post office, stood a pay phone with winglike sound shields. Above the phone, mounted on the wall of the building, was a security light behind a wire cage.

When I hung my hat on the cage, shadows fell.

I figured that Manuel Ramirez would still be at home. When I phoned him, his mother, Rosalina, said that he had been gone for hours. He was working a double shift because another officer had called in sick. This evening he was on desk duty; later, after midnight, he would be on patrol.

I punched in the main number of the Moonlight Bay Police and asked the operator if I could speak to Officer Ramirez.

Manuel, in my judgment the best cop in town, is three inches shorter than I am, thirty pounds heavier, twelve years older, and a Mexican-American. He loves baseball; I never follow sports because I have an acute sense of time slipping away and a reluctance to use my precious hours in too many passive activities. Manuel prefers country music; I like rock. He is a staunch Republican; I have no interest in politics. In movies, his guilty pleasure is Abbott and Costello; mine is the immortal Jackie Chan. We are friends.

'Chris, I heard about your dad,' Manuel said when he came on the line. 'I don't know what to say.'

'Neither do I, really.'

'No, there never is anything to say, is there?'

'Not that matters.'

'You going to be okay?'

To my surprise, I couldn't speak. My terrible loss seemed suddenly to be a surgeon's needle that stitched shut my throat and sewed my tongue to the roof of my mouth.

Curiously, immediately after Dad's death, I'd been able to answer this same question from Dr. Seth Cleveland without hesitation.

I felt closer to Manuel than to the physician. Friendship thaws the nerves, making it possible for pain to be felt.

'You come over some evening when I'm off duty,'

Manuel said. 'We'll drink some beer, eat some tamales, watch a couple of Jackie Chan movies.'

In spite of baseball and country music, we have much in common, Manuel Ramirez and I. He works the graveyard shift, from midnight until eight in the morning, sometimes doubling on the swing shift when, as on this March evening, there are personnel shortages. He likes the night as I do, but he also works it by necessity. Because the graveyard shift is less desirable than daytime duty, the pay is higher. More important, he is able to spend afternoons and evenings with his son, Toby, whom he cherishes. Sixteen years ago, Manuel's wife, Carmelita, died minutes after bringing Toby into the world. The boy is gentle, charming – and a victim of Down's syndrome. Manuel's mother moved into his house immediately after Carmelita's death and still helps to look after Toby. Manuel Ramirez knows about limitations. He feels the hand of fate every day of his life, in an age when most people no longer believe in purpose or destiny. We have much in common, Manuel Ramirez and I.

'Beer and Jackie Chan sound great,' I agreed. 'But who'll make the tamales – you or your mother?'

'Oh, not *mi madre*, I promise.'

Manuel is an exceptional cook, and his mother *thinks* that she is an exceptional cook. A comparison of their cooking provides a fearsomely illuminating example of the difference between a good deed and a good intention.

A car passed in the street behind me, and when I looked down, I saw my shadow pull at my unmoving feet, stretching from my left side around to my right, growing not merely longer but blacker on the concrete sidewalk, straining to tear loose of me and flee – but then snapping back to the left when the car passed.

'Manuel, there's something you can do for me, something more than tamales.'

'You name it, Chris.'

After a long hesitation, I said, 'It involves my dad . . . his body.'

Manuel matched my hesitation. His thoughtful silence was the equivalent of a cat's ears pricking with interest.

He heard more in my words than they appeared to convey. His tone was different when he spoke this time, still the voice of a friend but also the harder voice of a cop. 'What's happened, Chris?'

'It's pretty weird.'

'Weird?' he said, savoring the word as though it were an unexpected taste.

'I'd really rather not talk about it on the phone. If I come over to the station, can you meet me in the parking lot?'

I couldn't expect the police to switch off all their office lights and take my statement by the glow of candles.

Manuel said, 'We're talking something criminal?'

'Deeply. And weird.'

'Chief Stevenson's been working late today. He's still here but not for much longer. You think maybe I should ask him to wait?'

In my mind rose the eyeless face of the dead hitchhiker.

'Yeah,' I said. 'Yeah, Stevenson should hear this.'

'Can you be here in ten minutes?'

'See you then.'

I racked the telephone handset, snatched my cap

off the light cage, turned to the street, and shielded my eyes with one hand as two more cars drove past. One was a late-model Saturn. The other was a Chevy pickup.

No white van. No hearse. No black Hummer.

I didn't actually fear that the search for me was still on. By now the hitchhiker would be charring in the furnace. With the evidence reduced to ashes, no obvious proof existed to support my bizarre story. Sandy Kirk, the orderlies, and all the nameless others would feel safe.

Indeed, any attempt to kill or abduct me would risk witnesses to *that* crime, who would then have to be dealt with, increasing the likelihood of still more witnesses. These mysterious conspirators were best served now by discretion rather than aggression – especially when their sole accuser was the town freak, who came out of his heavily curtained house only between dusk and dawn, who feared the sun, who lived by the grace of cloaks and veils and hoods and masks of lotion, who crawled even the night town under a carapace of cloth and chemicals.

Considering the outrageous nature of my accusations, few would find my story credible, but I was sure that Manuel would know that I was telling the truth. I hoped the chief would believe me, too.

I stepped away from the telephone outside the post office and headed for the police station. It was only a couple of blocks away.

As I hurried through the night, I rehearsed what I would tell Manuel and his boss, Lewis Stevenson, who was a formidable figure for whom I wanted to be well prepared. Tall, broad-shouldered, athletic, Stevenson had a face noble enough to be stamped in profile on ancient Roman coins. Sometimes he seemed to be but an actor playing the role of dedicated police chief, although if it was a performance, then it was of award caliber. At fifty-two, he gave the impression – without appearing to try – that he was far wiser than his years, easily commanding respect and trust. There was something of the psychologist and something of the priest in him – qualities everyone in his position needed but few possessed. He was that rare person who enjoyed having power but did not abuse it, who exercised authority with good judgment and compassion, and he'd been chief of police for fourteen years without a hint of scandal, ineptitude, or inefficiency in his department.

Thus I came through lampless alleys lit by a moon riding higher in the sky than it had been earlier, came past fences and footpaths, past gardens and garbage cans, came mentally murmuring the words with which I hoped to tell a convincing story, came in two minutes instead of the ten that Manuel had suggested, came to the parking lot behind the municipal building and saw Chief Stevenson in a conspiratorial moment that stripped away the fine qualities that I'd projected onto him. Revealed now was a man who, regardless of his noble face, did not deserve to be honored by coins or by monuments or even by having his photograph hung in the station house next to those of the mayor, the governor, and the President of the United States.

Stevenson stood at the far end of the municipal building, near the back entrance to the police station, in a cascade of bluish light from a hooded security lamp above the door. The man with whom he conferred stood a few feet away, only half revealed in blue shadows.

I crossed the parking lot, heading toward them. They didn't see me coming because they were deeply engrossed in conversation. Furthermore, I was mostly screened from them as I passed among the street-department trucks and squad cars and water-department trucks and personal vehicles, while also staying as much as possible out of the direct light from the three tall pole lamps.

Just before I would have stepped into the open, Stevenson's visitor moved closer to the chief, shedding the shadows, and I halted in shock. I saw his shaved head, his hard face. Red-plaid flannel shirt, blue jeans, work shoes.

At this distance, I wasn't able to see his pearl earring.

I was flanked by two large vehicles, and I quickly retreated a few steps to shelter more completely in the oily darkness between them. One of the engines was still hot; it pinged and ticked as it cooled.

Although I could hear the voices of the two men, I could not make out their words. An onshore breeze still romanced the trees and quarreled against all the works of man, and this ceaseless whisper and hiss screened the conversation from me.

I realized that the vehicle to my right, the one with the hot engine, was the white Ford van in which the bald man had driven away from Mercy Hospital earlier in the night. With my father's mortal remains.

I wondered if the keys might be in the ignition. I pressed my face to the window in the driver's door, but I couldn't see much of the interior.

If I could steal the van, I would most likely have possession of crucial proof that my story was true. Even if my father's body had been taken elsewhere and was no longer in this van, forensic evidence might remain – not least, some of the hitchhiker's blood.

I had no idea how to hot-wire an engine.

Hell, I didn't know how to *drive*.

And even if I discovered that I possessed a natural talent for the operation of motor vehicles that was the equivalent of Mozart's brilliance at musical composition, I wouldn't be able to drive twenty miles south along the coast or thirty miles north to another police jurisdiction. Not in the glare of oncoming headlights. Not without my precious sunglasses, which lay broken far away in the hills to the east.

Besides, if I opened the van door, the cab lights would wink on. The two men would notice.

They would come for me.

They would kill me.

The back door of the police station opened. Manuel Ramirez stepped outside.

Lewis Stevenson and his conspirator broke off their urgent conversation at once. From this distance, I wasn't able to discern whether Manuel knew the bald man, but he appeared to address only the chief.

I couldn't believe that Manuel – good son of Rosalina, mourning widower of Carmelita, loving father of Toby – would be a part of any business that involved murder and graverobbing. We can never know many of the people in our lives, not truly *know* them, regardless of how deeply we believe that we see into them. Most of them are murky ponds, containing infinite layers of suspended particles, stirred by strange currents in their greatest depths. But I was willing to bet my life that Manuel's clear-water heart concealed no capacity for treachery.

I wasn't willing to bet *his* life, however, and if I called out to him to search the back of the white van with me, to impound the vehicle for an exhaustive forensics workup, I might be signing his death warrant as well as mine. In fact, I was sure of it.

Abruptly Stevenson and the bald man turned from Manuel to survey the parking lot. I knew then that he had told them about my telephone call.

I dropped into a crouch and shrank deeper into the gloom between the van and the water-department truck.

At the back of the van, I tried to read the license plate. Although usually I was plagued by too much light, this time I was hampered by too little.

Frantically, I traced the seven numbers and letters with my fingertips. I wasn't able to memorize them by Braille reading, however, at least not quickly enough to avoid discovery.

I knew that the bald man, if not Stevenson, was coming to the van. Was already on the move. The bald man, the butcher, the trader in bodies, the thief of eyes.

Staying low, I retraced the route by which I had come through the ranks of parked trucks and cars, returning to the alley and then scurrying onward, using rows of trash cans as cover, all but crawling to a Dumpster and past it, to a corner and around, into the other alleyway, out of sight of the municipal building, rising to my full height now, running once more, as fleet as the cat, gliding like an owl, creature of the night, wondering if I would find safe shelter before dawn or would still be afoot in the open to curl and blacken under the hot rising sun.

10

I assumed that I could safely go home but that I might be foolish to linger there too long. I wouldn't be overdue at the police station for another two minutes, and they would wait for me at least ten minutes past the appointed time before Chief Stevenson realized that I must have seen him with the man who had stolen my father's body.

Even then, they might not come to the house in search of me. I was still not a serious threat to them – and not likely to become one. I had no proof of anything that I'd seen.

Nevertheless, they seemed inclined to take extreme measures to prevent the exposure of their inscrutable conspiracy. They might be loath to leave even the smallest of loose ends – which meant a knot in my neck.

I expected to find Orson in the foyer when I unlocked the front door and stepped inside, but he was not waiting for me. I called his name, but he didn't appear; and if he had been approaching through the gloom, I would have heard his big paws thumping on the floor.

He was probably in one of his dour moods. For the most part, he is good-humored, playful and companionable, with enough energy in his tail to sweep all the streets in Moonlight Bay. From time to time, however, the world weighs heavily on him, and then he lies as limp as a rug, sad eyes open but fixed on some doggy memory or on some doggy vision beyond this world, making no sound other than an occasional attenuated sigh.

More rarely, I have found Orson in a state of what seems to be bleakest dejection. This ought to be a condition too profound for any dog to wear, although it fits him well.

He once sat before a mirrored closet door in my bedroom, staring at his reflection for nearly half an hour – an eternity to the dog mind, which generally experiences the world as a series of two-minute wonders and three-minute enthusiasms. I hadn't been able to tell what fascinated him in his image, although I ruled out both canine vanity and simple puzzlement; he seemed full of sorrow, all drooping ears and slumped shoulders and wagless tail. I swear, at times his eyes brimmed with tears that he was barely able to hold back.

'Orson?' I called.

The switch operating the staircase chandelier was fitted with a rheostat, as were most of the switches throughout the house. I dialed up the minimum light that I needed to climb the stairs.

Orson wasn't on the landing. He wasn't waiting in the second-floor hall.

In my room, I dialed a wan glow. Orson wasn't here, either.

I went directly to the nearest nightstand. From the top drawer I withdrew an envelope in which I kept a supply of knocking-around money. It contained only a hundred and eighty dollars, but this was better than nothing. Though I didn't know why I might need the cash, I intended to be prepared, so I transferred the entire sum to one of the pockets of my jeans.

As I slid shut the nightstand drawer, I noticed a dark object on the bedspread. When I picked it up, I was surprised that it was actually what it had appeared to be in the shadows: a pistol.

I had never seen this weapon before.

My father had never owned a gun.

Acting on instinct, I put down the pistol and used a corner of the bedspread to wipe my prints off it. I suspected that I was being set up to take a fall for something I had not done.

Although any television emits ultraviolet radiation, I've seen a lot of movies over the years, because I'm safe if I sit far enough from the screen. I know all of the great stories of innocent men – from Cary Grant and James Stewart to Harrison Ford – relentlessly hounded for crimes they never committed and incarcerated on trumped-up evidence.

Stepping quickly into the adjacent bathroom, I switched on the low-watt bulb. No dead blonde in the bathtub.

No Orson, either.

In the bedroom once more, I stood very still and listened to the house. If other people were present, they were only ghosts drifting in ectoplasmic silence.

I returned to the bed, hesitated, picked up the pistol, and fumbled with it until I ejected the magazine. It was fully loaded. I slammed the magazine back into the butt. Being inexperienced with handguns, I found the piece heavier than I had expected: It weighed at least a pound and a half.

Next to where I'd found the gun, a white envelope

lay on the cream-colored bedspread. I hadn't noticed it until now.

I withdrew a penlight from a nightstand drawer and focused the tight beam on the envelope. It was blank except for a professionally printed return address in the upper left corner: Thor's Gun Shop here in Moonlight Bay. The unsealed envelope, which bore neither a stamp nor a postmark, was slightly crumpled and stippled with curious indentations.

When I picked up the envelope, it was faintly damp in spots. The folded papers inside were dry.

I examined these documents in the beam of the penlight. I recognized my father's careful printing on the carbon copy of the standard application, on which he had attested to the local police that he had no criminal record or history of mental illness that would be grounds to deny him the right to own this firearm. Also included was a carbon copy of the original invoice for the weapon, indicating that it was a 9mm Glock 17 and that my father had purchased it with a check.

The date on the invoice gave me a chill: January 18, two years previous. My father had bought the Glock just three days after my mother had been killed in the car crash on Highway 1. As though he thought he needed protection.

In the study across the hallway from the bedroom, my compact cellular phone was recharging. I unplugged it and clipped it to my belt, at my hip.

Orson was not in the study.

Earlier, Sasha had stopped by the house to feed him. Maybe she had taken him with her when she'd gone. If Orson had been as somber as he'd been when I'd left for the hospital – and especially if he had settled into an even blacker mood – Sasha might not have been able to leave the poor beast here alone, because as much compassion as blood flows through her veins.

Even if Orson had gone with Sasha, who had transferred the 9mm Glock from my father's room to my bed? Not Sasha. She wouldn't have known the gun existed, and she wouldn't have prowled through my dad's belongings.

The desk phone was connected to an answering machine. Next to the blinking message light, the counter window showed two calls.

According to the machine's automatic time-and-date voice, the first call had come in only half an hour ago. It lasted nearly two minutes, although the caller spoke not a word.

Initially, he drew slow deep breaths and let them out almost as slowly, as though he possessed the magical power to inhale the myriad scents of my rooms even across a telephone line, and thereby discover if I was home or out. After a while, he began to hum as though he had forgotten that he was being recorded and was merely humming to himself in the manner of a daydreamer lost in thought, humming a tune that seemed to be improvised, with no coherent melody, spiraling and low, eerie and repetitive, like the song that a madman might hear when he believes that angels of destruction, in choirs, are singing to him.

I was sure he was a stranger. I believed that I would have been able to recognize the voice of a friend even from nothing more than the humming. I was also sure that he had not reached a wrong number; somehow he was involved with the events following my father's death.

By the time the first caller disconnected, I discovered that I had tightened my hands into fists. I was holding useless air in my lungs. I exhaled a hot dry gust, inhaled a cool sweet draft, but could not yet unclench my hands.

The second call, which had come in only minutes before I had returned home, was from Angela Ferryman, the nurse who had been at my father's bedside. She didn't identify herself, but I recognized her thin yet musical voice: Through her message, it quickened like an increasingly restless bird hopping from picket point to picket point along a fence.

'Chris, I'd like to talk to you. *Have* to talk. As soon as it's convenient. Tonight. If you can, tonight. I'm in the car, on my way home now. You know where I live. Come see me. Don't call. I don't trust phones. Don't even like making this call. But I've got to see you. Come to the back door. No matter how late you get this, come anyway. I won't be asleep. Can't sleep.'

I put a new message tape on the machine. I hid the original cassette under the crumpled sheets of writing paper at the bottom of the wastebasket beside my desk.

These two brief tape recordings wouldn't convince a cop or a judge of anything. Nevertheless, they were the only scraps of evidence I possessed to indicate that something extraordinary was happening to me – something even more extraordinary than my birth into this tiny sunless caste. More extraordinary than surviving twenty-eight years unscathed by xeroderma pigmentosum.

≈   ≈   ≈

I had been home less than ten minutes. Nevertheless, I was lingering too long.

As I searched for Orson, I more than half expected to hear a door being forced or glass breaking on the lower floor and then footsteps on the stairs. The house remained quiet, but this was a tremulous silence like the surface tension on a pond.

The dog wasn't moping in Dad's bedroom or bathroom. Not in the walk-in closet, either.

Second by second, I grew more worried about the mutt. Whoever had put the 9mm Glock pistol on my bed might also have taken or harmed Orson.

In my room again, I located a spare pair of sunglasses in a bureau drawer. They were in a soft case with a Velcro seal, and I clipped the case in my shirt pocket.

I glanced at my wristwatch, on which the time was displayed by light-emitting diodes.

Quickly, I returned the invoice and the police questionnaire to the envelope from Thor's Gun Shop. Whether it was more evidence or merely trash, I hid it between the mattress and box springs of my bed.

The date of purchase seemed significant. Suddenly *everything* seemed significant.

I kept the pistol. Maybe this was a setup, just like in the movies, but I felt safer with a weapon. I wished that I knew how to use it.

The pockets of my leather jacket were deep enough to conceal the gun. It hung in the right pocket not like a weight of dead steel but like a thing alive, like a torpid but not entirely dormant snake. When I moved, it seemed to writhe slowly: fat and sluggish, an oozing tangle of thick coils.

As I was about to go downstairs to search for Orson, I recalled one July night when I had watched him from my bedroom window as he sat in the backyard, his head tilted to lift his snout to the breeze, transfixed by something in the heavens, deep in one of his most puzzling moods. He had not been howling, and in any event the summer sky had been moonless; the sound he made was neither a whine nor a whimper but a mewling of singular and disturbing character.

Now I raised the blind at that same window and saw him in the yard below. He was busily digging a black hole in the moon-silvered lawn. This was peculiar, because he was a well-behaved dog and never a digger.

As I looked on, Orson abandoned the patch of earth at which he had been furiously clawing, moved a few feet to the right, and began to dig a new hole. A quality of frenzy marked his behavior.

'What's happened, boy?' I wondered, and in the yard below, the dog dug, dug, dug.

On my way downstairs, with the Glock coiling heavily in my jacket pocket, I remembered that July night when I had gone into the backyard to sit beside the mewling dog . . .

His cries grew as thin as the whistle-hiss of a glass-blower shaping a vase over a flame, so soft that they did not even disturb the nearest of our neighbors, yet there was such wretchedness in the sound that I was shaken by it. With his cries, he shaped a misery darker than the darkest glass and stranger in form than anything a blower could blow.

He was uninjured and did not appear to be ill. For all I could tell, the sight of the stars themselves was the thing that filled him with torment. Yet if the vision of dogs is as poor as we are taught, they can't see the stars well or at all. And why should stars cause Orson such anguish, anyway, or the night that was no deeper than other nights before it? Nevertheless, he gazed skyward and made tortured sounds and didn't respond to my reassuring voice.

When I put a hand on his head and stroked his back, I felt hard shudders passing through him. He sprang to his feet and padded away, only to turn and stare at me from a distance, and I swear that for a while he hated me. He loved me as always; he was still my dog, after all, and could not escape loving me; but at the same time, he hated me intensely. In the warm July air, I could virtually feel the cold hatred radiating off him. He paced the yard, alternately staring at me – holding my gaze as only he among all dogs is able to hold it – and looking at the sky, now stiff and shaking with rage, but now weak and mewling with what seemed despair.

When I'd told Bobby Halloway about this, he'd said that dogs are incapable of hating anyone or of feeling anything as complex as genuine despair, that their emotional lives are as simple as their intellectual lives. When I insisted on my interpretation of what I'd experienced, Bobby had said, 'Listen, Snow, if you're going to keep coming here to bore my ass off with this New Age crap, why don't you just buy a shotgun and blow my brains out? That would be more merciful than the excruciatingly slow death you're dealing out now, bludgeoning me with your tedious little stories and your moronic philosophies. There are limits to human endurance, St. Francis – even to mine.'

I know what I know, however, and I know Orson hated me that July night, hated me and loved me. And I know that something in the sky tormented him and filled him with despair: the stars, the blackness, or perhaps something he imagined.

Can dogs imagine? Why not?

I know they dream. I've watched them sleep, seen their legs kick as they chase dream rabbits, heard them sigh and whimper, heard them growl at dream adversaries.

Orson's hatred that night did not make me fear him, but I feared *for* him. I knew his problem was not distemper or any physical ailment that might have made him dangerous to me, but was instead a malady of the soul.

Bobby raves brilliantly at the mention of souls in animals and splutters ultimately into a tremendously entertaining incoherence. I could sell tickets. I prefer to open a bottle of beer, lean back, and have the whole show to myself.

Anyway, throughout that long night, I sat in the yard, keeping Orson company even though he might not have wanted it. He glowered at me, remarked upon the vaulted sky with razor-thin cries, shuddered uncontrollably, circled the yard, circled and circled until near dawn, when at last he came to me, exhausted, and put his head in my lap and did not hate me anymore.

Just before sunrise, I went upstairs to my room, ready for bed hours earlier than usual, and Orson came with me. Most of the time, when he chooses to sleep to my schedule, he curls near my feet, but on this occasion he lay on his side with his back to me, and until he slept, I stroked his burly head and smoothed his fine black coat.

I myself slept not at all that day. I lay thinking about the hot summer morning beyond the blinded windows. The sky like an inverted blue porcelain bowl with birds in flight around its rim. Birds of the day, which I had seen only in pictures. And bees and butterflies. And shadows ink-pure and knife-sharp at the edges as they never can be in the night. Sweet sleep couldn't pour into me because I was filled to the brim with bitter yearning.

≈ ≈ ≈

Now, nearly three years later, as I opened the kitchen door and stepped onto the back porch, I hoped that Orson wasn't in a despondent mood. This night, we had no time for therapy either for him or for me.

My bicycle was on the porch. I walked it down the steps and rolled it toward the busy dog.

In the southwest corner of the yard, he had dug half a dozen holes of various diameters and depths, and I had to be careful not to twist an ankle in one of them. Across that quadrant of the lawn were scattered ragged clumps of uprooted grass and clods of earth torn loose by his claws.

'Orson?'

He did not respond. He didn't even pause in his frenzied digging.

Giving him a wide berth to avoid the spray of dirt that fanned out behind his excavating forepaws, I went around the current hole to face him.

'Hey, pal,' I said.

The dog kept his head down, his snout in the ground, sniffing inquisitively as he dug.

The breeze had died, and the full moon hung like a child's lost balloon in the highest branches of the melaleucas.

Overhead, nighthawks dived and soared and barrel-looped, crying *peent-peent-peent* as they harvested flying ants and early-spring moths from the air.

Watching Orson at work, I said, 'Found any good bones lately?'

He stopped digging but still didn't acknowledge me. Urgently he sniffed the raw earth, the scent of which rose even to me.

'Who let you out here?'

Sasha might have brought him outside to toilet, but I was sure that she would have returned him to the house afterward.

'Sasha?' I asked nevertheless.

If Sasha were the one who had left him loose to wreak havoc on the landscaping, Orson was not going to rat on her. He wouldn't meet my eyes lest I read the truth in them.

Abandoning the hole he had just dug, he returned to a previous pit, sniffed it, and set to work again, seeking communion with dogs in China.

Maybe he knew that Dad was dead. Animals know things, as Sasha had noted earlier. Maybe this industrious digging was Orson's way of working off the nervous energy of grief.

I lowered my bicycle to the grass and hunkered down in front of the burrowing fiend. I gripped his collar and gently forced him to pay attention to me.

'What's wrong with you?'

His eyes had in them the darkness of the ravaged soil, not the brighter glimmering darkness of the starry sky. They were deep and unreadable.

'I've got places to go, pal,' I told him. 'I want you to come with me.'

He whined and twisted his head to look at the devastation all around him, as though to say that he was loath to leave this great work unfinished.

'Come morning, I'm going to stay at Sasha's place, and I don't want to leave you here alone.'

His ears pricked, although not at the mention of Sasha's name or at anything I had said. He wrenched his powerful body around in my grip to look toward the house.

When I let go of his collar, he raced across the yard but then stopped well short of the back porch. He stood at attention, head raised high, utterly still, alert.

'What is it, fella?' I whispered.

From a distance of fifteen or twenty feet, even with the breeze dead and the night hushed, I could barely hear his low growl.

On my way out of the house, I had dialed the switches all the way off, leaving lightless rooms behind me. Blackness still filled the place, and I could see no ghostly face pressed to any of the panes.

Orson sensed someone, however, because he began to back away from the house. Suddenly he spun around with the agility of a cat and raced toward me.

I raised my bike off its side, onto its wheels.

Tail low but not tucked between his legs, ears flattened against his head, Orson shot past me to the back gate.

Trusting in the reliability of canine senses, I joined the dog at the gate without delay. The property is surrounded by a silvered cedar fence as tall as I am, and the gate is cedar, too. The gravity latch was cold under my fingers. Quietly I slipped it open and silently cursed the squeaking hinges.

Beyond the gate is a hard-packed dirt footpath bordered by houses on one side and by a narrow grove of old red-gum eucalyptuses on the other. As we pushed through the gate, I half expected someone to be waiting for us, but the path was deserted.

To the south, beyond the eucalyptus grove, lies a golf course and then the Moonlight Bay Inn and Country Club. At this hour on a Friday night, viewed between the trunks of the tall trees, the golf course was as black and rolling as the sea, and the glittering amber windows of the distant inn were like the portals on a magnificent cruise ship forever bound for far Tahiti.

To the left, the footpath led uphill toward the heart of town, ultimately terminating in the graveyard adjacent to St. Bernadette's, the Catholic church. To the right, it led downhill toward the flats, the harbor, and the Pacific.

I shifted gears and cycled uphill, toward the graveyard, with the eucalyptus perfume reminding me of the light at a crematorium window and of a beautiful young mother lying dead upon a mortician's gurney, but with good Orson trotting alongside my bike and with the faint strains of dance music filtering across the golf course from the inn, and with a baby crying in one of our neighbors' houses to my left, but with the weight of the Glock pistol in my pocket and with nighthawks overhead snapping insects in their sharp beaks: the living and the dead all together in the trap of land and sky.

11

I wanted to talk to Angela Ferryman, because her message on my answering machine had seemed to promise revelations. I was in the mood for revelations.

First, however, I had to call Sasha, who was waiting to hear about my father.

I stopped in St. Bernadette's cemetery, one of my favorite places, a harbor of darkness in one of the more brightly lighted precincts of town. The trunks of six giant oaks rise like columns, supporting a ceiling formed by their interlocking crowns, and the quiet space below is laid out in aisles similar to those in any library; the gravestones are like rows of books bearing the names of those who have been blotted from the pages of life, who may be forgotten elsewhere but are remembered here.

Orson wandered, though not far from me, sniffing the spoor of the squirrels that, by day, gathered acorns off the graves. He was not a hunter tracking prey but a scholar satisfying his curiosity.

From my belt, I unclipped my cellular phone, switched it on, and keyed in Sasha Goodall's mobile number. She answered on the second ring.

'Dad's gone,' I said, meaning more than she could know.

Earlier, in anticipation of Dad's death, Sasha had expressed her sorrow. Now her voice tightened slightly with grief so well controlled that only I could have heard it: 'Did he . . . did he go easy at the end?'

'No pain.'

'Was he conscious?'

'Yeah. We had a chance to say good-bye.'

Fear nothing.

Sasha said, 'Life stinks.'

'It's just the rules,' I said. 'To get in the game, we have to agree to stop playing someday.'

'It still stinks. Are you at the hospital?'

'No. Out and about. Rambling. Working off some energy. Where're you?'

'In the Explorer. Going to Pinkie's Diner to grab breakfast and work on my notes for the show.' She would be on the air in three and a half hours. 'Or I could get takeout, and we could go eat somewhere together.'

'I'm not really hungry,' I said truthfully. 'I'll see you later though.'

'When?'

'You go home from work in the morning, I'll be there. I mean, if that's okay.'

'That's perfect. Love you, Snowman.'

'Love you,' I replied.

'That's our little mantra.'

'It's our truth.'

I pushed *end* on the keypad, switched off the phone, and clipped it to my belt again.

When I cycled out of the cemetery, my four-legged companion followed but somewhat reluctantly at first. His head was full of squirrel mysteries.

≈ ≈ ≈

I made my way to Angela Ferryman's house as far as possible by alleyways where I was not likely to encounter much traffic and on streets with widely spaced lampposts. When I had no choice but to pass under clusters of streetlamps, I pedaled hard.

Faithfully, Orson matched his pace to mine. He seemed happier than he had been earlier, now that he could trot at my side, blacker than any nightshadow that I could cast.

We encountered only four vehicles. Each time, I squinted and looked away from the headlights.

Angela lived on a high street in a charming Spanish bungalow that sheltered under magnolia trees not yet in bloom. No lights were on in the front rooms.

An unlocked side gate admitted me to an arbor-covered passage. The walls and arched ceiling of the arbor were entwined with star jasmine. In summer, sprays of the tiny five-petaled white flowers would be clustered so abundantly that the lattice would seem to be draped with multiple layers of lace. Even this early in the year, the hunter-green foliage was enlivened by those pinwheel-like blooms.

While I breathed deeply of the jasmine fragrance, savoring it, Orson sneezed twice.

I wheeled my bike out of the arbor and around to the back of the bungalow, where I leaned it against one of the redwood posts that supported the patio cover.

'Be vigilant,' I told Orson. 'Be big. Be bad.'

He chuffed as though he understood his assignment. Maybe he *did* understand, no matter what Bobby Halloway and the Rationality Police would say.

Beyond the kitchen windows and the translucent curtains was a slow pulse of candlelight.

The door featured four small panes of glass. I rapped softly on one of them.

Angela Ferryman drew aside the curtain. Her quick nervous eyes peeked at me – and then at the patio beyond me to confirm that I had come alone.

With a conspiratorial demeanor, she ushered me inside, locking the door behind us. She adjusted the curtain until she was convinced that no gap existed through which anyone could peer in at us.

Though the kitchen was pleasantly warm, Angela was wearing not only a gray sweat suit but a navy-blue wool cardigan over the sweats. The cable-knit cardigan might have belonged to her late husband; it hung to her knees, and the shoulder seams were halfway to her elbows. The sleeves had been rolled so often that the resultant cuffs were as thick as great iron manacles.

Even in this bulk of clothing, Angela appeared diminutive and thin. Evidently she remained chilly; she was virtually colorless, shivering.

She hugged me. As always it was a fierce, sharp-boned, *strong* hug, though I sensed in her an uncharacteristic fatigue.

She sat at the polished-pine table and invited me to take the chair opposite hers.

I took off my cap and considered removing my jacket as well. The kitchen was too warm. The pistol was in my pocket, however, and I was afraid that it might fall out on the floor or knock against the chair as I pulled my arms from the coat sleeves. I didn't want to alarm Angela, and she was sure to be frightened by the gun.

In the center of the table were three votive candles in little ruby-red glass containers. Arteries of shimmering red light crawled across the polished pine.

A bottle of apricot brandy also stood on the table. Angela had provided me with a cordial glass, and I half filled it.

Her glass was full to the brim. This wasn't her first serving, either.

She held the glass in both hands, as if taking warmth from it, and when she raised it with both hands to her lips, she looked more waiflike than ever. In spite of her gauntness, she could have passed for thirty-five, nearly fifteen years younger than her true age. At this moment, in fact, she seemed almost childlike.

'From the time I was a little girl, all I ever really wanted to be was a nurse.'

'And you're the best,' I said sincerely.

She licked apricot brandy from her lips and stared into her glass. 'My mother had rheumatoid arthritis. It progressed more quickly than usual. So fast. By the time I was six, she was in leg braces and using crutches. Shortly after my twelfth birthday, she was bedridden. She died when I was sixteen.'

I could say nothing meaningful or helpful about that. No one could have. Any words, no matter how sincerely meant, would have tasted as false as vinegar is bitter.

Sure enough, she had something important to tell me, but she needed time to marshall all the words into orderly ranks and march them across the table at me. Because whatever she had to tell me – it scared her. Her fear was visible: brittle in her bones and waxy in her skin.

Slowly working her way to her true subject, she said, 'I liked to bring my mother things when she couldn't get them easily herself. A glass of iced tea. A sandwich. Her medicine. A pillow for her chair. Anything. Later, it was a bedpan. And toward the end, fresh sheets when she was incontinent. I never minded that, either. She always smiled at me when I brought her things, smoothed my hair with her poor swollen hands. I couldn't heal her, or make it possible for her to run again or dance, couldn't relieve her pain or her fear, but I could *attend* her, make her comfortable, monitor her condition – and doing those things was more important to me than . . . than anything.'

The apricot brandy was too sweet to be called brandy but not as sweet as I had expected. Indeed, it was potent. No amount of it could make me forget my parents, however, or Angela her mother.

'All I ever wanted to be was a nurse,' she repeated. 'And for a long time it was satisfying work. Scary and sad, too, when we lost a patient, but mostly rewarding.' When she looked up from the brandy, her eyes were pried wide open by a memory. 'God, I was so scared when you had appendicitis. I thought I was going to lose my little Chris.'

'I was nineteen. Not too little.'

'Honey, I've been your visiting nurse since you were diagnosed when you were a toddler. You'll always be a little boy to me.'

I smiled. 'I love you too, Angela.'

Sometimes I forget that the directness with which I express my best emotions is unusual, that it can startle people and – as in this case – move them more deeply than I expect.

Her eyes clouded with tears. To repress them, she bit her lip, but then she resorted to the apricot brandy.

Nine years ago, I'd had one of those cases of appendicitis in which the symptoms do not manifest whatsoever until the condition is acute. After breakfast, I suffered mild indigestion. Before lunch, I was vomiting, red-faced, and gushing sweat. Stomach pain twisted me into the curled posture of a shrimp in the boiling oil of a french fryer.

My life was put at risk because of the delay caused by the need for extraordinary preparations at Mercy Hospital. The surgeon was not, of course, amenable to the idea of cutting open my abdomen and conducting the procedure in a dark – or even dimly lighted – operating room. Yet protracted exposure to the bright lights of the surgery was certain to result in a severe burn to any skin not protected from the glare, risking melanoma but also inhibiting the healing of the incision. Covering everything below the point of incision – from my groin to my toes – was easy: a triple layer of cotton sheeting pinned to prevent it from slipping aside. Additional sheeting was used to improvise complex tenting over my head and upper body, designed in such a way as to protect me from the light but also to allow the anesthesiologist to slip under from time to time, with a penlight, to take my blood pressure and my temperature, to adjust the gas mask, and to ensure that the electrodes from the electrocardiograph remained securely in place on my chest and wrists to permit continued monitoring of my heart. Their standard procedure required that my abdomen be draped except for a window of exposed skin at the site of the surgery, but in my case this rectangular window had to be reduced to the narrowest possible slit. With self-retaining retractors to keep the incision open and judicial use of tape to shield the skin to the very lip of the cut, they dared to slice me. My guts could take all the light that my doctors wanted to pour into them – but by the time they got that far, my appendix had burst. In spite of a meticulous cleanup, peritonitis ensued; an abscess developed and was swiftly followed by septic shock, requiring a second surgical procedure two days later.

After I recovered from septic shock and was in no danger of imminent death, I lived for months with the expectation that what I had endured might trigger one of the neurological problems related to XP. Generally these conditions develop after a burn or following long-term cumulative exposure to light – or for reasons not understood – but sometimes they apparently can be engendered by severe physical trauma or shock. Tremors of the head or the hands. Hearing loss. Slurred speech. Even mental impairment. I waited for the first signs of a progressive, irreversible neurological disorder – but they never came.

William Dean Howells, the great poet, wrote that death is at the bottom of everyone's cup. But there is still some sweet tea in mine.

And apricot brandy.

After taking another thick sip from her cordial glass, Angela said, 'All I ever wanted was to be a nurse, but look at me now.'

She wanted me to ask, and so I did: 'What do you mean?'

Gazing at captive flames through a curve of ruby glass, she said, 'Nursing is about life. I'm about death now.'

I didn't know what she meant, but I waited.

'I've done terrible things,' she said.

'I'm sure you haven't.'

'I've seen others do terrible things, and I haven't tried to stop them. The guilt's the same.'

'Could you have stopped them if you'd tried?'

She thought about that a while. 'No,' she said, but she looked no less troubled.

'No one can carry the whole world on her shoulders.'

'Some of us better try,' she said.

I gave her time. The brandy was fine.

She said, 'If I'm going to tell you, it has to be now. I don't have much time. I'm becoming.'

'Becoming?'

'I feel it. I don't know who I'll be a month from now, or six months. Someone I won't like to be. Someone who terrifies me.'

'I don't understand.'

'I know.'

'How can I help?' I asked.

'No one can help. Not you. Not me. Not God.' Having shifted her gaze from the votive candles to the golden liquid in her glass, she spoke quietly but fiercely: 'We're screwing it up, Chris, like we always do, but this is bigger than we've ever screwed up before. Because of pride, arrogance, envy. We're losing it, all of it. Oh, God, we're losing it, and already there's no way to turn back, to undo what's been done.'

Although her voice was not slurred, I suspected that she had drunk more than one previous glass of apricot brandy. I tried to take comfort in the thought that drink had led her to exaggerate, that whatever looming catastrophe she perceived was not a hurricane but only a squall magnified by mild inebriation.

Nevertheless, she had succeeded in countering the warmth of the kitchen and the cordial. I no longer considered removing my jacket.

'I can't stop them,' she said. 'But I can stop keeping secrets for them. You deserve to know what happened to your mom and dad, Chris – even if pain comes with the knowledge. Your life's been hard enough, plenty hard, without this, too.'

Truth is, I don't believe my life has been especially hard. It has been *different*. If I were to rage against this difference and spend my nights yearning for so-called normalcy, then I would surely make life as hard as granite and break myself on it. By embracing difference, by choosing to thrive on it, I lead a life no harder than most others and easier than some.

I didn't say a word of this to Angela. If she was motivated by pity to make these pending revelations, then I would compose my features into a mask of suffering and present myself as a figure of purest tragedy. I would be Macbeth. I would be mad Lear. I would be Schwarzenegger in *Terminator 2*, doomed to the vat of molten steel.

'You've got so many friends . . . but there're enemies you don't know about,' Angela continued. 'Dangerous bastards. And some of them are strange . . . They're becoming.'

That word again. *Becoming*.

When I rubbed the back of my neck, I discovered that the spiders I felt were imaginary.

She said, 'If you're going to have a chance . . . any chance at all . . . you need to know the truth. I've been wondering where to begin, how to tell you. I think I should start with the monkey.'

'The monkey?' I echoed, certain I had not heard her correctly.

'The monkey,' she confirmed.

In this context, the word had an inescapable comic quality, and I wondered again about Angela's sobriety.

When at last she looked up from her glass, her eyes were desolate pools in which lay drowned some vital part of the Angela Ferryman whom I had known since childhood. Meeting her stare – its bleak gray sheen – I felt the nape of my neck shrink, and I no longer found any comic potential whatsoever in the word *monkey*.

12

'It was Christmas Eve four years ago,' she said. 'About an hour after sunset. I was here in the kitchen, baking cookies. Using both ovens. Chocolate-chip in one. Walnut-oatmeal in the other. The radio was on. Somebody like Johnny Mathis singing "Silver Bells."'

I closed my eyes to try to picture the kitchen on that Christmas Eve – but also to have an excuse to shut out Angela's haunted stare.

She said, 'Rod was due home any minute, and we both were off work the entire holiday weekend.'

Rod Ferryman had been her husband.

Over three and a half years ago, six months after the Christmas Eve of which Angela was speaking, Rod had committed suicide with a shotgun in the garage of this house. Friends and neighbors had been stunned, and Angela had been devastated. He was an outgoing man with a good sense of humor, easy to like, not depressive, with no apparent problems that could have driven him to take his own life.

'I'd decorated the Christmas tree earlier in the day,' Angela said. 'We were going to have a candlelight dinner, open some wine, then watch *It's a Wonderful Life*. We loved that movie. We had gifts to exchange, lots of little gifts. Christmas was our favorite time of year, and we were like kids about the gifts . . .'

She fell silent.

When I dared to look, I saw that she had closed her eyes. Judging by her wrenched expression, her quicksilver memory had slipped from that Christmas night to the evening in the following June when she found her husband's body in the garage.

Candlelight flickered across her eyelids.

In time, she opened her eyes, but for a while they remained fixed on a faraway sight. She sipped her brandy.

'I was happy,' she said. 'The cookie smells. The Christmas music. And the florist had delivered a huge poinsettia from my sister, Bonnie. It was there on the end of the counter, so red and cheerful. I felt wonderful, really wonderful. It was the last time I ever felt wonderful – and the last time I ever will. So . . . I was spooning cookie batter onto a baking sheet when I heard this sound behind me, an odd little chirrup, and then something like a sigh, and when I turned, there was a monkey sitting right on this table.'

'Good heavens.'

'A rhesus monkey with these awful dark-yellow eyes. Not like their normal eyes. Strange.'

'Rhesus? You recognized the species?'

'I paid for my nurse's schooling by working as a lab assistant for a scientist at UCLA. The rhesus is one of the most commonly used animals in experiments. I saw a lot of them.'

'And suddenly one of them is sitting right here.'

'There was a bowl of fruit on the table – apples and tangerines. The monkey was peeling and eating one of the tangerines. Neat as you please, this big monkey placing the peelings in a tidy pile.'

'Big?' I asked.

'You're probably thinking of an organ grinder's monkey, one of those tiny cute little things. Rhesuses aren't like that.'

'How big?'

'Probably two feet tall. Maybe twenty-five pounds.'

Such a monkey would seem enormous when encountered, unexpected, in the middle of a kitchen table.

I said, 'You must have been pretty surprised.'

'More than surprised. I was a little scared. I know how strong those buggers are for their size. Mostly they're peaceable, but once in a while you get one with a mean streak, and he's a real handful.'

'Not the kind of monkey anyone would keep as a pet.'

'God, no. Not anyone normal – at least not in my book. Well, I'll admit that rhesuses can be cute sometimes, with their pale little faces and that ruff of fur. But this one wasn't cute.' Clearly, she could see it in her mind's eye. 'No, not this one.'

'So where did it come from?'

Instead of answering, Angela stiffened in her chair and cocked her head, listening intently to the house.

I couldn't hear anything out of the ordinary.

Apparently, neither did she. Yet when she spoke again, she did not relax. Her thin hands were locked clawlike on the cordial glass. 'I couldn't figure how the thing got inside, into the house. December wasn't overly warm that year. No windows or doors were open.'

'You didn't hear it enter the room?'

'No. I was making noise with the cookie sheets, the

mixing bowls. Music on the radio. But the damn thing must've been sitting on the table a minute or two, anyway, because by the time I realized it was there, it had eaten half the tangerine.'

Her gaze swept the kitchen, as though from the corner of her eye she had seen purposeful movement in the shadows at the periphery.

After steadying her nerves with brandy once more, she said, 'Disgusting – a monkey right on the kitchen table, of all places.'

Grimacing, she brushed one trembling hand across the polished pine, as though a few of the creature's hairs might still be clinging to the table four years after the incident.

'What did you do?' I pressed.

'I edged around the kitchen to the back door, opened it, hoping the monkey would run out.'

'But it was enjoying the tangerine, feeling pretty comfortable where it was,' I guessed.

'Yeah. It looked at the open door, then at me – and it actually seemed to laugh. This little tittering noise.'

'I swear I've seen dogs laugh now and then. Monkeys probably do, too.'

Angela shook her head. 'Can't remember any of them laughing in the lab. Of course, considering what their lives were like . . . they didn't have much reason to be in high spirits.'

She looked up uneasily at the ceiling, on which three small overlapping rings of light quivered like the smoldering eyes of an apparition: images of the trio of ruby-red glasses on the table.

Encouraging her to continue, I said, 'It wouldn't go outside.'

Instead of responding, she rose from her chair,

stepped to the back door, and tested the deadbolt to be sure it was still engaged.

'Angela?'

Hushing me, she pulled aside the curtain to peer at the patio and the moonlit yard, pulled it aside with trembling caution and only an inch, as if she expected to discover a hideous face pressed to the far side of the pane, gazing in at her.

My cordial glass was empty. I picked up the bottle, hesitated, and then put it down without pouring more.

When Angela turned away from the door, she said, 'It wasn't just a laugh, Chris. It was this frightening sound I could never adequately describe to you. It was an evil . . . an evil little cackle, a vicious edge to it. Oh, yes, I know what you're thinking – this was just an animal, just a monkey, so it couldn't be either good or evil. Maybe mean but not vicious, because animals *can* be bad-tempered, sure, but not consciously malevolent. That's what you're thinking. Well, I'm telling you, this one was more than just mean. This laugh was the coldest sound I've ever heard, the coldest and the ugliest – and evil.'

'I'm still with you,' I assured her.

Instead of returning to her chair from the door, she moved to the kitchen sink. Every square inch of glass in the windows above the sink was covered by the curtains, but she plucked at those panels of yellow fabric to make doubly sure that we were fully screened from spying eyes.

Turning to stare at the table as though the monkey sat there even now, Angela said, 'I got the broom, figuring I'd shoo the thing onto the floor and then toward the door. I mean, I didn't take a whack at it or anything, just brushed at it. You know?'

'Sure.'

'But it wasn't intimidated,' she said. 'It *exploded* with rage. Threw down the half-eaten tangerine and grabbed the broom and tried to pull it away from me. When I wouldn't let go, it started to climb the broom straight toward my hands.'

'Jesus.'

'Nimble as anything. So *fast*. Teeth bared and screeching, spitting, coming straight at me, so I let go of the broom, and the monkey fell to the floor with it, and I backed up until I bumped into the refrigerator.'

She bumped into the refrigerator again. The muffled clink of bottles came from the shelves within.

'It was on the floor, right in front of me. It knocked the broom aside. Chris, it was so *furious*. Fury out of proportion to anything that had happened. I hadn't hurt it, hadn't even touched it with the broom, but it wasn't going to take any crap from me.'

'You said rhesuses are basically peaceable.'

'Not this one. Lips skinned back from its teeth, screeching, running at me and then back and then at me again, hopping up and down, tearing at the air, glaring at me so hatefully, pounding the floor with its fists . . .'

Both of her cardigan sleeves had partly unrolled, and she drew her hands into them, out of sight. This memory monkey was so vivid that apparently she half expected it to fling itself at her right here, right now, and bite off the tips of her fingers.

'It was like a troll,' she said, 'a gremlin, some wicked thing out of a storybook. Those dark-yellow eyes.'

I could almost see them myself. Smoldering.

'And then suddenly, it leaps up the cabinets, onto the counter near me, all in a wink. It's right *there*' – she pointed – 'beside the refrigerator, inches from me, at eye level when I turn my head. It hisses at me, a mean hiss, and its breath smells like tangerines. That's how close we are. I knew—'

She interrupted herself to listen to the house again. She turned her head to the left to look toward the open door to the unlighted dining room.

Her paranoia was contagious. And because of what had happened to me since sundown, I was vulnerable to the infection.

Tensing in my chair, I cocked my head to allow any sinister sound to fall into the upturned cup of my ear.

The three rings of reflected light shimmered soundlessly on the ceiling. The curtains hung silently at the windows.

After a while Angela said, 'Its breath smelled like tangerines. It hissed and hissed. I knew it could kill me if it wanted, kill me somehow, even though it was only a monkey and hardly a fourth my weight. When it had been on the floor, maybe I could have drop-kicked the little son of a bitch, but now it was right in my face.'

I had no difficulty imagining how frightened she had been. A seagull, protecting its nest on a seaside bluff, diving repeatedly out of the night sky with angry shrieks and a hard *burrrr* of wings, pecking at your head and snaring strands of hair, is a fraction the weight of the monkey that she'd described but nonetheless terrifying.

'I considered running for the open door,' she said, 'but I was afraid I would make it angrier. So I froze here. My back against the refrigerator. Eye to eye with the hateful thing. After a while, when it was sure I was intimidated, it jumped off the counter, shot across the kitchen, pushed the back door shut, climbed quick onto the table again, and picked up the unfinished tangerine.'

I poured another shot of apricot brandy for myself.

'So I reached for the handle of this drawer here beside the fridge,' she continued. 'There's a tray of knives in it.'

Keeping her attention on the table, as she had that Christmas Eve, Angela skinned back the cardigan sleeve and reached blindly for the drawer again, to show me which one contained the knives. Without taking a step to the side, she had to lean and stretch.

'I wasn't going to attack it, just get something I could defend myself with. But before I could put my hand on anything, the monkey leaped to its feet on the table, screaming at me again.'

She groped for the drawer handle.

'It snatches an apple out of the bowl and throws it at me,' she said, 'really whales it at me. Hits me on the mouth. Splits my lip.' She crossed her arms over her face as if she were even now under assault. 'I try to protect myself. The monkey throws another apple, then a third, and it's shrieking hard enough to crack crystal if there were any around.'

'Are you saying it knew what was in that drawer?'

Lowering her arms from the defensive posture, she said, 'It had some intuitive sense what was in there, yeah.'

'And you didn't try for the knife again?'

She shook her head. 'The monkey moved like lightning. Seemed like it could be off that table and all over me even as I was pulling the drawer open, biting my hand before I could get a good grip on the handle of a knife. I didn't want to be bitten.'

'Even if it wasn't foaming at the mouth, it might have been rabid,' I agreed.

'Worse,' she said cryptically, rolling up the cuffs of the cardigan sleeves again.

'Worse than rabies?' I asked.

'So I'm standing at the refrigerator, bleeding from the lip, scared, trying to figure what to do next, and Rod comes home from work, comes through the back door there, whistling, and walks right into the middle of this weirdness. But he doesn't do anything you might expect. He's surprised – but not surprised. He's surprised to see the monkey *here*, yeah, but not surprised by the monkey itself. Seeing it here, that's what rattles him. Do you understand what I'm saying?'

'I think so.'

'Rod – damn him – he knows this monkey. He doesn't say, *A monkey?* He doesn't say, *Where the hell did a monkey come from?* He says, *Oh, Jesus.* Just, *Oh, Jesus.* It's cool that night, there's a threat of rain, he's wearing a trench coat, and he takes a pistol out of one of his coat pockets – as if he was expecting something like this. I mean, yeah, he's coming home from work, and he's in uniform, but he doesn't wear a sidearm at the office. This is peacetime. He's not in a war zone, for God's sake. He's stationed right outside Moonlight Bay, at a desk job, pushing papers and claiming he's bored, just putting on weight and waiting for retirement, but suddenly he's got this pistol on him that I don't even know he's been carrying until I see it now.'

Colonel Roderick Ferryman, an officer in the United States Army, had been stationed at Fort Wyvern, which had long been one of the big economic engines that powered the entire county. The base had been closed eighteen months ago and now stood abandoned, one of the many military facilities that, deemed superfluous, had been decommissioned following the end of the Cold War.

Although I had known Angela – and to a far lesser extent, her husband – since childhood, I had never known what, exactly, Colonel Ferryman did in the army.

Maybe Angela hadn't really known, either. Until he came home that Christmas Eve.

'Rod – he's holding the gun in his right hand, arm out straight and stiff, the muzzle trained square on the monkey, and he looks more scared than I am. He looks grim. Lips tight. All the color is gone from his face, just gone, he looks like bone. He glances at me, sees my lip starting to swell and blood all over my chin, and he doesn't even ask about that, looks right back at the monkey, afraid to take his eyes off it. The monkey's holding the last piece of tangerine but not eating now. It's staring very hard at the gun. Rod says, *Angie, go to the phone. I'm going to give you a number to call.*'

'Do you remember the number?' I asked.

'Doesn't matter. It's not in service these days. I recognized the exchange, 'cause it was the same first three digits as his office number on the base.'

'He had you call Fort Wyvern.'

'Yes. But the guy who answers – he doesn't identify himself or say which office he's in. He just says hello, and I tell him Colonel Ferryman is calling. Then Rod reaches for the phone with his left hand, the pistol still in his right. He tells the guy, *I just found the rhesus here at my house, in my kitchen*. He listens, keeping his eyes on the monkey, and then he says, *Hell if I know, but it's here, all right, and I need help to bag it.*'

'And the monkey's just watching all this?'

'When Rod hangs up the phone, the monkey raises its ugly little eyes from the gun, looks straight at him, a challenging and angry look, and then coughs out that damn sound, that awful little laugh that makes your skin crawl. Then it seems to lose interest in Rod and me, in the gun. It eats the last segment of the tangerine and starts to peel another one.'

As I lifted the apricot brandy that I had poured but not yet touched, Angela returned to the table and picked up her half-empty glass. She surprised me by clinking her glass against mine.

'What're we toasting?' I asked.

'The end of the world.'

'By fire or ice?'

'Nothing that easy,' she said.

She was as serious as stone.

Her eyes seemed to be the color of the brushed stainless-steel drawer fronts in the cold-holding room at Mercy Hospital, and her stare was too direct until, mercifully, she shifted it from me to the cordial glass in her hand.

'When Rod hangs up the phone, he wants me to tell him what happened, so I do. He has a hundred questions, and he keeps asking about my bleeding lip, about whether the monkey touched me, bit me, as if he can't quite believe the business with the apple. But he won't answer any of my questions. He just says, *Angie, you don't want to know.* Of course I want to know, but I understand what he's telling me.'

'Privileged information, military secrets.'

'My husband had been involved in sensitive projects before, national security matters, but I thought that was behind him. He said he couldn't talk about this. Not to me. Not to anyone outside the office. Not a word.'

Angela continued to stare at her brandy, but I sipped mine. It didn't taste as pleasing as it had been before. In fact, this time I detected an underlying bitterness, which reminded me that apricot pits were a source of cyanide.

Toasting the end of the world tends to focus the mind on the dark potential in all things, even in a humble fruit.

Asserting my incorrigible optimism, I took another long sip and concentrated on tasting only the flavor that had pleased me previously.

Angela said, 'Not fifteen minutes passed before three guys respond to Rod's phone call. They must've driven in from Wyvern using an ambulance or something for cover, though there wasn't any siren. None of them are wearing uniforms, either. Two of them come around to the back, open the door, and step into the kitchen without knocking. The third guy must have picked the lock on the front door and come in that way, quiet as a ghost, because he steps into the dining-room doorway the same time as the other two come in the back. Rod's still got the pistol trained on the monkey – his arms shaking with fatigue – and all three of the others have tranquilizer-dart guns.'

I thought of the quiet lamplit street out front, the charming architecture of this house, the pair of matched magnolia trees, the arbor hung with star jasmine. No one passing the place that night would have guessed at the strange drama playing out within these ordinary stucco walls.

'The monkey seems like he's expecting them,' Angela said, 'isn't concerned, doesn't try to get away. One of them shoots him with a dart. He bares his teeth and hisses but doesn't even try to pluck the needle out. He drops what's left of the second tangerine, struggles hard to swallow the bite he has in his mouth, then just curls up on the table, sighs, goes to sleep. They leave with the monkey, and Rod goes with them, and I never see the monkey again. Rod doesn't come back until three o'clock in the morning, until Christmas Eve is over, and we never do exchange gifts until late Christmas Day, and then it's no fun. By then we're in Hell and nothing's ever going to be the same. No way out, and I know it.'

Finally she tossed back her remaining brandy and put the glass down on the table so hard that it sounded like a gunshot.

Until this moment she had exhibited only fear and melancholy, both as deep as cancer in the bone. Now came anger from a still deeper source.

'I had to let them take their goddamn blood samples the day after Christmas.'

'Who?'

'The project at Wyvern.'

'Project?'

'And once a month ever since – their sample. Like my body isn't mine, like I've got to pay a rent in blood just to be allowed to go on living in it.'

'Wyvern has been closed a year and a half.'

'Not all of it. Some things don't die. Can't die. No matter how much we wish them dead.'

Although she was thin almost to the point of gaunt-ness, Angela had always been pretty in her way. Porcelain skin, a graceful brow, high cheekbones, sculpted nose, a generous mouth that balanced the otherwise vertical lines of her face and paid out a wealth of smiles – these qualities, combined with her selfless heart, made her lovely in spite of the fact that her skull was too near the skin and her skeleton too ill-concealed beneath the illusion of immortality that the flesh provides. Now, however, her face was hard and cold and ugly, fiercely sharpened at every edge by the grinding wheel of anger.

'If I ever refuse to give them the monthly sample, they'll kill me. I'm sure of that. Or lock me away in some secret hospital out there where they can keep a closer watch on me.'

'What's the sample for? What're they afraid of?'

She seemed about to tell me, but then she pressed her lips together.

'Angela?'

I gave a sample every month myself, for Dr. Cleveland, and often Angela drew it. In my case it was for an experimental procedure that might detect early indications of skin and eye cancers from subtle changes in blood chemistry. Although giving the samples was painless and for my own good, I resented the invasion, and I could imagine how deeply I would resent it if it was compulsory rather than voluntary.

She said, 'Maybe I shouldn't tell you. Even though you need to know to . . . to defend yourself. Telling you all of it is like lighting a fuse. Sooner or later, your whole world blows up.'

'Was the monkey carrying a disease?'

'I wish it were a disease. Wouldn't that be nice? Maybe I'd be cured by now. Or dead. Some days I think dead would be better than what's coming.'

She snatched up her empty cordial glass, made a fist around it, and for a moment I thought that she would hurl it across the room.

'The monkey never bit me,' she insisted, 'never clawed me, never even touched me, for God's sake. But they won't believe me. I'm not sure even Rod believed me. They won't take any chances. They made me . . . *Rod* made me submit to sterilization.'

Tears stood in her eyes, unshed but shimmering like the votive light in the red glass candleholders.

'I was forty-five years old then,' she said, 'and I'd never had a child, because I was *already* sterile. We'd tried so hard to have a baby – fertility doctors, hormone therapy, everything, everything – and nothing worked.'

Oppressed by the suffering in Angela's voice, I was barely able to remain in my chair, looking passively up at her. I had the urge to stand, to put my arms around her. To be the nurse this time.

With a tremor of rage in her voice, she said, 'And still the bastards made me have the surgery, *permanent* surgery, didn't just tie my tubes but removed my ovaries, cut me, cut out all hope.' Her voice almost broke, but she was strong. 'I was forty-five, and I'd given up hope anyway, or pretended to give it up. But to have it *cut* out of me . . . The humiliation of it, the hopelessness. They wouldn't even tell me *why*. Rod took me out to the base the day after Christmas, supposedly for an interview about the monkey, about its behavior. He wouldn't elaborate. Very mysterious. He took me into this place . . . this place out there that even most people on the base didn't know existed. They sedated me against my will, performed the surgery without my permission. And when it was all over, the sons of bitches *wouldn't even tell me why*!'

I pushed my chair away from the table and got to my feet. My shoulders ached, and my legs felt weak. I hadn't been expecting to hear a story of this weight.

Although I wanted to comfort her, I didn't attempt to

approach Angela. The cordial glass was still sealed in the hard shell of her fist. Grinding anger had sharpened her once-pretty face into a collection of knives. I didn't think that she would want me to touch her just then.

Instead, after standing awkwardly at the table for seconds that were interminable, not sure what to do, I went at last to the back door and checked the deadbolt to confirm that it was engaged.

'I know Rod loved me,' she said, although the anger in her voice didn't soften with those words. 'It broke his heart, just broke him entirely, to do what he had to do. Broke his heart to cooperate with them, tricking me into surgery. He was never the same after that.'

I turned and saw that her fist was cocked. The blades of her face were polished by candlelight.

'And if his superiors had understood how close Rod and I had always been, they would have known he couldn't go on keeping secrets from me, not when I'd suffered so much for them.'

'Eventually he told you all of it,' I guessed.

'Yes. And I forgave him, truly forgave him for what had been done to me, but he was still in despair. There was nothing I could do to nurse him out of it. So deep in despair . . . and so scared.' Now her anger was veined with pity and with sorrow. 'So scared he had no joy in anything anymore. Finally he killed himself . . . and when he was dead, there was nothing left to cut out of me.'

She lowered her fist. She opened it. She stared at the cordial glass – and then carefully set it on the table.

'Angela, what was wrong with the monkey?' I asked. She didn't reply.

Images of candle flames danced in her eyes. Her solemn face was like a stone shrine to a dead goddess.

I repeated the question: 'What was wrong with the monkey?'

When at last Angela spoke, her voice was hardly louder than a whisper: 'It wasn't a monkey.'

I knew that I had heard her correctly, yet her words made no sense. 'Not a monkey? But you said—'

'It appeared to be a monkey.'

'Appeared?'

'And it was a monkey, of course.'

Lost, I said nothing.

'Was and wasn't,' she whispered. 'And that's what was wrong with it.'

She did not seem entirely rational. I began to wonder if her fantastic story had been more fantasy than truth – and if she knew the difference.

Turning away from the votive candles, she met my eyes. She was not ugly anymore, but she wasn't pretty again, either. Hers was a face of ashes and shadows. 'Maybe I shouldn't have called you. I was emotional about your dad dying. I wasn't thinking clearly.'

'You said I need to know . . . to defend myself.'

She nodded. 'You do. That's right. You need to know. You're hanging by such a thin thread. You need to know who hates you.'

I held out my hand to her, but she didn't take it.

'Angela,' I pleaded, 'I want to know what really happened to my parents.'

'They're dead. They're gone. I loved them, Chris, loved them as friends, but they're gone.'

'I still need to know.'

'If you're thinking that somebody has to pay for their

deaths . . . then you have to realize that nobody ever will. Not in your lifetime. Not in anyone's. No matter how much of the truth you learn, no one will be made to pay. No matter what you try to do.'

I found that I had drawn my hand back and had curled it into a fist on the table. After a silence, I said, 'We'll see.'

'I've quit my job at Mercy this evening.' Revealing this sad news, she appeared to shrink, until she resembled a child in adult clothing, once more the girl who had brought iced tea, medicine, and pillows to her disabled mother. 'I'm not a nurse anymore.'

'What will you do?'

She didn't answer.

'It was all you ever wanted to be,' I reminded her.

'Doesn't seem any point to it now. Bandaging wounds in a war is vital work. Bandaging wounds in the middle of Armageddon is foolish. Besides, I'm becoming. I'm becoming. Don't you see?'

In fact, I didn't see.

'I'm becoming. Another me. Another Angela. Someone I don't want to be. Something I don't dare think about.'

I still didn't know what to make of her apocalyptic talk. Was it a rational response to the secrets of Wyvern or the result of the personal despair arising from the loss of her husband?

She said, 'If you insist on knowing about this, then once you know, there's nothing to do but sit back, drink what pleases you most, and watch it all end.'

'I insist anyway.'

'Then I guess it's time for show and tell,' Angela said with evident ambivalence. 'But . . . oh, Chris, it's going to break your heart.' Sadness elongated her features.

'I think you need to know . . . but it's going to break your heart.'

When she turned from me and crossed the kitchen, I began to follow her.

She stopped me. 'I'll have to turn some lights on to get what I need. You better wait here, and I'll bring everything back.'

I watched her navigate the dark dining room. In the living room, she switched on a single lamp, and from there she moved out of sight.

Restlessly, I circled this room to which I had been confined, my mind spinning as I prowled. The monkey was and was not a monkey, and its wrongness lay in this simultaneous wasness and notness. This would seem to make sense only in a Lewis Carroll world, with Alice at the bottom of a magical rabbit hole.

At the back door, I tried the deadbolt. Locked.

I drew the curtain aside and surveyed the night. I could not see Orson.

Trees were stirring. The wind had returned.

Moonlight was on the move. Apparently, new weather was coming in from the Pacific. As the wind flung tattered clouds across the face of the moon, a silvery radiance appeared to ripple across the nightscape. In fact, what traveled were the dappling shadows of the clouds, and the movement of the light was but an illusion. Nevertheless, the backyard was transformed into a winter stream, and the light purled like water moving under ice.

From elsewhere in the house came a brief wordless cry. It was as thin and forlorn as Angela herself.

13

The cry was so short-lived and so hollow that it might have been no more real than the movement of the moonlight across the backyard, merely a ghost of sound haunting a room in my mind. Like the monkey, it possessed a quality of both wasness and notness.

As the door curtain slipped through my fingers and fell silently across the glass, however, a muffled thump sounded elsewhere in the house and shuddered through the walls.

The second cry was briefer and thinner than the first – but it was unmistakably a bleat of pain and terror.

Maybe she had merely fallen off a step stool and sprained her ankle. Maybe I'd heard only wind and birds in the eaves. Maybe the moon is made of cheese and the sky is a chocolate nonpareil with sugar stars.

I called loudly to Angela.

She didn't answer.

The house was not so large that she could have failed to hear me. Her silence was ominous.

Cursing under my breath, I drew the Glock from my jacket pocket. I held it in the candlelight, searching desperately for safeties.

I found only one switch that might be what I wanted. When I pressed it down, an intense beam of red light shot out of a smaller hole below the muzzle and painted a bright dot on the refrigerator door.

My dad, wanting a weapon that was user friendly even to gentle professors of literature, had paid extra for laser sighting. Good man.

Although I didn't know much about handguns, I knew some models of pistols featured 'safe action' systems with only internal safety devices that disengaged as the trigger was pulled and, after firing, engaged again. Maybe this was one of those weapons. If not, then I would either find myself unable to get off a shot when confronted by an assailant – or, fumbling in panic, would shoot myself in the foot.

I didn't like the way my hands were shaking, but I sure as hell couldn't pause for deep-breathing exercises or meditation.

Although I wasn't trained for this work, there was no one but me to do the job. Admittedly, I thought about getting out of there, climbing on my bike, riding to safety, and placing an anonymous emergency call to the police. Thereafter, however, I would never be able to look at myself in a mirror – or even meet Orson's eyes.

As I crossed the kitchen to the open door at the dining room, I considered returning the pistol to my pocket and taking a knife from the cutlery drawer. Telling the story of the monkey, Angela had shown me where the blades were kept.

Reason prevailed. I was no more practiced with knives than I was expert with firearms.

Besides, using a knife, slashing and gouging at another human being, seemed to require a ruthlessness greater than that needed to pull a trigger. I figured I could do whatever was necessary if my life – or Angela's – was on the line, but I couldn't rule out the possibility that I was better suited to the comparatively dry business of shooting than to the up-close-and-personal wet work of evisceration. In a desperate confrontation, a flinch might be fatal.

As a thirteen-year-old boy, I had been able to look into the crematorium. Yet all these years later, I still wasn't ready to watch the grimmer show in an embalming chamber.

Swiftly crossing the dining room, I called out to Angela once more. Again, she failed to respond.

I wouldn't call her a third time. If indeed an intruder were in the house, I would only be revealing my position each time I shouted Angela's name.

In the living room, I didn't pause to switch off the lamp, but I stepped wide of it and averted my face.

Squinting in the stinging rain of foyer light, I glanced through the open door to the study. No one was in there.

The powder-room door was ajar. I pushed it all the way open. I didn't need to turn on a light to see that no one was in there, either.

Feeling naked without my cap, which I had left on the kitchen table, I switched off the ceiling fixture in the foyer. Blessed gloom fell.

I peered up at the landing where the shadowy stairs turned back and disappeared overhead. As far as I could tell, no lights were lit on the upper floor – which was fine with me. My dark-adapted eyes were my biggest advantage.

The cellular phone was clipped to my belt. As I started up the stairs, I considered calling the police.

After my failure to keep our appointment earlier in the evening, however, Lewis Stevenson might be looking for me. If so, then the chief himself would answer this call. Maybe the bald man with the earring would come along for the ride.

Manuel Ramirez couldn't assist me himself, because he was the duty officer this evening, restricted to the station. I didn't feel safe asking for any other officer. As far as I knew, Chief Stevenson might not be the only compromised cop in Moonlight Bay; perhaps every member of the force, except Manuel, was involved in this conspiracy. In fact, in spite of our friendship, I couldn't trust Manuel, either, not until I knew a lot more about this situation.

Climbing the stairs, I gripped the Glock with both hands, ready to press the laser-sighting switch if someone moved. I kept reminding myself that playing hero meant trying not to shoot Angela by mistake.

I turned at the landing and saw that the upper flight was darker than the lower. No ambient light from the living room reached this high. I ascended quickly and silently.

My heart was doing more than idling; it was revving nicely, but I was surprised that it wasn't racing. Only yesterday, I could not have imagined that I would be able to adapt so rapidly to the prospect of imminent violence. I was even beginning to recognize within myself a disconcerting *enthusiasm* for danger.

Four doors opened off the upstairs hall. Three were closed. The fourth – the door farthest from the stairs – was ajar, and from the room beyond came a soft light.

I disliked passing the three closed rooms without confirming that they were deserted. I would be leaving my back vulnerable.

Given my XP, however, and especially considering how quickly my eyes would sting and water when exposed to very bright light, I'd be able to search those spaces only with the pistol in my right hand and the penlight in my left. This would be awkward, time-consuming, and dangerous. Each time that I stepped into a room, no matter how low I crouched and how fast I moved, the penlight would instantly pinpoint my location for any would-be assailant before I found him with the narrow beam.

My best hope was to play to my strengths, which meant using the darkness, blending with the shadows. Moving sideways along the hall, keeping a watch in both directions, I made no sound, and neither did anyone else in the house.

The second door on the left was open only a crack, and the narrow wedge of light revealed little of the room beyond. Using the gun barrel, I pushed the door inward.

The master bedroom. Cozy. The bed was neatly made. A gaily colored afghan draped one arm of an easy chair, and on the footstool waited a folded newspaper. On the bureau, a collection of antique perfume bottles sparkled.

One of the nightstand lamps was aglow. The bulb was not strong, and the pleated-fabric shade screened most of the rays.

Angela was nowhere to be seen.

A closet door stood open. Perhaps Angela had come upstairs to fetch something from there. I couldn't see anything but hanging clothes and shoe boxes.

The door to the adjacent bathroom was ajar, and the bathroom was dark. To anyone in there, looking out, I was a well-lit target.

I approached the bathroom as obliquely as possible, aiming the Glock at the black gap between the door and the jamb. When I pushed on the door, it opened without resistance.

The smell stopped me from crossing the threshold.

Because the glow of the nightstand lamp didn't illuminate much of the space before me, I fished the penlight from my pocket. The beam glistered across a red pool on a white tile floor. The walls were sprayed with arterial gouts.

Angela Ferryman was slumped on the floor, head bent backward over the rim of the toilet bowl. Her eyes were as wide, pale, and flat as those of a dead seagull that I had once found on the beach.

At a glance, I thought her throat appeared to have been slashed repeatedly with a half-sharp knife. I couldn't bear to look at her too closely or for too long.

The smell was not merely blood. Dying, she had fouled herself. A draft bathed me in the stench.

A casement window was cranked all the way open. It wasn't a typically small bathroom window but large enough to have provided escape for the killer, who must have been liberally splashed with his victim's blood.

Perhaps Angela had left the window open. If there was a first-story porch roof under it, the killer could have entered as well as exited by this route.

Orson had not barked – but then this window was toward the front of the house, and the dog was at the back.

Angela's hands were at her sides, almost lost in the sleeves of the cardigan. She looked so innocent. She looked twelve.

All of her life, she had given of herself to others. Now someone, unimpressed by her selfless giving, had cruelly taken all that was left.

Anguished, shaking uncontrollably, I turned away from the bathroom.

I hadn't approached Angela with questions. I hadn't brought her to this hideous end. She had called me, and although she had used her car phone, someone had known that she needed to be silenced permanently and quickly. Maybe these faceless conspirators decided that her despair made her dangerous. She had quit her job at the hospital. She felt that she had no reason to live. And she was terrified of *becoming*, whatever that meant. She was a woman with nothing to lose, uncontrollable. They would have killed her even if I had not responded to her call.

Nevertheless, I was awash in guilt, drowning in cold currents, robbed of breath, and I stood gasping.

Nausea followed those currents, rippling like a fat slippery eel through my gut, swimming up my throat and almost surging into my mouth. I choked it down.

I needed to get out of here, yet I couldn't move. I was half crushed under a weight of terror and guilt.

My right arm hung at my side, pulled as straight as a plumb line by the weight of the gun. The penlight, clutched in my left hand, stitched jagged patterns on the wall.

I could not think clearly. My thoughts rolled thickly, like tangled masses of seaweed in a sludge tide.

On the nearer nightstand, the telephone rang.

I kept my distance from it. I had the queer feeling that this caller was the deep-breather who had left the message on my answering machine, that he would try to steal some vital aspect of me with his bloodhound inhalations, as if my very soul could be vacuumed out of me and drawn away across the open telephone line. I didn't want to hear his low, eerie, tuneless humming.

When at last the phone fell silent, my head had been somewhat cleared by the strident ringing. I clicked off the penlight, returned it to my pocket, raised the big pistol from my side – and realized that someone had switched on the light in the upstairs hall.

Because of the open window and the blood smeared on the frame, I had assumed I was alone in the house with Angela's body. I was wrong. An intruder was still present – waiting between me and the stairs.

The killer couldn't have slipped out of the master bath by way of the bedroom; a messy trail of blood would have marked his passage across the cream-colored carpet. Yet why would he have escaped from the upstairs only to return immediately through a ground-floor door or window?

If, after fleeing, he had changed his mind about leaving a potential witness and had decided to come back to get me, he wouldn't have turned on the light to announce his presence. He would have preferred to take me by surprise.

Cautiously, squinting against the glare, I stepped into the hallway. It was deserted.

The three doors that had been closed when I had first come upstairs were now standing wide open. The rooms beyond them were forbiddingly bright.

14

Like blood out of a wound, silence welled up from the bottom of the house into this upstairs hall. Then a sound rose, but it came from outside: the keening of the wind under the eaves.

A strange game seemed to be under way. I didn't know the rules. I didn't know the identity of my adversary. I was screwed.

Flicking a wall switch, I brought forth a soothing flow of shadows to the hall, which made the lights in the three open rooms seem brighter by comparison.

I wanted to run for the stairs. Get down, out, away. But I didn't dare leave unexplored rooms at my back this time. I'd end up like Angela, throat slashed from behind.

My best chance of staying alive was to remain calm. Think. Approach each door with caution. Inch my way out of the house. Make sure my back was protected every step of the way.

I squinted less, listened more, heard nothing, and moved to the doorway opposite the master bedroom. I didn't cross the threshold but remained in the shadows, using my left hand as a visor to shade my eyes from the harsh overhead light before me.

This might have been a son's or daughter's room

if Angela had been able to have children. Instead, it contained a tool cabinet with many drawers, a bar stool with a back, and two high work tables placed to form an L. Here she spent time at her hobby: doll-making.

A quick glance along the hallway. Still alone.

Keep moving. Don't be an easy target.

I pushed the hobby-room door all the way open. No one was hiding behind it.

I stepped briefly into the brightly lighted room, staying sideways to the hall to cover both spaces.

Angela was a fine dollmaker, as proved by the thirty dolls on the shelves of an open display cabinet at the far end of the hobby room. Her creations were attired in richly imagined, painstakingly realized costumes that Angela herself had sewn: cowboy and cowgirl outfits, sailor suits, party dresses with petticoats . . . The wonder of the dolls, however, was their faces. She sculpted each head with patience and real talent, and she fired it in a kiln in the garage. Some were matt-finish bisque. Others were glazed. All were hand-painted with such attention to detail that their faces looked real.

Over the years, Angela had sold some of her dolls and had given many away. These remaining were evidently her favorites, with which she had been most reluctant to part. Even under the circumstances, alert for the approach of a psychopath with a half-sharp knife, I saw that each face was unique – as though Angela wasn't merely making dolls but was lovingly imagining the possible faces of the children whom she had never carried in her womb.

I switched off the ceiling fixture, leaving only a work-table lamp. In the sudden swelling of shadows, the dolls appeared to shift on the shelves, as if preparing to leap to the floor. Their painted eyes – some bright with points of reflected light and some with a fixed inky glare – seemed watchful and intent.

I had the heebie-jeebies. Big time.

The dolls were only dolls. They were no threat to me.

Back into the corridor, sweeping the Glock left, right, left again. No one.

Next along this side of the hall was a bathroom. Even with my eyes narrowed to slits to filter out the dazzle of porcelain and glass and mirrors and yellow ceramic tile, I could see into every corner. No one was waiting there.

As I reached inside to switch off the bathroom lights, a noise rose behind me. Back toward the master bedroom. A quick rapping like knuckles on wood. From the corner of my eye, I saw movement.

I spun toward the sound, bringing up the Glock in a two-hand grip again, as if I knew what the hell I was doing, imitating Willis and Stallone and Schwarzenegger and Eastwood and Cage from a hundred jump-run-shoot-chase movies, as if I actually believed that *they* knew what the hell they were doing. I expected to see a hulking figure, demented eyes, an upraised arm, an arcing knife, but I was still alone in the hallway.

The movement I'd seen was the master-bedroom door being pushed shut from the inside. In the diminishing wedge of light between the moving door and the jamb, a twisted shadow loomed, writhed, shrank. The door fell shut with a solid sound like the closing of a bank vault.

That room had been deserted when I left it, and no one had come past me since I'd stepped into the hallway. Only the murderer could be in there – and only if he'd returned through the bathroom window from a porch roof where he'd been when I'd discovered Angela's body.

If the killer was already in the master bedroom again, however, he couldn't also have slipped behind me, moments earlier, to turn on the second-floor lights. So there were two intruders. I was caught between them.

Go forward or back? Lousy choice. Deep shit either way, and me without rubber boots.

They would expect me to run for the stairs. But it was safer to do the unexpected, so without hesitation I rushed to the master-bedroom door. I didn't bother with the knob, kicked hard, sprung the latch, and pushed inside with the Glock in front of me, ready to squeeze off four or five shots at anything that moved.

I was alone.

The nightstand lamp was still lit.

No bloody footprints stained the carpet, so no one could have re-entered the splattered bathroom from outside and then returned here by that route to close the hall door.

I checked the bathroom anyway. I left the penlight in my pocket this time, relying on an influx of faint light from the bedroom lamp, because I didn't need – or want – to see all the vivid details again. The casement window remained open. The smell was as repulsive as it had been two minutes ago. The shape slumped against the toilet was Angela. Although she was mercifully veiled in gloom, I could see her mouth gaping as though in amazement, her wide eyes unblinking.

I turned away and glanced nervously at the open door to the hall. No one had followed me in here.

Baffled, I retreated to the middle of the bedroom.

The draft from the bathroom window was not strong

enough to have blown the bedroom door shut. Besides, no draft had cast the twisted shadow that I had glimpsed.

Although the space under the bed might have been large enough to hide a man, he would have been uncomfortably compressed between the floor and the box springs, with frame slats banding his back. Besides, no one could have squirmed into that hiding place before I'd kicked my way into the room.

I could see through the open door to the walk-in closet, which obviously did not harbor an intruder. I took a closer look anyway. The penlight revealed an attic access in the closet ceiling. Even if a fold-down ladder was fitted to the back of that trap door, no one could have been spider-quick enough to climb into the attic and pull the ladder after himself in the two or three seconds that I had taken to burst in from the hallway.

Two draped windows flanked the bed. Both proved to be locked from the inside.

He hadn't gone out that way, but maybe I could. I wanted to avoid returning to the hall.

Keeping the bedroom door in view, I tried to open a window. It was painted shut. These were French windows with thick mullions, so I couldn't just break a pane and climb out.

My back was to the bathroom. Suddenly I felt as though spiders were twitching through the hollows of my spine. In my mind's eye, I saw Angela behind me, not lying by the toilet any longer but risen, red and dripping, eyes as bright and flat as silver coins. I expected to hear the wound bubbling in her throat as she tried to speak.

When I turned, tingling with dread, she was not behind me, but the hot breath of relief that erupted from me proved how seriously I'd been gripped by this fantastic expectation.

I was *still* gripped by it: I expected to hear her thrash to her feet in the bathroom. Already, my anguish over her death had been supplanted by fear for my own life. Angela was no longer a person to me. She was a thing, death itself, a monster, a fist-in-the-face reminder that we all perish and rot and turn to dust. I'm ashamed to say that I hated her a little because I'd felt obliged to come upstairs to help her, hated her for having put me in this vise, hated myself for hating her, my loving nurse, hated her for making me hate myself. This greasy emotional spiral was actually less about hatred than about panic, but it involved hatred nonetheless.

Sometimes there is no darker place than our own thoughts: the moonless midnight of the mind.

My hands were clammy. The butt of the pistol was slick with cold perspiration.

I stopped chasing ghosts and reluctantly returned to the upstairs hallway. A doll was waiting for me.

This was one of the largest from Angela's hobby-room shelves, nearly two feet high. It sat on the floor, legs splayed, facing me in the light that came through the open door from the only room that I hadn't yet explored, the one opposite the hall bath. Its arms were outstretched, and something hung across both of its hands.

This was not good.

I know *not good* when I see it, and this was fully, totally, radically *not good*.

In the movies, a development like the appearance of this doll was inevitably followed by the dramatic entrance of a really big guy with a bad attitude. A really big guy wearing a cool hockey mask. Or a hood. He'd be carrying an even cooler chainsaw or a compressed-air nail gun or, in an unplugged mood, an ax big enough to decapitate a *T. rex*.

I glanced into the hobby room, which was still half illuminated by the worktable lamp. No intruder lurked there.

Move. To the hall bathroom. It was still deserted. I needed to use the facilities. Not a convenient time. Move.

Now to the doll, which was dressed in black sneakers, black jeans, and a black T-shirt. The object in its hands was a navy-blue cap with two words embroidered in ruby-red thread above the bill: *Mystery Train*.

For a moment I thought it was a cap like mine. Then I saw that it *was* my own, which I'd left downstairs on the kitchen table.

Between glances at the head of the stairs and at the open door to the only room that I hadn't searched, expecting trouble from one source or the other, I plucked the cap from the small china hands. I pulled it on my head.

In the right light and circumstances, any doll can have an eerie or evil aspect. This was different, because not a single feature in this bisque face struck me as malevolent, yet the skin on the back of my neck creped like Halloween-party bunting.

What spooked me was not any strangeness about the doll but an uncanny familiarity: It had my face. It had been modeled after me.

I was simultaneously touched and creeped out. Angela had cared for me enough to sculpt my features meticulously, to memorialize me lovingly in one of her creations and keep it upon her shelves of favorites. Yet unexpectedly coming upon such an image of oneself wakes primitive fears – as if I might touch this fetish and instantly find my mind and soul trapped within it, while some malignant spirit, previously immobilized in the doll, came forth to establish itself in my flesh. Gleeful at its release, it would lurch into the night to crack virgins' skulls and eat the hearts of babies in my name.

In ordinary times – if such times exist – I am entertained by an unusually vivid imagination. Bobby Halloway calls it, with some mockery, 'the three-hundred-ring circus of your mind.' This is no doubt a quality I inherited from my mother and father, who were intelligent enough to know that little could be known, inquisitive enough never to stop learning, and perceptive enough to understand that all things and all events contain infinite possibilities. When I was a child, they read to me the writing of A. A. Milne and Beatrix Potter but also, certain that I was precocious, Donald Justice and Wallace Stevens. Thereafter, my imagination has always churned with images from lines of verse: from Timothy Tim's ten pink toes to fireflies twitching in the blood. In extraordinary times – such as this night of stolen cadavers – I am too imaginative for my own good, and in the three-hundred-ring circus of my mind, all the tigers wait to kill their trainers and all the clowns hide butcher knives and evil hearts under their baggy clothes.

Move.

One more room. Check it out, protect my back, then straight down the stairs.

Superstitiously avoiding contact with the doppel-gänger doll, stepping wide of it, I went to the open door of the room opposite the hall bath. A guest bedroom, simply furnished.

Tucking my capped head down and squinting against the glare from the ceiling fixture, I saw no intruder. The bed had side rails and a footboard behind which the spread was tucked, so the space under it was revealed.

Instead of a closet, there were a long walnut bureau with banks of drawers and a massive armoire with a pair of side-by-side drawers below and two tall doors above. The space behind the armoire doors was large enough to conceal a grown man with or without a chainsaw.

Another doll awaited me. This one was sitting in the center of the bed, arms outstretched like the arms of the Christopher Snow doll behind me, but in the shrouding brightness, I couldn't tell what it held in its pink hands.

I switched off the ceiling light. One nightstand lamp remained lit to guide me.

I backed into the guest room, prepared to respond with gunfire to anyone who appeared in the hall.

The armoire hulked at the edge of my vision. If the doors began to swing open, I wouldn't even need the laser sighting to chop holes in them with a few 9-millimeter rounds.

I bumped into the bed and turned from both the hall door and the armoire long enough to check out the doll. In each upturned hand was an eye. Not a hand-painted eye. Not a glass-button eye taken from the dollmaker's supply cabinet. A human eye.

The armoire doors hung unmoving on piano hinges.

Nothing but time moved in the hall.

I was as still as ashes in an urn, but life continued within me: My heart raced as it had never raced before, no longer merely revving nicely, but spinning with panic in its squirrel cage of ribs.

Once more I looked at the offering of eyes that filled those small china hands – bloodshot brown eyes, milky and moist, startling and startled in their lidless nakedness. I knew that one of the last things ever seen through them was a white van pulling to a stop in response to an upturned thumb. And then a man with a shaven head and one pearl earring.

Yet I was sure that I wasn't dealing with that same bald man here, now, in Angela's house. This game-playing wasn't his style, this taunting, this hide-and-seek. Quick, vicious, violent action was more to his taste.

Instead, I felt as though I had stumbled into a sanitarium for sociopathic youth, where psychotic children had savagely overthrown their keepers and, giddy with freedom, were now at play. I could almost hear their hidden laughter in other rooms: macabre silvery giggles stifled behind small cold hands.

I refused to open the armoire.

I had come up here to help Angela, but there was no helping her now or ever. All I wanted was to get downstairs, outside, onto my bicycle, and away.

As I started toward the door, the lights went out. Someone had thrown a breaker in a junction box.

This darkness was so bottomless that it didn't welcome even me. The windows were heavily draped, and the milk-pitcher moon couldn't find gaps through which to pour itself. All was blackness on blackness.

Blindly, I rushed toward the door. Then I angled to one side of it when I was overcome by the conviction that someone was in the hall and that I would encounter the thrust of a sharp blade at the threshold.

I stood with my back to the bedroom wall, listening. I held my breath but was unable to quiet my heart, which clattered like horses' hooves on cobblestones, a runaway *parade* of horses, and I felt betrayed by my own body.

Nevertheless, over the thundering stampede of my heart, I heard the creak of the piano hinges. The armoire doors were coming open.

Jesus.

It was a prayer, not a curse. Or maybe both.

Holding the Glock in a two-hand grip again, I aimed toward where I thought the big armoire stood. Then I reconsidered and swung the muzzle three inches to the left. Only to swing it immediately back to the right.

I was disoriented in the absolute blackness. Although I was certain that I would hit the armoire, I couldn't be sure that I would put the round straight through the center of the space above the two drawers. The first shot had to count, because the muzzle flash would give away my position.

I couldn't risk pumping out rounds indiscriminately. Although a spray of bullets would probably waste the bastard, whoever he might be, there was a chance that I would only wound him – and a smaller but still very real chance that I would merely piss him off.

When the pistol magazine was empty – then what?

Then what?

I sidled to the hallway, risking an encounter there, but it didn't happen. As I crossed the threshold, I pulled the guest-room door shut behind me, putting it between me and whoever had come out of the armoire – assuming that I hadn't imagined the creaking of the piano hinges.

The ground-floor lights were evidently on their own circuit. A glow rose through the stairwell at the end of the black hall.

Instead of waiting to see who, if anyone, would burst out of the guest room, I ran to the stairs.

I heard a door open behind me.

Gasping, descending two stairs at a time, I was almost to the landing when my head in miniature sailed past. It shattered against the wall in front of me.

Startled, I brought an arm up to shield my eyes. China shrapnel tattooed my face and chest.

My right heel landed on the bullnose edge of a step and skidded off. I nearly fell, pitched forward, slammed into the landing wall, but kept my balance.

On the landing, crunching shards of my glazed face underfoot, I whipped around to confront my assailant.

The decapitated body of the doll, appropriately attired in basic black, hurtled down. I ducked, and it passed over my head, thumping against the wall behind me.

When I looked up and covered the dark top of the stairs with the gun, there was no one to shoot – as if the doll had torn off its own head to throw at me and then had hurled itself into the stairwell.

The downstairs lights went out.

Through the forbidding blackness came the smell of something burning.

15

Groping in the impenetrable gloom, I finally found the handrail. I clutched at the smooth wood with one sweaty hand and started down the lower flight of stairs toward the foyer.

This darkness had a strange sinuosity, seemed to coil and writhe around me as I descended through it. Then I realized that it was the air, not the darkness, that I was feeling: serpentine currents of hot air swarming up the stairwell.

An instant later, tendrils and then tentacles and then a great pulsing mass of foul-smelling smoke poured into the stairwell from below, invisible but palpable, enveloping me as some giant sea anemone might envelop a diver. Coughing, choking, struggling to breathe, I reversed directions, hoping to escape through a second-floor window, although not through the master bathroom where Angela waited.

I returned to the landing and clambered up three or four steps of the second flight before halting. Through smoke-stung eyes flooded with tears – and through the pall of smoke itself – I saw a throbbing light above.

Fire.

Two fires had been set, one above and one below. These unseen psychotic children were busy in their mad play, and there seemed to be so *many* of them. I was reminded of the veritable platoon of searchers that appeared to spring out of the ground at the mortuary, as though Sandy Kirk possessed the power to summon the dead from their graves.

Downward, once more and quickly, I plunged toward the only hope of nourishing air. I would find it, if anywhere, at the lowest point of the structure, because smoke and fumes rise while the blaze sucks in cooler air at its base in order to feed itself.

Each inhalation caused a spasm of coughing, increased my feeling of suffocation, and fed my panic, so I held my breath until I reached the foyer. There, I dropped to my knees, stretched out on the floor, and discovered that I could breathe. The air was hot and smelled sour, but all things being relative, I was more thrilled by it than I had ever been by the crisp air coming off the scrub board of the Pacific.

I didn't lie there and surrender to an orgy of respiration. I hesitated just long enough to draw several deep breaths to clear my soiled lungs, and to work up enough saliva to spit some of the soot out of my mouth.

Then I raised my head to test the air and to learn how deep the precious safe zone might be. Not deep. Four to six inches. Nevertheless, this shallow pool ought to be enough to sustain me while I found my way out of the house.

Wherever the carpet was afire, of course, there would be no safe-air zone whatsoever.

The lights were still out, the smoke was blindingly thick, and I squirmed on my stomach, frantically heading toward where I believed that I would find the front door, the nearest exit. The first thing I encountered in the murk was a sofa, judging by the feel of it, which meant that I had passed through the archway and into the living room, at least ninety degrees off the course that I imagined I'd been following.

Now luminous orange pulses passed through the comparatively clear air near the floor, underlighting the curdled masses of smoke as if they were thunderheads looming over a plain. From my eye-to-the-carpet perspective, the beige nylon fibers stretched away like a vast flat field of dry grass, fitfully brightened by an electrical storm. This narrow, life-sustaining realm under the smoke seemed to be an alternate world into which I had fallen after stepping through a door between dimensions.

The ominous throbs of light were reflections of fire elsewhere in the room, but they didn't relieve the gloom enough to help me find the way out. The stroboscopic flickering only contributed to my confusion and scared the hell out of me.

As long as I couldn't see the blaze, I could pretend that it was in a distant corner of the house. Now I no longer had the refuge of pretense. Yet there was no advantage to glimpsing the reflected fire, because I wasn't able to tell if the flames were inches or feet from me, whether they were burning toward or away from me, so the light increased my anxiety without providing guidance.

Either I was suffering worse effects of smoke inhalation than I realized, including a distorted perception of time, or the fire was spreading with unusual swiftness. The arsonists had probably used an accelerant, maybe gasoline.

Determined to get back into the foyer and then to the front door, I sucked desperately at the increasingly acrid air near the floor and squirmed across the room, digging my elbows into the carpet to pull myself along, ricocheting off furniture, until I cracked my forehead solidly against the raised brick hearth of the fireplace. I was farther than ever from the foyer, and yet I couldn't picture myself crawling into the fireplace and up the chimney like Santa Claus on his way back to the sleigh.

I was dizzy. A headache split my skull on a diagonal from my left eyebrow to the part in my hair on the right. My eyes stung from the smoke and the salty sweat that poured into them. I wasn't choking again, but I was gagging on the pungent fumes that flavored even the clearer air near the floor, and I was beginning to think that I might not survive.

Trying hard to remember where the fireplace was situated in relationship to the foyer arch, I squirmed along the raised hearth and then angled off into the room again.

It seemed absurd to me that I couldn't find my way out of this place. This wasn't a mansion, for God's sake, not a castle, merely a modest house with seven rooms, none of them large, and two-point-five baths, and not even the cleverest realtor in the country could have described it in such a way as to give the impression that it had enough rattling-around space to satisfy the Prince of Wales and his retinue.

On the evening news, from time to time, you see stories about people dying in house fires, and you can never quite understand why they couldn't make it to a door or window, when one or the other was surely within a dozen steps. Unless they were, of course, drunk. Or wasted on drugs. Or foolish enough to rush back into the flames to rescue Fluffy, the kitten. Which may sound ungrateful of me after I myself was this same night rescued, in a sense, by a cat. But now I understood how people died in these circumstances: The smoke and churning darkness were more disorienting than drugs or booze, and the longer you breathed the tainted air, the less nimble your mind became, until your thoughts rambled and even panic couldn't focus them.

When I had first climbed the stairs to see what had happened to Angela, I had been amazed at how calm and collected I was in spite of the threat of imminent violence. With a fat dollop of male pride as cloying as a cupful of mayonnaise, I had even sensed in my heart a disconcerting *enthusiasm* for danger.

What a difference ten minutes can make. Now that it was brutally apparent to me that I was never going to acquit myself in these situations with even half the aplomb of Batman, the romance of danger failed to stir me.

Suddenly, creeping out of the dismal blear, something brushed against me and nuzzled my neck, my chin: something *alive*. In the three-hundred-ring circus of my mind, I pictured Angela Ferryman on her belly, reanimated by some evil voodoo, slithering across the floor to meet me, and planting a cold-lipped, bloody kiss on my throat. The effects of oxygen deprivation were becoming so severe that even this hideous and electrifying image was not sufficient to shock me into a clearer state of mind, and I reflexively squeezed off a shot.

Thank God, I fired entirely in the wrong direction, because even as the crack of the shot echoed through the living room, I recognized the cold nose at my throat and the warm tongue in my ear as those of my one and only dog, my faithful companion, my Orson.

'Hey, pal,' I said, but it came out as a meaningless croak.

He licked my face. He had dog's breath, but I couldn't really blame him for that.

I blinked furiously to clear my vision, and red light pulsed through the room brighter than ever. Still, I got no better than a bleary impression of his furry face pressed to the floor in front of mine.

Then I realized that if he could get into the house and find me, he could show me the way out before we caught fire with a stink of burning denim and fur.

I gathered sufficient strength to rise shakily to my feet. That stubborn eel of nausea swam up my throat again, but as before I choked it down.

Squeezing my eyes shut, trying not to think about the wave of intense heat that abruptly broke over me, I reached down and gripped Orson's thick leather collar, which was easy to find because he was pressed against my legs.

Orson kept his snout close to the floor, where he could breathe, but I had to hold my breath and ignore the nostril-tickling smoke as the dog led me through the house. He walked me into as few pieces of furniture as he could manage, and I have no suspicion whatever that he was amusing himself in the midst of such tragedy and terror. When I smacked my face into a door frame, I didn't knock out any teeth. Nevertheless, during that short journey, I thanked God repeatedly for testing me with XP rather than with blindness.

Just when I thought that I might pass out if I didn't drop to the floor to get some air, I felt a cold draft on my face, and when I opened my eyes, I could see. We were in the kitchen, into which the fire had not yet reached. There was no smoke, either, because the breeze coming in the open back door drove it all into the dining room.

On the table were the three votive candles in ruby-red

holders, two cordial glasses, and the open bottle of apricot brandy. Blinking at this cozy tableau, I could half believe that the events of the past several minutes had been only a monstrous dream and that Angela, still lost in her dead husband's cardigan, would sit here with me once more, refill her glass, and finish her strange story.

My mouth was so dry and foul that I almost took the bottle of brandy with me. Bobby Halloway would have beer, however, and that would be better.

The deadbolt on the kitchen door was disengaged now. As clever as Orson might be, I doubted that he could have opened a locked door to reach me; for one thing, he didn't have a key. Evidently the killers had fled by this route.

Outside, wheezing to expel a few final traces of smoke from my lungs, I shoved the Glock in my jacket pocket. I nervously surveyed the backyard for assailants as I blotted my damp hands on my jeans.

Like fishes schooling below the silvered surface of a pond, cloud shadows swam across the moonlit lawn.

Nothing else moved except the wind-shaken vegetation.

Grabbing my bicycle and wheeling it across the patio toward the arbor-covered passageway, I looked up at the house in astonishment, amazed that it was not entirely engulfed in flames. Instead, from the exterior, there were as yet only minor indications of the blaze growing from room to room inside: bright vines of flames twining up the draperies at two upstairs windows, white petals of smoke flowering from attic vent holes in the eaves.

Except for the bluster and grumble of the inconstant wind, the night was preternaturally silent. Moonlight

Bay is no city, but it usually has a distinct night voice nonetheless: a few cars on the move, distant music from a cocktail lounge or a kid practicing guitar on a back porch, a barking dog, the whisking sound of the big brushes on the street-cleaning machine, voices of strollers, laughter from the high-school kids gathered outside the Millennium Arcade down on Embarcadero Way, now and then a melancholy whistle as an Amtrak passenger train or a chain of freight cars approaches the Ocean Avenue crossing . . . Not at this moment, however, and not on this night. We might as well have been in the deadest neighborhood of a ghost town deep in the Mojave desert.

Apparently, the crack of the single gunshot that I had fired in the living room had not been loud enough out here to draw anyone's attention.

Under the lattice arch, through the sweet fragrance of jasmine, walking the bicycle, its wheel bearings clicking softly, my heart thudding not softly at all, I hurried after Orson to the front gate. He leaped up and pawed open the latch, a trick of his that I'd seen before. Together we followed the walkway to the street, moving quickly but not running.

We were in luck: no witnesses. No traffic was either approaching or receding along the street. No one was on foot, either.

If a neighbor saw me running from the house just as it went up in flames, Chief Stevenson might decide to use that as an excuse to come looking for me. To shoot me down when I resisted arrest. Whether I resisted or not.

I swung onto my bike, balancing it by keeping one foot on the pavement, and looked back at the house. The wind trembled the leaves of the huge magnolia trees, and through the branches, I could see fire at several of the downstairs and upstairs windows.

Full of grief and excitement, curiosity and dread, sorrow and dark wonder, I raced along the pavement, heading for a street with fewer lamps. Panting loudly, Orson sprinted at my side.

We had gone nearly a block when I heard the windows begin to explode at the Ferryman house, blown out by the fierce heat.

16

Stars between branches, leaf-filtered moonlight, giant oaks, a nurturing darkness, the peace of gravestones – and, for one of us, the eternally intriguing scent of hidden squirrels: We were back in the cemetery adjacent to St. Bernadette's Catholic Church.

My bike was propped against a granite marker topped by the haloed head of a granite angel. I was sitting – sans halo – with my back against another stone that featured a cross at its summit.

Blocks away, sirens shrieked into sudden silence as fire-department vehicles arrived at the Ferryman residence.

I hadn't cycled all the way to Bobby Halloway's house, because I'd been hit by a persistent fit of coughing that hampered my ability to steer. Orson's gait had grown wobbly, too, as he expelled the stubborn scent of the fire with a series of violent sneezes.

Now, in the company of a crowd too dead to be offended, I hawked up thick soot-flavored phlegm and spat it among the gnarled surface roots of the nearest oak, with the hope that I wasn't killing this mighty tree that had survived two centuries of earthquakes, storms, fires, insects, disease, and – more recently – modern America's passion for erecting a mini-mall with doughnut shop on every street corner. The taste in my mouth could not have been much different if I had been eating charcoal briquettes in a broth of starter fluid.

Having been in the burning house a shorter time than his more reckless master, Orson recovered faster than I. Before I was half done hawking and spitting, he was padding back and forth among the nearest tombstones, diligently sniffing out arboreal bushy-tailed rodents.

Between spells of hacking and expectorating, I talked to Orson if he was in sight, and sometimes he lifted his noble black head and pretended to listen, occasionally wagging his tail to encourage me, though often he was unable to tear his attention away from squirrel spoor.

'What the hell happened in that house?' I asked. 'Who killed her, why were they playing games with me, what was the point of all that business with the dolls, why didn't they just slit my throat and burn me with her?'

Orson shook his head, and I made a game of interpreting his response. He didn't know. Shook his head in bafflement. Clueless. He was clueless. He didn't know why they hadn't slit my throat.

'I don't think it was the Glock. I mean, there were more than one of them, at least two, probably three, so they could easily have overpowered me if they'd wanted. And though they slashed her throat, they must have been carrying guns of their own. I mean, these are serious bastards, vicious killers. They cut people's eyes out for the fun of it. They wouldn't be squeamish about carrying guns, so they wouldn't be intimidated by the Glock.'

Orson cocked his head, considering the issue. *Maybe it was the Glock. Maybe it wasn't. Then again, maybe it was. Who knew? What's a Glock, anyway? And what's that smell? Such an amazing smell. Such a luxurious fragrance. Is that squirrel piss? Excuse me, Master Snow. Business. Business to attend to here.*

'I don't think they set the house afire to kill me. They didn't really care whether they killed me or not. If they cared, they would have made a more direct effort to get me. They set the fire to cover up Angela's murder. That was the reason, nothing more.'

Sniff, sniff, sniff-sniff-sniff: out with the remaining bad air of the burning house, in with the revitalizing scent of squirrel, out with the bad, in with the good.

'God, she was such a good person, so giving,' I said bitterly. 'She didn't deserve to die like that, to die at all.'

Orson paused in his sniffing but only briefly. *Human suffering. Terrible. Terrible thing. Misery, death, despair. But nothing to be done. Nothing to be done about it. Just the way of the world, the nature of human existence. Terrible. Come smell the squirrels with me, Master Snow. You'll feel better.*

A lump rose in my throat, not poignant grief but something more prosaic, so I hacked with tubercular violence and finally planted a black oyster among the tree roots.

'If Sasha were here,' I said, 'I wonder if right now I'd remind her so much of James Dean?'

My face felt greasy and tender. I wiped at it with a hand that also felt greasy.

Across the thin grass on the graves and across the polished surfaces of the granite markers, the moonshadows of wind-trembled leaves danced like cemetery fairies.

Even in this peculiar light, I could see that the palm of

the hand I had put to my face was smeared with soot. 'I must stink to high heaven.'

Immediately, Orson lost interest in the squirrel spoor and came eagerly to me. He sniffed vigorously at my shoes, along my legs, across my chest, finally sticking his snout under my jacket and into my armpit.

Sometimes I suspect that Orson not only understands more than we expect a dog to understand, but that he has a sense of humor and a talent for sarcasm.

Forcibly withdrawing his snout from my armpit, holding his head in both hands, I said, 'You're no rose yourself, pal. And what kind of guard dog are you, anyway? Maybe they were already in the house with Angela when I arrived, and she didn't know it. But how come you didn't bite them in the ass when they left the place? If they escaped by the kitchen door, they went right past you. Why didn't I find a bunch of bad guys rolling around on the backyard, clutching their butts and howling in pain?'

Orson's gaze held steady, his eyes deep. He was shocked by the question, the implied accusation. Shocked. He was a peaceful dog. A dog of peace, he was. A chaser of rubber balls, a licker of faces, a philosopher and boon companion. *Besides, Master Snow, the job was to prevent villains from entering the house, not to prevent them from leaving. Good riddance to villains. Who wants them around, anyway? Villains and fleas. Good riddance.*

As I sat nose-to-nose with Orson, staring into his eyes, a sense of the uncanny came over me – or perhaps it was a transient madness – and for a moment I imagined that I could read his *true* thoughts, which were markedly different from the dialogue that I invented for him. Different and unsettling.

I dropped my bracketing hands from his head, but he chose not to turn away from me or to lower his gaze.

I was unable to lower mine.

To express a word of this to Bobby Halloway would have been to elicit a recommendation of lobotomy: Nevertheless, I sensed that the dog feared for me. Pitied me because I was struggling so hard not to admit the true depth of my pain. Pitied me because I could not acknowledge how profoundly the prospect of being alone scared me. More than anything, however, he *feared* for me, as though he saw an oncoming juggernaut of which I was oblivious: a great white blazing wheel, as big as a mountain, that would grind me to dust and leave the dust burning in its wake.

'What, when, where?' I wondered.

Orson's stare was intense. Anubis, the dog-headed Egyptian god of tombs, weigher of the hearts of the dead, could not have stared more piercingly. This dog of mine was no Lassie, no carefree Disney pooch with strictly cute moves and an unlimited capacity for mischievous fun.

'Sometimes,' I told him, 'you spook me.'

He blinked, shook his head, leaped away from me, and padded in circles among the tombstones, busily sniffing the grass and the fallen oak leaves, pretending to be just a dog again.

Maybe it wasn't Orson who had spooked me. Maybe I had spooked myself. Maybe his lustrous eyes had been mirrors in which I'd seen my own eyes; and in the reflections of my eyes, perhaps I had seen truths in my own heart that I was unwilling to look upon directly.

'That would be the Halloway interpretation,' I said.

With sudden excitement, Orson pawed through a drift of fragrant leaves still damp from an afternoon watering by the sprinkler system, burrowed his snout among them as though engaged in a truffle hunt, chuffed, and beat the ground with his tail.

Squirrels. Squirrels had sex. Squirrels had sex, had sex right here. Squirrels. Right here. *Squirrel-heat-musk smell here, right here, Master Snow, here, come smell here, come smell, quick quick quick quick, come smell squirrel sex.*

'You confound me,' I told him.

My mouth still tasted like the bottom of an ashtray, but I was no longer hacking up the phlegm of Satan. I should be able to steer to Bobby's place now.

Before fetching my bike, I rose onto my knees and turned to face the headstone against which I had been leaning. 'How're things with you, Noah? Still resting in peace?'

I didn't have to use the penlight to read the engraving on the stone. I'd read it a thousand times before, and I'd spent hours pondering the name and the dates under it.

NOAH JOSEPH JAMES
June 5, 1888 – July 2, 1984

Noah Joseph James, the man with three first names. It's not your name that amazes me; it's your singular longevity.

Ninety-six years of life.

Ninety-six springs, summers, autumns, winters.

Against daunting odds, I have thus far lived twenty-eight years. If Lady Fortune comes to me with both hands full, I might make thirty-eight. If the physicians prove to be bad prognosticators, if the laws of probability are suspended, if fate takes a holiday, perhaps I'll live to be forty-eight. Then I would have enjoyed one half the span of life granted to Noah Joseph James.

I don't know who he was, what he did with the better part of a century here on earth, whether he had one wife with whom to share his days or outlived three, whether the children whom he fathered became priests or serial killers, and I don't want to know. I've fantasized a rich and wondrous life for this man. I believe him to have been well traveled, to have been to Borneo and Brazil, to Mobile Bay during Jubilee and to New Orleans during Mardi Gras, to the sun-washed isles of Greece and to the secret land of Shangri-la high in the fastness of Tibet. I believe that he loved truly and was deeply loved in return, that he was a warrior and a poet, an adventurer and a scholar, a musician and an artist and a sailor who sailed all the seven seas, who boldly cast off what limitations – if any – were placed upon him. As long as he remains only a name to me and is otherwise a mystery, he can be whatever I want him to be, and I can vicariously experience his long, long life in the sun.

Softly I said, 'Hey, Noah, I'll bet when you died back there in 1984, undertakers didn't carry guns.'

I rose to my feet and stepped to the adjacent tombstone, where my bicycle was propped under the guardian gaze of the granite angel.

Orson let out a low growl. Abruptly he was tense, alert. His head was raised high, ears pricked. Although the light was poor, his tail seemed to be tucked between his legs.

I followed the direction of his coaly gaze and saw a tall, stoop-shouldered man stalking among the tombstones. Even in the softening shadows, he was a collection of angles and sharp edges, like a skeleton in a black suit, as if one of Noah's neighbors had climbed out of his casket to go visiting.

The man stopped in the very row of graves in which Orson and I stood, and he consulted a curious object in his left hand. It appeared to be the size of a cellular telephone, with an illuminated display screen.

He tapped on the instrument's keypad. The eerie music of electronic notes carried briefly through the cemetery, but these were different from telephone tones.

Just as a scarf of cloud blew off the moon, the stranger brought the sour-apple-green screen closer to his face for a better look at whatever data it provided, and those two soft lights revealed enough for me to make an identification. I couldn't see the red color of his hair or his russet eyes, but even in profile the whippet-lean face and thin lips were chillingly familiar: Jesse Pinn, assistant mortician.

He was not aware of Orson and me, though we stood only thirty or forty feet to his left.

We played at being granite. Orson wasn't growling anymore, even though the soughing of the breeze through the oaks would easily have masked his grumble.

Pinn raised his face from the hand-held device, glanced to his right, at St. Bernadette's, and then consulted the screen again. Finally he headed toward the church.

He remained unaware of us, although we were little more than thirty feet from him.

I looked at Orson.

He looked at me.

Squirrels forgotten, we followed Pinn.

17

The mortician hurried to the back of the church, never glancing over his shoulder. He descended a broad set of stone stairs that led to a basement door.

I followed closely to keep him in sight. Halting only ten feet from the head of the stairs and at an angle to them, I peered down at him.

If he turned and looked up, he would see me before I could move out of sight, but I was not overly concerned. He seemed so involved in the task at hand that the summons of celestial trumpets and the racket of the dead rising from their graves might not have drawn his attention.

He studied the mysterious device in his hand, switched it off, and tucked it into an inside coat pocket. From another pocket he extracted a second instrument, but the light was too poor to allow me to see what he held; unlike the first item, this one incorporated no luminous parts.

Even above the susurration of wind and oak leaves, I heard a series of clicks and rasping noises. These were followed by a hard snap, another snap, and then a third.

On the fourth snap, I thought that I recognized the distinctive sound. A Lockaid lock-release gun. The device had a thin pick that you slipped into the key channel, under the pin tumblers. When you pulled the trigger, a flat steel spring jumped upward and lodged some of the pins at the sheer line.

A few years ago, Manuel Ramirez gave me a Lockaid demonstration. Lock-release guns were sold only to law-enforcement agencies, and the possession of one by a civilian was illegal.

Although Jesse Pinn could hang a consoling expression on his mug as convincingly as could Sandy Kirk, he incinerated murder victims in a crematorium furnace to assist in the cover-up of capital crimes, so he was not likely to be fazed by laws restricting Lockaid ownership. Maybe he had limits. Maybe, for instance, he wouldn't push a nun off a cliff for no reason whatsoever. Nevertheless, recalling Pinn's sharp face and the stiletto flicker of his red-brown eyes as he had approached the crematorium window earlier this evening, I wouldn't have put money on the nun at any odds.

The undertaker needed to fire the lock-release gun five times to clear all the pins and disengage the deadbolt. After cautiously trying the door, he returned the Lockaid to his pocket.

When he pushed the door inward, the windowless basement proved to be lighted. Silhouetted, he stood listening on the threshold for perhaps half a minute, his bony shoulders canted to the left and his half-hung head cocked to the right, wind-spiked hair bristling like straw; abruptly he jerked himself into a better posture, like a suddenly animated scarecrow pulling loose of its supporting cross, and he went inside, pushing the door only half shut behind him.

'Stay,' I whispered to Orson.

I went down the stairs, and my ever-obedient dog followed me.

When I put one ear to the half-open door, I heard nothing from the basement.

Orson stuck his snout through the eighteen-inch gap, sniffing, and although I rapped him lightly on the top of the head, he didn't withdraw.

Leaning over the dog, I put my snout through the gap, too, not for a sniff but far enough inside to see what lay beyond. Squinting against the fluorescent glare, I saw a twenty-by-forty-foot room with concrete walls and ceiling, lined with equipment that served the church and the attached wing of Sunday-school rooms: five gas-fired furnaces, a big water heater, electric-service panels, and machinery that I didn't recognize.

Jesse Pinn was three-quarters of the way across this first room, approaching a closed door in the far wall, his back to me.

Stepping away from the door, I unclipped the glasses case from my shirt pocket. The Velcro closure peeled open with a sound that made me think of a snake breaking wind, though I don't know why, as I'd never in my life *heard* a snake breaking wind. My aforementioned flamboyant imagination had taken a scatological turn.

By the time I put on the glasses and peered inside again, Pinn had disappeared into the second basement room. That farther door stood half open as well, and light blazed beyond.

'It's a concrete floor in there,' I whispered. 'My Nikes won't make a sound, but your claws will tick. Stay.'

I pressed open the door before me and eased into the basement.

Orson remained outside, at the foot of the stairs. Perhaps he was obedient this time because I'd given him a logical reason to be.

Or perhaps, because of something he had smelled, he knew that proceeding farther was ill advised. Dogs have an olfactory sense thousands of times sharper than ours, bringing them more data than all human senses combined.

With the sunglasses, I was safe from the light, yet I could see more than well enough to navigate the room. I avoided the open center, staying close to the furnaces and the other equipment, where I could duck into a niche and hope to hide if I heard Jesse Pinn returning.

Time and sweat had by now diminished the effectiveness of the sunscreen on my face and hands, but I was counting on my layer of soot to protect me. My hands appeared to be sheathed in black silk gloves, and I assumed that my face was equally masked.

When I reached the inner door, I heard two distant voices, both male, one belonging to Pinn. They were muffled, and I couldn't understand what was being said.

I glanced at the outside door, where Orson peered in at me, one ear at attention and the other at ease.

Beyond the inner door was a long, narrow, largely empty room. Only a few of the overhead lights were aglow, suspended on chains between exposed water pipes and heating ducts, but I didn't remove my sunglasses.

At the end, this chamber proved to be part of an L-shaped space, and the next length, which opened to the right, was longer and wider than the first, although still dimly lighted. This second section was used as a storeroom, and seeking the voices, I crept past boxes of supplies, decorations for various holidays and celebrations, and file cabinets full of church records. Everywhere shadows gathered like convocations of robed and cowled monks, and I removed my sunglasses.

The voices grew louder as I proceeded, but the acoustics were terrible, and I still couldn't discern any words. Although he was not shouting, Pinn was angry, which I deduced from a low menace in his voice. The other man sounded as though he were trying to placate the undertaker.

A complete life-size creche was arrayed across half the width of the room: not merely Joseph and the Holy Virgin at a cradle with the Christ child, but the entire manger scene with wise men, camels, donkeys, lambs, and heralding angels. The stable was made of lumber, and the bales of hay were real; the people and animals were plaster over chicken wire and lath, their clothes and features painted by a gifted artist, protected by a waterproof lacquer that gave them a supernatural glow even in this poor light. Judging by the tools, paint, and other supplies at the periphery of the collection, repairs were being made, after which the creche would be put under dropcloths until next Christmas.

Beginning to make out scattered words of Pinn's conversation with the unknown man, I moved among the figures, some of which were taller than I am, and the scene was disorienting because none of the elements was staged for display, none in its proper relationship to the others. One of the wise men stood with his face in the bell of an angel's raised trumpet, and Joseph appeared to be engaged in a conversation with a camel. Baby Jesus lay unattended in His cradle, which stood on a bale of hay to one side. Mary sat with a beatific smile and an adoring gaze, but the object of her attention, rather than being her holy child, was a galvanized bucket. Another wise man seemed to be looking up a camel's butt.

I wended through this disorganized creche, and near the end of it, I used a lute-playing angel for cover. I was in shadows, but peering past the curve of a half-furled wing, I saw Jesse Pinn in the light about twenty feet away, hectoring another man near the stairs that led up to the main floor of the church.

'You've been warned,' Pinn said, raising his voice until it was almost a snarl. 'How many *times* have you been warned?'

At first I could not see the other man, who was blocked by Pinn. He spoke quietly, evenly, and I could not hear what he said.

The undertaker reacted in disgust and began to pace agitatedly, combing one hand through his disarranged hair.

Now I saw that the second man was Father Tom Eliot, rector of St. Bernadette's.

'You fool, you stupid shit,' Pinn said furiously, bitterly. 'You prattling, God-gushing *moron*.'

Father Tom was five feet eight, plump, with the expressive and rubbery face of a natural-born comedian. Although I wasn't a member of his – or any – church, I'd spoken with him on several occasions, and he seemed to be a singularly good-natured man with a self-deprecating sense of humor and an almost childlike enthusiasm for life. I had no trouble understanding why his parishioners adored him.

Pinn did not adore him. He raised one skeletal hand and pointed a bony finger at the priest: 'You make me sick, you self-righteous son of a bitch.'

Evidently Father Tom had decided to weather this outrageous verbal assault without response.

As he paced, Pinn chopped at the air with the sharp edge of one hand, as though struggling – with considerable frustration – to sculpt his words into a truth that the priest could understand. 'We're not taking any more of your crap, no more of your interference. I'm not going to threaten to kick your teeth out myself, though I'd sure as hell enjoy doing it. Never liked to dance, you know, but I'd sure like to dance on your stupid *face*. But no threats like before, no, not this time, not ever again. I'm not even going to threaten to send *them* after you, because I think that would actually appeal to you. Father Eliot the martyr, suffering for God. Oh, you'd like that – wouldn't you? – being a martyr, suffering such a rotten death without complaint.'

Father Tom stood with his head bowed, his eyes downcast, his arms straight at his sides, as though waiting patiently for this storm to pass.

The priest's passivity inflamed Pinn. The mortician made a sharp-knuckled fist of his right hand and pounded it into the palm of his left, as if he needed to hear the hard snap of flesh on flesh, and now his voice was as rich with scorn as with fury. 'You'd wake up some night, and they'd be all over you, or maybe they'd take you by surprise in the bell tower or in the sacristy when you're kneeling at the *prie-dieu*, and you'd surrender yourself to them in ecstasy, in a sick ecstasy, *reveling* in the pain, suffering for your God – that's the way you'd see it – suffering for your dead God, suffering your way straight into Heaven. You dumb bastard. You hopeless retard. You'd even pray for them, pray your heart out for them as they tore you to pieces. Wouldn't you, priest?'

To all of this, the chubby priest responded with lowered eyes and mute endurance.

Keeping my own silence required effort. I had questions for Jesse Pinn. Lots of questions.

Here, however, there was no crematory fire to which I could hold his feet to force answers out of him.

Pinn stopped pacing and loomed over Father Tom. 'No more threats against you, priest. No point to it. Just gives you a thrill to think of suffering for the Lord. So this is what'll happen if you don't stay out of our way – we'll waste your sister. Pretty Laura.'

Father Tom raised his head and met Pinn's eyes, but still he said nothing.

'I'll kill her myself,' Pinn promised. 'With this gun.'

He withdrew a pistol from inside his suit coat, evidently from a shoulder holster. Even at a distance and in this poor light, I could see that the barrel was unusually long.

Defensively, I put my hand into my jacket pocket, on the butt of the Glock.

'Let her go,' said the priest.

'We'll never let her go. She's too . . . interesting. Fact is,' Pinn said, 'before I kill Laura, I'll rape her. She's still a good-looking woman, even if she's getting strange.'

Laura Eliot, who had been a friend and colleague of my mother's, was indeed a lovely woman. Although I hadn't seen her in a year, her face came readily to mind. Supposedly, she had obtained employment in San Diego when Ashdon eliminated her position. Dad and I had received a letter from Laura, and we'd been disappointed that she hadn't come around to say goodbye in person. Evidently that was a cover story and she was still in the area – being held against her will.

Finding his voice at last, Father Tom said, 'God help you.'

'I don't need help,' Pinn said. 'When I jam the gun in her mouth, just before I pull the trigger, I'll tell her that her brother says he'll see her soon, see her soon in Hell, and then I'll blow her brains out.'

'God help me.'

'What did you say, priest?' Pinn inquired mockingly.

Father Tom didn't answer.

'Did you say, "God help me"?' Pinn taunted. '"God help me"? Not very damn likely. After all, you aren't one of His anymore, are you?'

This curious statement caused Father Tom to lean back against the wall and cover his face with his hands. He might have been weeping; I couldn't be sure.

'Picture your lovely sister's face,' said Pinn. 'Now picture her bone structure twisting, distorting, and the top of her skull blowing out.'

He fired the pistol at the ceiling. The barrel was long because it was fitted with a sound suppressor, and instead of a loud report, there was nothing but a noise like a fist hitting a pillow.

In the same instant and with a hard *clang*, the bullet struck the rectangular metal shade of the lamp suspended directly above the mortician. The fluorescent tube didn't shatter, but the lamp swung wildly on its long chains; an icy blade of light like a harvesting scythe cut bright arcs through the room.

In the rhythmic sweep of light, though Pinn himself did not at first move, his scarecrow shadow leaped at other shadows that flapped like blackbirds. Then he holstered the pistol under his coat.

As the chains of the swinging light fixture torqued, the links twisted against one another with enough friction to cause an eerie ringing, as if lizard-eyed altar boys in blood-soaked cassocks and surplices were ringing the unmelodious bells of a satanic mass.

The shrill music and the capering shadows seemed to excite Jesse Pinn. An inhuman cry issued from him, primitive and psychotic, a caterwaul of the sort that sometimes wakes you in the night and leaves you wondering about the species of origin. As that spittle-rich sound sprayed from his lips, he hammered his fists into the priest's midsection, two hard punches.

Quickly stepping out from behind the lute-playing angel, I tried to draw the Glock, but it caught on the lining of my jacket pocket.

As Father Tom doubled over from the two blows, Pinn locked his hands and clubbed them against the back of the priest's neck.

Father Tom dropped to the floor, and I finally ripped the pistol out of my pocket.

Pinn kicked the priest in the ribs.

I raised the Glock, aimed at Pinn's back, and engaged the laser sighting. As the mortal red dot appeared between his shoulder blades, I was about to say *enough,* but the mortician relented and stepped away from the priest.

I kept my silence, but to Father Tom, Pinn said, 'If you're not part of the solution, you're part of the problem. If you can't be part of the future, then get the hell out of the way.'

That sounded like a parting line. I switched off the laser sighting and retreated behind the angel just as the undertaker turned away from Father Tom. He didn't see me.

To the singing of the chains, Jesse Pinn walked back the way he had come, and the jittery sound seemed to issue not from overhead but from within him, as though locusts were swarming in his blood. His shadow repeatedly darted ahead of him and then leaped behind until he passed beyond the arcing sword of light from the swinging fixture, became one with the darkness, and rounded the corner into the other arm of the L-shaped room.

I returned the Glock to my jacket pocket.

From the cover of the dysfunctional creche, I watched Father Tom Eliot. He was lying at the foot of the stairs, in the fetal position, curled around his pain.

I considered going to him to determine if he was seriously hurt, and to learn what I could about the circumstances that lay behind the confrontation I had just witnessed, but I was reluctant to reveal myself. I stayed where I was.

Any enemy of Jesse Pinn should be an ally of mine – but I could not be certain of Father Tom's goodwill. Although adversaries, the priest and the mortician were players in some mysterious underworld of which I had been utterly unaware until this very night, so each of them had more in common with the other than with me. I could easily imagine that, at the sight of me, Father Tom would scream for Jesse Pinn, and that the undertaker would fly back, black suit flapping, with the inhuman caterwaul vibrating between his thin lips.

Besides, Pinn and his crew evidently were holding the priest's sister somewhere. Possession of her gave them a lever and fulcrum with which to move Father Tom, while I had no leverage whatsoever.

The chilling music of the torquing chains gradually faded, and the sword of light described a steadily diminishing arc.

Without a protest, without even an involuntary groan, the priest drew himself to his knees, gathered himself to his feet. He was not able to stand fully erect. Hunched like an ape and no longer comic in any aspect of face or body, with one hand on the railing, he began to pull himself laboriously up the steep, creaking steps toward the church above.

When at last he reached the top, he would switch off the lights, and I would be left here below in a darkness that even St. Bernadette herself, miracle worker of Lourdes, would find daunting. Time to go.

Before retracing my path through the life-size figures of the creche, I raised my eyes for the first time to the painted eyes of the lute-playing angel in front of me – and thought I saw a blue to match my own. I studied the rest of the lacquered-plaster features and, although the light was weak, I was sure that this angel and I shared a face.

This resemblance paralyzed me with confusion, and I struggled to understand how this Christopher Snow angel could have been here waiting for me. I have rarely seen my own face in brightness, but I know its reflection from the mirrors of my dimly lit rooms, and this was a similar light. This was unquestionably me: beatific as I am not, idealized, but me.

Since my experience in the hospital garage, every incident and object seemed to have significance. No longer could I entertain the possibility of coincidence. Everywhere I looked, the world oozed uncanniness.

This was, of course, the route to madness: viewing *all* of life as one elaborate conspiracy conducted by elite manipulators who see all and know all. The sane understand that human beings are incapable of sustaining conspiracies on a grand scale, because some of our most defining qualities as a species are inattention to detail, a tendency to panic, and an inability to keep our mouths shut. Cosmically speaking, we are barely able to tie our shoes. If there is, indeed, some secret order to the universe, it is not of our doing, and we are probably not even capable of apprehending it.

The priest was a third of the way up the stairs.

Stupefied, I studied the angel.

Many nights during the Christmas season, year after year, I had cycled along the street on which St. Bernadette's stood. The creche had been arranged on the front lawn of the church, each figure in its proper place, none of the gift-bearing magi posing as a proctologist to camels – and this angel had not been there. Or I hadn't realized that it was there. The likely explanation, of course, was that the display was too brightly lighted for me to risk admiring it; the Christopher Snow angel had been part of the scene, but I had always turned my face from it, squinted my eyes.

The priest was halfway up the stairs and climbing faster.

Then I remembered that Angela Ferryman had attended Mass at St. Bernadette's. Undoubtedly, considering her doll-making, she had been prevailed upon to lend her talent to the making of the creche.

End of mystery.

I still couldn't understand why she would have assigned my face to an angel. If my features belonged anywhere in the manger scene, they should have been on the donkey. Clearly, her opinion of me had been higher than I warranted.

Unwanted, an image of Angela rose in my mind's eye: Angela as I had last seen her on the bathroom floor, her eyes fixed on some last sight farther away than Andromeda, head tilted backward into the toilet bowl, throat slashed.

Suddenly I was certain that I had missed an important detail when I'd found her poor torn body. Repulsed by the gouts of blood, gripped by grief, in a state of shock and fear, I had avoided looking long at her – just as, for years, I had avoided looking at the figures in the brightly lighted creche outside the church. I had seen a vital clue, but it had not registered consciously. Now my subconscious taunted me with it.

As Father Tom reached the top of the steps, he broke into sobs. He sat on the landing and wept inconsolably.

I could not hold fast to a mental image of Angela's face. Later there would be time to confront and, reluctantly, explore that Grand Guignol memory.

From angel to camel to magi to Joseph to donkey to Holy Virgin to lamb to Lamb, I wove silently through the creche, then past file cabinets and boxes of supplies, into the shorter and narrower space where little was stored, and onward toward the door of the utilities room.

The sounds of the priest's anguish resonated off the concrete walls, fading until they were like the cries of some haunting entity barely able to make itself heard through the cold barrier between this world and the next.

Grimly, I recalled my father's wrenching grief in the cold-holding room at Mercy Hospital, on the night of my mother's death.

For reasons I don't entirely understand, I keep my own anguish private. When one of those wild cries threatens to arise, I bite hard until I chew the energy out of it and swallow it unspoken.

In my sleep I grind my teeth – no surprise – until I wake some nights with aching jaws. Perhaps I am fearful of giving voice in dreams to sentiments I choose not to express when awake.

On the way out of the church basement, I expected the undertaker – waxy and pale, with eyes like day-old blood blisters – to drop on me from above or to soar out of the shadows around my feet or to spring like an evil jack-in-the-box from a furnace door. He was not waiting anywhere along my route.

Outside, Orson came to me from among the tombstones, where he had hidden from Pinn. Judging by the dog's demeanor, the mortician was gone.

He stared at me with great curiosity – or I imagined that he did – and I said, 'I don't really know what happened in there. I don't know what it meant.'

He appeared dubious. He has a gift for looking dubious: the blunt face, the unwavering eyes.

'Truly,' I insisted.

With Orson padding at my side, I returned to my bicycle. The granite angel guarding my transportation did not resemble me in the least.

The fretful wind had again subsided into a caressing breeze, and the oaks stood silent.

A shifting filigree of clouds was silver across the silver moon.

A large flock of chimney swifts swooped down from the church roof and alighted in the trees, and a few nightingales returned, too, as though the cemetery had not been sanctified until Pinn had departed it.

Holding my bike by the handlebars, I pondered the ranks of tombstones and said: '". . . the dark grew solid around them, finally changing to earth." That's Louise Glück, a great poet.'

Orson chuffed as if in agreement.

'I don't know what's happening here, but I think a lot of people are going to die before this is over – and some of them are likely to be people we love. Maybe even me. Or you.'

Orson's gaze was solemn.

I looked past the cemetery at the streets of my hometown, which were suddenly a lot scarier than any boneyard.

'Let's get a beer,' I said.

I climbed on my bike, and Orson danced a dog dance across the graveyard grass, and for the time being, we left the dead behind.

Three

MIDNIGHT HOUR

18

The cottage is the ideal residence for a boardhead like Bobby. It stands on the southern horn of the bay, far out on the point, the sole structure within three-quarters of a mile. Point-break surf surrounds it.

From town, the lights of Bobby Halloway's house appear to be so far from the lights along the inner curve of the bay that tourists assume they are seeing a boat anchored in the channel beyond our sheltered waters. To longtime residents, the cottage is a landmark.

The place was constructed forty-five years ago, before many restrictions were placed on coastal building, and it never acquired neighbors because, in those days, there was an abundance of cheap land along the shore, where the wind and the weather were more accommodating than on the point, and where there were streets and convenient utility hookups. By the time the shore lots – then the hills behind them – filled up, regulations issued by the California Coastal Commission had made building on the bay horns impossible.

Long before the house came into Bobby's possession, a grandfather clause in the law preserved it's existence. Bobby intended to die in this singular place, he said, shrouded in the sound of breaking surf – but not until well past the middle of the first century of the new millennium.

No paved or graveled road leads along the horn, only a wide rock track flanked by low dunes precariously held in place by tall, sparse shore grass.

The horns that embrace the bay are natural formations, curving peninsulas: They are the remnants of the rim of a massive extinct volcano. The bay itself is a volcanic crater layered with sand by thousands of years of tides. Near shore, the southern horn is three to four hundred feet wide, but it narrows to a hundred at the point.

When I was two-thirds of the way to Bobby's house, I had to get off my bike and walk it. Soft drifts of sand, less than a foot deep, sloped across the rock trail. They would pose no obstacle to Bobby's four-wheel-drive Jeep wagon, but they made pedaling difficult.

This walk was usually peaceful, encouraging meditation. Tonight the horn was serene, but it seemed as alien as a spine of rock on the moon, and I kept glancing back, expecting to see someone pursuing me.

The one-story cottage is of teak, with a cedar-shingle roof. Weathered to a lustrous silver-gray, the wood takes the caress of moonlight as a woman's body receives a lover's touch. Encircling three sides of the house is a deep porch furnished with rocking chairs and gliders.

There are no trees. The landscaping consists only of sand and wild shore grass. Anyway, the eye is impatient with the nearer view and favors the sky, the sea, and the shimmering lights of Moonlight Bay, which look more distant than three-quarters of a mile.

Buying time to settle my nerves, I leaned my bike against the front porch railing and walked past the cottage, to the end of the point. There, I stood with Orson at the top of a slope that dropped thirty feet to the beach.

The surf was so slow that you would have to work hard to catch a wave, and the ride wouldn't last long. It was almost a neap tide, though this was the fourth quarter of the moon. The surf was a little sloppy, too, because of the onshore wind, which was blustery enough to cause some chop out here, even though it was all but dead in town.

Offshore wind is best, smoothing the ocean surface. It blows spray from the crest of the waves, makes them hold up longer, and causes them to hollow out before they break.

Bobby and I have been surfing since we were eleven: him by day, both of us by night. Lots of surfers hit the waves by moonlight, fewer when the moon is down, but Bobby and I like it best in storm waves without even stars.

We were grommets together, totally annoying surf mongrels, but we graduated to surf nazis before we were fourteen, and we were mature boardheads by the time Bobby graduated high school and I took my equivalency degree for home education. Bobby is more than just a boardhead now; he's a surf mensch, and people all over the world turn to him to find out where the big waves will be breaking next.

God, I love the sea at night. It is darkness distilled into a liquid, and nowhere in this world do I feel more at home than in these black swells. The only light that ever arises in the ocean is from bioluminescent plankton, which become radiant when disturbed, and although they can make an entire wave glow an intense lime green, their brightness is friendly to my eyes. The night sea contains nothing from which I must hide or from which I must even look away.

By the time I walked back to the cottage, Bobby was standing in the open front door. Because of our friendship, all the lights in his house are on rheostats; now he had dimmed them to the level of candlelight.

I haven't a clue as to how he knew that I had arrived. Neither I nor Orson had made a sound. Bobby just always knows.

He was barefoot, even in March, but he was wearing jeans instead of swim trunks or shorts. His shirt was Hawaiian; he owns no other style; but he had made a concession to the season by wearing a long-sleeve, crewneck, white cotton sweater under the short-sleeve shirt, which featured bright quizzical parrots and lush palm fronds.

As I climbed the steps to the porch, Bobby gave me a shaka, the surfer hand signal that's easier to make than the sign they exchange on *Star Trek*, which is probably based on the shaka. Fold your middle three fingers to your palm, extend your thumb and little finger, and lazily waggle your hand. It means a lot of things – hello, what's up, hang loose, great ride – all friendly, and it will never be taken as an insult unless you wave it at someone who isn't a surfer, such as an L.A. gang member, in which case it might get you shot dead.

I was eager to tell him about everything that had transpired since sundown, but Bobby values a laid-back approach to life. If he were any more laid back, he'd be dead. Except when riding a wave, he values tranquility. Treasures it. If you're going to be a friend of Bobby Halloway's, you have to learn to accept his view of life: Nothing that happens farther than half a mile from the beach is of sufficient importance to worry about, and no event is solemn enough or stylish enough to justify the wearing of a necktie. He responds to languid conversation better than to chatter, to indirection better than to direct statements.

'Flow me a beer?' I asked.

Bobby said, 'Corona, Heineken, Löwenbräu?'

'Corona for me.'

Leading the way across the living room, Bobby said, 'Is the one with the tail drinking tonight?'

'He'll have a Heinie.'

'Light or dark?'

'Dark,' I said.

'Must've been a rough night for dogs.'

'Full-on gnarly.'

The cottage consists of a large living room, an office where Bobby tracks waves worldwide, a bedroom, a kitchen, and one bath. The walls are well-oiled teak, dark and rich, the windows are big, the floors are slate, and the furniture is comfortable.

Ornamentation – other than the natural setting – is limited to eight astonishing watercolors by Pia Klick, a woman whom Bobby still loves, though she left him to spend time in Waimea Bay, on the north shore of Oahu. He wanted to go with her, but she said she needed to be alone in Waimea, which she calls her spiritual home; the harmony and beauty of the place are supposed to give her the peace of mind that she requires in order to decide whether or not to live with her fate. I don't know what that means. Neither does Bobby. Pia said she'd be gone a month or two. That was three years ago. The swell at Waimea comes out of extremely deep water. The waves are high, wall-like. Pia says they are the green of translucent jade. Some days I dream of walking that shore and hearing the thunder of those breakers. Once a month, Bobby calls Pia or she calls him. Sometimes they talk for a few minutes, sometimes for hours. She isn't with another man, and she does love Bobby. Pia is one of the kindest, gentlest, smartest people I have ever known. I don't understand why she's doing this. Neither does Bobby. The days go by. He waits.

In the kitchen, Bobby plucked a bottle of Corona from the refrigerator and handed it to me.

I twisted off the cap and took a swallow. No lime, no salt, no pretension.

He opened a Heineken for Orson. 'Half or all?'

I said, 'It's a radical night.' In spite of my dire news, I was deep in the tropical rhythms of Bobbyland.

He emptied the bottle into a deep, enameled-metal bowl on the floor, which he keeps for Orson. On the bowl he has painted ROSEBUD in block letters, a reference to the child's sled in Orson Welles' *Citizen Kane*.

I have no intention of inducing my canine companion to become an alcoholic. He doesn't get beer every day, and usually he splits a bottle with me. Nevertheless, he has his pleasures, and I don't intend to deny him what he enjoys. Considering his formidable body weight, he doesn't become inebriated on a single beer. Dare to give him two, however, and he redefines the term 'party animal.'

As Orson noisily lapped up the Heineken, Bobby opened a Corona for himself and leaned against the refrigerator.

I leaned against the counter near the sink. There was a table with chairs, but in the kitchen, Bobby and I tend to be leaners.

We are alike in many ways. We're the same height, virtually the same weight, and the same body type.

Although he has very dark brown hair and eyes so raven black that they seem to have blue highlights, we have been mistaken for brothers.

We both have a collection of surf bumps, too, and as he leaned against the refrigerator, Bobby was absentmindedly using the bottom of one bare foot to rub the bumps on the top of the other. These are knotty calcium deposits that develop from constant pressure against a surfboard; you get them on your toes and the tops of your feet from paddling while in a prone position. We have them on our knees, as well, and Bobby has them on his bottom ribs.

I am not tanned, of course, Bobby is. He's beyond tanned. He's a maximum brown sun god, year round, and in summer he's well-buttered toast. He does the mambo with melanoma, and maybe one day we'll die of the same sun that he courts and I reject.

'There were some unreal zippers out there today,' he said. 'Six footers, perfect shape.'

'Looks way slow now.'

'Yeah. Mellowed out around sunset.'

We sucked at our beers. Orson happily licked his chops.

'So,' Bobby said, 'your dad died.'

I nodded. Sasha must have called him.

'Good,' he said.

'Yeah.'

Bobby is not cruel or insensitive. He meant it was good that the suffering was over for my father.

Between us, we often say a lot with a few words. People have mistaken us for brothers not merely because we are the same height, weight, and body type.

'You got to the hospital in time. So it was cool.'

'It was.'

He didn't ask me how I was handling it. He knew.

'So after the hospital,' he said, 'you sang a couple numbers in a minstrel show.'

I touched one sooty hand to my sooty face. 'Someone killed Angela Ferryman, set her house on fire to cover it. I almost caught the great *onaula-loa* in the sky.'

'Who's the someone?'

'Wish I knew. Same people stole Dad's body.'

Bobby drank some beer and said nothing.

'They killed a drifter, swapped his body for Dad's. You might not want to know about this.'

For a while, he weighed the wisdom of ignorance against the pull of curiosity. 'I can always forget I heard it, if that seems smart.'

Orson belched. Beer makes him gaseous.

When the dog wagged his tail and looked up beseechingly, Bobby said, 'No more for you, furface.'

'I'm hungry,' I said.

'You're filthy, too. Catch a shower, take some of my clothes. I'll throw together some clucking tacos.'

'Thought I'd clean up with a swim.'

'It's nipple out there.'

'Feels about sixty degrees.'

'I'm talking water temp. Believe me, the nip factor is high. Shower's better.'

'Orson needs a makeover, too.'

'Take him in the shower with you. There're plenty of towels.'

'Very broly of you,' I said. *Broly* meaning brotherly.

'Yeah, I'm so Christian, I don't ride the waves anymore – I just walk on them.'

After a few minutes in Bobbyland, I was relaxed and willing to ease into my news even if Angela was right and the world was coming to an end. Bobby's more than a beloved friend. He's a tranquilizer.

Suddenly he stood away from the refrigerator and cocked his head, listening.

'Something?' I asked.

'Someone.'

I hadn't heard anything but the steadily diminishing voice of the wind. With the windows closed and the surf so slow, I couldn't even hear the sea, but I noticed that Orson was alert, too.

Bobby headed out of the kitchen to see who the visitor might be, and I said, 'Bro,' and offered him the Glock.

He stared dubiously at the pistol, then at me. 'Stay casual.'

'That drifter. They cut out his eyes.'

'Why?'

I shrugged. 'Because they could.'

For a moment Bobby considered what I'd said. Then he took a key from a pocket of his jeans and unlocked a broom closet, which to the best of my recollection had never featured a lock before. From the narrow closet, he took a pistol-grip, pump-action shotgun.

'That's new,' I said.

'Goon repellent.'

This was not life as usual in Bobbyland. I couldn't resist: 'Stay casual.'

Orson and I followed Bobby across the living room and onto the front porch. The onshore flow smelled faintly of kelp.

The cottage faced north. No boats were on the bay – or at least none with running lights. To the east, the town twinkled along the shore and up the hills.

Surrounding the cottage, the end of the horn featured

low dunes and shore grass frosted with moonlight. No one was in sight.

Orson moved to the top of the steps and stood rigid, his head raised and thrust forward, sniffing the air and catching a scent more interesting than kelp.

Relying perhaps on a sixth sense, Bobby didn't even look at the dog to confirm his own suspicion. 'Stay here. If I flush anyone out, tell him he can't leave till we validate his parking ticket.'

Barefoot, he descended the steps and crossed the dunes to look down the steep incline to the beach. Someone could have been lying on that slope, watching the cottage from concealment.

Bobby walked along the crest of the embankment, heading toward the point, studying the slope and the beach below, turning every few steps to survey the territory between him and the house. He held the shotgun ready in both hands and conducted the search with military methodicalness.

Obviously, he had been through this routine more than once before. He hadn't told me that he was being harassed by anyone or troubled by intruders. Ordinarily, if he were having a serious problem, he would have shared it with me.

I wondered what secret he was keeping.

19

Having turned away from the steps and pushed his snout between a pair of balusters at the east end of the porch, Orson was looking not west toward Bobby but back along the horn toward town. He growled deep in his throat.

I followed the direction of his gaze. Even in the fullness of the moon, which the snarled rags of cloud didn't currently obscure, I was unable to see anyone.

With the steadiness of a grumbling motor, the dog's low growl continued uninterrupted.

To the west, Bobby had reached the point, still moving along the crest of the embankment. Although I could see him, he was little more than a gray shape against the stark-black backdrop of sea and sky.

While I had been looking the other way, someone could have cut Bobby down so suddenly and violently that he had been unable to cry out, and I wouldn't have known. Now, rounding the point and beginning to approach the house along the southern flank of the horn, this blurry gray figure could have been anyone.

To the growling dog, I said, 'You're spooking me.'

Although I strained my eyes, I still couldn't discern anyone or any threat to the east, where Orson's attention remained fixed. The only movement was the flutter of the tall, sparse grass. The fading wind wasn't even strong enough to blow sand off the well-compacted dunes.

Orson stopped grumbling and thumped down the porch steps, as though in pursuit of quarry. Instead, he scampered into the sand only a few feet to the left of the steps, where he raised one hind leg and emptied his bladder.

When he returned to the porch, visible tremors were passing through his flanks. Looking eastward again, he didn't resume his growling; instead, he whined nervously.

This change in him disturbed me more than if he had begun to bark furiously.

I sidled across the porch to the western corner of the cottage, trying to watch the sandy front yard but also wanting to keep Bobby – if, indeed, it was Bobby – in sight as long as possible. Soon, however, still edging along the southern embankment, he disappeared behind the house.

When I realized that Orson had stopped whining, I turned toward him and discovered that he was gone.

I thought he must have chased after something in the night, though it was remarkable that he had sprinted off so soundlessly. Anxiously moving back the way I had come, across the porch toward the steps, I couldn't see the dog anywhere out there among the moon-lit dunes.

Then I found him at the open front door, peering out warily. He had retreated into the living room, just inside the threshold. His ears were flattened against his skull. His head was lowered. His hackles bristled as if he had sustained an electrical shock. He was neither growling nor whining, but tremors still passed through his flanks.

Orson is many things – not least of all, strange – but he is not cowardly or stupid. Whatever he was retreating from must have been worthy of his fear.

'What's the problem, pal?'

Failing to acknowledge me with even as little as a quick glance, the dog continued to obsess on the barren landscape beyond the porch. Although he drew his black lips away from his teeth, no snarl came from him. Clearly he no longer harbored any aggressive intent; rather, his bared teeth appeared to express extreme distaste, repulsion.

As I turned to scan the night, I glimpsed movement from the corner of my eye: the fuzzy impression of a man running in a half crouch, passing the cottage from east to west, progressing swiftly with long fluid strides through the last rank of dunes that marked the top of the slope to the beach, about forty feet away from me.

I swung around, bringing up the Glock. The running man had either gone to ground or had been a phantom.

Briefly I wondered if it was Pinn. No. Orson would not have been fearful of Jesse Pinn or of any man like him.

I crossed the porch, descended the three wooden steps, and stood in the sand, taking a closer look at the surrounding dunes. Scattered sprays of tall grass undulated in the breeze. Some of the shore lights shimmered across the lapping waters of the bay. Nothing else moved.

Like a tattered bandage unraveling from the dry white face of a mummified pharaoh, a long narrow cloud wound away from the chin of the moon.

Perhaps the running man was merely a cloud shadow. Perhaps. But I didn't think so.

I glanced back toward the open door of the cottage. Orson had retreated farther from the threshold, deeper into the front room. For once, he was not at home in the night.

I didn't feel entirely at home, either.

Stars. Moon. Sand. Grass. And a feeling of being watched.

From the slope that dropped to the beach or from a shallow swale between dunes, through a screen of grass, someone was watching me. A gaze can have weight, and this one was coming at me like a series of waves, not like slow surf but like fully macking double overheads, hammering at me.

Now the dog wasn't the only one with raised hackles.

Just when I began to worry that Bobby was taking a mortally long time, he appeared around the east end of the cottage. As he approached, sand pluming around his bare feet, he never looked at me but let his gaze travel ceaselessly from dune to dune.

I said, 'Orson haired out.'

'Don't believe it,' Bobby said.

'Totally haired out. He's never done that before. He's pure guts, that dog.'

'Well, if he did,' Bobby said, 'I don't blame him. Almost haired out myself.'

'Someone's out there.'

'More than one.'

'Who?'

Bobby didn't reply. He adjusted his grip on the shotgun but continued to hold it at the ready while he studied the surrounding night.

'They've been here before,' I guessed.

'Yeah.'

'Why? What do they want?'

'I don't know.'

'Who are they?' I asked again.

As before, he didn't answer.

'Bobby?' I pressed.

A great pale mass, a few hundred feet high, gradually resolved out of the darkness over the ocean to the west: A fog bank, revealed in lunar whitewash, extended far to the north and the south. Whether it came to land or hung offshore all night, the fog pushed a quieting pressure ahead of it. On silent wings, a formation of pelicans flew low over the peninsula and vanished across the black waters of the bay. As the remaining onshore breeze faded, the long grass drooped and was still, and I could better hear the slow surf breaking along the bay shore, although the sound was less a rumble than a lulling hushaby.

From out at the point, a cry as eerie as the call of a loon carved this deepening silence. An answering cry, equally sharp and chilling, arose from the dunes nearer the house.

I was reminded of those old Western movies in which the Indians call to one another in the night, imitating birds and coyotes, to coordinate their moves immediately before attacking the circled wagons of the homesteaders.

Bobby fired the shotgun into a nearby mound of sand, startling me so much that I nearly blew an aortic valve.

When echoes of the crash rebounded from the bay and receded again, when the last reverberations were absorbed by the vast pillow of fog in the west, I said, 'Why'd you do that?'

Instead of answering me at once, Bobby chambered another shell and listened to the night.

I remembered Pinn firing the handgun into the ceiling of the church basement to punctuate the threat that he had leveled against Father Tom Eliot.

Finally, when no more loonlike cries arose, Bobby said, almost as if talking to himself, 'Probably isn't necessary, but once in a while it doesn't hurt to float the idea of buckshot past them.'

'Who? Who are you warning off?'

I had known him to be mysterious in the past, but never quite so enigmatic as this.

The dunes continued to command his attention, and another minute of mental hang time passed before Bobby suddenly looked at me as if he had forgotten that I was standing beside him. 'Let's go inside. You scrub off the bad Denzel Washington disguise, and I'll slam together some killer tacos.'

I knew better than to press the issue any further. He was being mysterious either to stoke my curiosity and enhance his treasured reputation for weirdness or because he had good reason to keep this secret even from me. In either case, he was in that special Bobby place, where he's as inaccessible as if he were on his board, halfway through a tube radical, in an insanely hollow wave.

As I followed him into the house, I was still aware of being watched. The attention of the unknown observer prickled my back, like hermit-crab tracks on a surf-smoothed beach. Before closing the front door, I scanned the night once more, but our visitors remained well hidden.

≈ ≈ ≈

The bathroom is large and luxurious: an absolute-black granite floor, matching countertops, handsome teak cabinetry, and acres of beveled-edge mirrors. The huge shower stall can accommodate four people, which makes it ideal for dog grooming.

Corky Collins – who built Bobby's fine house long before Bobby's birth – was an unpretentious guy, but he indulged in amenities. Like the four-person, marble-lined spa in the corner diagonally across the room from the shower. Maybe Corky – whose name had been Toshiro Tagawa before he changed it – fantasized about orgies with three beach girls or maybe he just liked to be totally, awesomely clean.

As a young man – a prodigy fresh out of law school in 1941, at the age of only twenty-one – Toshiro had been interned in Manzanar, the camp where loyal Japanese-Americans remained imprisoned throughout World War II. Following the war, angered and humiliated, he became an activist, committed to securing justice for the oppressed. After five years, he lost faith in the possibility of equal justice and also came to believe that most of the oppressed, given a chance, would become enthusiastic oppressors in their own right.

He switched to personal-injury law. Because his learning curve was as steep as the huge monoliths macking in from a South Pacific typhoon, he rapidly became the most successful personal-injury attorney in the San Francisco area.

In another four years, having banked some serious cash, he walked away from his law practice. In 1956, at the age of thirty-six, he built this house on the southern horn of Moonlight Bay, bringing in underground power, water, and phone lines at considerable expense. With a dry sense of humor that prevented his cynicism from becoming bitterness, Toshiro Tagawa legally changed his name to Corky Collins on the day that he moved into the cottage, and he dedicated every day of the rest of his life to the beach and the ocean.

He grew surf bumps on the tops of his toes and feet, below his knee caps, and on his bottom ribs. Out of a desire to hear the unobstructed thunder of the waves, Corky didn't always use ear plugs when he surfed, so he developed exostosis; the channel to the inner ear constricts when filled with cold water, and because of repeated abuse, a benign bony tumor narrows the ear canal. By the time he was fifty, Corky was intermittently deaf in his left ear. Every surfer experiences faucet nose after a thrashing skim session, when your sinuses empty explosively, pouring forth all the seawater forced up your nostrils during wipeouts; this grossness usually happens when you're talking to an outrageously fine girl who's wearing a bun-floss bikini; after twenty years of epic hammering and subsequent nostril Niagaras, Corky developed exostosis in his sinus passages, requiring surgery to alleviate headaches and to restore proper drainage. On every anniversary of this operation, he had thrown a Proper Drainage Party. From years of exposure to the glaring sun and the salt water, Corky was also afflicted with surfer's eye – pterygium – a winglike thickening of the conjunctiva over the white of the eye, eventually extending across the cornea. His vision gradually deteriorated.

Nine years ago, he was spared ophthalmological surgery when he was killed – not by melanoma, not by a shark, but by Big Mama herself, the ocean. Though Corky was sixty-nine at the time, he went out in monster storm waves, twenty-foot behemoths, quakers, rolling thunder that most surfers a third his age wouldn't have tried, and according to witnesses, he was a party of one, hooting with joy, repeatedly almost airborne, racing the lip, carving truly sacred rail slashes, repeatedly getting barreled – until he wiped out big time and was held down by a breaking wave. Monsters that size can weigh thousands of tons, which is a lot of water, too much to struggle against, and even a strong swimmer can be held on the bottom half a minute or longer, maybe a lot longer, before he can get air. Worse, Corky surfaced at the wrong moment, just in time to be hammered deep by the next wave in the set, and he drowned in a two-wave hold-down.

Surfers from one end of California to the other shared the opinion that Corky Collins had led the perfect life and had died the perfect death. Exostosis of the ear, exostosis of the sinuses, pterygium in both eyes – none of that meant shit to Corky, and all of it was better than boredom or heart disease, better than a fat pension check that had to be earned by spending a lifetime in an office. Life was surf, death was surf, the power of nature vast and enfolding, and the heart stirred at the thought of Corky's enviably sweet passage through a world that was so much trouble for so many others.

Bobby inherited the cottage.

This development astonished Bobby. We had both known Corky Collins since we were eleven and first ventured to the end of the horn with board racks on our bikes. He was mentor to every surf rat who was ravenous for experience and eager to master the point break. He didn't act like the point was his, but everyone respected Corky as much as if he actually owned the beach from Santa Barbara all the way to Santa Cruz. He was impatient with any gyrospaz who ripped and slashed up a good wave, ruining it for everyone, and he had only disdain for freeway surfers and wish-wases of all types, but he was a friend and an inspiration to all of us who were in love with the sea and in sync with its rhythms. Corky had legions of friends and admirers, some of whom he had known for more than three decades, so we were baffled as to why he had bequeathed all his worldly possessions to Bobby, whom he had known only eight years.

As explanation, the executor of the estate presented to Bobby a letter from Corky that was a masterpiece of succinctness:

Bobby,
What most people find important, you do not. This is wisdom.
To what you believe is important, you are ready to give your mind, heart, and soul. This is grace.
We have only the sea, love, and time. God gave you the sea. By your own actions you will find love always. So I give you time.

Corky saw in Bobby someone who had an innate understanding, from boyhood, of those truths that Corky himself had not learned until he was thirty-seven. He wanted to honor and encourage that understanding. God bless him for it.

The summer following his freshman year at Ashdon College, when Bobby inherited, after taxes, the house and a modest sum of cash, he dropped out of school. This infuriated his parents. He was able to shrug off their fury, however, because the beach and the sea and the future were his.

Besides, his folks have been furious about one thing

or another all of their lives, and Bobby is inured to it. They own and edit the town newspaper, and they fancy themselves tireless crusaders for enlightened public policy, which means that they think most citizens are either too selfish to do the right thing or too stupid to know what is best for them. They expected Bobby to share what they called their 'passion for the great issues of our time,' but Bobby wanted to escape from his family's loudly announced idealism – and from all the poorly concealed envy, rancor, and egotism that was a part of it. All Bobby wanted was peace. His folks wanted peace, too, for the entire planet, peace in every corner of Spaceship Earth, but they weren't capable of providing it within the walls of their own home.

With the cottage and the seed money to launch the business that now supported him, Bobby found peace.

The hands of every clock are shears, trimming us away scrap by scrap, and every timepiece with a digital readout blinks us toward implosion. Time is so precious that it can't be purchased. What Corky had given Bobby was not time, really, but the chance to live without clocks, without an awareness of clocks, which seems to make time pass more gently, with less shearing fury.

My parents tried to give the same thing to me. Because of my XP, however, I occasionally hear ticking. Maybe Bobby occasionally hears it, too. Maybe there's no way any of us can entirely escape an awareness of clocks.

In fact, Orson's night of despair, when he had regarded the stars with such despondency and had refused all my efforts to comfort him, might have been caused by an awareness of his own days ticking away. We are told that the simple minds of animals are not capable of encompassing the concept of their own mortality. Yet every animal possesses a survival instinct and recognizes danger. If it struggles to survive, it understands death, no matter what the scientists and the philosophers might say.

This is not New Age sentimentalism. This is simply common sense.

Now, in Bobby's shower, as I scrubbed the soot off Orson, he continued to shiver. The water was warm. The shivers had nothing to do with the bath.

By the time I blotted the dog with several towels and fluffed him with a hair dryer that Pia Klick had left behind, his shakes had passed. While I dressed in a pair of Bobby's blue jeans and a long-sleeve, blue cotton sweater, Orson glanced at the frosted window a few times, as if leery of whoever might be out there in the night, but his confidence appeared to be returning.

With paper towels, I wiped off my leather jacket and my cap. They still smelled of smoke, the cap more than the jacket.

In the dim light, I could barely read the words above the bill: *Mystery Train*. I rubbed the ball of my thumb across the embroidered letters, recalling the windowless concrete room where I'd found the cap, in one of the more peculiar abandoned precincts of Fort Wyvern.

Angela Ferryman's words came back to me, her response to my statement that Wyvern had been closed for a year and a half: *Some things don't die. Can't die. No matter how much we wish them dead.*

I had another flashback to the bathroom at Angela's house: a mental image of her death-startled eyes and the silent surprised *oh* of her mouth. Again, I was gripped by the conviction that I had overlooked an important detail regarding the condition of her body, and as before, when I tried to summon a more vivid memory of her blood-spattered face, it grew not clearer in my mind but fuzzier.

We're screwing it up, Chris . . . bigger than we've ever screwed up before . . . and already there's no way . . . to undo what's been done.

~ ~ ~

The tacos – packed with shredded chicken, lettuce, cheese, and salsa – were delicious. We sat at the kitchen table to eat, instead of leaning over the sink, and we washed down the food with beer.

Although Sasha had fed him earlier, Orson cadged a few bits of chicken, but he couldn't charm me into giving him another Heineken.

Bobby had turned on the radio, and it was tuned to Sasha's show, which had just come on the air. Midnight had arrived. She didn't mention me or introduce the song with a dedication, but she played 'Heart Shaped World' by Chris Isaak, because it's a favorite of mine.

Enormously condensing the events of the evening, I told Bobby about the incident in the hospital garage, the scene in Kirk's crematorium, and the platoon of faceless men who pursued me through the hills behind the funeral home.

Throughout all of this, he only said, 'Tabasco?'

'What?'

'To hotten up the salsa.'

'No,' I said. 'This is killer just the way it is.'

He got a bottle of Tabasco sauce from the refrigerator and sprinkled it into his half-eaten first taco.

Now Sasha was playing 'Two Hearts' by Chris Isaak.

For a while I repeatedly glanced through the window beside the table, wondering whether anyone outside was watching us. At first I didn't think Bobby shared my concern, but then I realized that from time to time, he glanced intently, though with seeming casualness, at the blackness out there.

'Lower the blind?' I suggested.

'No. They might think I cared.'

We were pretending not to be intimidated.

'Who are they?'

He was silent, but I outwaited him, and at last he said, 'I'm not sure.'

That wasn't an honest answer, but I relented.

When I continued my story, rather than risk Bobby's scorn, I didn't mention the cat that led me to the culvert in the hills, but I described the skull collection arranged on the final two steps of the spillway. I told him about Chief Stevenson talking to the bald guy with the earring and about finding the pistol on my bed.

'Bitchin' gun,' he said, admiring the Glock.

'Dad opted for laser sighting.'

'Sweet.'

Sometimes Bobby is as self-possessed as a rock, so calm that you have to wonder if he is actually listening to you. As a boy, he was occasionally like this, but the older he has gotten, the more that this uncanny composure has settled over him. I had just brought him astonishing news of bizarre adventures, and he reacted as if he were listening to basketball scores.

Glancing at the darkness beyond the window, I wondered if anyone out there had me in a gun sight, maybe in the cross hairs of a night scope. Then I figured that if they had meant to shoot us, they would have cut us down when we were out in the dunes.

I told Bobby everything that had happened at Angela Ferryman's house.

He grimaced. 'Apricot brandy.'

'I didn't drink much.'

He said, 'Two glasses of that crap, you'll be talking to the seals,' which was surfer lingo for vomiting.

By the time I had told him about Jesse Pinn terrorizing Father Tom at the church, we had gone through three tacos each. He built another pair and brought them to the table.

Sasha was playing 'Graduation Day.'

Bobby said, 'It's a regular Chris Isaak festival.'

'She's playing it for me.'

'Yeah, I didn't figure Chris Isaak was at the station holding a gun to her head.'

Neither of us said anything more until we finished the final round of tacos.

When at last Bobby asked a question, the only thing he wanted to know about was something that Angela had said: 'So she told you it was a monkey and it wasn't.'

'Her exact words, as I recall, were . . . "It appeared to be a monkey. And it was a monkey. Was and wasn't. And that's what was wrong with it."'

'She seem totally zipped up to you?'

'She was in distress, scared, way scared, but she wasn't kooked out. Besides, somebody killed her to shut her up, so there must have been something to what she said.'

He nodded and drank some beer.

He was silent for so long that I finally said, 'Now what?'

'You're asking me?'

'I wasn't talking to the dog,' I said.

'Drop it,' he said.

'What?'

'Forget about it, get on with life.'

'I knew you'd say that,' I admitted.

'Then why ask me?'

'Bobby, maybe my mom's death wasn't an accident.'

'Sounds like more than a maybe.'

'And maybe there was more to my dad's cancer than just cancer.'

'So you're gonna hit the vengeance trail?'

'These people can't get away with murder.'

'Sure they can. People get away with murder all the time.'

'Well, they shouldn't.'

'I didn't say they should. I only said they do.'

'You know, Bobby, maybe life isn't just surf, sex, food, and beer.'

'I never said it was. I only said it should be.'

'Well,' I said, studying the darkness beyond the window, '*I'm* not hairing out.'

Bobby sighed and leaned back in his chair. 'If you're waiting to catch a wave, and conditions are epic, really big smokers honing up the coast, and along comes a set of twenty-footers, and they're pushing your limit but you know you can stretch to handle them, yet you sit in the lineup, just being a buoy through the whole set, then you're hairing out. But say, instead, what comes along all of a sudden is a long set of thirty-footers, massive pumping mackers that are going to totally prosecute you, that are going to blast you off the board and hold you down and make you suck kelp and pray to Jesus. If your choice is to be snuffed or be a buoy, then you're not hairing out if you sit in the lineup and soak through the whole set. You're exhibiting mature judgment. Even a total surf rebel needs a little of that. And the dude who tries the wave even though he knows he's going over the falls, knows he's going to be totally quashed – well, he's an asshole.'

I was touched by the length of his speech, because it meant that he was deeply worried about me.

'So,' I said, 'you're calling me an asshole.'

'Not yet. Depends on what you do about this.'

'So I'm an asshole waiting to happen.'

'Let's just say that your asshole potential is off the Richter.'

I shook my head. 'Well, from where I sit, this doesn't look like a thirty-footer.'

'Maybe a forty.'

'It looks like a twenty max.'

He rolled his eyes up into his head, as if to say that the only place he was going to see any common sense was inside his own skull. 'From what Angela said, this all goes back to some project at Fort Wyvern.'

'She went upstairs to get something she wanted to show me – some sort of proof, I guess, something her husband must have squirreled away. Whatever it was, it was destroyed in the fire.'

'Fort Wyvern. The army. The military.'

'So?'

'We're talking about the government here,' Bobby said. 'Bro, the government isn't even a thirty-footer. It's a hundred. It's a tsunami.'

'This is America.'

'It used to be.'

'I have a duty here.'

'What duty?'

'A moral duty.'

Beetling his brow, pinching the bridge of his nose

with thumb and forefinger, as though listening to me had given him a headache, he said, 'I guess if you turn on the evening news and hear there's a comet going to destroy the earth, you pull on your tights and cape and fly into outer space to deflect that sucker toward the other end of the galaxy.'

'Unless the cape is at the dry cleaner.'

'Asshole.'

'Asshole.'

20

'Look here,' Bobby said. 'Data coming down right now. This is from a British government weather satellite. Process it, and you can measure the height of any wave, anywhere in the world, to within a few centimeters.'

He had not turned on any lights in his office. The oversize video displays at the various computer workstations provided enough illumination for him and more than enough for me. Colorful bar graphs, maps, enhanced satellite photos, and flow charts of dynamic weather situations moved on the screens.

I have not embraced the computer age and never will. With UV-proof sunglasses, I can't easily read what's on a video display, and I can't risk spending hours in front of even a filtered screen with all of those UV rays pumping out at me. They are low-level emissions to you, but considering cumulative damage, a few hours at a computer would be a lightstorm to me. I do my writing by hand in legal tablets: the occasional article, the best-selling book that resulted in the long *Time* magazine article about me and XP.

This computer-packed room is the heart of Surfcast, Bobby's surf forecasting service, which provides daily predictions by fax to subscribers all over the world, maintains a Web site, and has a 900-number for surf information. Four employees work out of offices in Moonlight Bay, networked with this room, but Bobby himself does the final data analysis and surf predictions.

Along the shores of the world's oceans, approximately six million surfers regularly ride the waves, and about five and a half million of these are content with waves that have faces – measured from trough to crest – of six or eight feet. Ocean swells hide their power below the surface, extending down as much as one thousand feet, and they are not waves until they shoal up and break to the shore; consequently, there was no way, until the late 1980s, to predict with any reliability even where and when six-foot humpers could be found. Surf junkies could spend days at the beach, waiting through surf that was mushy or soft or even flat, while a few hundred miles up or down the coast, plunging breakers were macking to shore, corduroy to the horizon. A significant percentage of those five and a half million boardheads would rather pay Bobby a few bucks to learn where the action will or won't be, rather than rely strictly on the goodwill of Kahuna, the god of all surf.

A few bucks. The 900 number alone draws eight hundred thousand calls each year, at two dollars a pop. Ironically, Bobby the slacker and surf rebel has probably become the wealthiest person in Moonlight Bay – although no one realizes this and although he gives away most of it.

'Here,' he said, dropping into a chair in front of one of the computers. 'Before you rush off to save the world and get your brains blown out, think about this.' As Orson cocked his head to watch the screen, Bobby hammered the keyboard, calling up new data.

Most of the remaining half million of those six million surfers sit out waves above, say, fifteen feet, and probably fewer than ten thousand can ride twenty-footers, but although these more awesomely skilled and ballsy types are fewer in number, a higher percentage of them want Bobby's surf forecasts. They live and die for the ride; to miss a session of epic monsters, especially in their neighborhood, would be nothing less than Shakespearean tragedy with sand.

'Sunday,' Bobby said, still tapping the keyboard.

'This Sunday?'

'Two nights from now, you'll want to be here. Rather than be dead, I mean.'

'Big surf coming?'

'It's gonna be sacred.'

Perhaps three hundred or four hundred surfers on the planet have the experience, talent, and *cojones* to mount waves above twenty feet, and a handful of them pay Bobby well to track truly giant surf, even though it is treacherous and likely to kill them. A few of these maniacs are wealthy men who will fly anywhere in the world to challenge storm waves, thirty- and even forty-foot behemoths, into which they are frequently towed by a helper on a Jet Ski, because catching such huge monoliths in the usual fashion is difficult and often impossible. Worldwide, you can find well-formed, ride-worthy waves thirty feet and higher no more than thirty days a year, and often they come to shore in exotic places. Using maps, satellite photos, and weather data from numerous sources, Bobby can provide two- or three-day warnings, and his predictions are so trustworthy that these most demanding of all clients have never complained.

'There.' Bobby pointed to a wave profile on the computer. Orson took a closer look at the screen as Bobby said, 'Moonlight Bay, point-break surf. It's going to be classic Sunday afternoon, evening, all the way until Monday dawn – fully pumping mackers.'

I blinked at the video display. 'Am I seeing twelve-footers?'

'Ten to twelve feet, with a possibility of some sets as high as fourteen. They're hitting Hawaii soon . . . then us.'

'That'll be *live*.'

'Entirely live. Coming off a big, slow-moving storm north of Tahiti. There's going to be an offshore wind, too, so these monsters are going to give you more dry, insanely hollow barrels than you've seen in your dreams.'

'Cool.'

He swiveled in his chair to look up at me. 'So what do you want to ride – the Sunday night surf rolling out of Tahiti or the tsunami pipeline of death rolling out of Wyvern?'

'Both.'

'Kamikaze,' he said scornfully.

'Duck,' I called him, with a smile – which is the same as saying 'buoy,' meaning one who sits in the lineup and never has the guts to take a wave.

Orson turned his head from one of us to the other, back and forth, as if watching a tennis match.

'Geek,' Bobby said.

'Decoy,' I said, which is the same as saying 'duck.'

'Asshole,' he said, which has identical definitions in surfer lingo and standard English.

'I take it you're not with me on this.'

Getting up from the chair, he said, 'You can't go to

the cops. You can't go to the FBI. They're all paid by the other side. What can you possibly hope to learn about some way-secret project at Wyvern?'

'I've already uncovered a little.'

'Yeah, and the next thing you learn is the thing that'll get you killed. Listen, Chris, you aren't Sherlock Holmes or James Bond. At best, you're Nancy Drew.'

'Nancy Drew had an unreal rate of case closure,' I reminded him. 'She nailed one hundred percent of the bastards she went after. I'd be honored to be considered the equal of a kick-ass crime fighter like Ms. Nancy Drew.'

'Kamikaze.'

'Duck.'

'Geek.'

'Decoy.'

Laughing softly, shaking his head, scratching his beard stubble, Bobby said, 'You make me sick.'

'Likewise.'

The telephone rang, and Bobby answered it. 'Hey, gorgeous, I totally get off on the new format – all Chris Isaak, all the time. Play "Dancin'" for me, okay?' He passed the handset to me. 'It's for you, Nancy.'

I like Sasha's disc-jockey voice. It's only subtly different from her real-world voice, marginally deeper and softer and silkier, but the effect is profound. When I hear Sasha-the-deejay, I want to curl up in bed with her. I want to curl up in bed with her anyway, as often as possible, but when she's using her radio voice, I want to curl up in bed with her *urgently*. The voice comes over her from the moment she enters the studio, and it's with her even when she is off-mike, until she leaves work.

'This tune ends in about a minute, I've got to do some patter between cuts,' she told me, 'so I'll be quick. Somebody came around here at the station a little while ago, trying to get in touch with you. Says it's life or death.'

'Who?'

'I can't use the name on the phone. Promised I wouldn't. When I said you were probably at Bobby's . . . this person didn't want to call you there or come there to see you.'

'Why?'

'I don't know why exactly. But . . . this person was really nervous, Chris. "I have been one acquainted with the night." Do you know who I mean?'

I have been one acquainted with the night.

It was a line from a poem by Robert Frost.

My dad instilled in me his passion for poetry. I infected Sasha.

'Yes,' I said. 'I think I know who you mean.'

'Wants to see you as soon as possible. Says it's life or death. What's going on, Chris?'

'Big surf coming in Sunday afternoon,' I said.

'That's not what I mean.'

'I know. Tell you the rest later.'

'Big surf. Can I handle it?'

'Twelve-footers.'

'I think I'll just Gidget-out and beach party.'

'Love your voice,' I said.

'Smooth as the bay.'

She hung up, and so did I.

Although he had only heard my half of the conversation, Bobby relied on his uncanny intuition to figure out the tone and intent of Sasha's call. 'What're you walking into?'

'Just Nancy stuff,' I said. 'You wouldn't be interested.'

~ ~ ~

As Bobby and I led a still-uneasy Orson onto the front porch, the radio in the kitchen began to swing with 'Dancin'' by Chris Isaak.

'Sasha is an awesome woman,' Bobby said.

'Unreal,' I agreed.

'You can't be with her if you're dead. She's not that kinky.'

'Point taken.'

'You have your sunglasses?'

I patted my shirt pocket. 'Yeah.'

'Did you use some of my sunscreen?'

'Yes, Mother.'

'Geek.'

I said, 'I've been thinking . . .'

'It's about time you started.'

'I've been working on the new book.'

'Finally got your lazy ass in gear.'

'It's about friendship.'

'Am I in it?'

'Amazingly, yes.'

'You're not using my real name, are you?'

'I'm calling you Igor. The thing is . . . I'm afraid readers might not relate to what I have to say, because you and I – all my friends – we live such different lives.'

Stopping at the head of the porch steps, regarding me with his patented look of scorn, Bobby said, 'I thought you had to be smart to write books.'

'It's not a federal law.'

'Obviously not. Even the literary equivalent of a

gyrospaz ought to know that every last one of us leads a different life.'

'Yeah? Maria Cortez leads a different life?'

Maria was Manuel Ramirez's younger sister, twenty-eight like Bobby and me. She was a beautician, and her husband worked as a car mechanic. They had two children, one cat, and a small tract house with a big mortgage.

Bobby said, 'She doesn't live her life in the beauty shop, doing someone's hair – or in her house, vacuuming the carpet. She lives her life between her ears. There's a *world* inside her skull, and probably way stranger and more bitchin' than you or I, with our shallow brain pans, can imagine. Six billion of us walking the planet, six billion smaller worlds on the bigger one. Shoe salesmen and short-order cooks who look boring from the outside – some have weirder lives than you. Six billion stories, every one an epic, full of tragedy and triumph, good and evil, despair and hope. You and me – we aren't so special, bro.'

I was briefly speechless. Then I fingered the sleeve of his parrot-and-palm-frond shirt and said, 'I didn't realize you were such a philosopher.'

He shrugged. 'That little gem of wisdom? Hell, that was just something I got in a fortune cookie.'

'Must've been a big honker of a cookie.'

'Hey, it was a huge monolith, dude,' he said, giving me a sly smile.

The great wall of moonlit fog loomed half a mile from the shore, no closer or farther away than it had been earlier. The night air was as still as that in the cold-holding room at Mercy Hospital.

As we descended the porch steps, no one shot at us. No one issued that loonlike cry, either.

They were still out there, however, hiding in the dunes or below the crest of the slope that fell to the beach. I could feel their attention like the dangerous energy pending release in the coils of a motionless, strike-poised rattlesnake.

Although Bobby had left his shotgun inside, he was vigilant. Surveying the night as he accompanied me to my bike, he began to reveal more interest in my story than he had admitted earlier: 'This monkey Angela mentioned . . .'

'What about it?'

'What was it like?'

'Monkeylike.'

'Like a chimpanzee, an orangutan, or what?'

Gripping the handlebars of my bicycle and turning it around to walk it through the soft sand, I said, 'It was a rhesus monkey. Didn't I say?'

'How big?'

'She said two feet high, maybe twenty-five pounds.'

Gazing across the dunes, he said, 'I've seen a couple myself.'

Surprised, leaning the bike against the porch railing again, I said, 'Rhesus monkeys? Out here?'

'Some kind of monkeys, about that size.'

There is, of course, no species of monkey native to California. The only primates in its woods and fields are human beings.

Bobby said, 'Caught one looking in a window at me one night. Went outside, and it was gone.'

'When was this?'

'Maybe three months ago.'

Orson moved between us, as if for comfort.

I said, 'You've seen them since?'

'Six or seven times. Always at night. They're

239

secretive. But they're also bolder lately. They travel in a troop.'

'Troop?'

'Wolves travel in a pack. Horses in a herd. With monkeys, it's called a troop.'

'You've been doing research. How come you haven't told me about this?'

He was silent, watching the dunes.

I was watching them, too. 'Is that what's out there now?'

'Maybe.'

'How many in this troop?'

'Don't know. Maybe six or eight. Just a guess.'

'You bought a shotgun. You think they're dangerous?'

'Maybe.'

'Have you reported them to anyone? Like animal control?'

'No.'

'Why not?'

Instead of answering me, he hesitated and then said, 'Pia's driving me nuts.'

Pia Klick. Out there in Waimea for a month or two, going on three years.

I didn't understand how Pia related to Bobby's failure to report the monkeys to animal-control officers, but I sensed that he would make the connection for me.

'She says she's discovered that she's the reincarnation of Kaha Huna,' Bobby said.

Kaha Huna is the mythical Hawaiian goddess of surfing, who was never actually incarnate in the first place and, therefore, incapable of being *re*.

Considering that Pia was not a *kamaaina*, not a

native of Hawaii, but a *haole*, who had been born in Oskaloosa, Kansas, and raised there until she left home at seventeen, she seemed an unlikely candidate to be a mythological *uber wahine*.

I said, 'She lacks some credentials.'

'She's dead-solid serious about this.'

'Well, she's way pretty enough to be Kaha Huna. Or any other goddess, for that matter.'

Standing beside Bobby, I couldn't see his eyes too well, but his face was bleak. I had never seen him bleak before. I hadn't even realized that bleakness was an option for him.

Bobby said, 'She's trying to decide whether being Kaha Huna requires her to be celibate.'

'Ouch.'

'She thinks she probably shouldn't ever live with an ordinary dude, meaning a mortal man. Somehow that would be a blasphemous rejection of her fate.'

'Brutal,' I said sympathetically.

'But it would be cool for her to shack up with the current reincarnation of Kahuna.'

Kahuna is the mythical *god* of surfing. He is largely a creation of modern surfers who extrapolate his legend from the life of an ancient Hawaiian witch doctor.

I said, 'And you aren't the reincarnation of Kahuna.'

'I refuse to be.'

From that response, I inferred that Pia was trying to convince him that he was, indeed, the god of surfing.

With audible misery and confusion, Bobby said, 'She's so smart, so talented.'

Pia had graduated *summa cum laude* from UCLA. She had paid her way through school by painting portraits; now her hyperrealist canvases sold for impressive prices, as quickly as she cared to produce them.

'How can she be so smart and talented,' Bobby demanded, 'and then . . . this?'

'Maybe you *are* Kahuna,' I said.

'This isn't funny,' he said, which was a striking statement, because to one degree or another, everything was funny to Bobby.

In the moonlight, the dune grass drooped, no blade so much as trembling in the now windless night. The soft rhythm of the surf, rising from the beach below, was like the murmured chanting of a distant, prayerful crowd.

This Pia business was fascinating, but understandably, I was more interested in the monkeys.

'These last few years,' Bobby said, 'with this New Age stuff from Pia . . . Well, sometimes it's okay, but sometimes it's like spending days in radical churly-churly.'

Churly-churly is badly churned-up surf heavy with sand and pea gravel, which smacks you in the face when you walk into it. This is not a pleasant surf condition.

'Sometimes,' Bobby said, 'when I get off the phone with her, I'm so messed up, missing her, wanting to be with her . . . I could almost convince myself she *is* Kaha Huna. She's so *sincere*. And she doesn't rave on about it, you know. It's this quiet thing with her, which makes it even more disturbing.'

'I didn't know you got disturbed.'

'I didn't know it, either.' Sighing, scuffing at the sand with one bare foot, he began to make the connection between Pia and the monkeys: 'When I saw the monkey at the window the first time, it was cool, made me laugh. I figured it was someone's pet that got loose . . . but the second time I saw more than one. And it was as weird as all this Kaha Huna shit, because they weren't behaving at all like monkeys.'

'What do you mean?'

'Monkeys are playful, goofing around. These guys . . . they weren't playful. Purposeful, solemn, creepy little geeks. Watching me and studying the house, not out of curiosity but with some agenda.'

'What agenda?'

Bobby shrugged. 'They were so strange . . .'

Words seemed to fail him, so I borrowed one from H. P. Lovecraft, for whose stories we had such enthusiasm when we were thirteen: 'Eldritch.'

'Yeah. They were eldritch to the max. I knew no one was going to believe me. I almost felt I was hallucinating. I grabbed a camera but couldn't get a picture. You know why?'

'Thumb over the lens?'

'They didn't want to be photographed. First sight of the camera, they ran for cover, and they're insanely fast.' He glanced at me, reading my reaction, then looked to the dunes again. 'They knew what the camera was.'

I couldn't resist: 'Hey, you're not anthropomorphizing them, are you? You know – ascribing human attributes and attitudes to animals?'

Ignoring me, he said, 'After that night, I didn't put the camera away in the closet. I kept it on a kitchen counter, close at hand. If they showed up again, I figured I might get a snapshot before they realized what was happening. One night about six weeks ago, it was pumping eight-footers with a good offshore, barrel after barrel, so even though it was way nipple out there, I put on my wet suit and spent a couple of hours totally tucked away. I didn't take the camera down to the beach with me.'

'Why not?'

'I hadn't seen the damn monkeys in a week. I figured maybe I'd never see them again. Anyway, when I came back to the house, I stripped out of the neoprene, went into the kitchen, and got a beer. When I turned away from the fridge, there were monkeys at two windows, hanging on the frames outside, looking in at me. So I reached for my camera – and it was gone.'

'You misplaced it.'

'No. It's gone for good. I left the door unlocked when I went to the beach that night. I don't leave it unlocked anymore.'

'You're telling me the monkeys took it?'

He said, 'The next day I bought a disposable camera. Put it on the counter by the oven again. That night I left the lights on, locked up, and took my stick down to the beach.'

'Good surf?'

'Slow. But I wanted to give them a chance. And they took it. While I was gone, they broke a pane, unlocked the window, and stole the disposable camera. Nothing else. Just the camera.'

Now I knew why the shotgun was kept in a locked broom closet.

This cottage on the horn, without neighbors, had always appealed to me as a fine retreat. At night, when the surfers left, the sky and the sea formed a sphere in which the house stood like a diorama in one of those glass paperweights that fills with whirling snow when you shake it, though instead of a blizzard there was deep peace and a glorious solitude. Now, however, the nurturing solitude had become an unnerving isolation. Rather than offering a sense of peace, the night was thick and still with expectation.

'And they left me a warning,' Bobby said.

I pictured a threatening note laboriously printed in crude block letters – WATCH YOUR ASS. Signed, THE MONKEYS.

They were too clever to leave a paper trail, however, and even more direct. Bobby said, 'One of them crapped on my bed.'

'Oh, nice.'

Bobby said, 'They're secretive, like I said. I've decided not even to try to photograph them. If I managed to get a flash shot of them some night . . . I think they'd be way pissed.'

'You're afraid of them. I didn't know you got disturbed, and I didn't know you were ever afraid. I'm learning a lot about you tonight, bro.'

He didn't admit to feeling fear.

'You bought the shotgun,' I pressed.

'Because I think it's good to challenge them from time to time, good to show the little bastards that I'm territorial, and that this is, by God, my territory. But I'm not afraid, really. They're just monkeys.'

'And then again – they're not.'

Bobby said, 'Some days I wonder if I've picked up some New Age virus over the telephone line from Pia, all the way from Waimea – and now while she's obsessed with being Kaha Huna, I'm obsessed with the monkeys of the new millennium. I suspect that's what the tabloids would call them, don't you?'

'The millennium monkeys. Has a ring to it.'

'That's why I haven't reported them. I'm not going to make myself a target of the press or anyone. I'm not going to be the geek who saw Big Foot or extraterrestrials in a spaceship shaped like a four-slice toaster. Life wouldn't ever be the same for me after that, would it?'

'You'd be a freak like me.'

'Exactly.'

My awareness of being watched became more intense. I almost borrowed a trick from Orson, almost growled low in my throat.

The dog, still standing between Bobby and me, remained alert and quiet, his head raised and one ear pricked. He was no longer shaking, but he was clearly respectful of whatever was observing us from the surrounding night.

'Now that I've told you about Angela, you know the monkeys have something to do with what was going on out at Fort Wyvern,' I said. 'This isn't just a tabloid fantasy anymore. This is real, this is totally *live*, and we can do something about it.'

'Still going on,' he said.

'What?'

'From what Angela told you, Wyvern's not entirely shut down.'

'But it was abandoned eighteen months ago. If there were still personnel staffing any operations at all out there, we'd know about it. Even if they lived on base, they'd come into town to shop, to go to a movie.'

'You said Angela called this Armageddon. It's the end of the world, she said.'

'Yeah. So?'

'So maybe if you're busily working on a project

to destroy the world, you don't have time to come into town for a movie. Anyway, like I said, this is a tsunami, Chris. This is the government. There's no way to surf these waters and survive.'

I gripped the handlebars of my bike and stood it upright again. 'In spite of these monkeys and what you've seen, you're going to just lay back?'

He nodded. 'If I stay cool, it's possible they'll eventually go away. They're not here every night, anyway. Once or twice a week. If I wait them out . . . I might get my life back like it was.'

'Yeah, but maybe Angela wasn't just smoking something. Maybe there's no chance, ever again, that anything will be like it was.'

'Then why put on your tights and cape if it's a lost cause?'

'To XP-Man,' I said with mock solemnity, 'there are no lost causes.'

'Kamikaze.'

'Duck.'

'Geek.'

'Decoy,' I said affectionately and walked the bicycle away from the house, through the soft sand.

Orson let out a thin whine of protest as we left the comparative safety of the cottage behind us, but he didn't try to hold back. He stayed close to me, sniffing the night air as we headed inland.

We'd gone about thirty feet when Bobby, kicking up small clouds of sand, sprinted in front of us and blocked the way. 'You know what your problem is?'

I said, 'My choice of friends?'

'Your problem is you want to make a mark on the world. You want to leave something behind that says, *I was here.*'

'I don't care about that.'

'Bullshit.'

'Watch your language. There's a dog present.'

'That's why you write the articles, the books,' he said. 'To leave a mark.'

'I write because I enjoy writing.'

'You're always bitching about it.'

'Because it's the hardest thing I've ever done, but it's also rewarding.'

'You know why it's so hard? Because it's unnatural.'

'Maybe to people who can't read and write.'

'We're not here to leave a mark, bro. Monuments, legacies, marks – that's where we always go wrong. We're here to revel in the world, to soak in the awesomeness of it, to enjoy the ride.'

'Orson, look, it's Philosopher Bob again.'

'The world's maximum perfect as it is, beauty from horizon to horizon. Any mark any of us tries to leave – hell, it's only graffiti. Nothing can improve on the world we've been given. Any mark anyone leaves is no better than vandalism.'

I said, 'The music of Mozart.'

'Vandalism,' Bobby said.

'The art of Michelangelo.'

'Graffiti.'

'Renoir,' I said.

'Graffiti.'

'Bach, the Beatles.'

'Aural graffiti,' he said fiercely.

As he followed our conversation, Orson was getting whiplash.

'Matisse, Beethoven, Wallace Stevens, Shakespeare.'

'Vandals, hooligans.'

'Dick Dale,' I said, dropping the sacred name of the King of the Surf Guitar, the father of all surf music.

Bobby blinked but said, 'Graffiti.'

'You are a sick man.'

'I'm the healthiest person you know. Drop this insanely useless crusade, Chris.'

'I must really be swimming in a school of slackers when a little curiosity is seen as a crusade.'

'Live life. Soak it up. Enjoy. That's what you're here to do.'

'I'm having fun in my own way,' I assured him. 'Don't worry – I'm just as big a bum and jerk-off as you are.'

'You wish.'

When I tried to walk the bike around him, he side-stepped into my path again.

'Okay,' he said resignedly. 'All right. But walk the bike with one hand and keep the Glock in the other until you're back on hard ground and can ride again. Then ride fast.'

I patted my jacket pocket, which sagged with the weight of the pistol. One round fired accidentally at Angela's. Nine left in the magazine. 'But they're just monkeys,' I said, echoing Bobby himself.

'And they're not.'

Searching his dark eyes, I said, 'You have something else that I should know?'

He chewed on his lower lip. Finally: 'Maybe I am Kahuna.'

'That's not what you were about to tell me.'

'No, but it's not as fully nutball as what I was going to say.' His gaze traveled over the dunes. 'The leader of the troop . . . I've only glimpsed him at a distance, in the darkness, hardly more than a shadow. He's bigger than the rest.'

'How big?'

His eyes met mine. 'I think he's a dude about my size.'

Earlier, as I had stood on the porch waiting for Bobby to return from his search of the beach scarp, I had glimpsed movement from the corner of my eye: the fuzzy impression of a man loping through the dunes with long fluid strides. When I'd swung around with the Glock, no one had been there.

'A man?' I said. 'Running with the millennium monkeys, leading the troop? Our own Moonlight Bay Tarzan?'

'Well, I hope it's a man.'

'And what's that supposed to mean?'

Breaking eye contact, Bobby shrugged. 'I'm just saying there aren't only the monkeys I've seen. There's someone or something big out there with them.'

I looked toward the lights of Moonlight Bay. 'Feels like there's a clock ticking somewhere, a bomb clock, and the whole town's sitting on explosives.'

'That's my point, bro. Stay out of the blast zone.'

Holding the bike with one hand, I drew the Glock from my jacket pocket.

'As you go about your perilous and foolish adventures, XP-Man,' Bobby said, 'here's something to keep in mind.'

'More boardhead wisdom.'

'Whatever was going on out there at Wyvern – and might still be going on – a big troop of scientists must have been involved. Hugely educated dudes with foreheads higher than your whole face. Government and military types, too, and lots of them. The elite of the system. Movers and shakers. You know why they were part of this before it all went wrong?'

'Bills to pay, families to support?'

'Every last one of them wanted to leave his mark.'

I said, 'This isn't about ambition. I just want to know why my mom and dad had to die.'

'Your head's as hard as an oyster shell.'

'Yeah, but there's a pearl inside.'

'It's not a pearl,' he assured me. 'It's a fossilized seagull dropping.'

'You've got a way with words. You should write a book.'

He squeezed out a sneer as thin as a shaving of lemon peel. 'I'd rather screw a cactus.'

'That's pretty much what it's like. But rewarding.'

'This wave is going to put you through the rinse cycle and then down the drain.'

'Maybe. But it'll be a totally cool ride. And aren't you the one who said we're here to enjoy the ride?'

Finally defeated, he stepped out of my way, raised his right hand, and made the shaka sign.

I held the bike with my gun hand long enough to make the Star Trek sign.

In response, he gave me the finger.

With Orson at my side, I walked the bike eastward through the sand, heading toward the rockier part of the peninsula. Before I'd gone far, I heard Bobby say something behind me, but I couldn't catch his words.

I stopped, turned, and saw him heading back toward the cottage. 'What'd you say?'

'Here comes the fog,' he repeated.

Looking beyond him, I saw towering white masses

descending out of the west, an avalanche of churning vapor patinaed with moonlight. Like some silently toppling wall of doom in a dream.

The lights of town seemed to be a continent away.

Four

DEEP NIGHT

21

By the time Orson and I walked out of the dunes and reached the sandstone portion of the peninsula, thick clouds swaddled us. The fog bank was hundreds of feet deep, and though a pale dusting of moonlight sifted through the mist all the way to the ground, we were in a gray murk more blinding than a starless, moonless night would have been.

The lights of town were no longer visible.

The fog played tricks with sound. I could still hear the rough murmur of breaking surf, but it seemed to come from all four sides, as though I were on an island instead of a peninsula.

I wasn't confident about being able to ride my bicycle in that cloying gloom. Visibility continuously shifted between zero and a maximum of six feet. Although no trees or other obstacles lay along the curved horn, I could easily become disoriented and ride off the edge of the beach scarp; the bike would pitch forward, and when the front tire plowed into the soft sand of the slope below the scarp, I would come to a sudden halt and take a header off the bike to the beach, possibly breaking a limb or even my neck.

Besides, to build speed and to keep my balance, I would have to steer the bike with two hands, which meant pocketing the pistol. After my conversation with Bobby, I was loath to let go of the Glock. In the fog, something could close to within a few feet of me before I became aware of it, which wouldn't leave me time enough to tear the gun out of my jacket pocket and get off a shot.

I walked at a relatively brisk pace, wheeling the bicycle with my left hand, pretending that I was carefree and confident, and Orson trotted slightly ahead of me. The dog was wary, no good at whistling in the graveyard either literally or figuratively, turning his head ceaselessly from side to side.

The click of the wheel bearings and the tick of the drive chain betrayed my position. There was no way to quiet the bicycle short of picking it up and carrying it, which I could do with one arm but only for short distances.

The noise might not matter, anyway. The monkeys probably had acute animal senses that detected the most meager stimuli; in fact, they were no doubt able to track me by scent.

Orson would be able to smell them, too. In this nebulous night, his black form was barely visible, and I couldn't see if his hackles were raised, which would be a sure sign that the monkeys were nearby.

As I walked, I wondered what it was about these creatures that made them different from an ordinary rhesus.

In appearance, at least, the beast in Angela's kitchen had been a typical example of its species, even if it had been at the upper end of the size range for a rhesus. She'd said only that it had 'awful dark-yellow eyes,' but as far as I knew, that was well within the spectrum of eye colors for this group of primates. Bobby hadn't mentioned anything strange about the troop that was bedeviling him, other than their peculiar behavior and the unusual size of their shadowy leader: no misshapen craniums, no third eyes in their foreheads, no bolts in their necks to indicate that they had been stitched and stapled together in the secret laboratory of Dr. Victor Frankenstein's megalomaniacal great-great-great-great-granddaughter, Heather Frankenstein.

The project leaders at Fort Wyvern had been worried that the monkey in Angela's kitchen had either scratched or bitten her. Considering the scientists' fear, it was logical to infer that the beast had carried an infectious disease transmitted by blood, saliva, or other bodily fluids. This inference was supported by the physical examinations to which she'd been subjected. For four years, they had also taken monthly blood samples from her, which meant that the disease had a potentially long incubation period.

Biological warfare. The leaders of every country on earth denied making preparations for such a hateful conflict. Evoking the name of God, warning of the judgment of history, they solemnly signed fat treaties guaranteeing never to engage in this monstrous research and development. Meanwhile, each nation was busily brewing anthrax cocktails, packaging bubonic-plague aerosols, and engineering such a splendiferous collection of exotic new viruses and bacteria that no line at any unemployment office anywhere on the planet would ever contain a single out-of-work mad scientist.

Nevertheless, I couldn't understand why they would have forcibly subjected Angela to sterilization. No doubt certain diseases increase the chances that one's offspring will suffer birth defects. Judging by what

Angela had told me, however, I didn't think that the people at Wyvern sterilized her out of a concern either for her or for any children that she might conceive. They appeared to have been motivated not by compassion but by fear swollen nearly to panic.

I had asked Angela if the monkey was carrying a disease. She had as much as denied it: *I wish it were a disease. Wouldn't that be nice? Maybe I'd be cured by now. Or dead. Some days I think dead would be better.*

But if not a disease, what?

Suddenly the loonlike cry that we had heard earlier now pierced the night and fog again, jolting me out of my ruminations.

Orson twitched to a full stop. I halted, too, and the click-tick of the bicycle fell silent.

The cry seemed to issue from the west and south, and after only a brief moment, an answering call came, as best I could tell, from the north and east. We were being stalked.

Because sound traveled so deceptively through the mist, I was not able to judge how far from us the cries arose. I would have bet one lung that they were close.

The rhythmic, heartlike pulse of the surf throbbed through the night. I wondered which Chris Isaak song Sasha was spinning across the airwaves at that moment.

Orson began to move again, and so did I, a little faster than before. We had nothing to gain by hesitating. We wouldn't be safe until we were off the lonely peninsula and back in town – and perhaps not even then.

When we had gone no more than thirty or forty feet, that eerie ululant cry rose again. It was answered, as before.

This time we kept moving.

My heart was racing, and it didn't slow when I reminded myself that these were only monkeys. Not predators. Eaters of fruits, berries, nuts. Members of a peaceable kingdom.

Suddenly, perversely, Angela's dead face flashed onto my memory screen. I realized what I had misinterpreted, in my shock and anguish, when I'd first found her body. Her throat appeared to have been slashed repeatedly with a half-sharp knife, because the wound was ragged. In fact, it hadn't been slashed: It had been bitten, torn, chewed. I could see the terrible wound more clearly now than I'd been willing to see it when standing on the threshold of the bathroom.

Furthermore, I half recalled other marks on her, wounds that I'd not had the stomach to consider at the time. Livid bite marks on her hands. Perhaps even one on her face.

Monkeys. But not ordinary monkeys.

The killers' actions in Angela's house – the business with the dolls, the game of hide and seek – had seemed like the play of demented children. More than one of these monkeys must have been in those rooms: small enough to hide in places where a man could not have been concealed, so inhumanly quick as to have seemed like ghosts.

Another cry arose in the murk and was answered by a low hooting from *two* other locations.

Orson and I kept moving briskly, but I resisted the urge to bolt. If I broke into a run, my haste might be interpreted – and rightly – as a sign of fear. To a predator, fear indicates weakness. If they perceived any weakness, they might attack.

I had the Glock, on which my grip was so tight that

the weapon seemed to be welded to my hand. But I didn't know how many of these creatures might be in this troop: perhaps only three or four, perhaps ten, maybe even more. Considering that I had never fired a gun before – except once, earlier this evening, entirely by accident – I was not going to be able to cut down all of these beasts before they overwhelmed me.

Although I didn't want to give my fevered imagination such dark material with which to work, I couldn't help wondering what a rhesus monkey's teeth were like. All blunt bicuspids? No. Even herbivores – assuming that the rhesus was indeed herbivorous – needed to tear at the peel of a fruit, at husks, at shells. They were sure to have incisors, maybe even pointy eyeteeth, as did human beings. Although these particular specimens might have stalked Angela, the rhesus itself hadn't evolved as a predator; therefore, they wouldn't be equipped with fangs. Certain apes had fangs, though. Baboons had enormous, wicked teeth. Anyway, the biting power of the rhesus was moot, because regardless of the nature of their dental armaments, these particular specimens had been well enough equipped to kill Angela Ferryman savagely and quickly.

At first I heard or sensed, rather than saw, movement in the fog a few feet to my right. Then I glimpsed a dark, undefined shape close to the ground, coming at me swiftly and silently.

I twisted toward the movement. The creature brushed against my leg and vanished into the fog before I could see it clearly.

Orson growled with restraint, as though to warn off something without quite challenging it to fight. He was facing the billowy wall of gray mist that scudded through the darkness on the other side of the bicycle, and I suspected that with light I would see not merely that his hackles were raised but that every hair on his back was standing stiffly on end.

I was looking low, toward the ground, half expecting to see the shining, dark-yellow gaze of which Angela had spoken. The shape that suddenly loomed in the fog was, instead, nearly as big as I am. Maybe bigger. Shadowy, amorphous, like a swooping angel of death hovering in a dream, it was more suggestion than substance, fearsome precisely because it remained mysterious. No baleful yellow eyes. No clear features. No distinct form. Man or ape, or neither: the leader of the troop, there and gone.

Orson and I had come to a halt again.

I turned my head slowly to survey the streaming murk around us, intent on picking up any helpful sound. But the troop moved as silently as the fog.

I felt as though I were a diver far beneath the sea, trapped in blinding currents rich with plankton and algae, having glimpsed a circling shark, waiting for the fish to reappear out of the gloom and bite me in half.

Something brushed against the back of my legs, plucked at my jeans, and it wasn't Orson because it made a wicked hissing sound. I kicked at it but didn't connect, and it vanished into the mist before I could get a look at it.

Orson yelped in surprise, as though he'd had an encounter of his own.

'Here, boy,' I said urgently, and he came at once to my side.

I let go of the bicycle, which clattered to the sand.

Gripping the pistol in both hands, I began to turn in a full circle, searching for something to shoot at.

Shrill, angry chittering arose. These seemed recognizably to be the voices of monkeys. At least half a dozen of them.

If I killed one, the others might flee in fear. Or they might react as the tangerine-eating monkey had reacted to the broom that Angela had brandished in her kitchen: With furious aggressiveness.

In any event, visibility was virtually zero, and I couldn't see their eyeshine or their shadows, so I dared not waste ammunition by firing blindly into the fog. When the Glock was empty, I would be easy prey.

As one, the chittering voices fell silent.

The dense, ceaselessly seething clouds now damped even the sound of the surf. I could hear Orson's panting and my own too-rapid breathing, nothing else.

The great black form of the troop leader swelled again through the vaporous gray shrouds. It swooped as if it were winged, although this appearance of flight was surely illusory.

Orson snarled, and I juked back, triggering the laser-sighting mechanism. A red dot rippled across the morphing face of the fog. The troop leader, no more defined than a fleeting shadow on a frost-crusted window, was swallowed entirely by the mist before I could pin the laser to its mercurial shape.

I recalled the collection of skulls on the concrete stairs of the spillway in the storm culvert. Maybe the collector wasn't some teenage sociopath in practice for his adult career. Maybe the skulls were trophies that had been gathered and arranged by the monkeys – which was a peculiar and disturbing notion.

An even more disturbing thought occurred to me:

Maybe my skull and Orson's – stripped of all flesh, hollow-eyed and gleaming – would be added to the display.

Orson howled as a screeching monkey burst through the veils of mist and leaped onto his back. The dog twisted his head, snapping his teeth, trying to bite his unwanted rider, simultaneously trying to thrash it off.

We were so close that even in the meager light and churning mist, I could see the yellow eyes. Radiant, cold, and fierce. Glaring up at me. I couldn't squeeze off a shot at the attacker without hitting Orson.

The monkey had hardly landed on Orson's back when it sprang off the dog. It slammed hard into me, twenty-five pounds of wiry muscle and bone, staggering me backward, clambering up my chest, using my leather jacket for purchase, and in the chaos I was unable to shoot it without a high risk of wounding myself.

For an instant, we were face-to-face, eye to murderous eye. The creature's teeth were bared, and it was hissing ferociously, breath pungent and repulsive. It was a monkey yet not a monkey, and the profoundly *alien* quality of its bold stare was terrifying.

It snatched my cap off my head, and I swatted at it with the barrel of the Glock. Clutching the cap, the monkey dropped to the ground. I kicked, and the kick connected, knocking the cap out of its hand. Squealing, the rhesus tumbled-scampered into the fog, out of sight.

Orson started after the beast, barking, all his fear forgotten. When I called him back, he did not obey.

Then the larger form of the troop leader appeared again, more fleetingly than before, a sinuous shape billowing like a flung cape, gone almost as soon as it appeared but lingering long enough to make Orson reconsider the wisdom of pursuing the rhesus that had tried to steal my cap.

'*Jesus*,' I said explosively as the dog whined and backed away from the chase.

I snatched the cap off the ground but didn't return it to my head. Instead, I folded it and jammed it into an inside pocket of my jacket.

Shakily, I assured myself that I was okay, that I hadn't been bitten. If I'd been scratched, I didn't feel the sting of it, not on my hands or face. No, I hadn't been scratched. Thank God. If the monkey was carrying an infectious disease communicable only by contact with bodily fluids, I couldn't have caught it.

On the other hand, I'd smelled its fetid breath when we were face-to-face, breathed the very air that it exhaled. If this was an airborne contagion, I was already in possession of a one-way ticket to the cold-holding room.

In response to a tinny clatter behind me, I swung around and discovered that my fallen bicycle was being dragged into the fog by something I couldn't see. Flat on its side, combing sand with its spokes, the rear wheel was the only part of the bike still in sight, and it almost disappeared into the murk before I reached down with one hand and grabbed it.

The hidden bicycle thief and I engaged in a brief tug of war, which I handily won, suggesting that I was pitted against one or two rhesus monkeys and not against the much larger troop leader. I stood the bike on its wheels, leaned it against my body to keep it upright, and once more raised the Glock.

Orson returned to my side.

Nervously, he relieved himself again, shedding the

last of his beer. I was half surprised that I hadn't wet my pants.

For a while I gasped noisily for breath, shaking so badly that even a two-hand grip on the pistol couldn't keep it from jigging up and down. Gradually I grew calmer. My heart worked less diligently to crack my ribs.

Like the hulls of ghost ships, gray walls of mist sailed past, an infinite flotilla, towing behind them an unnatural stillness. No chittering. No squeals or shrieks. No loonlike cries. No sigh of wind or sough of surf. I felt almost as though, without realizing it, I had been killed in the recent confrontation, as though I now stood in a chilly antechamber outside the corridor of life, waiting for a door to open into Judgment.

As time eased by with the peace unbroken, the encounter with the monkeys should have seemed less real second by second. Instead, it grew more vivid in my mind, and I felt as if those terrible yellow eyes had not merely seared their radiant image into my memory but had left their mark on my soul.

Finally it became apparent that the games were over for a while. Holding the Glock with only one hand, I began to walk the bicycle east along the horn. Orson padded at my side.

I was sure that the troop was still monitoring us, although from a greater distance than before. I saw no stalking shapes in the fog, but they were out there, all right.

Monkeys. But not monkeys. Apparently escaped from a laboratory at Wyvern.

The end of the world, Angela had said.

Not by fire.

Not by ice.

Something worse.

Monkeys. The end of the world by monkeys.

Apocalypse with primates.

Armageddon. The end, *fini*, omega, doomsday, close the door and turn out the lights forever.

This was totally, fully, way crazy. Every time I tried to get my mind around the facts and pull them into some intelligible order, I wiped out big time, got radically clamshelled by a huge wave of imponderables.

Bobby's attitude, his relentless determination to distance himself from the insoluble troubles of the modern world and be a champion slacker, had always struck me as a legitimate lifestyle choice. Now it seemed to be not merely legitimate but reasoned, logical, and wise.

Because I was not expected to survive to adulthood, my parents raised me to play, to have fun, to indulge my sense of wonder, to live as much as possible without worry and without fear, to live in the moment with little concern for the future: in short, to trust in God and to believe that I, like everyone, am here for a purpose; to be as grateful for my limitations as for my talents and blessings, because both are part of a design beyond my comprehension. They recognized the need for me to learn self-discipline, of course, and respect for others. But, in fact, those things come naturally when you truly believe that your life has a spiritual dimension and that you are a carefully designed element in the mysterious mosaic of life. Although there had appeared to be little chance that I would outlive both parents, Mom and Dad prepared for this eventuality when I was first diagnosed: They purchased a large second-to-die life-insurance policy, which would now provide handsomely for me even if I never earned another cent from my books and articles. Born for play and fun and wonder, destined never to have to hold a job, destined never to be burdened by the responsibilities that weigh down most people, I could give up my writing and become such a total surf bum that Bobby Halloway, by comparison, would appear to be a compulsive workaholic with no more capacity for fun than a cabbage. Furthermore, I could embrace absolute slackerhood with no guilt whatsoever, with no qualms or doubts, because I was raised to be what all humanity might have been if we hadn't violated the terms of the lease and been evicted from Eden. Like all who are born of man and woman, I live by the whims of fate: Because of my XP, I'm just more acutely aware of the machinations of fate than most people are, and this awareness is liberating.

Yet, as I walked my bicycle eastward along the peninsula, I persevered in my search for meaning in all that I'd seen and heard since sunset.

Before the troop had arrived to torment Orson and me, I'd been trying to pin down exactly what was different about these monkeys; now I returned to that riddle. Unlike ordinary rhesuses, these were bold rather than shy, brooding rather than lighthearted. The most obvious difference was that these monkeys were hot-tempered, vicious. Their potential for violence was not, however, the primary quality that separated them from other rhesuses; it was only a consequence of another, more profound difference that I recognized but that I was inexplicably reluctant to consider.

The curdled fog was as thick as ever, but gradually it began to brighten. Smears of blurry light appeared in the murk: buildings and streetlamps along the shore.

Orson whined with delight – or just relief – at these signs of civilization, but we weren't any safer in town than out of it.

When we left the southern horn entirely and entered Embarcadero Way, I paused to take my cap from the jacket pocket in which I had tucked it. I put it on and gave the visor a tug. The Elephant Man adjusts his costume.

Orson peered up at me, cocked his head consideringly, and then chuffed as though in approval. He was the Elephant Man's dog, after all, and as such, a measure of his own self-image was dependent upon the style and grace with which I comported myself.

Because of the streetlamps, visibility had increased to perhaps a hundred feet. Like the ghost tides of an ancient and long-dead sea, fog surged off the bay and into the streets; each fine drop of mist refracted the golden sodium-vapor light and translated it to the next drop.

If members of the troop still accompanied us, they would be forced to lurk at a greater distance here than they had on the barren peninsula, to avoid being seen. Like players in a recasting of Poe's 'The Murders in the Rue Morgue,' they would have to confine their skulking to parks, unilluminated alleyways, balconies, high ledges, parapets, and rooftops.

At this late hour, no pedestrians or motorists were in sight. The town appeared to have been abandoned.

I was overcome by the disturbing notion that these silent and empty streets foreshadowed a real, frightening desolation that would befall Moonlight Bay in the not too distant future. Our little burg was preparing to be a ghost town.

I climbed onto my bike and headed north on

Embarcadero Way. The man who had contacted me through Sasha, at the radio station, was waiting on his boat at the marina.

As I pedaled along the deserted avenue, my mind returned to the millennium monkeys. I was sure that I had identified the most fundamental difference between ordinary rhesuses and this extraordinary troop that secretly roamed the night, but I was reluctant to accept my own conclusion, inevitable though it seemed: *These monkeys were smarter than ordinary monkeys.*

Way smarter, radically smarter.

They had understood the purpose of Bobby's camera, and they had stolen it. They filched his new camera, too.

They recognized my face among the faces of the forty dolls in Angela's workroom, and they used that one to taunt me. Later, they set a fire to conceal Angela's murder.

The big brows at Fort Wyvern might have been engaged in secret bacteriological-warfare research, but that didn't explain why their laboratory monkeys were markedly smarter than any monkeys that had previously walked the earth.

Just how smart *was* 'markedly smarter'? Maybe not smart enough to win a bundle on *Jeopardy*. Maybe not smart enough to teach poetry at the university level or to successfully manage a radio station or to track the patterns of surf worldwide, maybe not even smart enough to write a *New York Times* best-seller – but perhaps smart enough to be the most dangerous, uncontrollable pest humanity had ever known. Imagine what damage rats could do, how rapidly their numbers would grow, if they were even half as smart as human beings and could learn how to avoid all traps and poisons.

Were these monkeys truly escapees from a laboratory, loose in the world and cleverly eluding capture? If so, how did they get to be so intelligent in the first place? What did they want? What was their agenda? Why hadn't a massive effort been launched to track them down, round them up, and return them to better cages from which they could never break free?

Or were they tools being used by someone at Wyvern? The way the cops use trained police dogs. The way the Navy uses dolphins to search for enemy submarines and, in wartime – it is rumored – even to plant magnetic packages of explosives on the hulls of targeted boats.

A thousand other questions swarmed through my mind. All of them were equally crazy.

Depending on the answers, the ramifications of these monkeys' heightened intelligence could be earth-shattering. The possible consequences to human civilization were especially alarming when you considered the viciousness of these animals and their apparently innate hostility.

Angela's prediction of doom might not have been farfetched, might actually have been *less* pessimistic than my assessment of the situation would be when – if ever – I knew all the facts. Certainly, doom had come to Angela herself.

I also intuited that the monkeys were not the entire story. They were but one chapter of an epic. Other astonishments were awaiting discovery.

Compared to the project at Wyvern, Pandora's fabled box, from which had been unleashed all the evils that plague humanity – wars, pestilence, diseases, famines, floods – might prove to have held only a collection of petty nuisances.

In my haste to get to the marina, I was cycling too fast to allow Orson to keep pace with me. He was sprinting full throttle, ears flapping, panting hard, but falling steadily behind.

In truth, I was cranking the bike to the max not because I was in a hurry to reach the marina but because, unconsciously, I wanted to outrace the tidal wave of terror sweeping toward us. There was no escaping it, however, and no matter how furiously I pedaled, I could outrun nothing but my dog.

Recalling Dad's final words, I stopped pedaling and coasted until Orson was able to stay at my side without heroic effort.

Never leave a friend behind. Friends are all we have to get us through this life – and they are the only things from this world that we could hope to see in the next.

Besides, the best way to deal with a rising sea of trouble is to catch the wave at the zero break and ride it out, slide along the face straight into the cathedral, get totally zip-locked in the green room, walk the board all the way through the barrel, hooting, showing no fear. That's not only cool: It's classic.

22

With a gentle and even tender sound, like flesh on flesh in a honeymoon bed, low waves slipped between the pilings and slapped against the sea wall. The damp air offered a faint and pleasant aromatic melange of brine, fresh kelp, creosote, rusting iron, and other fragrances I couldn't quite identify.

The marina, tucked into the sheltered northeast corner of the bay, offers docking for fewer than three hundred vessels, only six of which are full-time residences for their owners. Although social life in Moonlight Bay does not center around boating, there is a long waiting list for any slip that becomes available.

I walked my bike toward the west end of the main pier, which ran parallel to shore. The tires swished and bumped softly across the dew-wet, uneven planks. Only one boat in the marina had lights in its windows at that hour. Dock lamps, though dim, showed me the way through the fog.

Because the fishing fleet ties up farther out along the northern horn of the bay, the comparatively sheltered marina is reserved for pleasure craft. There are sloops and ketches and yawls ranging from modest to impressive – although more of the former than the latter –

motor yachts mostly of manageable length and price, a few Boston Whalers, and even two houseboats. The largest sailing yacht – in fact, the largest boat – docked here is currently *Sunset Dancer*, a sixty-foot Windship cutter. Of the motor yachts, the largest is *Nostromo*, a fifty-six-foot Bluewater coastal cruiser; and it was to this boat that I was headed.

At the west end of the pier, I took a ninety-degree turn onto a subsidiary pier that featured docking slips on both sides. The *Nostromo* was in the last berth on the right.

I have been one acquainted with the night.

That was the code Sasha had used to identify the man who had come to the radio station seeking me, who hadn't wanted his name used on the phone, and who had been reluctant to come to Bobby's house to talk with me. It was a line from a poem by Robert Frost, one that most eavesdroppers would be unlikely to recognize, and I had assumed that it referred to Roosevelt Frost, who owned the *Nostromo*.

As I leaned my bicycle against the dock railing near the gangway to Roosevelt's slip, tidal action caused the boats to wallow in their berths. They creaked and groaned like arthritic old men murmuring feeble complaints in their sleep.

I had never bothered to chain my bike when I left it unattended, because until this night Moonlight Bay had been a refuge from the crime that infected the modern world. By the time this weekend passed, our picturesque town might lead the country in murders, mutilations, and priest beatings, per capita, but we probably didn't have to worry about a dramatic increase in bicycle theft.

The gangway was steep because the tide was not

high, and it was treacherously slippery with condensation. Orson descended as carefully as I did.

We were two-thirds of the way down to the portside finger of the slip when a low voice, hardly more than a gruff whisper, seeming to originate magically from the fog directly over my head, demanded, *'Who goes there?'*

Startled, I almost fell, but I clutched the dripping gangway handrail and kept my feet under me.

The Bluewater 563 is a sleek, white, low-profile, double-deck cruiser with an upper helm station that is enclosed by a hard top and canvas walls. The only light aboard came from behind the curtained windows of the aft stateroom and the main cabin amidships, on the lower deck. The open upper deck and the helm station were dark and fog-wrapped, and I couldn't see who had spoken.

'Who goes there?' the man whispered again, no louder but with a harder edge to his voice.

I recognized the voice now as that of Roosevelt Frost.

Taking my cue from him, I whispered: 'It's me, Chris Snow.'

'Shield your eyes, son.'

I made a visor of my hand and squinted as a flashlight blazed, pinning me where I stood on the gangway. It switched off almost at once, and Roosevelt said, still in a whisper, 'Is that your dog with you?'

'Yes, sir.'

'And nothing else?'

'I'm sorry?'

'Nothing else with you, no one else?'

'No, sir.'

'Come aboard, then.'

I could see him now, because he had moved closer to the railing on the open upper deck, aft of the helm station. I couldn't identify him even from this relatively short distance, however, because he was screened by the pea-soup fog, the night, and his own darkness.

Urging Orson to precede me, I boarded the boat through the gap in the port railing, and we quickly climbed the open steps to the upper deck.

When we got to the top, I saw that Roosevelt Frost was holding a shotgun. Pretty soon the National Rifle Association would move its headquarters to Moonlight Bay. He wasn't aiming the gun at me, but I was sure that he'd been covering me with it until he had been able to identify me in the beam of the flashlight.

Even without the shotgun, he was a formidable figure. Six feet four. Neck like a dock piling. Shoulders as wide as a staysail boom. Deep chest. With a two-hand spread way bigger than the diameter of the average helm wheel. This was the guy who Ahab should have called to cold-cock Moby Dick. He had been a football star in the sixties and early seventies, when sports writers routinely referred to him as 'the Sledge-hammer.' Though he was now sixty-three, a successful businessman who owned a men's clothing store, a mini-mall, and half interest in the Moonlight Bay Inn and Country Club, he appeared capable of pulverizing any of the genetic-mutant, steroid-pumped behemoths who played some of the power positions on contemporary teams.

'Hello, dog,' he murmured.

Orson chuffed.

'Hold this, son,' Frost whispered, handing the shotgun to me.

A pair of curious-looking, high-tech binoculars hung

on a strap around his neck. He brought them to his eyes and, from this top-deck vantage point overlooking surrounding craft, surveyed the pier along which I had recently approached the *Nostromo*.

'How can you see anything?' I wondered.

'Night-vision binoculars. They magnify available light eighteen thousand times.'

'But the fog . . .'

He pressed a button on the glasses, and as a mechanism purred inside them, he said, 'They also have an infra-red mode, shows you only heat sources.'

'Must be lots of heat sources around the marina.'

'Not with boat engines off. Besides, I'm interested only in heat sources *on the move*.'

'People.'

'Maybe.'

'Who?'

'Whoever might've been following you. Now hush, son.'

I hushed. As Roosevelt patiently scanned the marina, I passed the next minute wondering about this former football star and local businessman who was not, after all, quite what he seemed.

I wasn't surprised, exactly. Since sundown, the people I'd encountered had revealed dimensions to their lives of which I had previously been unaware. Even Bobby had been keeping secrets: the shotgun in the broom closet, the troop of monkeys. When I considered Pia Klick's conviction that she was the reincarnation of Kaha Huna, which Bobby had been keeping to himself, I better understood his bitter, disputatious response to any view that he felt smacked of New Age thinking, including my occasional innocent comments about my strange dog. At least Orson, if no one else, had remained in character throughout the night – although, considering the way things were going, I wouldn't have been bowled over if suddenly he revealed an ability to stand on his hind paws and tap dance with mesmerizing showmanship.

'No one's trailing after you,' said Roosevelt as he lowered the night glasses and took back his shotgun. 'This way, son.'

I followed him aft across the sun deck to an open hatch on the starboard side.

Roosevelt paused and looked back, over the top of my head, to the port railing where Orson still lingered. 'Here now. Come along, dog.'

The mutt hung behind, but not because he sensed anything lurking on the dock. As usual, he was curiously and uncharacteristically shy around Roosevelt.

Our host's hobby was 'animal communication' – a quintessential New Age concept that had been fodder for most daytime television talk shows, although Roosevelt was discreet about his talent and employed it only at the request of neighbors and friends. The mere mention of animal communication had been able to start Bobby foaming at the mouth even long before Pia Klick had decided that she was the goddess of surfing in search of her Kahuna. Roosevelt claimed to be able to discern the anxieties and desires of troubled pets that were brought to him. He didn't charge for this service, but his lack of interest in money didn't convince Bobby: *Hell, Snow, I never said he was a charlatan trying to make a buck. He's well meaning. But he just ran headfirst into a goal post once too often.*

According to Roosevelt, the only animal with which he had never been able to communicate was my dog.

He considered Orson a challenge, and he never missed an opportunity to try to chat him up. 'Come here now, old pup.'

With apparent reluctance, Orson finally accepted the invitation. His claws clicked on the deck.

Carrying the shotgun, Roosevelt Frost went through the open hatch and down a set of molded fiberglass stairs lit only by a faint pearly glow at the bottom. He ducked his head, hunched his huge shoulders, pulled his arms against his sides to make himself smaller, but nevertheless appeared at risk of becoming wedged in the tight stairway.

Orson hesitated, tucked his tail between his legs, but finally descended behind Roosevelt, and I went last. The steps led to a porch-style afterdeck overhung by the cantilevered sun deck.

Orson was reluctant to go into the stateroom, which looked cozy and welcoming in the low light of a nightstand lamp. After Roosevelt and I stepped inside, however, Orson vigorously shook the condensed fog off his coat, spraying the entire afterdeck, and then followed us. I could almost believe that he'd hung back out of consideration, to avoid splattering us.

When Orson was inside, Roosevelt locked the door. He tested it to be sure it was secure. Then tested it again.

Beyond the aft stateroom, the main cabin included a galley with bleached-mahogany cabinets and matching faux-mahogany floor, a dining area, and a salon in one open and spacious floorplan. Out of respect for me, it was illuminated only by one downlight in a living-room display case full of football trophies and by two fat green candles standing in saucers on the dinette table.

The air was redolent of fresh-brewed coffee, and when Roosevelt offered a cup, I accepted.

'Sorry to hear about your dad,' he said.

'Well, at least it's over.'

He raised his eyebrows. 'Is it really?'

'I mean, for him.'

'But not for you. Not after what you've seen.'

I frowned. 'How do you know what I've seen?'

'The word's around,' he said cryptically.

'What do you—'

He held up one hubcap-size hand. 'We'll talk about it in a minute. That's why I asked you to come here. But I'm still trying to think through what I need to tell you. Let me get around to it in my own way, son.'

Coffee served, the big man took off his nylon windbreaker, hung it on the back of a chair, and sat at the table. He indicated that I should sit catercorner to him, and with his foot, he pushed out another chair. 'Here you go, dog,' he said, offering the third seat to Orson.

Although this was standard procedure when we visited Roosevelt, Orson pretended incomprehension. He settled onto the floor in front of the refrigerator.

'That is unacceptable,' Roosevelt quietly informed him.

Orson yawned.

With one foot, Roosevelt gently rattled the chair that he had pushed away from the table for the dog. 'Be a good puppy.'

Orson yawned more elaborately than before. He was overplaying his disinterest.

'If I have to, pup, I'll come over there, pick you up, and put you in this chair,' Roosevelt said, 'which will be an embarrassment to your master, who would like you to be a courteous guest.'

He was smiling good-naturedly, and no slightest threatening tone darkened his voice. His broad face was that of a black Buddha, and his eyes were full of kindness and amusement.

'Be a good puppy,' Roosevelt repeated.

Orson swept the floor with his tail, caught himself, and stopped wagging. He shyly shifted his stare from Roosevelt to me and cocked his head.

I shrugged.

Once more Roosevelt lightly rattled the offered chair with his foot.

Although Orson got up from the floor, he didn't immediately approach the table.

From a pocket of the nylon windbreaker that hung on his chair, Roosevelt extracted a dog biscuit shaped like a bone. He held it in the candlelight so that Orson could see it clearly. Between his big thumb and forefinger, the biscuit appeared to be almost as tiny as a trinket from a charm bracelet, but it was in fact a large treat. With ceremonial solemnity, Roosevelt placed it on the table in front of the seat that was reserved for the dog.

With wanting eyes, Orson followed the biscuit hand. He padded toward the table but stopped short of it. He was being more than usually standoffish.

From the windbreaker, Roosevelt extracted a second biscuit. He held it close to the candles, turning it as if it were an exquisite jewel shining in the flame, and then he put it on the table beside the first biscuit.

Although he whined with desire, Orson didn't come to the chair. He ducked his head shyly and then looked up from under his brow at our host. This was the only man into whose eyes Orson was sometimes reluctant to stare.

Roosevelt took a third biscuit from the windbreaker pocket. Holding it under his broad and oft-broken nose, he inhaled deeply, lavishly, as if savoring the incomparable aroma of the bone-shaped treat.

Raising his head, Orson sniffed, too.

Roosevelt smiled slyly, winked at the dog – and then popped the biscuit into his mouth. He crunched it with enormous delight, rinsed it down with a swig of coffee, and let out a sigh of pleasure.

I was impressed. I had never seen him do this before. 'What did that taste like?'

'Not bad. Sort of like shredded wheat. Want one?'

'No, sir. No thank you,' I said, content to sip my coffee.

Orson's ears were pricked; Roosevelt now had his undivided attention. If this towering, gentle-voiced, giant black human truly enjoyed the biscuits, there might be fewer for any canine who played too hard to get.

From the windbreaker draped on the back of his chair, Roosevelt withdrew another biscuit. He held this one under his nose, too, and inhaled so expansively that he was putting me in danger of oxygen deprivation. His eyelids drooped sensuously. A shiver of pretended pleasure swept him, almost swelled into a swoon, and he seemed about to fall into a biscuit-devouring frenzy.

Orson's anxiety was palpable. He sprang off the floor, into the chair across the table from mine, where Roosevelt wanted him, sat on his hindquarters, and craned his neck forward until his snout was only two inches from Roosevelt's nose. Together, they sniffed the endangered biscuit.

Instead of popping this one into his mouth, Roosevelt carefully placed it on the table beside the two that were already arranged in front of Orson's seat. 'Good old pup.'

I wasn't sure that I believed in Roosevelt Frost's supposed ability to communicate with animals, but in my opinion, he was indisputably a first-rate dog psychologist.

Orson sniffed the biscuits on the table.

'Ah, ah, ah,' Roosevelt warned.

The dog looked up at his host.

'You mustn't eat them until I say you may,' Roosevelt told him.

The dog licked his chops.

'So help me, pup, if you eat them without my permission,' said Roosevelt, 'there will never, ever, ever again be biscuits for you.'

Orson issued a thin, pleading whine.

'I mean it, dog,' Roosevelt said quietly but firmly. 'I can't make you talk to me if you don't want to. But I can insist that you display a minimum of manners aboard my boat. You can't just come in here and wolf down the canapes as if you were some wild beast.'

Orson gazed into Roosevelt's eyes as though trying to judge his commitment to this no-wolfing rule.

Roosevelt didn't blink.

Apparently convinced that this was no empty threat, the dog lowered his attention to the three biscuits. He gazed at them with such desperate longing that I thought I ought to try one of the damn things, after all.

'Good pup,' said Roosevelt.

He picked up a remote-control device from the table and jabbed one of the buttons on it, although the tip of his finger seemed too large to press fewer than three buttons at once. Behind Orson, motorized tambour doors rolled up and out of sight on the top half of a built-in hutch, revealing two stacks of tightly packed electronic gear gleaming with light-emitting diodes.

Orson was interested enough to turn his head for a moment before resuming worship of the forbidden biscuits.

In the hutch, a large video monitor clicked on. The quartered screen showed murky views of the fog-shrouded marina and the bay on all four sides of the *Nostromo*.

'What's this?' I wondered.

'Security.' Roosevelt put down the remote control. 'Motion detectors and infra-red sensors will pick up anyone approaching the boat and alert us at once. Then a telescopic lens automatically isolates and zooms in on the intruder before he gets here, so we'll know what we're dealing with.'

'What *are* we dealing with?'

The man mountain took two slow, dainty sips of his coffee before he said, 'You might already know too much about that.'

'What do you mean? Who are you?'

'I'm nobody but who I am,' he said. 'Just old Rosie Frost. If you're thinking that maybe I'm one of the people behind all this, you're wrong.'

'What people? Behind what?'

Looking at the four security-camera views on the quartered video monitor, he said, 'With any luck, they're not even aware that I know about them.'

'Who? People at Wyvern?'

He turned to me again. 'They're not just at Wyvern anymore. Townspeople are in it now. I don't know how many. Maybe a couple of hundred, maybe five hundred, but probably not more than that, at least not yet. No doubt it's gradually spreading to others . . . and it's already beyond Moonlight Bay.'

Frustrated, I said, 'Are you *trying* to be inscrutable?'

'As much as I can, yes.'

He got up, fetched the coffeepot, and without further comment freshened our cups. Evidently he intended to make me wait for morsels of information in much the way that poor Orson was being made to wait patiently for his snack.

The dog licked the tabletop around the three biscuits, but his tongue never touched the treats.

When Roosevelt returned to his chair, I said, 'If you're not involved with these people, how do you know so much about them?'

'I don't know all that much.'

'Apparently a lot more than I do.'

'I know only what the animals tell me.'

'What animals?'

'Well, not your dog, for sure.'

Orson looked up from the biscuits.

'He's a regular sphinx,' Roosevelt said.

Although I hadn't been aware of doing so, sometime soon after sunset, I had evidently walked through a magic looking-glass.

Deciding to play by the lunatic rules of this new kingdom, I said, 'So . . . aside from my phlegmatic dog, what do these animals tell you?'

'You shouldn't know all of it. Just enough so you realize it's best that you forget what you saw in the hospital garage and up at the morgue.'

I sat up straighter in my chair, as though pulled erect by my tightening scalp. 'You *are* one of them.'

'No. Relax, son. You're safe with me. How long have we been friends? More than two years now since you first came here with your dog. And I think you know you can trust me.'

In fact, I was at least half convinced that I could still trust Roosevelt Frost, even though I was no longer as sure of my character judgment as I had once been.

'But if you don't forget what you saw,' he continued, 'if you try to contact authorities outside town, you'll endanger lives.'

As my chest tightened around my heart, I said, 'You just told me I could trust you, and now you're threatening me.'

He looked wounded. 'I'm your friend, son. I wouldn't threaten you. I'm only telling you—'

'Yeah. What the animals said.'

'It's the people from Wyvern who want to keep a lid on this at any cost, not me. Anyway, you aren't *personally* in any danger even if you try to go to outside authorities, at least not at first. They won't touch you. Not you. You're revered.'

This was one of the most baffling things that he had said yet, and I blinked in confusion. 'Revered?'

'Yes. They're in awe of you.'

I realized that Orson was staring at me intently, temporarily having forgotten the three promised biscuits.

Roosevelt's statement was not merely baffling: It was downright whacky. 'Why would anyone be in awe of me?' I demanded.

'Because of who you are.'

My mind looped and spun and tumbled like a capering seagull. 'Who am I?'

Roosevelt frowned and pulled thoughtfully at his

face with one hand before finally saying, 'Damned if I know. I'm only repeating what I've been told.'

What the animals told you. The black Dr. Dolittle.

Some of Bobby's scorn was creeping into me.

'The point is,' he said, 'the Wyvern crowd won't kill you unless you give them no choice, unless it's absolutely the only way to shut you up.'

'When you talked to Sasha earlier tonight, you told her this was a matter of life and death.'

Roosevelt nodded solemnly. 'And it is. For her and others. From what I hear, these bastards will try to control you by killing people you love until you agree to cease and desist, until you forget what you saw and just get on with your life.'

'People I love?'

'Sasha. Bobby. Even Orson.'

'They'll kill my friends to shut me up?'

'*Until* you shut up. One by one, they'll kill them one by one until you shut up to save those who are left.'

I was willing to risk my own life to find out what had happened to my mother and father – and why – but I couldn't put the lives of my friends on the line. 'This is monstrous. Killing innocent—'

'That's who you're dealing with.'

My skull felt as though it would crack to relieve the pressure of my frustration: 'Who *am* I dealing with? I need something more specific than just the people at Wyvern.'

Roosevelt sipped his coffee and didn't answer.

Maybe he was my friend, and maybe the warning he'd given me would, if I heeded it, save Sasha's life or Bobby's, but I wanted to punch him. I might have done it, too, might have hammered him with a merciless series of blows if there had been any chance whatsoever that I wouldn't have broken my hands.

Orson had put one paw on the table, not with the intention of sweeping his biscuits to the floor and absconding with them but to balance himself as he leaned sideways in his chair to look past me. Something in the salon, beyond the galley and dining area, had drawn his attention.

When I turned in my chair to follow Orson's gaze, I saw a cat sitting on the arm of the sofa, backlit by the display case full of football trophies. It appeared to be pale gray. In the shadows that masked its face, its eyes glowed green and were flecked with gold.

It could have been the same cat that I had encountered in the hills behind Kirk's Funeral Home earlier in the night.

23

Like an Egyptian sculpture in a pharaoh's sepulcher, the cat sat motionless and seemed prepared to spend eternity on the arm of the sofa.

Although it was only a cat, I was uncomfortable with my back to the animal. I moved to the chair opposite Roosevelt Frost, from which I could see, to my right, the entire salon and the sofa at the far end of it.

'When did you get a cat?' I asked.

'It's not mine,' Roosevelt said. 'It's just visiting.'

'I think I saw this cat earlier tonight.'

'Yes, you did.'

'That's what it told you, huh?' I said with a touch of Bobby's scorn.

'Mungojerrie and I had a talk, yes,' Roosevelt confirmed.

'Who?'

Roosevelt gestured toward the cat on the sofa. 'Mungojerrie.' He spelled it for me.

The name was exotic yet curiously familiar. Being my father's son in more than blood and name, I needed only a moment to recognize the source. 'It's one of the cats in *Old Possum's Book of Practical Cats*, the T. S. Eliot collection.'

'Most of these cats like those names from Eliot's book.'

'These cats?'

'These new cats like Mungojerrie here.'

'New cats?' I asked, struggling to follow him.

Rather than explain what he meant by that term, Roosevelt said, 'They prefer those names. Couldn't tell you why – or how they came by them. I know one named Rum Tum Tugger. Another is Rumpelteazer. Coricopat and Growltiger.'

'Prefer? You make it sound almost as if they choose their own names.'

'Almost,' Roosevelt said.

I shook my head. 'This is radically bizarre.'

'After all these years of animal communication,' Roosevelt said, 'I sometimes still find it bizarre myself.'

'Bobby Halloway thinks you were hit in the head once too often.'

Roosevelt smiled. 'He's not alone in that opinion. But I was a football player, you know, not a boxer. What do you think, Chris? Has half my brain turned to gristle?'

'No, sir,' I admitted. 'You're as sharp as anyone I've ever known.'

'On the other hand, intelligence and flakiness aren't mutually exclusive, are they?'

'I've met too many of my parents' fellow academics to argue that one with you.'

From the living room, Mungojerrie continued to watch us, and from his chair, Orson continued to monitor the cat not with typical canine antagonism but with considerable interest.

'I ever tell you how I got into this animal-communication thing?' Roosevelt wondered.

'No, sir. I never asked.' Calling attention to such

an eccentricity had seemed as impolite as mentioning a physical deformity, so I had always pretended to accept this aspect of Roosevelt as though it were not in the least remarkable.

'Well,' he said, 'about nine years ago I had this really great dog named Sloopy, black and tan, about half the size of your Orson. He was just a mutt, but he was special.'

Orson had shifted his attention from the cat to Roosevelt.

'Sloopy had a terrific disposition. He was always a playful, good-tempered dog, not one bad day in him. Then his mood changed. Suddenly he became withdrawn, nervous, even depressed. He was ten years old, not nearly a pup anymore, so I took him to a vet, afraid I was going to hear the worst kind of diagnosis. But the vet couldn't find anything much wrong with him. Sloopy had a little arthritis, something an aging ex-linebacker with football knees can identify with, but he didn't have it bad enough to inhibit him much, and that was the only thing wrong. Yet week after week, he wallowed in his funk.'

Mungojerrie was on the move. The cat had climbed from the arm to the back of the sofa and was stealthily approaching us.

'So one day,' Roosevelt continued, 'I read this human-interest story in the paper about this woman in Los Angeles who called herself a pet communicator. Name was Gloria Chan. She'd been on a lot of TV talk shows, counseled a lot of movie people on their pets' problems, and she'd written a book. The reporter's tone was smart-ass, made Gloria sound like your typical Hollywood flake. For all I knew, he probably had her pegged. You remember, after the football career was over, I did a few movies. Met a lot of celebrities, actors and rock stars and comedians. Producers and directors, too. Some of them were nice folks and some were even smart, but frankly a lot of them and a lot of the people who hung out with them *were* so bugshit crazy you wouldn't want to be around them unless you were carrying a major concealed weapon.'

After creeping the length of the sofa, the cat descended to the nearer arm. It shrank into a crouch, muscles taut, head lowered and thrust forward, ears flattened against its skull, as if it was going to spring at us across the six feet between the sofa and the table.

Orson was alert, focused again on Mungojerrie, both Roosevelt and the biscuits forgotten.

'I had some business in L.A.,' Roosevelt said, 'so I took Sloopy with me. We went down by boat, cruised the coast. I didn't have the *Nostromo* then. I was driving this really sweet sixty-foot Chris Craft Roamer. I docked her at Marina Del Rey, rented a car, took care of business for two days. I got Gloria's number through some friends in the film business, and she agreed to see me. She lived in the Palisades, and I drove out there with Sloopy late one morning.'

On the sofa arm, the cat was still crouched to spring. Its muscles were coiled even tighter than before. Little gray panther.

Orson was rigid, as still as the cat. He made a high-pitched, thin, anxious sound and then was silent again.

Roosevelt said, 'Gloria was fourth-generation Chinese-American. A petite, doll-like person. Beautiful, really beautiful. Delicate features, huge eyes. Like something a Chinese Michelangelo might have carved out of luminous amber jade. You expected her to have a little-girl voice, but she sounded like Lauren Bacall, this deep smoky voice coming from this tiny woman. Sloopy instantly liked her. Before I knew it, she's sitting with him in her lap, face-to-face with him and talking to him, petting him, and telling me what he's so moody about.'

Mungojerrie leaped off the sofa arm, not to the dinette but to the deck, and then instantly sprang from the deck to the seat of the chair that I had abandoned when I had moved one place around the table to keep an eye on him.

Simultaneously, as the spry cat landed on the chair, Orson and I twitched.

Mungojerrie stood with his hind paws on the chair, forepaws on the table, staring intently at my dog.

Orson issued that brief, thin, anxious sound again – and didn't take his eyes off the cat.

Unconcerned about Mungojerrie, Roosevelt said, 'Gloria told me that Sloopy was depressed mostly because I wasn't spending any time with him anymore. "You're always out with Helen," she said. "And Sloopy knows Helen doesn't like him. He thinks you're going to have to choose between him and Helen, and he knows you'll have to choose her." Now, son, I'm stunned to be hearing all this, because I was, in fact, dating a woman named Helen here in Moonlight Bay, but no way could Gloria Chan have known about her. And I *was* obsessed with Helen, spending most of my free time with her, and she didn't like dogs, which meant Sloopy always got left behind. I figured she would come around to liking Sloopy, 'cause even Hitler couldn't have helped having a soft spot in his heart for that mutt. But as it turned out, Helen was already turning as sour on me as she was on dogs, though I didn't know it yet.'

Staring intently at Orson, Mungojerrie bared his fangs.

Orson pulled back in his chair, as if afraid the cat was going to launch itself at him.

'Then Gloria tells me a few other things bothering Sloopy, one of which was this Ford pickup I'd bought. His arthritis was mild, but the poor dog couldn't get in and out of the truck as easy as he could a car, and he was scared of breaking a bone.'

Still baring his fangs, the cat hissed.

Orson flinched, and a brief keening sound of anxiety escaped him, like a burst of steam whistling out of a teakettle.

Evidently oblivious to this feline-canine drama, Roosevelt said, 'Gloria and I had lunch and spent the whole afternoon talking about her work as an animal communicator. She told me she didn't have any special talent, that it wasn't any paranormal psychic nonsense, just a sensitivity to other species that we all have but that we've repressed. She said anyone could do it, that I could do it myself if I learned the techniques and spent enough time at it, which sounded preposterous to me.'

Mungojerrie hissed again, somewhat more ferociously, and again Orson flinched, and then I swear the cat smiled or came as close to smiling as any cat can.

Stranger yet, Orson appeared to break into a wide grin – which requires no imagination to picture because all dogs are able to grin. He was panting happily, grinning at the smiling cat, as though their confrontation had been an amusing joke.

'I ask you, son, who wouldn't want to learn such a thing?' said Roosevelt.

'Who indeed?' I replied numbly.

'So Gloria taught me, and it took a frustratingly long time, months and months, but I eventually got as good at it as she was. The first big hurdle is believing you can actually do it. Putting aside your doubt, your cynicism, all your preconceived notions about what's possible and what isn't. Most of all, hardest of all, you have to stop worrying about looking foolish, 'cause fear of being humiliated really limits you. Lots of folks could never get past all that, and I'm sort of surprised that I got past it myself.'

Shifting forward in his chair, Orson leaned over the table and bared his teeth at Mungojerrie.

The cat's eyes widened with fear.

Silently but threateningly, Orson gnashed his teeth.

Wistfulness filled Roosevelt's deep voice: 'Sloopy died three years later. God, how I grieved for him. But what a fascinating and wonderful three years they were, being so in tune with him.'

Teeth still bared, Orson growled softly at Mungojerrie, and the cat whimpered. Orson growled again, the cat bawled a pitiful meow of purest fear – and then both grinned.

'What the hell is going on here?' I wondered.

Orson and Mungojerrie seemed to be perplexed by the nervous tremor in my voice.

'They're just having fun,' Roosevelt said.

I blinked at him.

In the candlelight, his face shone like darkly stained and highly polished teak.

'Having fun mocking their stereotypes,' he explained.

I couldn't believe I was hearing him correctly. Considering how completely I must be misperceiving his words, I was going to need a high-pressure hose and a plumber's drain snake to clean out my ears. 'Mocking their stereotypes?'

'Yes, that's right.' He bobbed his head in confirmation. 'Of course they wouldn't put it in those terms, but that's what they're doing. Dogs and cats are supposed to be mindlessly hostile. These guys are having fun mocking that expectation.'

Now Roosevelt was grinning at me as stupidly as the dog and the cat were grinning at me. His lips were so dark red that they were virtually black, and his teeth were as big and white as sugar cubes.

'Sir,' I told him, 'I take back what I said earlier. After careful reconsideration, I've decided you're totally awesomely crazy, whacked-out to the max.'

He bobbed his head again, continuing to grin at me. Suddenly, like the darkling beams of a black moon, lunacy rose in his face. He said, 'You wouldn't have any damn trouble believing me if I were *white*,' and as he snarled the final word, he slammed one massive fist into the table so hard that our coffee cups rattled in their saucers and nearly tipped over.

If I could have reeled backward while in a chair, I would have done so, because his accusation stunned me. I had never heard either of my parents use an ethnic slur or make a racist statement; I'd been raised without prejudice. Indeed, if there was an ultimate outcast in this world, it was *me*. I was a minority all to myself, a minority of one: 'the Nightcrawler,' as certain bullies had called me when I was a little kid, before I'd ever met Bobby and had someone who would stand beside me. Though not an albino, though my skin was pigmented, I was stranger, in many people's eyes, than Bo Bo the Dog-Faced Boy. To some I was merely unclean, tainted, as if my genetic vulnerability to ultraviolet light could be passed to others with a sneeze, but some people feared and despised me more than they would fear or despise a three-eyed Toad Man in any carnival freak show from sea to shining sea, if only because I lived next door.

Half rising out of his chair, leaning across the table, shaking a fist as big as a cantaloupe, Roosevelt Frost spoke with a hatred that astonished and sickened me: 'Racist! You mealy racist bastard!'

I could barely find my voice. 'W-When did race ever matter to me? *How* could it ever matter to me?'

He looked as if he would reach across the table, tear me out of my chair, and strangle me until my tongue unraveled to my shoes. He bared his teeth and growled at me, growled like a dog, very much like a dog, suspiciously like a dog.

'What the hell is going on here?' I asked again, but this time I found myself asking the dog and cat.

Roosevelt growled at me again, and when I only gaped stupidly at him, he said, 'Come on, son, if you can't call me a name, at least give me a little growl. Give me a little growl. Come on, son, you can do it.'

Orson and Mungojerrie watched me expectantly.

Roosevelt growled once more, giving his snarl an interrogatory inflection at the end, and finally I growled back at him. He growled louder than before, and I growled louder, too.

Smiling broadly, he said, 'Hostility. Dog and cat. Black and white. Just having a little fun mocking stereotypes.'

As Roosevelt settled into his chair again, my bewilderment began to give way to a tremulous sense of the miraculous. I was aware of a looming revelation that would rock my life forever, expose dimensions of the world that I could not now imagine; but although I strained to grasp it, this understanding remained elusive, tantalizingly just beyond the limits of my reach.

I looked at Orson. Those inky, liquid eyes.

I looked at Mungojerrie.

The cat bared his teeth at me.

Orson bared his, too.

A faint cold fear thrilled through my veins, as the Bard of Avon would put it, not because I thought the dog and cat might bite me but because of what this amused baring of teeth implied. Not just fear shivered through me, either, but also a delicious chill of wonder and giddy excitement.

Although such an act would have been out of character for him, I actually wondered if Roosevelt Frost had spiked the coffee. Not with brandy. With hallucinogenics. I was simultaneously disoriented and clearer of mind than I'd ever been, as if I were in a heightened state of consciousness.

The cat hissed at me, and I hissed at the cat.

Orson growled at me, and I growled at him.

In the most astonishing moment of my life to this point, we sat around the dinette table, grinning men and beasts, and I was reminded of those cute but corny paintings that were popular for a few years: scenes of dogs playing poker. Only one of us was a dog, of course, and none of us had cards, so the painting in my mind's eye didn't seem to apply to this situation, and yet the longer I dwelled on it, the closer I came to revelation, to epiphany, to understanding all of the ramifications of what had happened at this table in the past few minutes—

—and then my train of thought was derailed by a

beeping that arose from the electronic security equipment in the hutch beside the table.

As Roosevelt and I turned to look at the video monitor, the four views on the screen resolved into one. The automated system zoomed in on the intruder and revealed it in the eerie, enhanced light of a night-vision lens.

The visitor stood in the eddying fog at the aft end of the port finger of the boat slip in which the *Nostromo* was berthed. It looked as though it had stepped directly out of the Jurassic Period into our time: Perhaps four feet tall, pterodactyl-like, with a long wicked beak.

My mind was so full of feverish speculations related to the cat and the dog – and I was so unnerved by the other events of the night – that I was prepared to see the uncanny in the ordinary, where it did not in fact exist. My heart raced. My mouth soured and went dry. If I hadn't been frozen by shock, I would have bolted to my feet, knocking my chair over. Given another five seconds, I still might have managed to make a fool of myself, but I was saved from mortification by Roosevelt. He was either by nature more deliberative than I was or he had lived so long with the uncanny that he was quick to differentiate genuine eldritch from faux eldritch.

'Blue heron,' he said. 'Doing a little night fishing.'

I was as familiar with the great blue heron as with any bird that thrived in and around Moonlight Bay. Now that Roosevelt had named our visitor, I recognized it for what it was.

Cancel the call to Mr. Spielberg. There is no movie here.

In my defense, I would note that for all its elegant physiology and its undeniable grace, this heron has a fierce predatory aura and a cold reptilian gaze that identify it as a survivor of the age of dinosaurs.

The bird was poised at the very edge of the slip finger, peering intently into the water. Suddenly it bent forward, its head darted down, its beak stabbed into the bay, it snatched up a small fish, and it threw its head back, swallowing the catch. Some die that others may live.

Considering how hastily I had ascribed preternatural qualities to this ordinary heron, I began to wonder if I were attributing more significance to the recent episode with the cat and the dog than it deserved. Certainty gave way to doubt. The onrushing, macking wave of epiphany abruptly receded without breaking, and a churly-churly tide of confusion slopped over me again.

Drawing my attention from the video display, Roosevelt said, 'In the years since Gloria Chan taught me interspecies communication, which is basically just being a cosmically good listener, my life has been immeasurably enriched.'

'Cosmically good listener,' I repeated, wondering if Bobby would still be able to execute one of his wonderfully entertaining riffs on a nutball phrase like that. Maybe his experiences with the monkeys had left him with a permanent deficit of both sarcasm and skepticism. I hoped not. Although change might be a fundamental principle of the universe, some things were meant to be timeless, including Bobby's insistence on a life that allowed only for things as basic as sand, surf, and sun.

'I've greatly enjoyed all the animals that have come to me over the years,' Roosevelt said as drily as if he were only a veterinarian reminiscing about a career in animal medicine. He reached out to Mungojerrie and stroked his head, scratched behind his ears. The cat leaned into the big man's hand and purred. 'But these new cats I've been encountering the last two years or so . . . they open a far more exciting dimension of communication.' He turned to Orson: 'And I'm sure that you are every bit as interesting as the cats.'

Panting, tongue lolling, Orson assumed an expression of perfect doggy vacuousness.

'Listen, dog, you have never fooled me,' Roosevelt assured him. 'And after your little game with the cat a moment ago, you might as well give up the act.'

Ignoring Mungojerrie, Orson looked down at the three biscuits in front of him, on the table.

'You can pretend to be all dog appetite, pretend nothing's more important to you than those tasty treats, but I know differently.'

Gaze locked on the biscuits, Orson whined longingly.

Roosevelt said, 'It was you who brought Chris here the first time, old pup, so why did you come if not to talk?'

On Christmas Eve, more than two years ago, not a month before my mother died, Orson and I had been roaming the night, according to our usual habits. He had been only a year old then. As a puppy, he had been frisky and playful, but he had never been as hyper as most very young dogs. Nevertheless, at the age of one, he was not always able to control his curiosity and not always as well behaved as he ultimately became. We were on the outdoor basketball court behind the high school, my dog and I, and I was shooting baskets. I was telling Orson that Michael Jordan should be *damn* glad that I'd been born with XP and was unable to compete under lights, when the mutt abruptly sprinted away from me. Repeatedly I called to him, but he only paused to glance back at me, then trotted away again. By the time I realized that he was not going to return, I didn't even have time to snug the ball into the net bag that was tied to the handlebars of my bicycle. I pedaled after the fugitive fur ball, and he led me on a wild chase: street to alley to street, through Quester Park, down to the marina, and ultimately along the docks to the *Nostromo*. Although he rarely barked, that night Orson flew into a barking frenzy as he leaped off the dock directly onto the porchlike afterdeck of the cruiser, and by the time I braked to a skidding halt on the damp dock planks, Roosevelt had come out of the boat to cuddle and calm the dog.

'You want to talk,' Roosevelt told Orson now. 'You originally came here wanting to talk, but I suspect you just don't trust me.'

Orson kept his head down, his eyes on the biscuits.

'Even after two years, you half suspect maybe I'm hooked up with the people at Wyvern, and you're not going to be anything but the most doggie of dogs until you're sure of me.'

Sniffing the biscuits, once more licking the table around them, Orson seemed not even to be aware that anyone was speaking to him.

Turning his attention to me, Roosevelt said, 'These new cats, they come from Wyvern. Some are first-generation, the original escapees, and some are second-generation who were born in freedom.'

'Lab animals?' I asked.

'The first generation were, yes. They and their off-spring are different from other cats. Different in lots of ways.'

'Smarter,' I said, remembering the behavior of the monkeys.

'You know more than I thought.'

'It's been a busy night. How smart are they?'

'I don't know how to calibrate that,' he said, and I could see that he was being evasive. 'But they're smarter and different in other ways, too.'

'Why? What was done to them out there?'

'I don't know,' he said.

'How'd they get loose?'

'Your guess is as good as mine.'

'Why haven't they been rounded up?'

'Beats me.'

'No offense, sir, but you're a bad liar.'

'Always have been,' Roosevelt said with a smile. 'Listen, son, I don't know everything, either. Only what the animals tell me. But it's not good for you to know even that much. The more you know, the more you'll want to know – and you've got your dog and those friends to worry about.'

'Sounds like a threat,' I said without animosity.

When he shrugged his immense shoulders, there should have been a low thunder of displaced air. 'If you think I've been co-opted by them at Wyvern, then it's a threat. If you believe I'm your friend, then it's advice.'

Although I wanted to trust Roosevelt, I shared Orson's doubt. I found it hard to believe that this man was capable of treachery. But here on the weird side of the magical looking-glass, I had to assume that every face was a false face.

Edgy from the caffeine but with a craving for more, I took my cup to the coffeemaker and refilled it.

'What I *can* tell you,' Roosevelt said, 'is there were

supposed to be dogs out at Fort Wyvern as well as cats.'

'Orson didn't come from Wyvern.'

'Where did he come from?'

I stood with my back against the refrigerator, sipping the hot coffee. 'One of my mom's colleagues gave him to us. Their dog had a lot of puppies, and they needed to find homes for them.'

'One of your mom's colleagues at the university?'

'Yeah. A professor at Ashdon.'

Roosevelt Frost stared, unspeaking, and a terrible cloud of pity crossed his face, darkened his eyes. I felt as though he could hear the rumbling of an apocalyptic storm that eluded my ears, and that all the lightning bolts of its assault were destined to strike me.

'What?' I asked, and heard a quavery note in my voice that I did not like.

He opened his mouth to speak, thought better of it, and kept his silence. Suddenly he seemed to want to avoid my eyes. Now both he and Orson were studying the damn dog biscuits.

The cat had no interest in the biscuits. Instead, it watched me.

If another cat made of pure gold with eyes of jewels, standing silent guard for millennia in the most sacred room of a pyramid far beneath a sea of sand, had suddenly come to life before my eyes, it would not have seemed more mysterious than this cat with his steady, somehow ancient gaze.

To Roosevelt, I said, 'You don't think that's where Orson came from? Not Wyvern? Why would my mother's colleague lie to her?'

He shook his head, as if he didn't know, but he knew all right.

I was frustrated by the way that he fluctuated between making disclosures and guarding his secrets. I didn't understand his game, couldn't grasp why he was alternately forthcoming and close-mouthed.

Under the gray cat's hieroglyphic gaze, in the draft-trembled candlelight, with the humid air thickened by mystery as manifest as incense, I said, 'All you need to complete your act is a crystal ball, silver hoop earrings, a Gypsy headband, and a Romanian accent.'

I couldn't get a rise out of him.

Returning to my chair at the table, I tried to use what little I knew to encourage him to believe that I knew even more. Maybe he would open up further if he thought some of his secrets weren't so secret, after all. 'There weren't only cats and dogs in the labs at Wyvern. There were monkeys.'

Roosevelt didn't reply, and he still avoided my eyes.

'You do know about the monkeys?' I asked.

'No,' he said, but he glanced from the biscuits to the security-camera monitor in the hutch.

'I suspect it's because of the monkeys that you got a mooring outside the marina three months ago.'

Realizing that he had betrayed his knowledge by looking at the monitor when I mentioned the monkeys, he returned his attention to the dog biscuits.

Only a hundred moorings were available in the bay waters beyond the marina, and they were nearly as prized as the dock slips, though it was a necessary inconvenience to travel to and from your moored boat in another craft. Roosevelt had subleased a space from Dieter Gessel, a fisherman whose trawler was docked farther out along the northern horn with the rest of the fishing fleet but who had kept a junk dinghy at the mooring against the day when he retired and acquired a pleasure boat. Rumor was that Roosevelt was paying five times what the lease was costing Dieter.

I had never before asked him about it because it wasn't any of my business unless he brought it up first.

Now I said, 'Every night, you move the *Nostromo* from this slip out to the mooring, and you sleep there. Every night without fail – except tonight, while you're waiting here for me. Folks thought you were going to buy a second boat, something smaller and fun, just to play with. When you didn't, when you just went out there every night to bunk down, they figured – "well, okay, he's a little eccentric anyway, old Roosevelt, talking to people's pets and whatnot."'

He remained silent.

He and Orson appeared to be so intensely and equally fascinated by those three dog biscuits that I could almost believe *either* of them might abruptly break discipline and gobble up the treats.

'After tonight,' I said, 'I think I know why you go out there to sleep. You figure it's safer. Because maybe monkeys don't swim well – or at least they don't enjoy it.'

As if he hadn't heard me, he said, 'Okay, dog, even if you won't talk to me, you can have your nibbles.'

Orson risked eye-to-eye contact with his inquisitor, seeking confirmation.

'Go ahead,' Roosevelt urged.

Orson looked dubiously at me, as if asking whether I thought Roosevelt's permission was a trick.

'He's the host,' I said.

The dog snatched up the first biscuit and happily crunched it.

Finally turning his attention to me, with that unnerving

pity still in his face and eyes, Roosevelt said, 'The people behind the project at Wyvern . . . they might have had good intentions. Some of them, anyway. And I think some good things might've come from their work.' He reached out to pet the cat again, which relaxed under his hand, though it never shifted its piercing eyes from me. 'But there was also a dark side to this business. A very dark side. From what I've been told, the monkeys are only one manifestation of it.'

'Only one?'

Roosevelt held my stare in silence for a long time, long enough for Orson to eat the second biscuit, and when at last he spoke, his voice was softer than ever: 'There were more than just cats and dogs and monkeys in those labs.'

I didn't know what he meant, but I said, 'I suspect you aren't talking about guinea pigs or white mice.'

His eyes shifted away from me, and he appeared to be staring at something far beyond the cabin of this boat. 'Lot of change coming.'

'They say change is good.'

'Some is.'

As Orson ate the third biscuit, Roosevelt rose from his chair. Picking up the cat, holding it against his chest, stroking it, he seemed to be considering whether I needed to – or should – know more.

When he finally spoke, he slid once again from a revelatory mood into a secretive one. 'I'm tired, son. I should have been in bed hours ago. I was asked to warn you that your friends are in danger if you don't walk away from this, if you keep probing.'

'The cat asked you to warn me.'

'That's right.'

As I got to my feet, I became more aware of the

wallowing motion of the boat. For a moment I was stricken by a spell of vertigo, and I gripped the back of the chair to steady myself.

This physical symptom was matched by mental turmoil, as well, and my grip on reality seemed increasingly tenuous. I felt as if I were spinning along the upper rim of a whirlpool that would suck me down faster, faster, faster, until I went through the bottom of the funnel – my own version of Dorothy's tornado – and found myself not in Oz but in Waimea Bay, Hawaii, solemnly discussing the fine points of reincarnation with Pia Klick.

Aware of the extreme flakiness of the question, I nevertheless asked, 'And the cat, Mungojerrie . . . he isn't in league with these people at Wyvern?'

'He escaped from them.'

Licking his chops to be sure that no precious biscuit crumbs adhered to his lips or to the fur around his muzzle, Orson got off the dinette chair and came to my side.

To Roosevelt, I said, 'Earlier tonight, I heard the Wyvern project described in apocalyptic terms . . . the end of the world.'

'The world as we know it.'

'You actually believe that?'

'It could play out that way, yes. But maybe when it all shakes down, there'll be more good changes than bad. The end of the world *as we know it* isn't necessarily the same as the end of the world.'

'Tell that to the dinosaurs after the comet impact.'

'I have my jumpy moments,' he admitted.

'If you're frightened enough to go to the mooring to sleep every night and if you really believe that what they were doing at Wyvern was so dangerous, why don't you get out of Moonlight Bay?'

'I've considered it. But my businesses are here. My life's here. Besides, I wouldn't be escaping. I'd only be buying a little time. Ultimately, nowhere is safe.'

'That's a bleak assessment.'

'I guess so.'

'Yet you don't seem depressed.'

Carrying the cat, Roosevelt led us out of the main cabin and through the aft stateroom. 'I've always been able to handle whatever the world threw at me, son, both the ups and the downs, as long as it was at least *interesting*. I've had the blessing of a full and varied life, and the only thing I really dread is boredom.' We stepped out of the boat onto the afterdeck, into the clammy embrace of the fog. 'Things are liable to get downright hairy here in the Jewel of the Central Coast, but whichever way it goes, for damn sure it won't be boring.'

Roosevelt had more in common with Bobby Halloway than I would have thought.

'Well, sir . . . thank you for the advice. I guess.' I sat on the coaming and swung off the boat to the dock a couple of feet below, and Orson leaped down to my side.

The big blue heron had departed earlier. The fog eddied around me, the black water purled under the boat slip, and all else was as still as a dream of death.

I had taken only two steps toward the gangway when Roosevelt said, 'Son?'

I stopped and looked back.

'The safety of your friends really is at stake here. But your happiness is on the line, too. Believe me, you don't want to know more about this. You've got enough problems . . . the way you have to live.'

'I don't have any problems,' I assured him. 'Just

different advantages and disadvantages from most people.'

His skin was so black that he might have been a mirage in the fog, a trick of shadow. The cat, which he held, was invisible but for its eyes, which appeared to be disembodied, mysterious, bright-green orbs floating in midair. 'Just different advantages . . . do you really believe that?' he asked.

'Yes, sir,' I said, although I wasn't sure whether I believed it because it was, in fact, the truth or because I had spent most of my life convincing myself that it was true. A lot of the time, reality is what you make it.

'I'll tell you one more thing,' he said. 'One more thing because it might convince you to let this go and get on with life.'

I waited.

At last, with sorrow in his voice, he said, 'The reason most of them don't want to harm you, the reason they'd rather try to control you by killing your friends, the reason most of them *revere* you is because of who your mother was.'

Fear, as death-white and cold as a Jerusalem cricket, crawled up the small of my back, and for a moment my lungs constricted so that I couldn't draw a breath – although I didn't know why Roosevelt's enigmatic statement should affect me so instantly and profoundly. Maybe I understood more than I thought I did. Maybe the truth was already waiting to be acknowledged in the canyons of the subconscious – or in the abyss of the heart.

When I could breathe, I said, 'What do you mean?'

'If you think about it for a while,' he said, 'really think about it, maybe you'll realize that you have nothing to gain by pursuing this thing – and so much to lose. Knowledge seldom brings us peace, son. A hundred years ago, we didn't know about atomic structure or DNA or black holes – but are we any happier and more fulfilled now than people were then?'

As he spoke that final word, fog filled the space where he had stood on the afterdeck. A cabin door closed softly; with a louder sound, a deadbolt was engaged.

24

Around the creaking *Nostromo*, the fog seethed in slow motion. Nightmare creatures appeared to form out of the mist, loom, and then dissolve.

Inspired by Roosevelt Frost's final revelation, more fearful things than fog monsters took shape from the mists in my mind, but I was reluctant to concentrate on them and thereby impart to them a greater solidity. Maybe he was right. If I learned everything that I wanted to know, I might wish that I had remained ignorant of the truth.

Bobby says that truth is sweet but dangerous. He says that people couldn't bear to go on living if they faced every cold truth about themselves.

In that case, I tell him, he'll never be suicidal.

As Orson preceded me up the gangway from the slip, I considered my options, trying to decide where to go and what to do next. There was a siren singing, and only I could hear her dangerous song; though I was afraid of wrecking on the rocks of truth, this hypnotic melody was one I couldn't resist.

When we reached the top of the gangway, I said to my dog, 'So . . . any time you want to start explaining all this to me, I'm ready to listen.'

Even if Orson could have answered me, he didn't seem to be in a communicative mood.

My bicycle was still leaning against the dock railing. The rubber handlebar grips were cold and slick, wet with condensation.

Behind us, the *Nostromo*'s engines turned over. When I glanced back, I saw the running lights of the boat diffused and ringed by halos in the fog.

I couldn't make out Roosevelt at the upper helm station, but I knew he was there. Though only a few hours of darkness remained, he was moving his boat out to his mooring even in this low visibility.

As I walked my bike shoreward through the marina, among the gently rocking boats, I looked back a couple of times, to see if I could spot Mungojerrie in the dim wash of the dock lights. If he was following us, he was being discreet. I suspected that the cat was still aboard the *Nostromo*.

. . . the reason most of them revere you is because of who your mother was.

When we turned right onto the main dock pier and headed toward the entrance to the marina, a foul odor rose off the water. Evidently the tide had washed a dead squid or a man-of-war or a fish in among the pilings. The rotting corpse must have gotten hung up above the water line on one of the jagged masses of barnacles that encrusted the concrete caissons. The stench became so ripe that the humid air seemed to be not merely scented but flavored with it, as repulsive as a broth from the devil's dinner table. I held my breath and kept my mouth tightly closed against the disgusting taste that had been imparted to the fog.

The grumble of the *Nostromo*'s engines had faded as it cruised out to the mooring. Now the muffled rhythmic thumping that came across the water sounded not like engine noise at all but like the ominous beat of a leviathan's heart, as though a monster of the deep might surface in the marina, sinking all the boats, battering apart the dock, and plunging us into a cold wet grave.

When we reached the midpoint of the main pier, I looked back and saw neither the cat nor a more fearsome pursuer.

Nevertheless, I said to Orson, 'Damn, but it's starting to *feel* like the end of the world.'

He chuffed in agreement as we left the stench of death behind us and walked toward the glow of the quaint ship lanterns that were mounted on massive teak pilasters at the main pier entrance.

Moving out of an almost liquid gloom beside the marina office, Lewis Stevenson, the chief of police, still in uniform as I had seen him earlier in the night, crossed into the light. He said, 'I'm in a mood here.'

For an instant, as he stepped from the shadows, something about him was so peculiar that a chill bored like a corkscrew in my spine. Whatever I had seen – or thought that I'd seen – passed in a blink, however, and I found myself shivering and keenly disturbed, overcome by an extraordinary perception of being in the presence of something unearthly and malevolent, without being able to identify the precise cause of this feeling.

Chief Stevenson was holding a formidable-looking pistol in his right hand. Although he was not in a shooting stance, his grip on the weapon wasn't casual. The muzzle was trained on Orson, who was two steps ahead of me, standing in the outer arc of the lantern light, while I remained in shadows.

'You want to guess what mood I'm in?' Stevenson asked, stopping no more than ten feet from us.

'Not good,' I ventured.

'I'm in a mood not to be screwed with.'

The chief didn't sound like himself. His voice was familiar, the timbre and the accent unchanged, but there was a hard note when before there had been quiet authority. Usually his speech flowed like a stream, and you found yourself almost floating on it, calm and warm and assured; but now the flow was fast and turbulent, cold and stinging.

'I don't feel good,' he said. 'I don't feel good at all. In fact, I feel like shit, and I don't have much patience for anything that makes me feel even worse. You understand me?'

Although I didn't understand him entirely, I nodded and said, 'Yes. Yes, sir, I understand.'

Orson was as still as cast iron, and his eyes never left the muzzle of the chief's pistol.

I was acutely aware that the marina was a desolate place at this hour. The office and the fueling station were not staffed after six o'clock. Only five boat owners, other than Roosevelt Frost, lived aboard their vessels, and they were no doubt sound asleep. The docks were no less lonely than the granite rows of eternal berths in St. Bernadette's cemetery.

The fog muffled our voices. No one was likely to hear our conversation and be drawn to it.

Keeping his attention on Orson but addressing me, Stevenson said, 'I can't get what I need, because I don't even know what it *is* I need. Isn't that a bitch?'

I sensed that this was a man at risk of coming apart, perilously holding himself together. He had lost his noble aspect. Even his handsomeness was sliding away as the planes of his face were pulled toward a new configuration by what seemed to be rage and an equally powerful anxiety.

'You ever feel this emptiness, Snow? You ever feel an emptiness so bad, and you've got to fill it or you'll die, but you don't know where the emptiness is or what in the name of God you're supposed to fill it *with*?'

Now I didn't understand him *at all*, but I didn't think that he was in a mood to explain himself, so I looked solemn and nodded sympathetically. 'Yes, sir. I know the feeling.'

His brow and cheeks were moist but not from the clammy air; he glistened with greasy sweat. His face was so supernaturally white that the mist seemed to pour from him, boiling coldly off his skin, as though he were the father of all fog. 'Comes on you bad at night,' he said.

'Yes, sir.'

'Comes on you anytime, but worse at night.' His face twisted with what might have been disgust. 'What kind of damn dog is this, anyway?'

His gun arm stiffened, and I thought I saw his finger tighten on the trigger.

Orson bared his teeth but neither moved nor made a sound.

I quickly said, 'He's just a Labrador mix. He's a good dog, wouldn't harm a cat.'

His anger swelling for no apparent reason, Stevenson said, 'Just a Labrador mix, huh? The hell he is. Nothing's *just* anything. Not here. Not now. Not anymore.'

I considered reaching for the Glock in my jacket. I was holding my bike with my left hand. My right hand was free, and the pistol was in my right-hand pocket.

Even as distraught as Stevenson was, however, he was nonetheless a cop, and he was sure to respond with deadly professionalism to any threatening move that I made. I didn't put much faith in Roosevelt's strange assurance that I was revered. Even if I let the bicycle fall over to distract him, Stevenson would shoot me dead before the Glock cleared my pocket.

Besides, I wasn't going to pull a gun on the chief of police unless I had no choice but to use it. And if I shot him, that would be the end of my life, a thwarting of the sun.

Abruptly Stevenson snapped his head up, looking away from Orson. He drew a deep breath, then several that were as quick and shallow as those of a hound following the spoor of its quarry. 'What's that?'

He had a keener sense of smell than I did, because I only now realized that an almost imperceptible breeze had brought us a faint hint of the stench from the decomposing sea creature back under the main pier.

Although Stevenson was already acting strangely enough to make my scalp crinkle into faux corduroy, he grew markedly stranger. He tensed, hunched his shoulders, stretched his neck, and raised his face to the fog, as though savoring the putrescent scent. His eyes were feverish in his pale face, and he spoke not with the measured inquisitiveness of a cop but with an eager, nervous curiosity that seemed perverse: 'What is that? You smell that? Something dead, isn't it?'

'Something back under the pier,' I confirmed. 'Some kind of fish, I guess.'

'Dead. Dead and rotting. Something . . . It's got an edge to it, doesn't it?' He seemed about to lick his lips. 'Yeah. Yeah. Sure does have an interesting edge to it.'

Either he heard the eerie current crackling through his voice or he sensed my alarm at his eccentric behavior, because he glanced worriedly at me and struggled to compose himself. It *was* a struggle. He was teetering on a crumbling ledge of emotion.

Finally the chief found his normal voice – or something that approximated it. 'I need to talk to you, reach an understanding. Now. Tonight. Why don't you come with me, Snow.'

'Come where?'

'My patrol car's out front.'

'But my bicycle—'

'I'm not arresting you. Just a quick chat. Let's make sure we understand each other.'

The last thing that I wanted to do was get in a patrol car with Stevenson. If I refused, however, he might make his invitation more formal by taking me into custody.

Then, if I tried to resist arrest, if I climbed on my bicycle and pumped the pedals hard enough to make the crank axle smoke – where would I go? With dawn only a few hours away, I had no time to flee as far as the next town on this lonely stretch of coast. Even if I had ample time, XP limited my world to the boundaries of Moonlight Bay, where I could return home by sunrise or find an understanding friend to take me in and give me darkness.

'I'm in a mood here,' Lewis Stevenson said again, through half-clenched teeth, the hardness returning to his voice. 'I'm in a real mood. You coming with me?'

'Yes, sir. I'm cool with that.'

Motioning with his pistol, he indicated that Orson and I were to precede him.

I walked my bike toward the end of the entrance pier, loath to have the chief behind me with the gun. I didn't need to be an animal communicator to know that Orson was nervous, too.

The pier planks ended in a concrete sidewalk flanked by flower beds full of ice plant, the blooms of which open wide in sunshine and close at night. In the low landscape lighting, snails were crossing the walkway, antennae glistening, leaving silvery trails of slime, some creeping from the right-hand bed of ice plant to the identical bed on the left, others laboriously making their way in the opposite direction, as if these humble mollusks shared humanity's restlessness and dissatisfaction with the terms of existence.

I weaved with the bike to avoid the snails, and although Orson sniffed them in passing, he stepped over them.

From behind us rose the crunching of crushed shells, the squish of jellied bodies tramped underfoot. Stevenson was stepping not only on those snails directly in his path but on every hapless gastropod in sight. Some were dispatched with a quick snap, but he *stomped* on others, came down on them with such force that the slap of shoe sole against concrete rang like a hammer strike.

I didn't turn to look.

I was afraid of seeing the cruel glee that I remembered too well from the faces of the young bullies who had tormented me throughout childhood, before I'd been wise enough and big enough to fight back. Although that expression was unnerving when a child wore it, the same look – the beady eyes that seemed perfectly reptilian even without elliptical pupils, the hate-reddened cheeks, the bloodless lips drawn back in a sneer from spittle-shined teeth – would be immeasurably more disturbing on the face of an adult, especially when the adult had a gun in his hand and wore a badge.

Stevenson's black-and-white was parked at a red curb thirty feet to the left of the marina entrance, beyond the reach of the landscape lights, in deep night shade under the spreading limbs of an enormous Indian laurel.

I leaned my bike against the trunk of the tree, on which the fog hung like Spanish moss. At last I turned warily to the chief as he opened the back door on the passenger side of the patrol car.

Even in the murk, I recognized the expression on his face that I had dreaded seeing: the hatred, the irrational but unassuageable anger that makes some human beings more deadly than any other beast on the planet.

Never before had Stevenson disclosed this malevolent aspect of himself. He hadn't seemed capable of unkindness let alone senseless hatred. If suddenly he had revealed that he wasn't the real Lewis Stevenson but an alien life-form mimicking the chief, I would have believed him.

Gesturing with the gun, Stevenson spoke to Orson: 'Get in the car, fella.'

'He'll be all right out here,' I said.

'Get in,' he urged the dog.

Orson peered suspiciously at the open car door and whined with distrust.

'He'll wait here,' I said. 'He never runs off.'

'I want him in the car,' Stevenson said icily. 'There's a leash law in this town, Snow. We've never enforced it with you. We always turn our heads, pretend not to see, because of . . . because a dog is exempted if he belongs to a disabled person.'

I didn't antagonize Stevenson by rejecting the term *disabled*. Anyway, I was interested less in that one word than in the six words I was sure he had almost said before catching himself: *because of who your mother was.*

'But this time,' he said, 'I'm not going to sit here while the damn dog trots around loose, crapping on the sidewalk, flaunting that he isn't on a leash.'

Although I could have noted the contradiction between the fact that the dog of a disabled person was exempt from the leash law and the assertion that Orson was flaunting his leashlessness, I remained silent. I couldn't win any argument with Stevenson while he was in this hostile state.

'If he won't get in the car when I tell him to,' Stevenson said, '*you* make him get in.'

I hesitated, searching for a credible alternative to meek cooperation. Second by second, our situation seemed more perilous. I'd felt safer than this when we had been in the blinding fog on the peninsula, stalked by the troop.

'*Get the goddamn dog in the goddamn car now!*' Stevenson ordered, and the venom in this command was so potent that he could have killed snails without stepping on them, sheerly with his voice.

Because his gun was in his hand, I remained at a disadvantage, but I took some thin comfort from the fact that he apparently didn't know that I was armed. For the time being, I had no choice but to cooperate.

'In the car, pal,' I told Orson, trying not to sound fearful, trying not to let my hammering heart pound a tremor into my voice.

Reluctantly the dog obeyed.

Lewis Stevenson slammed the rear door and then opened the front. 'Now you, Snow.'

I settled into the passenger seat while Stevenson

walked around the black-and-white to the driver's side and got in behind the wheel. He pulled his door shut and told me to close mine, which I had hoped to avoid doing.

Usually I don't suffer from claustrophobia in tight spaces, but no coffin could have been more cramped than this patrol car. The fog pressing at the windows was as psychologically suffocating as a dream about premature burial.

The interior of the car seemed chillier and damper than the night outside. Stevenson started the engine in order to be able to switch on the heater.

The police radio crackled, and a dispatcher's static-filled voice croaked like frog song. Stevenson clicked it off.

Orson stood on the floor in front of the backseat, forepaws on the steel grid that separated him from us, peering worriedly through that security barrier. When the chief pressed a console button with the barrel of his gun, the power locks on the rear doors engaged with a hard sound no less final than the *thunk* of a guillotine blade.

I had hoped that Stevenson would holster his pistol when he got into the car, but he kept a grip on it. He rested the weapon on his leg, the muzzle pointed at the dashboard. In the dim green light from the instrument panel, I thought I saw that his forefinger was now curled around the trigger guard rather than around the trigger itself, but this didn't lessen his advantage to any appreciable degree.

For a moment he lowered his head and closed his eyes, as though praying or gathering his thoughts.

Fog condensed on the Indian laurel, and drops of water dripped from the points of the leaves, snapping with an unrhythmical *ponk-pank-ping* against the roof and hood of the car.

Casually, quietly, I tucked both hands into my jacket pockets. I closed my right hand around the Glock.

I told myself that, because of my overripe imagination, I was exaggerating the threat. Stevenson was in a foul mood, yes, and from what I had seen behind the police station, I knew that he was not the righteous arm of justice that he had long pretended to be. But this didn't mean that he had any violent intentions. He might, indeed, want only to talk, and having said his piece, he might turn us loose unharmed.

When at last Stevenson raised his head, his eyes were servings of bitter brew in cups of bone. As his gaze flowed to me, I was again chilled by an impression of inhuman malevolence, as I had been when he'd first stepped out of the gloom beside the marina office, but this time I knew why my harp-string nerves thrummed with fear. Briefly, at a certain angle, his liquid stare rippled with a yellow luminance similar to the eyeshine that many animals exhibit at night, a cold and mysterious inner light like nothing I had ever seen before in the eyes of man or woman.

25

The electric and electrifying radiance passed through Chief Stevenson's eyes so fleetingly, as he turned to face me, that on any night before this one, I might have dismissed the phenomenon as merely a queer reflection of the instrument-panel lights. But since sundown, I had seen monkeys that were not merely monkeys, a cat that was somehow more than a cat, and I had waded through mysteries that flowed like rivers along the streets of Moonlight Bay, and I had learned to expect significance in the seemingly insignificant.

His eyes were inky again, glimmerless. The anger in his voice was now an undertow, while the surface current was gray despair and grief. 'It's all changed now, all changed, and no going back.'

'What's changed?'

'I'm not who I used to be. I can hardly remember what I used to be like, the kind of man I was. It's lost.'

I felt that he was talking as much to himself as to me, grieving aloud for this loss of self that he imagined.

'I don't have anything to lose. Everything that matters has been taken from me. I'm a dead man walking, Snow. That's all I am. Can you imagine how that feels?'

'No.'

'Because even you, with your shitty life, hiding from the day, coming out only at night like some slug crawling out from under a rock – even you have reasons to live.'

Although the chief of police was an elected official in our town, Lewis Stevenson didn't seem to be concerned about winning my vote.

I wanted to tell him to go copulate with himself. But there is a difference between showing no fear and begging for a bullet in the head.

As he turned his face away from me to gaze at the white sludge of fog sliding thickly across the windshield, that cold fire throbbed in his eyes again, a briefer and fainter flicker than before yet more disturbing because it could no longer be dismissed as imaginary.

Lowering his voice as though afraid of being overheard, he said, 'I have terrible nightmares, terrible, full of sex and blood.'

I had not known exactly what to expect from this conversation; but revelations of personal torment would not have been high on my list of probable subjects.

'They started well over a year ago,' he continued. 'At first they came only once a week, but then with increasing frequency. And at the start, for a while, the women in the nightmares were no one I'd ever seen in life, just pure fantasy figures. They were like those dreams you have during puberty, silken girls so ripe and eager to surrender . . . except that in these dreams, I didn't just have sex with them . . .'

His thoughts seemed to drift with the bilious fog into darker territory.

Only his profile was presented to me, dimly lit and glistening with sour sweat, yet I glimpsed a savagery that made me hope that he would not favor me with a full-face view.

Lowering his voice further still, he said, 'In these dreams, I beat them, too, punch them in the face, punch and punch and *punch* them until there's nothing left of their faces, choke them until their tongues swell out of their mouths . . .'

As he had begun to describe his nightmares, his voice had been marked by dread. In addition to this fear, an unmistakable perverse excitement now rose in him, evident not only in his husky voice but also in the new tension that gripped his body.

'. . . and when they cry out in pain, I love their screams, the agony on their faces, the sight of their blood. So delicious. So *exciting*. I wake shivering with pleasure, swollen with need. And sometimes . . . though I'm fifty-two, for God's sake, I climax in my sleep or just as I'm waking.'

Orson dropped away from the security grille and retreated to the back seat.

I wished that I, too, could put more distance between myself and Lewis Stevenson. The cramped patrol car seemed to close around us, as though it were being squashed in one of those salvage-yard hydraulic crushers.

'Then Louisa, my wife, began to appear in the dreams . . . and my two . . . my two daughters. Janine. Kyra. They are afraid of me in these dreams, and I give them every reason to be, because their terror excites me. I'm disgusted but . . . but also thrilled at what I'm doing with them, to them . . .'

The anger, the despair, and the perverse excitement were still to be detected in his voice, in his slow heavy breathing, in the hunch of his shoulders – and in the subtle but ghastly reconstruction of his face, obvious even in profile. But among those powerfully conflicted desires that were at war for control of his mind, there was also a desperate hope that he could avoid plunging into the abyss of madness and savagery on the brink of which he appeared to be so precariously balanced, and this hope was clearly expressed in the anguish that now became as evident in his voice and demeanor as were his anger, despair, and depraved need.

'The nightmares got so bad, the things I did in them so sick and filthy, so repulsive, that I was afraid to go to sleep. I'd stay awake until I was exhausted, until no amount of caffeine could keep me on my feet, until even an ice cube held against the back of my neck couldn't stop my burning eyes from slipping shut. Then when I finally slept, my dreams would be more intense than ever, as though exhaustion drove me into sounder sleep, into a deeper darkness inside me where worse monsters lived. Rutting and slaughter, ceaseless and vivid, the first dreams I ever had in color, such *intense* colors, and sounds as well, their pleading voices and my pitiless replies, their screams and weeping, their convulsions and death rattles when I tore their throats out with my teeth even as I thrust into them.'

Lewis Stevenson seemed to see these hideous images where I could see only the lazily churning fog, as if the windshield before him were a screen on which his demented fantasies were projected.

'And after a while . . . I no longer fought sleep. For a time, I just endured it. Then somewhere along the way – I can't remember the precise night – the dreams ceased to hold any terror for me and became *purely* enjoyable, when previously they inspired far more guilt than pleasure. Although at first I couldn't admit it to myself, I began to look forward to bedtime. These women were so precious to me when I was awake, but when I slept . . . then . . . *then* I thrilled at the chance to debase them, humiliate them, torture them in the most imaginative ways. I no longer woke in fear from these nightmares . . . but in a strange bliss. And I'd lie in the dark, wondering how much better it might feel to commit these atrocities for real than just to dream of them. Merely *thinking* about acting out my dreams, I became aware of this awesome *power* flowing into me, and I felt so free, utterly free, as never before. In fact, it seemed as if I'd lived my life in huge iron manacles, wrapped in chains, weighted down by blocks of stone. It seemed that giving in to these desires wouldn't be criminal, would have no moral dimension whatsoever. Neither right nor wrong. Neither good nor bad. But tremendously *liberating*.'

Either the air in the patrol car was growing increasingly stale or I was sickened by the thought of inhaling the same vapors that the chief exhaled: I'm not sure which. My mouth filled with a metallic taste, as if I had been sucking on a penny, my stomach cramped around a lump of something as cold as arctic rock, and my heart was sheathed in ice.

I couldn't understand why Stevenson would lay bare his troubled soul to me, but I had a premonition that these confessions were only a prelude to a hateful revelation that I would wish I'd never heard. I wanted to silence him before he sprang that ultimate secret on me, but I could see that he was forcefully compelled to relate these horrific fantasies – perhaps because I was the first to whom he had dared to unburden himself. There was no way to shut him up short of killing him.

'Lately,' he continued in a hungry whisper that would haunt *my* sleep for the rest of my life, 'these dreams all focus on my granddaughter. Brandy. She's ten. A pretty girl. A very pretty girl. So slim and pretty. The things I do to her in dreams. Ah, the things I do. You can't imagine such merciless brutality. Such exquisitely vicious *inventiveness*. And when I wake up, I'm beyond exhilaration. Transcendent. In a *rapture*. I lie in bed, beside my wife, who sleeps on without guessing what strange thoughts obsess me, who can't possibly ever know, and I *thrum* with power, with the awareness that absolute freedom is available to me any time I want to seize it. Any time. Next week. Tomorrow. *Now*.'

Overhead, the silent laurel spoke as, in quick succession, at least a double score of pointed green tongues trembled with too great a weight of condensed fog. Each loosed its single watery note, and I twitched at the sudden rataplan of fat droplets beating on the car, half surprised that what streamed down the windshield and across the hood was not blood.

In my jacket pocket, I closed my right hand more tightly around the Glock. After what Stevenson had told me, I couldn't imagine any circumstances in which he could allow me to leave this car alive. I shifted slightly in my seat, the first of several small moves that shouldn't make him suspicious but would put me in a position to shoot him through my jacket, without having to draw the pistol from the pocket.

'Last week,' the chief whispered, 'Kyra and Brandy came over for dinner with us, and I had trouble taking my eyes off the girl. When I looked at her, in my mind's eye she was naked, as she is in the dreams. So slim. So fragile. Vulnerable. I became aroused by her vulnerability, by her tenderness, her weakness, and had to hide my condition from Kyra and Brandy. From Louisa. I wanted . . . wanted to . . . *needed* to . . .'

His sudden sobbing startled me: Waves of grief and despair swept through him once more, as they had washed through him when first he had begun to speak. His eerie needfulness, his obscene hunger, was drowned in this tide of misery and self-hatred.

'A part of me wants to kill myself,' Stevenson said, 'but only the smaller part, the smaller and weaker part, the fragment that's left of the man I used to be. This predator I've become will never kill himself. Never. He's too *alive*.'

His left hand, clutched into a fist, rose to his open mouth, and he crammed it between his teeth, biting so fiercely on his clenched fingers that I wouldn't have been surprised if he had drawn his own blood; he was biting and choking back the most wretched sobs that I'd ever heard.

In this new person that Lewis Stevenson seemed to have become, there was none of the calm and steady bearing that had always made him such a credible figure of authority and justice. At least not tonight, not in this bleak mood that plagued him. Raw emotion appeared always to be flowing through him, one current or another, without any intervals of tranquil water, the tide always running, battering.

My fear of him subsided to make room for pity. I almost reached out to put a comforting hand on his shoulder, but I restrained myself because I sensed that the monster I'd been listening to a moment ago had not been vanquished or even chained.

Lowering his fist from his mouth, turning his head toward me, Stevenson revealed a face wrenched by such abysmal torment, by such agony of the heart and mind, that I had to look away.

He looked away, too, facing the windshield again, and as the laurel shed the scattershot distillate of fog, his sobs faded until he could speak. 'Since last week, I've been making excuses to visit Kyra, to be around Brandy.' A tremor distorted his words at first, but it quickly faded, replaced by the hungry voice of the soulless troll. 'And sometimes, late at night, when this damn mood hits me, when I get to feeling so cold and hollow inside that I want to scream and never stop screaming, I think the way to fill the emptiness, the only way to stop this awful gnawing in my gut . . . is to do what makes me happy in the dreams. And I'm going to do it, too. Sooner or later, I'm going to do it. Sooner than later.' The tide of emotion had now turned entirely from guilt and anguish to a quiet but demonic glee. 'I'm going to do it and do it. I've been looking for girls Brandy's age, just nine or ten years old, as slim as she is, as pretty as she is. It'll be safer to start with someone who has no connection to me. Safer but no less satisfying. It's going to feel good. It's going to feel *so* good, the power, the destruction, throwing off all the shackles they make you live with, tearing down the walls, being totally free, totally free at last. I'm going to bite her, this girl, when I get her alone, I'm going to bite her and bite her. In the dreams I lick their skin, and it's got a salty taste, and then I bite them, and I can feel their screams vibrating in my teeth.'

Even in the dim light, I could see the manic pulse throbbing in his temples. His jaw muscles bulged, and the corner of his mouth twitched with excitement. He seemed to be more animal than human – or something less than both.

My hand clutched the Glock so ferociously that my arm ached all the way to my shoulder. Abruptly I realized that my finger had tightened on the trigger and that I was in danger of unintentionally squeezing off a shot, though I had not yet fully adjusted my position to bring the muzzle toward Stevenson. With considerable effort, I managed to ease off the trigger.

'What made you like this?' I asked.

As he turned his head to me, the transient luminosity shimmered through his eyes again. His gaze, when the eyeshine passed, was dark and murderous. 'A little delivery boy,' he said cryptically. 'Just a little delivery boy that wouldn't die.'

'Why tell me about these dreams, about what you're going to do to some girl?'

'Because, you damn freak, I've got to give you an ultimatum, and I want you to understand how serious it is, how dangerous I am, how little I have to lose and how much I'll enjoy gutting you if it comes to that. There's others who won't touch you—'

'Because of who my mother was.'

'So you know that much already?'

'But I don't know what it means. Who *was* my mother in all this?'

Instead of answering, Stevenson said, 'There's others who won't touch you and who don't want me to touch you, either. But if I have to, I will. You keep pushing your nose into this, and I'll smash your skull open, scoop your brain out, and toss it in the bay for fish food. Think I won't?'

'I believe you,' I said sincerely.

'With the book you wrote being a best-seller, you can maybe get certain media types to listen to you. If you make any calls trying to stir up trouble, I'll get my hands on that deejay bitch first. I'll turn her inside out in more ways than one.'

His reference to Sasha infuriated me, but it also scared me so effectively that I held my silence.

Now it was clear that Roosevelt Frost's warning had indeed been only advice. *This* was the threat that Roosevelt, claiming to speak for the cat, had warned me to expect.

The pallor was gone from Stevenson's face, and he was flushed with color – as though, the moment that he had decided to surrender to his psychotic desires, the cold and empty spaces within him had been filled with fire.

He reached to the dashboard controls and he switched off the car heater.

Nothing was surer than that he would abduct a little girl before the next sunset.

I found the confidence to push for answers only because I had shifted sufficiently in my seat to bring the pocketed pistol to bear on him. 'Where's my father's body?'

'At Fort Wyvern. There has to be an autopsy.'

'Why?'

'You don't need to know. But to put an end to this stupid little crusade of yours, I'll at least tell you it *was* cancer that killed him. Cancer of a kind. There's no one for you to get even with, the way you were talking to Angela Ferryman.'

'Why should I believe you?'

'Because I could kill you as easily as give you an answer – so why would I lie?'

'What's happening in Moonlight Bay?'

The chief cracked a grin the likes of which had seldom been seen beyond the walls of an asylum. As if the prospect of catastrophe was nourishment to him, he sat up straighter and appeared to fatten as he said, 'This whole town's on a roller coaster straight to Hell, and it's going to be an *incredible* ride.'

'That's no answer.'

'It's all you'll get.'

'Who killed my mother?'

'It was an accident.'

'I thought so until tonight.'

His wicked grin, thin as a razor slash, became a wider wound. 'All right. One more thing if you insist. Your mother was killed, like you suspect.'

My heart rolled, as heavy as a stone wheel. 'Who killed her?'

'She did. She killed herself. Suicide. Cranked that Saturn of hers all the way up to a hundred and ran it head-on into the bridge abutment. There wasn't any mechanical failure. The accelerator didn't stick. That was all a cover story we concocted.'

'You lying son of a bitch.'

Slowly, slowly, Stevenson licked his lips, as if he found his smile to be sweet. 'No lie, Snow. And you know what? If I'd known two years ago what was going to happen to me, how much everything was going to change, I'd have happily killed your old lady. Killed her because of the part she played in this. I'd have taken her somewhere, cut her heart out, filled the hole in her chest with salt, burned her at a stake – whatever you do to make sure a witch is dead. Because what difference is there between what she did and a witch's curse? Science or magic? What's it matter when the result is the same? But I didn't know what was coming then, and she did, so she saved me the trouble and took a high-speed header into eighteen-inch-thick concrete.'

Oily nausea welled in me, because I could hear the truth in his voice as clearly as I had ever heard it spoken. I understood only a fraction of what he was saying, yet I understood too much.

He said, 'You've got nothing to avenge, freak. No one killed your folks. In fact, one way you look at it, your old lady did them both – herself and your old man.'

I closed my eyes. I couldn't bear to look at him, not merely because he took pleasure in the fact of my mother's death but because he clearly believed – with reason? – that there had been justice in it.

'Now what I want you to do is crawl back under your rock and stay there, live the rest of your days there. We won't allow you to blow this wide open. If the world finds out what's happened here, if the knowledge goes beyond those at Wyvern and us, outsiders will quarantine the whole county. They'll seal it off, kill every last one of us, burn every building to the ground, poison every bird and every coyote and every house cat – and then probably nuke the place a few times for good measure. And that would all be for nothing, anyway, because the plague has already spread far beyond this place, to the other end of the continent and beyond. We're the original source, and the effects are more obvious here and compounding faster, but now it'll go on spreading without us. So none of us is ready to die just so the scum-sucking politicians can claim to have taken action.'

When I opened my eyes, I discovered that he'd raised his pistol and was covering me with it. The muzzle was less than two feet from my face. Now my only advantage was that he didn't know I was armed, and it was a useful advantage only if I was the first to pull the trigger.

Although I knew it was fruitless, I tried to argue with him – perhaps because arguing was the only way that I could distract myself from what he had revealed about my mother. 'Listen, for God's sake, only a few minutes ago, you said you had nothing to live for, anyway. Whatever's happened here, maybe if we get help—'

'I was in a *mood*,' he interrupted sharply. 'Weren't you listening to me, freak? I told you I was in a mood. A seriously ugly mood. But now I'm in a different mood. A better mood. I'm in the mood to be all that I can be, to embrace what I'm becoming instead of trying to resist it. Change, little buddy. That's what it's all about, you know. Change, glorious change, everything changing, always and forever, change. This new world coming – it's going to be *dazzling*.'

'But we can't—'

'If you did solve your mystery and told the world, you'd just be signing your own death warrant. You'd be killing your sexy little deejay bitch and all your friends. Now get out of the car, get on your bike, and haul your skinny ass home. Bury whatever ashes Sandy Kirk chooses to give you. Then if you can't live with not knowing more, if you maybe picked up too much curiosity from a cat bite, go down to the beach for a few days and catch some sun, work up a really *bitchin'* tan.'

I couldn't believe that he was going to let me go.

Then he said, 'The dog stays with me.'

'No.'

He gestured with his pistol. 'Out.'

'He's my dog.'

'He's nobody's dog. And this isn't a debate.'

'What do you want with him?'

'An object lesson.'

'What?'

'Gonna take him down to the municipal garage. There's a wood-chipping machine parked there, to grind up tree limbs.'

'No way.'

'I'll put a bullet in the mutt's head—'

'No.'

'—toss him in the chipper—'

'Let him out of the car now.'

'—bag the slush that comes out the other end, and drop it by your house as a reminder.'

Staring at Stevenson, I knew that he was not merely a changed man. He was not the same man at all. He was someone new. Someone who had been born out of the old Lewis Stevenson, like a butterfly from a chrysalis, except that this time the process was hideously reversed: the butterfly had gone into the chrysalis, and a worm had emerged. This nightmarish metamorphosis had been underway for some time but had culminated before my eyes. The last of the former chief was gone forever, and the person whom I now challenged eye to eye was driven entirely by need and desire, uninhibited by a conscience, no longer capable of sobbing as he had sobbed only minutes ago, and as deadly as anyone or anything on the face of the earth.

If he carried a laboratory-engineered infection that could induce such a change, would it pass now to me?

My heart fought itself, throwing hard punch after hard punch.

Although I had never imagined myself capable of killing another human being, I thought I was capable of wasting this man, because I'd be saving not only Orson but also untold girls and women whom he intended to welcome into his nightmare.

With more steel in my voice than I had expected, I said, 'Let the dog out of the car *now*.'

Incredulous, his face splitting with that familiar rattlesnake smile, he said, 'Are you forgetting who's the cop? Huh, freak? You forgetting who's got the gun?'

If I fired the Glock, I might not kill the bastard instantly, even at such close range. Even if the first round stopped his heart in an instant, he might reflexively squeeze off a round that, from a distance of less than two feet, couldn't miss me.

He broke the impasse: 'All right, okay, you want to *watch* while I do it?'

Incredibly, he half turned in his seat, thrust the barrel of his pistol through one of the inch-square gaps in the steel security grille, and fired at the dog.

The blast rocked the car, and Orson squealed.

'*No!*' I shouted.

As Stevenson jerked his gun out of the grille, I shot him. The slug punched a hole through my leather jacket and tore open his chest. He fired wildly into the ceiling. I shot him again, in the throat this time, and the window behind him shattered when the bullet passed out of the back of his neck.

26

I sat stunned, as if spellbound by a sorcerer, unable to move, unable even to blink, my heart hanging like an iron plumb bob in my chest, numb to emotion, unable to feel the pistol in my hand, unable to see anything whatsoever, not even the dead man whom I knew to be at the other end of the car seat, briefly blinded by shock, baffled and bound by blackness, temporarily deafened either by the gunfire or perhaps by a desperate desire not to hear even the inner voice of my conscience chattering about consequences.

The only sense that I still possessed was the sense of smell. The sulfurous-carbon stink of gunfire, the metallic aroma of blood, the acidic fumes of urine because Stevenson had fouled himself in his death throes, and the fragrance of my mother's rose-scented shampoo whirled over me at once, a storm of odor and malodor. All were real except the attar of roses, which was long forgotten but now summoned from memory with all its delicate nuances. *Extreme terror gives us back the gestures of our childhood,* said Chazal. The smell of that shampoo was my way, in my terror, of reaching out to my lost mother with the hope that her hand would close reassuringly around mine.

In a rush, sight, sound, and all sensation returned to

me, jolting me almost as hard as – but less mortally than – the pair of 9-millimeter bullets had jolted Lewis Stevenson. I cried out and gasped for breath.

Shaking uncontrollably, I pressed the console button that the chief had pressed earlier. The electric locks on the back doors clicked when they disengaged.

I shoved open the door at my side, clambered out of the patrol car, and yanked open the rear door, frantically calling Orson's name, wondering how I could carry him to the veterinarian's office in time to save him if he was wounded, wondering how I was going to cope if he was dead. He couldn't be dead. He was no ordinary dog: He was Orson, my dog, strange and special, companion and friend, only with me for three years but now as essential a part of my dark world as was anyone else in it.

And he *wasn't* dead. He bounded out of the car with such relief that he nearly knocked me off my feet. His piercing squeal, in the wake of the gunshot, had been an expression of terror, not pain.

I dropped to my knees on the sidewalk, let the Glock slip out of my hand, and pulled the dog into my arms. I held him fiercely, stroking his head, smoothing his black coat, reveling in his panting, in the fast thudding of his heart, in the swish of his tail, reveling even in the dampish reek of him and in the stale-cereal smell of his biscuit-scented breath.

I didn't trust myself to speak. My voice was a key-stone mortared in my throat. If I managed to break it loose, an entire dam might collapse, a babble of loss and longing might pour out of me, and all the unshed tears for my father and for Angela Ferryman might come in a flood.

I do not allow myself to cry. I would rather be a

bone worn to dry splinters by the teeth of sorrow than a sponge wrung ceaselessly in its hands.

Besides, even if I could have trusted myself to speak, words weren't important here. Though he was certainly a special dog, Orson wasn't going to join me in spirited conversation – at least not if and until I shed enough of my encumbering reason to ask Roosevelt Frost to teach me animal communication.

When I was able to let go of Orson, I retrieved the Glock and rose to my feet to survey the marina parking lot. The fog concealed most of the few cars and recreational vehicles owned by the handful of people who lived on their boats. No one was in sight, and the night remained silent except for the idling car engine.

Apparently the sound of gunfire had been largely contained in the patrol car and suppressed by the fog. The nearest houses were outside the commercial marina district, two blocks away. If anyone aboard the boats had been awakened, they'd evidently assumed that those four muffled explosions had been nothing more than an engine backfiring or dream doors slamming between the sleeping and the waking worlds.

I wasn't in immediate danger of being caught, but I couldn't cycle away and expect to escape blame and punishment. I had killed the chief of police, and though he had no longer been the man whom Moonlight Bay had long known and admired, though he had metamorphosed from a conscientious servant of the people into someone lacking all the essential elements of humanity, I couldn't *prove* that this hero had become the very monster that he was sworn to oppose.

Forensic evidence would convict me. Because of the identity of the victim, first-rate police-lab technicians from both county and state offices would become involved, and when they processed the patrol car, they wouldn't miss anything.

I could never tolerate imprisonment in some narrow candlelit cell. Though my life is limited by the presence of light, no walls must enclose me between the sunset and the dawn. None ever will. The darkness of closed spaces is profoundly different from the darkness of the night; the night has no boundaries, and it offers endless mysteries, discoveries, wonders, opportunities for joy. Night is the flag of freedom under which I live, and I will live free or die.

I was sickened by the prospect of getting back into the patrol car with the dead man long enough to wipe down everything on which I might have left a fingerprint. It would be a futile exercise, anyway, because I'd surely overlook one critical surface.

Besides, a fingerprint wasn't likely to be the only evidence that I'd left behind. Hairs. A thread from my jeans. A few tiny fibers from my Mystery Train cap. Orson's hairs in the back seat, the marks of his claws on the upholstery. And no doubt other things equally or more incriminating.

I'd been damn lucky. No one had heard the shots. But by their nature, both luck and time run out, and although my watch contained a microchip rather than a mainspring, I swore that I could hear it ticking.

Orson was nervous, too, vigorously sniffing the air for monkeys or another menace.

I hurried to the back of the patrol car and thumbed the button to release the trunk lid. It was locked, as I'd feared.

Tick, tick, tick.

Steeling myself, I returned to the open front door. I inhaled deeply, held my breath, and leaned inside.

Stevenson sat twisted in his seat, head tipped back against the door post. His mouth shaped a silent gasp of ecstasy, and his teeth were bloody, as though he had fulfilled his dreams, had been biting young girls.

Drawn by a meager cross-draft, entering through the shattered window, a scrim of fog floated toward me, as if it were steam rising off the still-warm blood that stained the front of the dead man's uniform.

I had to lean in farther than I hoped, one knee on the passenger seat, to switch off the engine.

Stevenson's black-olive eyes were open. No life or unnatural light glimmered in them, yet I half expected to see them blink, swim into focus, and fix on me.

Before the chief's clammy gray hand could reach out to clutch at me, I plucked the keys from the ignition, backed out of the car, and finally exhaled explosively.

In the trunk I found the large first-aid kit that I expected. From it, I extracted only a thick roll of gauze bandage and a pair of scissors.

While Orson patrolled the entire perimeter of the squad car, diligently sniffing the air, I unrolled the gauze, doubling it again and again into a collection of five-foot loops before snipping it with the scissors. After twisting the strands tightly together, I tied a knot at the upper end, another in the middle, and a third at the lower end. After repeating this exercise, I joined the two multiple-strand lengths together with a final knot – and had a fuse approximately ten feet long.

Tick, tick, tick.

I coiled the fuse on the sidewalk, opened the fuel port on the side of the car, and removed the tank cap. Gasoline fumes wafted out of the neck of the tank.

At the trunk again, I replaced the scissors and what remained of the roll of gauze in the first-aid kit. I closed the kit and then the trunk.

The parking lot remained deserted. The only sounds were the drops of condensation plopping from the Indian laurel onto the squad car and the soft ceaseless padding of my worried dog's paws.

Although it meant another visit with Lewis Stevenson's corpse, I returned the keys to the ignition. I'd seen a few episodes from the most popular crime series on television, and I knew how easily even fiendishly clever criminals could be tripped up by an ingenious homicide detective. Or by a best-selling, female mystery novelist who solves real murders as a hobby. Or a retired, spinster schoolteacher. All this between the opening credits and the final commercial for a vaginal deodorant. I intended to give them – both the professionals and the meddlesome hobbyists – damned little with which to work.

The dead man croaked at me as a bubble of gas broke deep in his esophagus.

'Rolaids,' I advised him, trying unsuccessfully to cheer myself.

I didn't see any of the four expended brass cartridges on the front seat. In spite of the platoons of amateur sleuths waiting to pounce, and regardless of whether having the brass might help them identify the murder weapon, I didn't have the nerve to search the floor, especially under Stevenson's legs.

Anyway, even if I found all the cartridges, there was still a bullet buried in his chest. If it wasn't too grossly distorted, this wad of lead would feature score marks that could be matched to the singularities of the bore of my pistol, but even the prospect of prison wasn't sufficient to make me take out my penknife and perform exploratory surgery to retrieve the incriminating slug.

If I'd been a different man than I am, with the stomach for such an impromptu autopsy, I wouldn't have risked it, anyway. Assuming that Stevenson's radical personality change – his newfound thirst for violence – was but one symptom of the weird disease he carried, and assuming that this illness could be spread by contact with infected tissues and bodily fluids, this type of grisly wet work was out of the question, which is also why I had been careful not to get any of his blood on me.

When the chief had been telling me about his dreams of rape and mutilation, I'd been sickened by the thought that I was breathing the same air that he'd used and exhaled. I doubted, however, that the microbe he carried was airborne. If it was *that* highly contagious, Moonlight Bay wouldn't be on a roller-coaster ride to Hell, as he had claimed the town was: It would long ago have arrived in the sulfurous Pit.

Tick, tick, tick.

According to the gauge on the instrument panel, the fuel tank was nearly full. Good. Perfect. Earlier in the night, at Angela's, the troop had taught me how to destroy evidence and possibly conceal a murder.

The fire should be so intense that the four brass cartridges, the sheet-metal body of the car, and even portions of the heavier frame would melt. Of the late Lewis Stevenson, little more than charred bones would remain, and the soft lead slug would effectively vanish. Certainly, none of my fingerprints, hairs, or clothes fibers would survive.

Another slug had passed through the chief's neck, pulverizing the window in the driver's door. It was now lying somewhere out in the parking lot or, with luck, was at rest deep in the ivy-covered slope that rose from the far end of the lot to the higher-situated Embarcadero Way, where it would be all but impossible to find.

Incriminating powder burns marred my jacket. I should have destroyed it. I couldn't. I loved that jacket. It was cool. The bullet hole in the pocket made it even cooler.

'Gotta give the spinster schoolteachers *some* chance,' I muttered as I closed the front and back doors of the car.

The brief laugh that escaped me was so humorless and bleak that it scared me almost as much as the possibility of imprisonment.

I ejected the magazine from the Glock, took one cartridge from it, which left six, and then slapped it back into the pistol.

Orson whined impatiently and picked up one end of the gauze fuse in his mouth.

'Yeah, yeah, yeah,' I said – and then gave him the double take that he deserved.

The mutt might have picked it up solely because he was curious about it, as dogs tend to be curious about everything.

Funny white coil. Like a snake, snake, snake . . . but not a snake. Interesting. Interesting. Master Snow's scent on it. Might be good to eat. Almost anything might be good to eat.

Just because Orson picked up the fuse and whined impatiently didn't necessarily mean that he understood the purpose of it or the nature of the entire scheme I'd concocted. His interest – and uncanny timing – might be purely coincidental.

Yeah. Sure. Like the purely coincidental eruption of fireworks every Independence Day.

Heart pounding, expecting to be discovered at any moment, I took the twisted gauze fuse from Orson and carefully knotted the cartridge to one end of it.

He watched intently.

'Do you approve of the knot,' I asked, 'or would you like to tie one of your own?'

At the open fuel port, I lowered the cartridge into the tank. The weight of it pulled the fuse all the way down into the reservoir. Like a wick, the highly absorbent gauze would immediately begin to soak up the gasoline.

Orson ran nervously in a circle: *Hurry, hurry. Hurry quick. Quick, quick, quick, Master Snow.*

I left almost five feet of fuse out of the tank. It hung along the side of the patrol car and trailed onto the sidewalk.

After fetching my bicycle from where I'd leaned it against the trunk of the laurel, I stooped and ignited the end of the fuse with my butane lighter. Although the exposed length of gauze was not gasoline-soaked, it burned faster than I expected. Too fast.

I climbed onto my bike and pedaled as if all of Hell's lawyers and a few demons of this earth were baying at my heels, which they probably were. With Orson sprinting at my side, I shot across the parking lot to the ramped exit drive, onto Embarcadero Way, which was deserted, and then south past the shuttered restaurants and shops that lined the bay front.

The explosion came too soon, a solid *whump* that wasn't half as loud as I'd anticipated. Around and even ahead of me, orange light bloomed; the initial flare of the blast was refracted a considerable distance by the fog.

Recklessly, I squeezed the hand brake, slid through

a hundred- and-eighty-degree turn, came to a halt with one foot on the blacktop, and looked back.

Little could be seen, no details: a core of hard yellow-white light surrounded by softer orange plumes, all softened by the deep, eddying mist.

The worst thing that I saw wasn't in the night but inside my head: Lewis Stevenson's face bubbling, smoking, streaming hot clear grease like bacon in a frying pan.

'Dear God,' I said in a voice that was so raspy and tremulous that I didn't recognize it.

Nevertheless, I could have done nothing else but light that fuse. Although the cops would know Stevenson had been killed, evidence of how it was done – and by whom – would now be obliterated.

I made the drive chain sing, leading my accomplice dog away from the harbor, through a spiraling maze of streets and alleyways, deeper into the murky, nautilus heart of Moonlight Bay. Even with the heavy Glock in one pocket, my unzipped leather jacket flapped as though it were a cape, and I fled unseen, avoiding light for more than one reason now, a shadow flowing liquidly through shadows, as though I were the fabled Phantom, escaped from the labyrinth underneath the opera house, now on wheels and hell-bent on terroriz-ing the world above ground.

Being able to entertain such a flamboyantly romantic image of myself in the immediate aftermath of murder doesn't speak well of me. In my defense, I can only say that by recasting these events as a grand adventure, with me in a dashing role, I was desperately trying to quell my fear and, more desperately still, struggling to suppress the memories of the shooting. I also needed to suppress the ghastly images of the burning body that my active imagination generated like an endless series of pop-up spooks leaping from the black walls of a funhouse.

Anyway, this shaky effort to romanticize the event lasted only until I reached the alleyway behind the Grand Theater, half a block south of Ocean Avenue, where a grime-encrusted security lamp made the fog appear to be brown and polluted. There, I swung off my bike, let it clatter to the pavement, leaned into a Dumpster, and brought up what little I had not digested of my midnight dinner with Bobby Halloway.

I had murdered a man.

Unquestionably, the victim had deserved to die. And sooner or later, relying on one excuse or another, Lewis Stevenson would have killed me, regardless of his co-conspirators' inclination to grant special dispensation to me; arguably, I acted in self-defense. And to save Orson's life.

Nevertheless, I'd killed a human being; even these qualifying circumstances didn't alter the moral essence of the act. His vacant eyes, black with death, haunted me. His mouth, open in a silent scream, his bloodied teeth. Sights are readily recalled from memory; recollections of sounds and tastes and tactile sensations are far less easily evoked; and it is virtually impossible to experience a scent merely by willing it to rise from memory. Yet earlier I'd recalled the fragrance of my mother's shampoo, and now the metallic odor of Stevenson's fresh blood lingered so pungently that it kept me hanging on the Dumpster as if I were at the railing of a yawing ship.

In fact, I was shaken not solely by having killed him but by having destroyed the corpse and all evidence with brisk efficiency and self-possession. Apparently I had a talent for the criminal life. I felt as though some of the darkness in which I'd lived for twenty-eight years had seeped into me and had coalesced in a previously unknown chamber of my heart.

Purged but feeling no better for it, I boarded the bicycle again and led Orson through a series of byways to Caldecott's Shell at the corner of San Rafael Avenue and Palm Street. The service station was closed. The only light inside came from a blue-neon wall clock in the sales office, and the only light outside was at the soft-drink vending machine.

I bought a can of Pepsi to cleanse the sour taste from my mouth. At the pump island, I opened the water faucet partway and waited while Orson drank his fill.

'What an awesomely lucky dog you are to have such a thoughtful master,' I said. 'Always tending to your thirst, your hunger, your grooming. Always ready to kill anyone who lifts a finger against you.'

The searching look that he turned on me was disconcerting even in the gloom. Then he licked my hand.

'Gratitude acknowledged,' I said.

He lapped at the running water again, finished, and shook his dripping snout.

Shutting off the faucet, I said, 'Where *did* Mom get you?'

He met my eyes again.

'What secret was my mother keeping?'

His gaze was unwavering. He knew the answers to my questions. He just wasn't talking.

27

I suppose God really might be loafing around in St. Bernadette's Church, playing air guitar with a companion band of angels, or games of mental chess. He might be there in a dimension that we can't quite see, drawing blueprints for new universes in which such problems as hatred and ignorance and cancer and athlete's-foot fungus will have been eliminated in the planning stage. He might be drifting high above the polished-oak pews, as if in a swimming pool filled with clouds of spicy incense and humble prayer instead of water, silently bumping into the columns and the corners of the cathedral ceiling as He dreamily meditates, waiting for parishioners in need to come to Him with problems to be solved.

This night, however, I felt sure God was keeping His distance from the rectory adjoining the church, which gave me the creeps when I cycled past it. The architecture of the two-story, stone house – like that of the church itself – was modified Norman, with enough of the French edge abraded away to make it fit more comfortably in the softer climate of California. The overlapping black slate tiles of the steep roof, wet with fog, were as armor-thick as the scales on the beetled brow of a dragon, and beyond the blank black eyes of window glass – including an oculus on each side of the front door – lay a soulless realm. The rectory had never appeared forbidding to me before, and I knew that I now viewed it with uneasiness only because of the scene I had witnessed between Jesse Pinn and Father Tom in the church basement.

I pedaled past both the rectory and the church, into the cemetery, under the oaks, and among the graves. Noah Joseph James, who'd had ninety-six years from birthday to deathbed, was just as silent as ever when I greeted him and parked my bike against his headstone.

I unclipped the cell phone from my belt and keyed in the number for the unlisted back line that went directly to the broadcasting booth at KBAY. I heard four rings before Sasha picked up, although no tone would have sounded in the booth; she would have been alerted to the incoming call solely by a flashing blue light on the wall that she faced when at her microphone. She answered it by pushing a hold button, and while I waited, I could hear her program over the phone line.

Orson began to sniff out squirrels again.

Shapes of fog drifted like lost spirits among the gravestones.

I listened to Sasha run a pair of twenty-second 'doughnut' spots – which are not ads for doughnuts but commercials with recorded beginnings and endings that leave a hole for live material in the center. She followed these with some way smooth historical patter about Elton John, and then brought up 'Japanese Hands' with a silky six-bar talk-over. Evidently the Chris Isaak festival had ended.

Taking me off hold, she said, 'I'm doing back-to-back tracks, so you've got just over five minutes, baby.'

'How'd you know it was me?'

'Only a handful of people have this number, and most of them are asleep at this hour. Besides, when it comes to you, I've got great intuition. The moment I saw the phone light flash, my nether parts started to tingle.'

'Your nether parts?'

'My female nether parts. Can't wait to see you, Snowman.'

'Seeing would be a good start. Listen, who else is working tonight?'

'Doogie Sassman.' He was her production engineer, operating the board.

'Just the two of you there alone?' I worried.

'You're jealous all of a sudden? How sweet. But you don't have to worry. I don't measure up to Doogie's standards.'

When Doogie wasn't parked in a command chair at an audio control panel, he spent most of his time with his massive legs wrapped around a Harley-Davidson. He was five feet eleven and weighed three hundred pounds. His wealth of untamed blond hair and his naturally wavy beard were so lush and silky that you had to resist the urge to pet him, and the colorful mural that covered virtually every inch of his arms and torso had put some tattooist's child through college. Yet Sasha wasn't entirely joking when she said that she didn't measure up to Doogie's standards. With the opposite sex, he had more bearish charm than Pooh to the tenth power. Since I'd met him six years ago, each of the four women with whom he'd enjoyed a relationship had been stunning enough to attend the Academy

Awards in blue jeans and a flannel shirt, sans makeup, and nevertheless outshine every dazzling starlet at the ceremony.

Bobby says that Doogie Sassman (pick one) has sold his soul to the devil, is the secret master of the universe, has the most astonishingly proportioned genitalia in the history of the planet, or produces sexual pheromones that are more powerful than Earth's gravity.

I was glad that Doogie was working the night shift, because I had no doubt that he was a lot tougher than any of the other engineers at KBAY.

'But I thought there'd be someone besides the two of you,' I said.

Sasha knew that I wasn't jealous of Doogie, and now she heard the concern in my voice. 'You know how things have tightened up here since Fort Wyvern closed and we lost the military audience at night. We're barely making money on this airshift even with a skeleton staff. What's wrong, Chris?'

'You keep the station doors locked, don't you?'

'Yeah. All us late-night jocks and jockettes are required to watch *Play Misty for Me* and take it to heart.'

'Even though it'll be after dawn when you leave, promise me you'll have Doogie or someone from the morning shift walk you out to your Explorer.'

'Who's on the loose – Dracula?'

'Promise me.'

'Chris, what the hell—'

'I'll tell you later. Just promise me,' I insisted.

She sighed. 'All right. But are you in some kind of trouble? Are you—'

'I'm all right, Sasha. Really. Don't worry. Just, damn it, promise me.'

'I did promise—'

'You didn't use the word.'

'Jesus. Okay, okay. I *promise*. Cross my heart and hope to die. But now I'm expecting a great story later, at least as spooky as the ones I used to hear around Girl-Scout campfires. You'll be waiting for me at home?'

'Will you wear your old Girl-Scout uniform?'

'The only part of it I could duplicate are the knee socks.'

'That's enough.'

'You're stirred by that picture, huh?'

'Vibrating.'

'You're a bad man, Christopher Snow.'

'Yeah, I'm a killer.'

'See you in a little while, killer.'

We disconnected, and I clipped the cell phone to my belt once more.

For a moment I listened to the silent cemetery. Not a single nightingale performed, and even the chimney swifts had gone to bed. No doubt the worms were awake and laboring, but they always conduct their solemn work in a respectful hush.

To Orson, I said, 'I find myself in need of some spiritual guidance. Let's pay a visit to Father Tom.'

As I crossed the cemetery on foot and went behind the church, I drew the Glock from my jacket pocket. In a town where the chief of police dreamed of beating and torturing little girls and where undertakers carried handguns, I could not assume that the priest would be armed solely with the word of God.

≈ ≈ ≈

The rectory had appeared dark from the street, but

from the backyard I saw two lighted windows in a rear room on the second floor.

After the scene that I'd witnessed in the basement of the church, from the cover of the creche, I wasn't surprised that the rector of St. Bernadette's was unable to sleep. Although it was nearly three o'clock in the morning, four hours since Jesse Pinn's visit, Father Tom was still reluctant to turn out the light.

'Make like a cat,' I whispered to Orson.

We crept up a set of stone steps and, as silently as possible, across the wooden floor of the back porch.

I tried the door, but it was locked. I had been hoping that a man of God would consider it a point of faith to trust in his Maker rather than in a deadbolt.

I didn't intend to knock or to go around to the front and ring the bell. With murder already under my belt, it seemed foolish to have qualms about engaging in criminal trespass. I hoped to avoid breaking and entering, however, because the sound of shattering glass would alert the priest.

Four double-hung windows faced onto the porch. I tried them one by one, and the third was unlocked. I had to tuck the Glock in my jacket pocket again, because the wood of the window was swollen with moisture and moved stiffly in the frame; I needed both hands to raise the lower sash, pressing first on the horizontal muntin and then hooking my fingers under the bottom rail. It slid upward with sufficient rasping and squeaking to lend atmosphere to an entire Wes Craven film.

Orson chuffed as though scornful of my skills as a lawbreaker. Everyone's a critic.

I waited until I was confident that the noise had not been heard upstairs, and I slipped through the open window into a room as black as the interior of a witch's purse.

'Come on, pal,' I whispered, for I didn't intend to leave him outside alone, without a gun of his own.

Orson sprang inside, and I slid the window shut as quietly as possible. I locked it, too. Although I didn't believe that we were currently being watched by members of the troop or by anyone else, I didn't want to make it easy for someone or something to follow us into the rectory.

A quick sweep with my penlight revealed a dining room. Two doors – one to my right, the other in the wall opposite the windows – led from the room.

Switching off the penlight, drawing the Glock again, I tried the nearer door, to the right. Beyond lay the kitchen. The radiant numerals of digital clocks on the two ovens and on the microwave cast just enough light to enable me to cross to the pivot-hinged hall door without walking into the refrigerator or the cooking island.

The hallway led past dark rooms to a foyer lit only by a single small candle. On a three-legged, half-moon table against one wall was a shrine to the Holy Mother. A votive candle in a ruby-red glass fluttered fitfully in the half-inch of wax that remained.

In this inconstant pulse of light, the face on the porcelain figure of Mary was a portrait less of beatific grace than of sorrow. She appeared to know that the resident of the rectory was, these days, more a captive of fear than a captain of faith.

With Orson at my side, I climbed the two broad flights of stairs to the second floor. The felon freak and his four-legged familiar.

The upstairs hall was in the shape of an L, with the

stairhead at the junction. The length to the left was dark. At the end of the hall directly ahead of me, a ladder had been unfolded from a ceiling trapdoor; a lamp was lit in a far corner of the attic, but only a ghostly glow stepped down the ladder treads.

Stronger light came from an open door to the right. I eased along the hall to the threshold, cautiously looked inside, and found Father Tom's starkly furnished bedroom, where a crucifix hung above the simple dark-pine bed. The priest was not here; he was evidently in the attic. The bedspread had been removed and the covers neatly folded back, but the sheets had not been disturbed.

Both nightstand lamps were lit, which made that area too bright for me, but I was more interested in the other end of the room, where a writing desk stood against the wall. Under a bronze desk lamp with a green glass shade lay an open book and a pen. The book appeared to be a journal or diary.

Behind me, Orson growled softly.

I turned and saw that he was at the bottom of the ladder, gazing up suspiciously at the dimly lighted attic beyond the open trapdoor. When he looked at me, I raised a finger to my lips, softly hushed him, and then motioned him to my side.

Instead of climbing like a circus dog to the top of the ladder, he came to me. For the time being, anyway, he still seemed to be enjoying the novelty of routine obedience.

I was certain that Father Tom would make enough noise descending from the attic to alert me long before his arrival. Nevertheless, I stationed Orson immediately inside the bedroom door, with a clear view of the ladder.

Averting my face from the light around the bed, crossing the room toward the writing desk, I glanced through the open door of the adjoining bathroom. No one was in there.

On the desk, in addition to the journal, was a decanter of what appeared to be Scotch. Beside the decanter was a double-shot glass more than half full of the golden liquid. The priest had been sipping it neat, no ice. Or maybe not just sipping.

I picked up the journal. Father Tom's handwriting was as tight and precise as machine-generated script. I stepped into the deepest shadows in the room, because my dark-adapted eyes needed little light by which to read, and I scanned the last paragraph on the page, which referred to his sister. He had broken off in mid sentence:

When the end comes, I might not be able to save myself. I know that I will not be able to save Laura, because already she is not fundamentally who she was. She is already gone. Little more than her physical shell remains – and perhaps even that is changed. Either God has somehow taken her soul home to His bosom while leaving her body inhabited by the entity into which she has evolved – or He has abandoned her. And will therefore abandon us all. I believe in the mercy of Christ. I believe in the mercy of Christ. I believe because I have nothing else to live for. And if I believe, then I must live by my faith and save whom I can. If I can't save myself or even Laura, I can at least rescue these pitiful creatures who come to me to be freed from torment and control. Jesse Pinn or those who give him orders may kill Laura, but she is not Laura anymore, Laura is long lost, and I can't

let their threats stop my work. They may kill me, but
until they do

Orson stood alertly at the open door, watching the hall.

I turned to the first page of the journal and saw that the initial entry was dated January first of this year:

Laura has been held for more than nine months now,
and I've given up all hope that I will ever see her again.
And if I were given the chance to see her again, I might
refuse, God forgive me, because I would be too afraid
of facing what she might have become. Every night, I
petition the Holy Mother to intercede with her Son to
take Laura from the suffering of this world.

For a full understanding of his sister's situation and condition, I would have to find the previous volume or volumes of this journal, but I had no time to search for them.

Something thumped in the attic. I froze, staring at the ceiling, listening. At the doorway, Orson pricked one ear.

When half a minute passed without another sound, I turned my attention once more to the journal. With a sense of time running out, I searched hurriedly through the book, reading at random.

Much of the contents concerned the priest's theological doubts and agonies. He struggled daily to remind himself – to convince himself, to plead with himself to remember – that his faith had long sustained him and that he would be utterly lost if he could not hold fast to his faith in this crisis. These sections were grim and might have been fascinating reading for the portrait of a tortured psyche that they provided, but they revealed nothing about the facts of the Wyvern conspiracy that had infected Moonlight Bay. Consequently, I skimmed through them.

I found one page and then a few more on which Father Tom's neat handwriting deteriorated into a loose scrawl. These passages were incoherent, ranting and paranoid, and I assumed that they had been composed after he'd poured down enough Scotch to start speaking with a burr.

More disturbing was an entry dated February fifth – three pages on which the elegant penmanship was obsessively precise:

I believe in the mercy of Christ. I believe in the mercy of Christ. I believe in the mercy of Christ. I believe in the mercy of Christ. I believe in the mercy of Christ . . .

Those seven words were repeated line after line, nearly two hundred times. Not a single one appeared to have been hastily penned; each sentence was so meticulously inscribed on the page that a rubber stamp and an ink pad could hardly have produced more uniform results. Scanning this entry, I could feel the desperation and terror that the priest had felt when he'd written it, as if his turbulent emotions had been infused into the paper with the ink, to radiate from it evermore.

I believe in the mercy of Christ.

I wondered what incident on the fifth of February had brought Father Tom to the edge of an emotional and spiritual abyss. What had he seen? I wondered if perhaps he had written this impassioned but despairing incantation after experiencing a nightmare similar to the dreams of rape and mutilation that had troubled – and ultimately delighted – Lewis Stevenson.

Continuing to page through the entries, I found an interesting observation dated the eleventh of February. It was buried in a long-tortured passage in which the priest argued with himself over the existence and nature of God, playing both skeptic and believer, and I would have skimmed over it if my eye had not been caught by the word *troop*.

This new troop, to whose freedom I have committed myself, gives me hope precisely because it is the antithesis of the original troop. There is no evil in these newest creatures, no thirst for violence, no rage—

A forlorn cry from the attic called my attention away from the journal. This was a wordless wail of fear and pain, so eerie *and* so pathetic that dread reverberated like a gong note through my mind simultaneously with a chord of sympathy. The voice sounded like that of a child, perhaps three or four years old, lost and afraid and in extreme distress.

Orson was so affected by the cry that he quickly padded out of the bedroom, into the hallway.

The priest's journal was slightly too large to fit into one of my jacket pockets. I tucked it under the waistband of my jeans, against the small of my back.

When I followed the dog into the hall, I found him at the foot of the folding ladder again, gazing up at the pleated shadows and soft light that hung in the rectory attic. He turned his expressive eyes on me, and I knew that if he could speak, he would say, *We've got to do something*.

This peculiar dog not only harbors a fleet of mysteries, not only exhibits greater cleverness than any dog should possess, but often seems to have a well-defined sense of moral responsibility. Before the events of which I write herein, I had sometimes half-seriously wondered if reincarnation might be more than superstition, because I could envision Orson as a committed teacher or dedicated police-man or even as a wise little nun in a former life, now reborn in a downsized body, furry, with tail.

Of course, ponderings of this nature have long qualified me as a candidate for the Pia Klick Award for exceptional achievement in the field of airheaded speculation. Ironically, Orson's true origins as I would soon come to understand them, although not super-natural, would prove to be more astonishing than any scenario that I and Pia Klick, in fevered collaboration, could have imagined.

Now the cry issued from above a second time, and Orson was so affected that he let out a whine of distress too thin to carry into the attic. Even more than the first time, the wailing voice seemed to be that of a small child.

It was followed by another voice, too low for the words to be distinct. Though I was sure that this must be Father Tom, I couldn't hear his tone well enough to tell if it was consoling or threatening.

28

If I'd trusted to instinct, I would have fled the rectory right then, gone directly home, brewed a pot of tea, spread lemon marmalade on a scone, popped a Jackie Chan movie on the TV, and spent the next couple of hours on the sofa, with an afghan over my lap and with my curiosity on hold.

Instead, because pride prevented me from admitting that I had a sense of moral responsibility less well developed than that of my dog, I signaled Orson to stand aside and wait. Then I went up the ladder with the 9mm Glock in my right hand and Father Tom's stolen journal riding uncomfortably against the small of my back.

Like a raven frantically beating its wings against a cage, dark images from Lewis Stevenson's descriptions of his sick dreams flapped through my mind. The chief had fantasized about girls as young as his granddaughter, but the cry that I'd just heard sounded as though it had come from a child much younger than ten. If the rector of St. Bernadette's was in the grip of the same dementia that had afflicted Stevenson, however, I had no reason to expect him to limit his prey to those aged ten or older.

Near the top of the ladder, one hand on the flimsy,

collapsible railing, I turned my head to peer down along my flank and saw Orson staring up from the hallway. As instructed, he had not tried to climb after me.

He'd been solemnly obedient for the better part of an hour, having commented on my commands with not a single sarcastic chuff or rolling of the eyes. This restraint marked a personal best for him. In fact, it was a personal best by a margin of at least half an hour, an Olympic-caliber performance.

Expecting to take a kick in the head from an ecclesiastical boot, I climbed higher nonetheless, into the attic. Evidently I'd been sufficiently stealthy to avoid drawing Father Tom's attention, because he wasn't waiting to kick my sinus bones deep into my frontal lobe.

The trapdoor lay at the center of a small clear space that was surrounded, as far as I could discern, by a maze of cardboard cartons of various sizes, old furniture, and other objects that I couldn't identify – all stacked to a height of about six feet. The bare bulb directly over the trap was not lit, and the only light came from off to the left, in the southeast corner, toward the front of the house.

I eased into the vast attic in a crouch, though I could have stood erect. The steeply pitched Norman roof provided plenty of clearance between my head and the rafters. Although I wasn't concerned about walking face-first into a roof beam, I still believed there was a risk of being clubbed on the skull or shot between the eyes or stabbed in the heart by a crazed cleric, and I was intent on keeping as low a profile as possible. If I could have slithered on my belly like a snake, I wouldn't even have been all the way up in a crouch.

The humid air smelled like time itself distilled and

bottled: dust, the staleness of old cardboard, a lingering woody fragrance from the rough-sawn rafters, mildew spooring, and the faint stink of some small dead creature, perhaps a bird or mouse, festering in a lightless corner.

To the left of the trapdoor were two entrances into the maze, one approximately five feet wide, and the other no wider than three feet. Assuming that the roomier passage provided the most direct route across the cluttered attic and, therefore, was the one that the priest regularly used to go to and from his captive – if indeed there was a captive – I slipped quietly into the narrower aisle. I preferred to take Father Tom by surprise rather than encounter him accidentally at some turning in this labyrinth.

To both sides of me were boxes, some tied with twine, others festooned with peeling lengths of shipping tape that brushed like insectile feelers against my face. I moved slowly, feeling my way with one hand, because the shadows were confounding, and I dared not bump into anything and set off a clatter.

I reached a T intersection but didn't immediately step into it. I stood at the brink, listening for a moment, holding my breath, but heard nothing.

Cautiously I leaned out of the first passageway, looking right and left along this new corridor in the maze, which was also only three feet wide. To the left, the lamplight in the southeast corner was slightly brighter than before. To the right lay deep sable gloom that wouldn't yield its secrets even to my night-loving eyes, and I had the impression that a hostile inhabitant of this darkness was within an arm's length, watching and set to spring.

Assuring myself that all trolls lived under bridges,

that wicked gnomes lived in caves and mines, that gremlins established housekeeping only in machinery, and that goblins – being demons – wouldn't dare to take up residence in a rectory, I stepped into the new passageway and turned left, putting my back to the impenetrable dark.

At once a squeal arose, so chilling that I swung around and thrust the pistol toward the blackness, certain that trolls, wicked gnomes, gremlins, goblins, ghosts, zombies, and several psychotic mutant altar boys were descending on me. Fortunately I didn't squeeze the trigger, because this transient madness passed, and I realized that the cry had arisen from the same direction as before: from the lighted area in the southeast corner.

This third wail, which had covered the noise that I'd made when turning to confront the imaginary horde, was from the same source as the first two, but here in the attic, it sounded different from how it had sounded when I'd been down in the second-floor hallway. For one thing, it didn't seem as much like the voice of a suffering child as it had earlier. More disconcerting: The weirdness factor was a lot higher, way off the top of the chart, as if several bars of theremin music had issued from a human throat.

I considered retracing my path to the ladder, but I was in too deep to turn back now. There was still a chance, however slim, that I was hearing a child in jeopardy.

Besides, if I retreated, my dog would know that I had haired out. He was one of my three closest friends in a world where only friends and family matter, and as I no longer had any family, I put enormous value on his high opinion of me.

The boxes on my left gave way to stacked wicker lawn chairs, a jumbled collection of thatched and lacquered baskets made of wicker and reed, a battered dresser with an oval mirror so grimy that I cast not even a shadowy reflection in it, unguessable items concealed by drop cloths, and then more boxes.

I turned a corner, and now I could hear Father Tom's voice. He was speaking softly, soothingly, but I couldn't make out a word of what he said.

I walked into a cobweb barrier, flinching as it clung to my face and brushed like phantom lips against my mouth. With my left hand I wiped the tattered strands from my cheeks and from the bill of my cap. The gossamer had a bitter-mushroom taste; grimacing, I tried to spit it out without making a sound.

Because I was hoping again for revelations, I was compelled to follow the priest's voice as irresistibly as I might have followed the music of a piper in Hamelin. All the while, I was struggling to repress the desire to sneeze, which was spawned by dust with a scent so dry that it must have come from the previous century.

After one more turn, I was in a last short length of passageway. About six feet beyond the end of this narrow corridor of boxes was the steeply pitched underside of the roof at the east flank – the front – of the building. The rafters, braces, collar beams, and the underside of the roof sheathing, to which the slate was attached, were revealed by muddy-yellow light issuing from a source out of sight to the right.

Creeping to the end of the passage, I was acutely aware of the faint creaking of the floorboards under me. It was no louder or more suspicious than the ordinary settling noises in this high redoubt, but it was nonetheless potentially betraying.

Father Tom's voice grew clearer, although I could catch only one word in five or six.

Another voice rose, higher-pitched and tremulous. It resembled the voice of a very young child – and yet was nothing as ordinary as that. Not as musical as the speech of a child. Not half as innocent. I couldn't make out what, if anything, it was saying. The longer that I listened, the eerier it became, until it made me pause – though I didn't dare pause for long.

My aisle terminated in a perimeter passage that extended along the eastern flank of the attic maze. I risked a peek into this long straight run.

To the left was darkness, but to the right was the southeast corner of the building, where I had expected to find the source of the light and the priest with his wailing captive. Instead, the lamp remained out of sight to the right of the corner, around one more turn, along the south wall.

I followed this six-foot-wide perimeter passage, half crouched by necessity now, for the wall to my left was actually the steeply sloped underside of the roof. To my right, I passed the dark mouth of another passageway between piles of boxes and old furniture – and then halted within two steps of the corner, with only the last wall of stored goods between me and the lamp.

Abruptly a squirming shadow leaped across the rafters and roof sheathing that formed the wall ahead of me: a fierce spiky thrashing of jagged limbs with a bulbous swelling at the center, so alien that I nearly shouted in alarm. I found myself holding the Glock in both hands.

Then I realized that the apparition before me was the distorted shadow of a spider suspended on a single silken thread. It must have been dangling so close to the source of the light that its image was projected, greatly enlarged, across the surfaces in front of me.

For a ruthless killer, I was far too jumpy. Maybe the caffeine-laden Pepsi, which I'd drunk to sweeten my vomit-soured breath, was to blame. Next time I killed someone and threw up, I'd have to use a caffeine-free beverage and lace it with Valium, in order to avoid tarnishing my image as an emotionless, efficient homicide machine.

Cool with the spider now, I also realized that I could at last hear the priest's voice clearly enough to understand his every word: '. . . hurts, yes, of course, it hurts very much. But now I've cut the transponder out of you, cut it out and crushed it, and they can't follow you anymore.'

I flashed back to the memory of Jesse Pinn stalking through the cemetery earlier in the night, holding the peculiar instrument in his hand, listening to faint electronic tones and reading data on a small, glowing green screen. He'd evidently been tracking the signal from a surgically implanted transponder in this creature. A monkey, was it? Yet not a monkey?

'The incision wasn't very deep,' the priest continued. 'The transponder was just under the subcutaneous fat. I've sterilized the wound and sewn it up.' He sighed. 'I wish I knew how much you understand me, if at all.'

In Father Tom's journal, he had referred to the members of a *new* troop that was less hostile and less violent than the first, and he had written that he was committed to their liberation. Why there should be a new troop, as opposed to an old one, or why they should be set loose in the world with transponders under their skin – even *how* these smarter monkeys of either troop could have come into existence in the first place – I couldn't fathom. But it was clear that the priest styled himself as a modern-day abolitionist fighting for the rights of the oppressed and that this rectory was a key stop on an underground railroad to freedom.

When he had confronted Father Tom in the church basement, Pinn must have believed that this current fugitive had already received superficial surgery and moved on, and that his hand-held tracker was picking up the signal from a transponder no longer embedded in the creature that it was meant to identify. Instead, the fugitive was recuperating here in the attic.

The priest's mysterious visitor mewled softly, as if in pain, and the cleric replied with a sympathetic patter perilously close to baby talk.

Taking courage from the memory of how meekly the priest had responded to the undertaker, I crossed the remaining couple of feet to the final wall of boxes. I stood with my back to the end of the row, knees bent only slightly to accommodate the slope of the roof. From here, to see the priest and the creature with him, I needed only to lean to my right, turn my head, and look into the perimeter aisle along the south flank of the attic where the light and the voices originated.

I hesitated to reveal my presence only because I recalled some of the odder entries in the priest's diary: the ranting and paranoid passages that bordered on incoherence, the two hundred repetitions of *I believe in the mercy of Christ*. Perhaps he wasn't always as meek as he had been with Jesse Pinn.

Overlaying the odors of mildew and dust and old cardboard was a new medicinal scent composed of rubbing alcohol, iodine, and an astringent antiseptic cleanser.

Somewhere in the next aisle, the fat spider reeled

itself up its filament, away from the lamplight, and the magnified arachnid shadow rapidly dwindled across the slanted ceiling, shrinking into a black dot and finally vanishing.

Father Tom spoke reassuringly to his patient: 'I have antibiotic powder, capsules of various penicillin derivatives, but no effective painkiller. I wish I did. But this world is about suffering, isn't it? This vale of tears. You'll be all right. You'll be just fine. I promise. God will look after you through me.'

Whether the rector of St. Bernadette's was a saint or villain, one of the few rational people left in Moonlight Bay or way insane, I couldn't judge. I didn't have enough facts, didn't understand the context of his actions.

I was certain of only one thing: Even if Father Tom might be rational and doing the right thing, his head nevertheless contained enough loose wiring to make it unwise to let him hold the baby during a baptism.

'I've had some very basic medical training,' the priest told his patient, 'because for three years after seminary, I was called to a mission in Uganda.'

I thought I heard the patient: a muttering that reminded me – but not quite – of the low cooing of pigeons blended with the more guttural purr of a cat.

'I'm sure you'll be all right,' Father Tom continued. 'But you really must stay here a few days so I can administer the antibiotics and monitor the healing of the wound. Do you understand me?' With a note of frustration and despair: 'Do you understand me at all?'

As I was about to lean to the right and peer around the wall of boxes, the Other replied to the priest. *The Other*: That was how I thought of the fugitive when I heard it speaking from such close range, because this was a voice that I was not able to imagine as being either that of a child or a monkey, or of anything else in *God's Big Book of Creation*.

I froze. My finger tightened on the trigger.

Certainly it sounded partly like a young child, a little girl, and partly like a monkey. It sounded partly like a lot of things, in fact, as though a highly creative Hollywood sound technician had been playing with a library of human and animal voices, mixing them through an audio console until he'd created the ultimate voice for an extraterrestrial.

The most affecting thing about the Other's speech was not the tonal range of it, not the pattern of inflections, and not even the earnestness and the emotion that clearly shaped it. Instead, what most jolted me was the perception that it had *meaning*. I was not listening merely to a babble of animal noises. This was not English, of course, not a word of it; and although I'm not multilingual, I'm certain it wasn't any foreign tongue, either, for it was not complex enough to be a true language. It was, however, a fluent series of exotic sounds crudely composed like words, a powerful but primitive *attempt* at language, with a small polysyllabic vocabulary, marked by urgent rhythms.

The Other seemed pathetically desperate to communicate. As I listened, I was surprised to find myself emotionally affected by the longing, loneliness, and anguish in its voice. These were not qualities that I imagined. They were as real as the boards beneath my feet, the stacked boxes against my back, and the heavy beating of my heart.

When the Other and the priest both fell silent, I wasn't able to look around the corner. I suspected that whatever the priest's visitor might look like, it would not pass for a real monkey, as did those members of the original troop that had been tormenting Bobby and that Orson and I had encountered on the southern horn of the bay. If it resembled a rhesus at all, the differences would be greater and surely more numerous than the baleful dark-yellow color of the other monkeys' eyes.

If I was afraid of what I might see, my fear had nothing whatsoever to do with the possible hideousness of this laboratory-born Other. My chest was so tight with emotion that I couldn't draw deep breaths, and my throat was so thick that I could swallow only with effort. What I feared was meeting the gaze of this entity and seeing my own isolation in its eyes, my own yearning to be normal, which I'd spent twenty-eight years denying with enough success to be happy with my fate. But my happiness, like everyone's, is fragile. I had heard a terrible longing in this creature's voice, and I felt that it was akin to the sharp longing around which I had ages ago formed a pearl of indifference and quiet resignation; I was afraid that if I met the Other's eyes, some resonance between us would shatter that pearl and leave me vulnerable once more.

I was shaking.

This is also why I cannot, dare not, *will* not express my pain or my grief when life wounds me or takes from me someone I love. Grief too easily leads to despair. In the fertile ground of despair, self-pity can sprout and thrive. I can't begin to indulge in self-pity, because by enumerating and dwelling upon my limitations, I will be digging a hole so deep that I'll never again be able to crawl out of it. I've got to be something of a cold bastard to survive, live with a chinkless shell around my heart at least when it comes to grieving for the dead. I'm able to express my love for the living, to embrace my friends without reservation, to give my heart without concern for how it might be abused. But on the day that my father dies, I must make jokes about death, about crematoriums, about life, about every damn thing, because I can't risk – *won't* risk – descending from grief to despair to self-pity and, finally, to the pit of inescapable rage and loneliness and self-hatred that is freakdom. I can't love the dead too much. No matter how desperately I want to remember them and hold them dear, I have to let them go – and quickly. I have to push them out of my heart even as they are cooling in their deathbeds. Likewise, I have to make jokes about being a killer, because if I think too long and too hard about what it really means to have murdered a man, even a monster like Lewis Stevenson, then I will begin to wonder if I am, in fact, the freak that those nasty little shitheads of my childhood insisted that I was: the Nightcrawler, Vampire Boy, Creepy Chris. I must not care too much about the dead, either those whom I loved or those whom I despised. I must not care too much about being alone. I must not care too much about what I cannot change. Like all of us in this storm between birth and death, I can wreak no great changes on the world, only small changes for the better, I hope, in the lives of those I love, which means that to live I must care not about what I am but about what I can become, not about the past but about the future, not even so much about myself as about the bright circle of friends who provide the only light in which I am able to flourish.

I was shaking as I contemplated turning the corner and facing the Other, in whose eyes I might see far too much of myself. I was clutching the Glock as if it were a talisman rather than a weapon, as though it were a crucifix with which I could ward off all that might destroy me, but I forced myself into action. I leaned to the right, turned my head – and saw no one.

This perimeter passage along the south side of the attic was wider than the one along the east flank, perhaps eight feet across; and on the plywood floor, tucked in against the eaves, was a narrow mattress and a tangle of blankets. The light came from a cone-shaped brass desk lamp plugged into a GFI recep-tacle that was mounted on an eave brace. Beside the mattress were a Thermos, a plate of sliced fruit and buttered bread, a pail of water, bottles of medica-tion and rubbing alcohol, the makings for bandages, a folded towel, and a damp wash cloth spotted with blood.

The priest and his guest seemed to have vanished as if they had whispered an incantation.

Although immobilized by the emotional impact of the longing in the Other's voice, I could not have been standing at the end of the box row for more than a minute after the creature had fallen silent, perhaps no more than half a minute. Yet neither Father Tom nor his visitor was in sight in the passageway ahead.

Silence ruled. I heard not a single footfall. Not any creak or pop or tick of wood that sounded more sig-nificant than the usual faint settling noises.

I actually looked up into the rafters toward the center of the space, overcome by the bizarre conviction that the missing pair had learned a trick from the clever spider and had drawn themselves up gossamer fila-ments, curling into tight black balls in the shadows overhead.

As long as I stayed close to the wall of boxes on my right side, I had sufficient headroom to stand erect. Soaring from the eaves to my left, the sharply pitched rafters cleared my head by six or eight inches. Nevertheless, I moved defensively in a modified crouch.

The lamp was not dangerously bright, and the brass cone focused the light away from me, so I moved to the mattress for a closer look at the items arrayed beside it. With the toe of one shoe, I disturbed the tangled blankets; although I'm not sure what I expected to find under them, what I did find was a lot of nothing.

I wasn't concerned that Father Tom would go downstairs and find Orson. For one thing, I didn't think he was finished with his work up here in the attic. Besides, my criminally experienced mutt would have the street savvy to duck for cover and lie low until escape was more feasible.

Suddenly, however, I realized that if the priest went below, he might fold away the ladder and close the trapdoor. I could force it open and release the ladder from above, but not without making almost as much racket as Satan and his conspirators had made when cast out of Heaven.

Rather than follow this passage to the next entrance to the maze and risk encountering the priest and the Other on the route they might have taken, I turned back the way I'd come, reminding myself to be light on my feet. The high-quality plyboard had few voids, and it was screwed rather than nailed to the floor joists, so I was virtually silent even in my haste.

When I turned the corner at the end of the row of boxes, plump Father Tom loomed from the shadows where I had stood listening only a minute or two ago.

He was dressed neither for Mass nor bed, but was wearing a gray sweatsuit and a sheen of sweat, as if he'd been fending off gluttonous urges by working out to an exercise video.

'*You!*' he said bitterly when he recognized me, as though I were not merely Christopher Snow but were the devil Baal and had stepped out of a conjurer's chalk pentagram without first asking permission or obtaining a lavatory pass.

The sweet-tempered, jovial, good-natured padre that I had known was evidently vacationing in Palm Springs, having given the keys of his parish to his evil twin. He poked me in the chest with the blunt end of a baseball bat, hard enough to hurt.

Because even XP Man is subject to the laws of physics, I was rocked backward by the blow, stumbled into the eaves, and cracked the back of my head against a rafter. I didn't see stars, not even a great character actor like M. Emmet Walsh or Rip Torn, but if not for the cushion provided by my James-Dean thatch of hair, I might have gone out cold.

Poking me again in the chest with the baseball bat, Father Tom said, 'You! You!'

Indeed, I was me, and I had never tried to claim otherwise, so I didn't know why he should be so incensed.

'*You!*' he said with a new rush of anger.

This time he rammed the damn bat into my stomach, which winded me but not as badly as it might have if I hadn't seen it coming. Just before the blow landed, I sucked in my stomach and tightened my abdominal muscles, and because I'd already thrown up what was left of Bobby's chicken tacos, the only consequence was a hot flash of pain from my groin to my breastbone, which I would have laughed off if I'd been wearing my armored Spandex superhero uniform under my street clothes.

I pointed the Glock at him and wheezed threateningly, but either he was a man of God with no fear of death – or he was nuts. Gripping the bat with both hands to put even more power behind it, he poked it savagely at my stomach again, but I twisted to the side and dodged the blow, although unfortunately I mussed my hair on a rough-sawn rafter.

I was nonplussed to be in a fight with a priest. The encounter seemed more absurd than frightening – though it was plenty frightening enough to make my heart race and to make me worry that I'd have to return Bobby's jeans with urine stains.

'*You! You!*' he said more angrily than ever and seemingly with more surprise, too, as though my appearance in his dusty attic were so outrageous and improbable that his astonishment would grow at an ever-accelerating rate until his brain went nova.

He swung at me again. He would have missed this time even if I hadn't wrenched myself away from the bat. He was a priest, after all, not a Ninja assassin. He was middle-aged and overweight, too.

The baseball bat smashed into one of the cardboard boxes with enough force to tear a hole in it and knock it out of the stack into the empty aisle beyond. Although woefully ignorant of even the basic principles of the martial arts and not gifted with the physique of a mighty warrior, the good father could not be faulted for a lack of enthusiasm.

I couldn't imagine shooting him, but I couldn't very well allow him to club me to death. I backed away from him, toward the lamp and the mattress in the wider aisle along the south side of the attic, hoping that he would recover his senses.

Instead, he came after me, swinging the bat from left to right, cutting the air with a *whoosh*, then immediately swinging it right to left, chanting, '*You!*' between each swing.

His hair was disarranged and hanging over his brow, and his face appeared to be contorted as much by terror as by rage. His nostrils dilated and quivered with each stentorian breath, and spittle flew from his mouth with each explosive repetition of the pronoun that seemed to comprise his entire vocabulary.

I was going to end up radically dead if I waited for Father Tom to recover his senses. If he even *had* senses left, the priest wasn't carrying them with him. They were put away somewhere, perhaps over in the church, locked up with a splinter of a saint's shin bone in the reliquary on the altar.

As he swung at me again, I searched for that animal eyeshine I'd seen in Lewis Stevenson, because a glimpse of that uncanny glow might justify meeting violence with violence. It would mean I was battling not a priest or an ordinary man, but something with one foot in the Twilight Zone. But I couldn't see a glimmer. Perhaps Father Tom was infected with the same disease that had corrupted the police chief's mind, but if so, he evidently wasn't yet as far gone as the cop.

Moving backward, attention on the baseball bat, I hooked the lamp cord with my foot. Proving myself a worthy victim for an aging, overweight priest, I fell flat on my back, drumming a nice paradiddle on the floor with the back of my skull.

The lamp fell over. Fortunately, it neither went out nor flung its light directly into my sensitive eyes.

I shook my foot out of the entangling cord and scooted backward on my butt as Father Tom rushed in and hammered the floor with the bat.

He missed my legs by inches, punctuating the assault with that now-familiar accusation in the second-person singular: *'You!'*

'You!' I said somewhat hysterically, casting it right back at him as I continued to scoot out of his way.

I wondered where all these people were who supposedly revered me. I was more than ready to be revered a little, but Stevenson and Father Tom Eliot certainly didn't qualify for the Christopher Snow Admiration Society.

Although the priest was streaming sweat and panting, he was out to prove that he had stamina. He approached in the stooped, hunch-shouldered, rolling lurch of a troll, as if he were on a work-release program from under the bridge to which he was usually committed. This cramped posture allowed him to raise the bat high over his head without cracking it against an overhanging rafter. He wanted to keep it high over his head because he clearly intended to play Babe Ruth with my skull and make my brains squirt out my ears.

Eyeshine or no eyeshine, I was going to have to blast the chubby little guy without delay. I couldn't scoot backward as fast as he could troll-walk toward me, and although I was a little hysterical – okay, *way* hysterical – I could figure the odds well enough to know that even the greediest bookie in Vegas wouldn't cover a bet on my survival. In my panic, hammered by terror and by a dangerously giddy sense of the absurd, I thought that the most humane course of action would be to shoot him in the gonads because he had taken a vow of celibacy, anyway.

Fortunately, I never had the opportunity to prove myself to be the expert marksman that such a perfectly placed shot would have required. I aimed in the general direction of his crotch, and my finger tightened on the trigger. No time to use the laser sighting. Before I could squeeze off a round, something monstrous growled in the passageway behind the priest, and a great dark snarling predator leaped on his back, causing him to scream and drop the baseball bat as he was driven to the attic floor.

For an instant, I was stunned that the Other should be so utterly unlike a rhesus and that it should attack Father Tom, its nurse and champion, rather than tear out *my* throat. But, of course, the great dark snarling predator was not the Other: It was Orson.

Standing on the priest's back, the dog bit at the sweat-suit collar. Fabric tore. He was snarling so viciously that I was afraid he'd actually maul Father Tom.

I called him off as I scrambled to my feet. The mutt obeyed at once, without inflicting a wound, not a fraction as bloodthirsty as he'd pretended to be.

The priest made no effort to get up. He lay with his head turned to one side, his face half covered with tousled, sweat-soaked hair. He was breathing hard and sobbing, and after every third or fourth breath, he said bitterly, *'You . . .'*

Obviously he knew enough about what was happening at Fort Wyvern and in Moonlight Bay to answer many if not all of my most pressing questions. Yet I didn't want to talk to him. I *couldn't* talk to him.

The Other might not have left the rectory, might still be here in the shadowy cloisters of the attic. Although I didn't believe that it posed a serious danger to me and

Orson, especially not when I had the Glock, I had not seen it and, therefore, couldn't dismiss it as a threat. I didn't want to stalk it – or be stalked by it – in this claustrophobic space.

Of course, the Other was merely an excuse to flee.

Those things that I truly feared were the answers Father Tom might give to my questions. I thought I was eager to hear them, but evidently I was not yet prepared for certain truths.

You.

He'd spoken that one word with seething hatred, with uncommonly dark emotion for a man of God but also for a man who was usually kind and gentle. He transformed the simple pronoun into a denunciation and a curse.

You.

Yet I'd done nothing to earn his enmity. I hadn't given life to the pitiable creatures that he had committed himself to freeing. I hadn't been a part of the program at Wyvern that had infected his sister and possibly him, as well. Which meant that he hated not me, as a person, but hated me because of who I was.

And who was I?

Who was I if not my mother's son?

According to Roosevelt Frost – and even Chief Stevenson – there were, indeed, those who revered me because I was my mother's son, though I'd yet to meet them. For the same lineage, I was hated.

Christopher Nicholas Snow, only child of Wisteria Jane (Milbury) Snow, whose own mother named her after a flower. Christopher born of Wisteria, come into this too-bright world near the beginning of the Disco Decade. Born in a time of tacky fashion trends and frivolous pursuits, when the country was eagerly winding down a war, and when the worst fear was mere nuclear holocaust.

What could my brilliant and loving mother possibly have done that would make me either revered or reviled?

Sprawled on the attic floor, racked by emotion, Father Tom Eliot knew the answer to that mystery and would almost certainly reveal it when he had regained his composure.

Instead of asking the question at the heart of all that had happened this night, I shakily apologized to the sobbing priest. 'I'm sorry. I . . . I shouldn't have come here. God. Listen. I'm so sorry. Please forgive me. Please.'

What had my mother done?

Don't ask.

Don't ask.

If he had started to answer my unspoken question, I would have clamped my hands to my ears.

I called Orson to my side and led him away from the priest, into the maze, proceeding as fast as I dared. The narrow passages twisted and branched until it seemed as though we were not in an attic at all but in a network of catacombs. In places the darkness was nearly blinding; but I'm the child of darkness, never thwarted by it. I brought us quickly to the open trapdoor.

Though Orson had climbed the ladder, he peered at the descending treads with trepidation and hesitated to find his way into the hall below. Even for a four-footed acrobat, going down a steep ladder was immeasurably more difficult than going up.

Because many of the boxes in the attic were large and because bulky furniture was also stored there, a second trap must exist, and it must be larger than the first, with an associated sling-and-pulley system for raising and lowering heavy objects to and from the second floor. I didn't want to search for it, but I wasn't sure how I could safely climb backward down an attic ladder while carrying a ninety-pound dog.

From the farthest end of the vast room, the priest called out to me – 'Christopher' – in a voice heavy with remorse. 'Christopher, I'm lost.'

He didn't mean that he was lost in his own maze. Nothing as simple as that, nothing as hopeful as that.

'Christopher, I'm lost. Forgive me. *I'm so lost.*'

From elsewhere in the gloom came the child-monkey-not-of-this-world voice that belonged to the Other: struggling toward language, desperate to be understood, charged with longing and loneliness, as bleak as any arctic icefield but also, worse, filled with a reckless hope that would surely never be rewarded.

This plaintive bleat was so unbearable that it drove Orson to try the ladder and may even have given him the balance to succeed. When he was only halfway to the bottom, he leaped over the remaining treads to the hallway floor.

The priest's journal had almost slipped out from under my belt and into the seat of my pants. As I descended the ladder, the book rubbed painfully against the base of my spine, and when I reached the bottom I clawed it from under my belt and held it in my left hand, as the Glock was still clamped fiercely in my right.

Together, Orson and I raced down through the rectory, past the shrine to the Blessed Virgin, where the guttering candle was extinguished by the draft of our passing. We fled along the lower hall, through the kitchen with its three green digital clocks, out the back door, across the porch, into the night and the fog, as if we were escaping from the House of Usher moments before it collapsed and sank into the deep dank tarn.

We passed the back of the church. Its formidable mass was a tsunami of stone, and while we were in its nightshadow, it seemed about to crest and crash and crush us.

I glanced back twice. The priest was not behind us. Neither was anything else.

Although I half expected my bicycle to be gone or damaged, it was propped against the headstone, where I had left it. No monkey business.

I didn't pause to say a word to Noah Joseph James. In a world as screwed up as ours, ninety-six years of life didn't seem to be as desirable as it had been only a day ago.

After pocketing the pistol and tucking the journal inside my shirt, I ran beside my bike along an aisle between rows of graves, swinging aboard it while on the move. Bouncing off the curb into the street, leaning forward over the handlebars, pedaling furiously, I bored like an auger through the fog, leaving a temporary tunnel in the churning mist behind me.

Orson had no interest in the spoor of squirrels. He was as eager as I was to put distance between us and St. Bernadette's.

We had gone several blocks before I began to realize that escape wasn't possible. The inevitable dawn restricted me to the boundaries of Moonlight Bay, and the madness in St. Bernadette's rectory was to be found in every corner of the town.

More to the point, I was trying to run away from a threat that could never be escaped even if I could fly to the most remote island or mountaintop in the world. Wherever I went, I would carry with me the thing that I feared: the need to know. I wasn't frightened merely of the answers that I might receive when I asked questions about my mother. More fundamentally, I was afraid of the questions themselves, because the very nature of them, whether they were eventually answered or not, would change my life forever.

29

From a bench in the park at the corner of Palm Street and Grace Drive, Orson and I studied a sculpture of a steel scimitar balanced on a pair of tumbling dice carved from white marble, which were in turn balanced on a highly polished representation of Earth hewn from blue marble, which itself was perched upon a large mound of bronze cast to resemble a pile of dog poop.

This work of art has stood at the center of the park, surrounded by a gently bubbling fountain, for about three years. We've sat here many nights, pondering the meaning of this creation, intrigued and edified and challenged – but not particularly enlightened – by it.

Initially we believed that the meaning was clear. The scimitar represents war or death. The tumbling dice represent fate. The blue marble sphere, which is Earth, is a symbol of our lives. Put it all together, and you have a statement about the human condition: We live or die according to the whims of fate, our lives on this world ruled by cold chance. The bronze dog poop at the bottom is a minimalist repetition of the same theme: Life is shit.

Many learned analyses have followed the first. The scimitar, for example, might not be a scimitar at all; it might be a crescent moon. The dice-like forms might be sugar cubes. The blue sphere might not be our nurturing planet – merely a bowling ball. What the various forms symbolize can be interpreted in a virtually infinite number of ways, although it is impossible to conceive of the bronze casting as anything but dog poop.

Seen as a moon, sugar cubes, and a bowling ball, this masterwork may be warning that our highest aspirations (reaching for the moon) cannot be achieved if we punish our bodies and agitate our minds by eating too many sweets or if we sustain lower-back injury by trying too hard to torque the ball when we're desperate to pick up a seven-ten split. The bronze dog poop, therefore, reveals to us the ultimate consequences of a bad diet combined with obsessive bowling: Life is shit.

Four benches are placed around the broad walkway that encircles the fountain in which the sculpture stands. We have viewed the piece from every perspective.

The park lamps are on a timer, and they are all extinguished at midnight to conserve city funds. The fountain stops bubbling as well. The gently splashing water is conducive to meditation, and we wish that it spritzed all night; although even if I were not an XPer, we would prefer no lamplight. Ambient light is not only sufficient but ideal for the study of this sculpture, and a good thick fog can add immeasurably to your appreciation of the artist's vision.

Prior to the erection of this monument, a simple bronze statue of Junipero Serra stood on the plinth at the center of the fountain for over a hundred years. He was a Spanish missionary to the Indians of California, two and a half centuries ago: the man who established the network of missions that are now landmark buildings, public treasures, and magnets for history-minded tourists.

Bobby's parents and a group of like-minded citizens had formed a committee to press for the banishment of the Junipero Serra statue on the grounds that a monument to a religious figure did not belong in a park created and maintained with public funds. Separation of church and state. The United States Constitution, they said, was clear on this issue.

Wisteria Jane (Milbury) Snow – *Wissy* to her friends, *Mom* to me – in spite of being a scientist and rationalist, led the opposing committee that wished to preserve the statue of Serra. 'When a society erases its past, for whatever reason,' she said, 'it cannot have a future.'

Mom lost the debate. Bobby's folks won.

The night that the decision came down, Bobby and I met in the most solemn circumstances of our long friendship, to determine if family honor and the sacred obligations of bloodline required us to conduct a vicious, unrelenting feud – in the manner of the legendary Hatfields and McCoys – until even the most distant cousins had been sent to sleep with the worms and until one or both of us was dead. After consuming enough beer to clear our heads, we decided that it was impossible to conduct a proper feud and still find the time to ride every set of glassy, pumping monoliths that the good sea sent to shore. To say nothing of all the time spent on murder and mayhem that might have been spent ogling girls in bun-floss bikinis.

Now I entered Bobby's number in the keypad on my phone and pressed *send*.

I turned the volume up a little so Orson might be able to hear both sides of the conversation. When I realized what I had done, I knew that unconsciously I had accepted the most fantastic possibility of the Wyvern project as proven fact – even if I was still pretending to have my doubts.

Bobby answered on the second ring: 'Go away.'

'You asleep?'

'Yeah.'

'I'm sitting here in Life Is Shit Park.'

'Do I care?'

'Some really bad stuff has gone down since I saw you.'

'It's the salsa on those chicken tacos,' he said.

'I can't talk about it on the phone.'

'Good.'

'I'm worried about you,' I said.

'That's sweet.'

'You're in real danger, Bobby.'

'I swear I flossed, Mom.'

Orson chuffed with amusement. The hell he didn't.

'Are you awake now?' I asked Bobby.

'No.'

'I don't think you were asleep in the first place.'

He was silent. Then: 'Well, there's been a way spooky movie on all night since you left.'

'*Planet of the Apes*?' I guessed.

'On a three-hundred-sixty-degree, wrap-around screen.'

'What're they doing?'

'Oh, you know, the usual monkeyshines.'

'Nothing more threatening?'

'They think they're cute. One of them's at the window right now, mooning me.'

'Yeah, but did you start it?'

'I get the feeling they're trying to irritate me until I come outside again.'

Alarmed, I said, 'Don't go.'

'I'm not a moron,' he said sourly.

'Sorry.'

'I'm an asshole.'

'That's right.'

'There's a critical difference between a moron and an asshole.'

'I'm clear on that.'

'I wonder.'

'Do you have the shotgun with you?'

'Jesus, Snow, didn't I just say I'm not a moron?'

'If we can ride this barrel until dawn, then I think we're safe until sundown tomorrow.'

'They're on the roof now.'

'Doing what?'

'Don't know.' He paused, listening. 'At least two of them. Running back and forth. Maybe looking for a way in.'

Orson jumped off the bench and stood tensely, one ear pricked toward the phone, a worried air about him. He seemed to be willing to shed some doggy pretenses if that didn't disturb me.

'*Is* there a way in from the roof?' I asked Bobby.

'The bathroom and kitchen vent ducts aren't large enough for these bastards.'

Surprisingly, considering all its other amenities, the cottage had no fireplace. Corky Collins – formerly Toshiro Tagawa – had most likely decided against a fireplace because, unlike the warm waters of a spa, the stone hearth and hard bricks of a firebox didn't provide an ideal spot to get it on with a couple of

naked beach girls. Thanks to his single-minded las-
civiousness, there was now no convenient chimney to
admit the monkeys.

I said, 'I've got some more Nancy work to squeeze
in before dawn.'

'How's that panning out?' Bobby asked.

'I'm awesomely good at it. Come morning, I'll spend
the day at Sasha's, and we'll both be at your place first
thing tomorrow evening.'

'You mean I've got to make dinner again?'

'We'll bring pizza. Listen, we're gonna get slammed,
I think. One of us, anyway. And the only way to
prevent it is hang together. Better get what sleep you
can during the day. Tomorrow night might be radically
hairy out there on the point.'

'So you've got a handle on this?' Bobby said.

'There isn't a handle on it.'

'You're not as cheerful as Nancy Drew.'

I wasn't going to lie to him, not to him any more than
to Orson or Sasha. 'There's no solution. There's no way
to zip it shut or put a button on it. Whatever's going
down here – we'll have to live with it the rest of our
lives. But maybe we can find a way to ride the wave,
even though it's a huge spooky slab.'

After a silence, Bobby said, 'What's wrong, bro?'

'Didn't I just say?'

'Not everything.'

'I told you, some of it's not for the phone.'

'I'm not talking about details. I'm talking about you.'

Orson put his head in my lap, as if he thought I
would take some consolation from petting him and
scratching behind his ears. In fact, I did. It always
works. A good dog is a medicine for melancholy and
a better stress reliever than Valium.

'You're doing cool,' Bobby said, 'but you're not being cool.'

'Bob Freud, bastard grandson of Sigmund.'

'Lie down on my couch.'

Smoothing Orson's coat in an attempt to smooth my nerves, I sighed and said, 'Well, what it boils down to is, I think maybe my mom destroyed the world.'

'Solemn.'

'It is, isn't it?'

'This science thing of hers?'

'Genetics.'

'Remember how I warned you against trying to leave your mark.'

'I think it's worse than that. I think maybe, at the start, she was trying to find a way to help me.'

'End of the world, huh?'

'End of the world as we know it,' I said, remembering Roosevelt Frost's qualification.

'Beaver Cleaver's mom never did much more than bake a cake.'

I laughed. 'How would I make it without you, bro?'

'There's only one important thing I ever did for you.'

'What's that?'

'Taught you perspective.'

I nodded. 'What's important and what isn't.'

'Most isn't,' he reminded me.

'Even this?'

'Make love to Sasha. Get some solid sleep. We'll have a bitchin' dinner tomorrow night. We'll kick some monkey ass. Ride some epic waves. A week from now, in your heart, your mom is just your mom again – if you want to let it be that way.'

'Maybe,' I said doubtfully.

'Attitude, bro. It's everything.'

'I'll work on it.'

'One thing surprises me, though.'

'What?'

'Your mom must've been really *pissed* about losing the fight to keep that statue in the park.'

Bobby broke the connection. I switched off my phone.

Is this really a wise strategy for living? Insisting that most of life isn't to be taken seriously. Relentlessly viewing it as a cosmic joke. Having only four guiding principles: one, do as little harm to others as possible; two, be there always for your friends; three, be responsible for yourself and ask nothing of others; four, grab all the fun you can. Put no stock in the opinions of anyone but those closest to you. Forget about leaving a mark on the world. Ignore the great issues of your time and thereby improve your digestion. Don't dwell in the past. Don't worry about the future. Live in the moment. Trust in the purpose of your existence and let meaning come to you instead of straining to discover it. When life throws a hard punch, roll with it – but roll with laughter. Catch the wave, dude.

This is how Bobby lives, and he is the happiest and most well-balanced person I have ever known.

I try to live as Bobby Halloway does, but I'm not as successful at it as he is. Sometimes I thrash when I should float. I spend too much time anticipating and too little time letting life surprise me. Maybe I don't try hard enough to live like Bobby. Or maybe I try too hard.

Orson went to the pool that surrounded the sculpture. He lapped noisily at the clear water, obviously savoring the taste and the coolness of it.

I remembered that July night in our backyard when he had stared at the stars and fallen into blackest despair. I had no accurate way to determine how much smarter Orson was than an ordinary dog. Because his intelligence had somehow been enhanced by the project at Wyvern, however, he understood vastly more than nature ever intended a dog to understand. That July night, recognizing his revolutionary potential yet – perhaps for the first time – grasping the terrible limitations placed on him by his physical nature, he'd sunk into a slough of despondency that almost claimed him permanently. To be intelligent but without the complex larynx and other physical equipment to make speech possible, to be intelligent but without the hands to write or make tools, to be intelligent but trapped in a physical package that will forever prevent the full expression of your intelligence: This would be akin to a human being born deaf, mute, and limbless.

I watched Orson now with astonishment, with a new appreciation for his courage, and with a tenderness that I had never felt before for anyone on this earth.

He turned from the pool, licking at the water that dripped from his chops, grinning with pleasure. When he saw me looking at him, he wagged his tail, happy to have my attention or just happy to be with me on this strange night.

For all of his limitations and in spite of all the good reasons why he should be perpetually anguished, my dog, for God's sake, was better at being Bobby Halloway than I was.

Does Bobby have a wise strategy for living? Does Orson? I hope one day to have matured enough to live as well by their philosophy as they do.

Getting up from the bench, I pointed to the sculpture.

'Not a scimitar. Not a moon. It's the smile of the invisible Cheshire cat from *Alice in Wonderland*.'

Orson turned to gaze up at the masterwork.

'Not dice. Not sugar cubes,' I continued. 'A pair of either the grow-small or grow-big pills that Alice took in the story.'

Orson considered this with interest. On video, he had seen Disney's animated version of this classic tale.

'Not a symbol of the earth. Not a blue bowling ball. A big blue eye. Put it all together and what does it mean?'

Orson looked at me for elucidation.

'The Cheshire smile is the artist laughing at the gullible people who paid him so handsomely. The pair of pills represent the drugs he was high on when he created this junk. The blue eye is his eye, and the reason you can't see his other eye is because he's winking it. The bronze pile at the bottom is, of course, dog poop, which is intended to be a pungent critical comment on the work – because, as everyone knows, dogs are the most perceptive of all critics.'

If the vigor with which Orson wagged his tail was a reliable indication, he enjoyed this interpretation enormously.

He trotted around the entire fountain pool, reviewing the sculpture from all sides.

Perhaps the purpose for which I was born is *not* to write about my life in search of some universal meaning that may help others to better understand their own lives – which, in my more egomaniacal moments, is a mission I have embraced. Instead of striving to make even the tiniest mark on the world, perhaps I should consider that, possibly, the sole purpose for which I was born is to amuse Orson, to be not his master but his loving brother, to make his strange and difficult life as easy, as full of delight, and as rewarding as it can be. This would constitute a purpose as meaningful as most and more noble than some.

Pleased by Orson's wagging tail at least as much as he seemed to be pleased by my latest riff on the sculpture, I consulted my wristwatch. Less than two hours remained until dawn.

I had two places I wanted to go before the sun chased me into hiding. The first was Fort Wyvern.

~ ~ ~

From the park at Palm Street and Grace Drive in the southeast quadrant of Moonlight Bay, the trip to Fort Wyvern takes less than ten minutes by bicycle, even allowing for a pace that will not tire your canine brother. I know a shortcut through a storm culvert that runs under Highway 1. Beyond the culvert is an open, ten-foot-wide, concrete drainage channel that continues deep into the grounds of the military base after being bisected by the chain-link fence – crowned with razor wire – that defines the perimeter of the facility.

Everywhere along the fence – and throughout the grounds of Fort Wyvern – large signs in red and black warn that trespassers will be prosecuted under federal statutes and that the minimum sentence upon conviction involves a fine of no less than ten thousand dollars and a prison sentence of no less than one year. I have always ignored these threats, largely because I know that because of my condition, no judge will sentence me to prison for this minor offense. And I can afford the ten thousand bucks if it comes to that.

One night, eighteen months ago, shortly after Wyvern officially closed forever, I used a bolt cutter to breach the chain-link where it descended into the drainage channel. The opportunity to explore this vast new realm was too enticing to resist.

If my excitement seems strange to you – considering that I was not an adventuresome boy at the time but a twenty-six-year-old man – then you are probably someone who can catch a plane to London if you wish, sail off to Puerto Vallarta on a whim, or take the Oriental Express from Paris to Istanbul. You probably have a driver's license and a car. You probably have not spent your entire life within the confines of a town of twelve thousand people, ceaselessly traveling it by night until you know its every byway as intimately as you know your own bedroom, and you are probably, therefore, not just a little crazy for new places, new experiences. So cut me some slack.

Fort Wyvern, named for General Harrison Blair Wyvern, a highly decorated hero of the First World War, was commissioned in 1939, as a training and support facility. It covers 134,456 acres, which makes it neither the largest nor by far the smallest military base in the state of California.

During the Second World War, Fort Wyvern established a school for tank warfare, offering training in the operation and maintenance of every tread-driven vehicle in use in the battlefields of Europe and in the Asian theater. Other schools under the Wyvern umbrella provided first-rate education in demolitions and bomb disposal, sabotage, field artillery, field medical service, military policing, and cryptography, as well as basic training to tens of thousands of infantrymen. Within its boundaries were an artillery range, a huge network of bunkers serving as an ammunition dump, an airfield, and more buildings than exist within the city limits of Moonlight Bay.

At the height of the Cold War, active-duty personnel assigned to Fort Wyvern numbered – officially – 36,400. There were also 12,904 dependents and over four thousand civilian personnel associated with the base. The military payroll was well over seven hundred million dollars annually, and the contract expenditures exceeded one hundred and fifty million per annum.

When Wyvern was shut down at the recommendation of the Defense Base Closure and Realignment Commission, the sound of money being sucked out of the county economy was so loud that local merchants were unable to sleep because of the noise and their babies cried in the night for fear of having no college tuition when eventually they would need it. KBAY, which lost nearly a third of its potential county-wide audience and fully half of its late-night listeners, was forced to trim staff, which was why Sasha found herself serving as both the post-midnight jock and the general manager and why Doogie Sassman worked eight hours of overtime per week for regular wage and never flexed his tattooed biceps in protest.

By no means continuous but nevertheless frequent major building projects of a high-security nature were undertaken on the grounds of Fort Wyvern by military contractors whose laborers were reportedly sworn to secrecy and remained, for life, at risk of being charged with treason for a slip of the tongue. According to rumor, because of its proud history as a center of military training and education, Wyvern was chosen as the site of a major chemical-biological warfare research facility constructed as a huge self-contained, biologically secure, subterranean complex.

Given the events of the past twelve hours, I felt confident in assuming that more than a scrap of truth underlay these rumors, although I have never seen a single thread of evidence that such a stronghold exists.

The abandoned base offers sights that are, however, as likely to amaze you, give you the creeps, and make you ponder the extent of human folly as anything that you will see in a cryobiological warfare laboratory. I think of Fort Wyvern, in its present state, as a macabre theme park, divided into various lands much the same as Disneyland is divided, with the difference that only one patron, along with his faithful dog, is admitted at any one time.

Dead Town is one of my favorites.

Dead Town is my name for it, not what it was called when Fort Wyvern thrived. It consists of more than three thousand single-family cottages and duplex bungalows in which married active-duty personnel and their dependents were housed if they chose to live on base. Architecturally, these humble structures have little to recommend them, and each is virtually identical to the one next door; they provided the minimum of comforts to the mostly young families who occupied them, each for only a couple of years at a time, over the war-filled decades. But in spite of their sameness, these are pleasant houses, and when you walk through their empty rooms, you can feel that life was lived well in them, with lovemaking and laughter and gatherings of friends.

These days the streets of Dead Town, laid out in a military grid, feature drifts of dust against the curbs and dry tumbleweeds waiting for wind. After the rainy season, the grass quickly turns brown and stays that shade most of the year. The shrubs are all withered, and many of the trees are dead, their leafless branches blacker than the black sky at which they seem to claw. Mice have the houses to themselves, and birds build nests on the front-door lintels, painting the stoops with their droppings.

You might expect that the structures would either be maintained against the real possibility of future need or efficiently razed, but there is no money for either solution. The materials and the fixtures of the buildings have less value than the cost of salvaging them, so no contract can be negotiated to dispose of them in that manner. For the time being, they are left to deteriorate in the elements much as the ghost towns of the gold-mining era were abandoned.

Wandering through Dead Town, you feel as though everyone in the world has vanished or died of a plague and that you are alone on the face of the earth. Or that you have gone mad and exist now in a grim solipsist fantasy, surrounded by people that you refuse to see. Or that you have died and gone to Hell, where your particular damnation consists of eternal isolation. When you see a scruffy coyote or two prowling between the houses, lean of flank, with long teeth and fiery eyes, they appear to be demons, and the Hades fantasy is the easiest one to believe. If your father was a professor of poetry, however, and if you are blessed or cursed with a three-hundred-ring circus of a mind, you can imagine countless scenarios to explain the place.

This night in March, I cycled through a couple of streets in Dead Town, but I didn't stop to visit. The fog had not reached this far inland, and the dry air was warmer than the humid murk along the coast;

though the moon had set, the stars were bright, and the night was ideal for sightseeing. To thoroughly explore even this one land in the theme park that is Wyvern, however, you need to devote a week to the task.

I was not aware of being watched. After what I'd learned in the past few hours, I knew that I must have been monitored at least intermittently on my previous visits.

Beyond the borders of Dead Town lay numerous barracks and other buildings. A once-fine commissary, a barber shop, a dry cleaner, a florist, a bakery, a bank: their signs peeling and caked with dust. A day-care center. High-school-age military brats attended classes in Moonlight Bay; but there are a kindergarten and an elementary school here. In the base library, the cobwebbed shelves are stripped of books except for one overlooked copy of *The Catcher in the Rye*. Dental and medical clinics. A movie theater with nothing on its flat marquee except a single enigmatic word: WHO. A bowling alley. An Olympic-size pool now drained and cracked and blown full of debris. A fitness center. In the rows of stables, which no longer shelter horses, the unlatched stall doors swing with an ominous chorus of rasping and creaking each time the wind stiffens. The softball field is choked with weeds, and the rotting carcass of a mountain lion that lay for more than a year in the batter's cage is at last only a skeleton.

I was not interested in any of these destinations, either. I cycled past them to the hangarlike building that stands over the warren of subterranean chambers in which I found the Mystery Train cap on a visit last autumn.

Clipped to the back rack of my bicycle is a police flashlight with a switch that allows the beam to be adjusted to three degrees of brightness. I parked at the hangar and unsnapped the flashlight from the rack.

Orson finds Fort Wyvern alternately frightening and fascinating, but regardless of his reaction on any particular night, he stays at my side, uncomplaining. This time, he was clearly spooked, but he didn't hesitate or whine.

The smaller man-size door in one of the larger hangar doors was unlocked. Switching on the flashlight, I went inside with Orson at my heels.

This hangar isn't adjacent to the airfield, and it's unlikely that aircraft were stored or serviced here. Overhead are the tracks on which a mobile crane, now gone, once moved from end to end of the structure. Judging by the sheer mass and complexity of the steel supports for these elaborate rails, the crane lifted objects of great weight. Steel bracing plates, still bolted to the concrete, once must have been surmounted by substantial machinery. Elsewhere, curiously shaped wells in the floor, now empty, appear to have housed hydraulic mechanisms of unknowable purpose.

In the passing beam of my flashlight, geometric patterns of shadow and light leaped off the crane tracks. Like the ideograms of an unknown language, they stenciled the walls and the Quonset-curve of the ceiling, revealing that half the panes in the high clerestory windows were broken.

Unnervingly, the impression wasn't of a vacated machine shop or maintenance center, but of an abandoned church. The oil and chemical stains on the floor gave forth an incenselike aroma. The penetrating cold was not solely a physical sensation but affected the spirit as well, as if this were a deconsecrated place.

A vestibule in one corner of the hangar houses a

set of stairs and a large elevator shaft from which the lift mechanism and the cab had been removed. I can't be sure, but judging from the aftermath left by those who had gutted the building, access to the vestibule had once been through another chamber; and I suspect that the existence of the stairs and elevator was kept secret from most of the personnel who had worked in the hangar or who'd had occasion to pass through it.

A formidable steel frame and threshold remain at the top of the stairwell, but the door is gone. With the flashlight beam, I chased spiders and pill bugs from the steps and led Orson downward through a film of dust that bore no footprints except those that we had left during other visits.

The steps serve three subterranean floors, each with a footprint considerably larger than the hangar above. This webwork of corridors and windowless rooms has been assiduously stripped of every item that might provide a clue to the nature of the enterprise conducted here. Stripped all the way to the bare concrete. Even the smallest elements of the air-filtration and plumbing systems have been torn out.

I have a sense that this meticulous eradication is only partly explained by their desire to prevent anyone from ascertaining the purpose of the place. Although I'm operating strictly on intuition, I believe that as they scrubbed away every trace of the work done here, they were motivated in part by *shame*.

I don't believe, however, that this is the chemical-biological warfare facility that I mentioned earlier. Considering the high degree of biological isolation required, that subterranean complex is surely in a more remote corner of Fort Wyvern, dramatically larger than these three immense floors, more elaborately hidden, and buried far deeper beneath the earth.

Besides, that facility is apparently still operative.

Nevertheless, I am convinced that dangerous and extraordinary activities of one kind or another were conducted beneath this hangar. Many of the chambers, reduced only to their basic concrete forms, have features that are at once baffling and – because of their sheer strangeness – profoundly disquieting.

One of these puzzling chambers is on the deepest level, down where no dust has yet drifted, at the center of the floor plan, ringed by corridors and smaller rooms. It is an enormous ovoid, a hundred and twenty feet long, not quite sixty feet in diameter at its widest point, tapering toward the ends. The walls, ceiling, and floor are curved, so that when you stand here, you feel as if you are within the empty shell of a giant egg.

Entrance is through a small adjacent space that might have been fitted out as an airlock. Rather than a door, there must have been a hatch; the only opening in the walls of this ovoid chamber is a circle five feet in diameter.

Moving across the raised, curved threshold and passing through this aperture with Orson, I swept the light over the width of the surrounding wall, marveling at it as always: five feet of poured-in-place, steel-reinforced concrete.

Inside the giant egg, the continuous smooth curve that forms the walls, the floor, and the ceiling is sheathed in what appears to be milky, vaguely golden, translucent glass at least two or three inches thick. It's not glass, however, because it's shatterproof and because, when tapped hard, it rings like tubular bells. Furthermore, no seams are evident anywhere.

This exotic material is highly polished and appears as slick as wet porcelain. The flashlight beam penetrates this coating, quivers and flickers through it, flares off the faint golden whorls within, and shimmers across its surface. Yet the stuff was not in the least slippery as we crossed to the center of the chamber.

My rubber-soled shoes barely squeaked. Orson's claws made faint elfin music, ringing off the floor with a *tink-ting* like finger bells.

On this night of my father's death, on this night of nights, I wanted to return to this place where I'd found my Mystery Train cap the past autumn. It had been lying in the center of the egg room, the only object left behind in the entire three floors below the hangar.

I had thought that the cap had merely been forgotten by the last worker or inspector to leave. Now I suspected that on a certain October night, persons unknown had been aware of me exploring this facility, that they had been following me floor to floor without my knowledge, and that they had eventually slipped ahead of me to place the cap where I would be sure to find it.

If this were the case, it seemed to be not a mean or taunting act but more of a greeting, perhaps even a kindness. Intuition told me that the words *Mystery Train* had something to do with my mother's work. Twenty-one months after her death, someone had given me the cap because it was a link to her, and whoever had made the gift was someone who admired my mother and respected me if only because I was her son.

This is what I wanted to believe: that there were, indeed, those involved in this seemingly impenetrable conspiracy who did not see my mother as a villain and who felt friendly toward me, even if they did not revere me as Roosevelt insisted. I wanted to believe that there were good guys in this, not merely bad, because when I learned what my mother had done to destroy the world as we know it, I preferred to receive that information from people who were convinced, at least, that her *intentions* had been good.

I didn't want to learn the truth from people who looked at me, saw my mother, and bitterly spat out that curse and accusation: *You!*

'Is anyone here?' I asked.

My question spiraled in both directions along the walls of the egg room and returned to me as two separate echoes, one to each ear.

Orson chuffed inquiringly. This soft sound lingered along the curved planes of the chamber, like a breeze whispering across water.

Neither of us received an answer.

'I'm not out for vengeance,' I declared. 'That's behind me.'

Nothing.

'I don't even intend to go to outside authorities anymore. It's too late to undo whatever's been done. I accept that.'

The echo of my voice gradually faded. As it some-times did, the egg room filled with an uncanny silence that felt as dense as water.

I waited a minute before breaking that silence again: 'I don't want Moonlight Bay wiped from the map – and me and my friends with it – for no good reason. All I want now is to understand.'

No one cared to enlighten me.

Well, coming here had been a long shot anyway.

I wasn't disappointed. I have rarely allowed myself

to feel disappointment about anything. The lesson of my life is patience.

Above these man-made caverns, dawn was rapidly approaching, and I couldn't spare more time for Fort Wyvern. I had one more essential stop to make before retreating to Sasha's house to wait out the reign of the murderous sun.

Orson and I crossed the dazzling floor, in which the flashlight beam was refracted along glimmering golden whorls like galaxies of stars underfoot.

Beyond the hatches' entry portal, in the drab concrete vault that might have once been an airlock, we found my father's suitcase. The one that I had put down in the hospital garage before hiding under the hearse, that had been gone when I'd come out of the cold-holding room.

It had not, of course, been here when we had passed through five minutes ago.

I stepped around the suitcase, into the room beyond the vault, and swept that space with the light. No one was there.

Orson waited diligently at the suitcase, and I returned to his side.

When I lifted the bag, it was so light that I thought it must be empty. Then I heard something tumble softly inside.

As I was releasing the latches, my heart clutched at the thought that I might find another pair of eyeballs in the bag. To counter this hideous image, I conjured Sasha's lovely face in my mind, which started my heart beating again.

When I opened the lid, the suitcase appeared to contain only air. Dad's clothes, toiletries, paperback books, and other effects were gone.

Then I saw the photograph in one corner of the bag. It was the snapshot of my mother that I had promised would be cremated with my father's body.

I held the picture under the flashlight. She was lovely. And such fierce intelligence shone from her eyes.

In her face, I saw certain aspects of my own countenance that made me understand why Sasha could, after all, look favorably on me. My mother was smiling in this picture, and her smile was so like mine.

Orson seemed to want to look at the photograph, so I turned it toward him. For long seconds his gaze traveled the image. His thin whine, when he looked away from her face, was the essence of sadness.

We *are* brothers, Orson and me. I am the fruit of Wisteria's heart and womb. Orson is the fruit of her mind. He and I share no blood, but we share things more important than blood.

When Orson whined again, I firmly said, 'Dead and gone,' with that ruthless focus on the future that gets me through the day.

Forgoing one more look at the photograph, I tucked it into my shirt pocket.

No grief. No despair. No self-pity.

Anyway, my mother is not entirely dead. She lives in me and in Orson and perhaps in others like Orson.

Regardless of any crimes against humanity of which my mother might stand accused by others, she is alive in us, alive in the Elephant Man and his freak dog. And with all due humility, I think that the world is better for us being in it, Orson and me. We are not the bad guys.

As we left the vault, I said 'thank you' to whoever had left the photograph for me, though I didn't know if they could hear and though I was only assuming that their intentions had been kind.

Above ground, outside the hangar, my bicycle was where I'd left it. The stars were where I'd left them, too.

I cycled back through the edge of Dead Town and toward Moonlight Bay, where the fog – and more – waited for me.

Five

NEAR DAWN

30

The Nantucket-style house, with dark wood-shingle siding and deep white porches, seems to have slid three thousand miles during an unnoticed tipping of the continent, coming to rest here in the California hills above the Pacific. Looking more suitable to the landscape than logic says it should, sitting toward the front of the one-acre lot, shaded by stone pines, the residence exudes the charm, grace, and warmth of the loving family that lives within its walls.

All the windows were dark, but before long, light would appear in a few of them. Rosalina Ramirez would rise early to prepare a lavish breakfast for her son, Manuel, who would soon return from a double shift of policework – assuming he wouldn't be delayed by the extensive paperwork associated with Chief Stevenson's immolation. As he was a better cook than his mother, Manuel would prefer to make his own breakfast, but he would eat what she gave him and praise it. Rosalina was still sleeping; she had the large bedroom that had once belonged to her son, a room that he'd not used since his wife died giving birth to Toby.

Beyond a deep backyard, shingled to match the house and with windows flanked by white shutters, stands a small barn with a gambrel roof. Because the property is at the extreme southern end of town, it offers access to riding trails and the open hills; the original owner had stabled horses in the barn. Now the structure is a studio, where Toby Ramirez builds his life from glass.

Approaching through the fog, I saw the windows glowing. Toby often wakes long before dawn and comes out to the studio.

I propped the bike against the barn wall and went to the nearest window. Orson put his forepaws on the windowsill and stood beside me, peering inside.

When I pay a visit to watch Toby create, I usually don't go into the studio. The fluorescent ceiling panels are far too bright. And because borosilicate glass is worked at temperatures exceeding twenty-two hundred degrees Fahrenheit, it emits significant amounts of intense light that can damage anyone's eyes, not just mine. If Toby is between tasks, he may turn the lights off, and then we talk for a while.

Now, wearing a pair of goggles with didymium lenses, Toby was in his work chair at the glassblowing table, in front of the Fisher Multi-Flame burner. He had just finished forming a graceful pear-shaped vase with a long neck, which was still so hot that it was glowing gold and red; now he was annealing it.

When a piece of glassware is removed suddenly from a hot flame, it will usually cool too quickly, develop stresses – and crack. To preserve the item, it must be annealed – that is, cooled in careful stages.

The flame was fed by natural gas mixed with pure oxygen from a pressurized tank that was chained to the glassblowing table. During the annealing process, Toby would feather out the oxygen, gradually reducing the temperature, giving the glass molecules time to shift to more stable positions.

Because of the numerous dangers involved in glassblowing, some people in Moonlight Bay thought it was irresponsible of Manuel to allow his Down's-afflicted son to practice this technically demanding art and craft. Fiery catastrophes were envisioned, predicted, and awaited with impatience in some quarters.

Initially, no one was more opposed to Toby's glass dream than Manuel. For fifteen years, the barn had served as a studio for Carmelita's older brother, Salvador, a first-rank glass artist. As a child, Toby had spent uncounted hours with his Uncle Salvador, wearing goggles, watching the master at work, on rare occasion donning Kevlar mittens to transfer a vase or bowl to or from the annealing oven. While he'd appeared to many to be passing those hours in stupefaction, with a dull gaze and a witless smile, he had actually been learning without being directly taught. To cope, the intellectually disadvantaged often must have superhuman patience. Toby sat day after day, year after year, in his uncle's studio, watching and slowly learning. When Salvador died two years ago, Toby – then only fourteen – asked his father if he might continue his uncle's work. Manuel had not taken the request seriously, and he'd gently discouraged his son from dwelling on this impossible dream.

One morning before dawn, he found Toby in the studio. At the end of the work table, standing on the fire-resistant Ceramfab top, was a family of simple, blown-glass swans. Beside the swans stood a newly formed and annealed vase into which had been introduced a calculated mixture of compatible impurities that imparted to the glass mysterious midnight-blue swirls with a silvery glitter like stars. Manuel knew at once that this piece was equal to the finest vases that Salvador had ever produced; and Toby was at that very moment flame-annealing an equally striking piece of work.

The boy had absorbed the technical aspects of glass craft from his uncle, and in spite of his mild retardation, he obviously knew the proper procedures for avoiding injury. The magic of genetics was involved, too, for he possessed a striking talent that could not have been learned. He wasn't merely a craftsman but an artist, and not merely an artist but perhaps an idiot savant to whom the inspiration of the artist and the techniques of the craftsman came with the ease of waves to the shore.

Gift shops in Moonlight Bay, Cambria, and as far north as Carmel sold all the glass Toby produced. In a few years, he might become self-supporting.

Sometimes, nature throws a bone to those she maims. Witness my own ability to compose sentences and paragraphs with some skill.

Now, in the studio, orange light flared and billowed from the large, bushy annealing flame. Toby took care to turn the pear-shaped vase so that it was bathed uniformly by the fire.

With a thick neck, rounded shoulders, and proportionately short arms and stocky legs, he might have been a storybook gnome before a watch fire deep in the earth. Brow sloped and heavy. Bridge of the nose flat. Ears set too low on a head slightly too small for his body. His soft features and the inner epicanthic folds of his eyes give him a perpetual dreamy expression.

Yet on his high work chair, turning the glass in

the flame, adjusting the oxygen flow with intuitive precision, face shimmering with reflected light, eyes concealed behind didymium goggles, Toby did not in any way seem below average, did not in any way impress me as being diminished by his condition. To the contrary, observed in his element, in the act of creation, he appeared exalted.

Orson snorted with alarm. He dropped his forepaws from the window, turned away from the studio, and tightened into a wary crouch.

Turning as well, I saw a shadowy figure crossing the backyard, coming toward us. In spite of the darkness and fog, I recognized him at once because of the easy way that he carried himself. It was Manuel Ramirez: Toby's dad, number two in the Moonlight Bay Police Department but now at least temporarily risen by succession to the top post, due to the fiery death of his boss.

I put both hands in my jacket pockets. I closed my right hand around the Glock.

Manuel and I were friends. I wouldn't feel comfortable pointing a gun at him, and I certainly couldn't shoot him. Unless he was not Manuel anymore. Unless, like Stevenson, he had become someone else.

He stopped eight or ten feet from us. In the annealing flame's coruscating orange glow, which pierced the nearby window, I could see that Manuel was wearing his khaki uniform. His service pistol was holstered on his right hip. Although he stood with his thumbs hooked in his gun belt, he would be able to draw his weapon at least as quickly as I could pull the Glock from my jacket.

'Your shift over already?' I asked, although I knew it wasn't.

Instead of answering me, he said, 'I hope you're not expecting beer, tamales, and Jackie Chan movies at this hour.'

'I just stopped by to say hello to Toby if he happened to be between jobs.'

Manuel's face, too worn with care for his forty years, had a naturally friendly aspect. Even in this Halloween light, his smile was still engaging, reassuring. As far as I could see, the only luminosity in his eyes was the reflected light from the studio window. Of course, that reflection might mask the same transient flickers of animal eyeshine that I'd seen in Lewis Stevenson.

Orson was reassured enough to ease out of his crouch. But he remained wary.

Manuel exhibited none of Stevenson's simmering rage or electric energy. As always, his voice was soft and almost musical. 'You never did come around to the station after you called.'

I considered my answer and decided to go with the truth. 'Yes, I did.'

'So when you phoned me, you were already close,' he guessed.

'Right around the corner. Who's the bald guy with the earring?'

Manuel mulled over his answer and followed my lead with some truth of his own. 'His name's Carl Scorso.'

'But who is he?'

'A total dirtbag. How far are you going to carry this?'

'Nowhere.'

He was silent, disbelieving.

'It started out as a crusade,' I admitted. 'But I know when I'm beaten.'

'That sure would be a new Chris Snow.'

'Even if I could contact an outside authority or the media, I don't understand the situation well enough to convince them of anything.'

'And you have no proof.'

'Nothing substantive. Anyway, I don't think I'd be allowed to make that contact. If I could get someone to come investigate, I don't think I or any of my friends would be alive to greet them when they got here.'

Manuel didn't reply, but his silence was all the answer I needed.

He might still be a baseball fan. He might still like country music, Abbott and Costello. He still understood as much as I did about limitations and still felt the hand of fate as I did. He might even still like me – but he was no longer my friend. If he wouldn't be sufficiently treacherous to pull the trigger on me himself, he would watch as someone else did.

Sadness pooled in my heart, a greasy despondency that I'd never felt before, akin to nausea. 'The entire police department has been co-opted, hasn't it?'

His smile had faded. He looked tired.

When I saw weariness in him rather than anger, I knew that he was going to tell me more than he should. Riven by guilt, he would not be able to keep all his secrets.

I already suspected that I knew one of the revelations he would make about my mother. I was so loath to hear it that I almost walked away. Almost.

'Yes,' he said. 'The entire department.'

'Even you.'

'Oh, *mi amigo*, especially me.'

'Are you infected by whatever bug came out of Wyvern?'

'"Infection" isn't quite the word.'

'But close enough.'

'Everyone else in the department has it. But not me. Not that I know. Not yet.'

'So maybe they had no choice. You did.'

'I decided to cooperate because there might be a lot more good that comes from this than bad.'

'From the end of the world?'

'They're working to undo what's happened.'

'Working out there at Wyvern, underground somewhere?'

'There and other places, yeah. And if they find a way to combat it . . . then wonderful things could come from this.'

As he spoke, his gaze moved from me to the studio window.

'Toby,' I said.

Manuel's eyes shifted to me again.

I said, 'This thing, this plague, whatever it is – you're hoping that if they can bring it under control, they'll be able to use it to help Toby somehow.'

'You have a selfish interest here, too, Chris.'

From the barn roof, as if suspicious of everyone in Moonlight Bay, an owl asked its single question of identity five times in quick succession.

I took a deep breath and said, 'That's the only reason my mother would work on biological research for military purposes. The only reason. Because there was a very good chance that something would come of it that might cure my XP.'

'And something may still come of it.'

'It was a weapons project?'

'Don't blame her, Chris. Only a weapons project

would have tens of billions of dollars behind it. She'd never have had a chance to do this work for the *right* reasons. It was just too expensive.'

This was no doubt true. Nothing but a weapons project would have the bottomless resources needed to fund the complex research that my mother's most profound concepts necessitated.

Wisteria Jane (Milbury) Snow was a theoretical geneticist. This means that she did the heavy thinking while other scientists did the heavy lifting. She didn't spend much of her time in laboratories or even working in the virtual lab of a computer. Her lab was her mind, and it was extravagantly equipped. She theorized, and with guidance from her, others sought to prove her theories.

I have said that she was brilliant but perhaps not that she was extraordinarily brilliant. Which she was. She could have chosen any university affiliation in the world. They all sought her.

My father loved Ashdon, but he would have followed her where she wished to go. He would have thrived in any academic environment.

She restricted herself to Ashdon because of me. Most of the truly great universities are in either major or midsize cities, where I'd be no more limited by day than I am in Moonlight Bay, but where I'd have no hope of a rich life by night. Cities are bright even after sunset. And the few dark precincts of a city are not places where a young boy on a bicycle could safely go adventuring between dusk and dawn.

She made less of her life in order to make more of mine. She confined herself to a small town, willing to leave her full potential unrealized, to give me a chance at realizing mine.

Tests to determine genetic damage in a fetus were rudimentary when I was born. If the analytic tools had been sufficiently advanced for my XP to have been detected in the weeks following my conception, perhaps she would have chosen not to bring me into the world.

How I love the world in all its beauty and strangeness.

Because of me, however, the world will grow ever stranger in the years to come – and perhaps less beautiful.

If not for me, she would have refused to put her mind to work for the project at Wyvern, would never have led them on new roads of inquiry. And we would not have followed one of those roads to the precipice on the brink of which we now stand.

As Orson moved to make room for him, Manuel came to the window. He stared in at his son, and with his face more brightly lit, I could see not a wild light in his eyes but only overwhelming love.

'Enhancing the intelligence of animals,' I said. 'How would that have military applications?'

'For one thing, what better spy than a dog as smart as a human being, sent behind enemy lines? An impenetrable disguise. And they don't check dogs' passports. What better scout on a battlefield?'

Maybe you engineer an exceptionally powerful dog that's smart but also savagely vicious when it needs to be. You have a new kind of soldier: a biologically designed killing machine with the capacity for strategizing.

'I thought intelligence depended on brain size.'

He shrugged. 'I'm just a cop.'

'Or on the number of folds in the brain surface.'

'Evidently they discovered different. Anyway,'

Manuel said, 'there was a previous success. Something called the Francis Project, several years ago. An amazingly smart golden retriever. The Wyvern operation was launched to capitalize on what they learned from that. And at Wyvern it wasn't just about animal intelligence. It was about enhancing human intelligence, about lots of things, *many* things.'

In the studio, hands covered with Kevlar gloves, Toby placed the hot vase into a bucket half filled with vermiculite. This was the next stage of the annealing process.

Standing at Manuel's side, I said, 'Many things? What else?'

'They wanted to enhance human agility, speed, longevity – by finding ways not just to transfer genetic material from one person to another but from species to species.'

Species to species.

I heard myself say, 'Oh, my God.'

Toby poured more of the granular vermiculite over the vase, until it was covered. Vermiculite is a superb insulator that allows the glass to continue cooling very slowly and at a constant rate.

I remembered something Roosevelt Frost had said: that the dogs, cats, and monkeys were not the only experimental subjects in the labs at Wyvern, that there was something worse.

'People,' I said numbly. 'They experimented on people?'

'Soldiers court-martialed and found guilty of murder, condemned to life sentences in military prisons. They could rot there . . . or take part in the project and maybe win their freedom as a reward.'

'But experimenting on people . . .'

'I doubt your mother knew anything about that. They didn't always share with her *all* the ways they applied her ideas.'

Toby must have heard our voices at the window, because he took off the insulated gloves and raised the big goggles from his eyes to squint at us. He waved.

'It all went wrong,' Manuel said. 'I'm no scientist. Don't ask me how. But it went wrong not just in one way. Many ways. It blew up in their faces. Suddenly things happened they weren't expecting. Changes they didn't contemplate. The experimental animals and the prisoners – their genetic makeup underwent changes that weren't desired and couldn't be controlled . . .'

I waited a moment, but he apparently wasn't prepared to tell me more. I pressed him: 'A monkey escaped. A rhesus. They found it in Angela Ferryman's kitchen.'

The searching look that Manuel turned on me was so penetrating that I was sure he had seen into my heart, knew the contents of my every pocket, and had an accurate count of the number of bullets left in the Glock.

'They recaptured the rhesus,' he said, 'but made the mistake of attributing its escape to human error. They didn't realize it had been let go, *released*. They didn't realize there were a few scientists in the project who were . . . becoming.'

'Becoming what?'

'Just . . . becoming. Something new. Changing.'

Toby switched off the natural gas. The Fisher burner swallowed its own flames.

'Changing how?' I asked Manuel.

'Whatever delivery system they developed to insert

new genetic material in a research animal or prisoner
. . . that system just took on a life of its own.'

Toby turned off all but one panel of fluorescents, so
I could go inside for a visit.

Manuel said, 'Genetic material from other species
was being carried into the bodies of the project
scientists without their being aware of it. Eventually,
some of them began to have a lot in common with the
animals.'

'Jesus.'

'Too much in common maybe. There was some
kind of . . . episode. I don't know the details. It was
extremely violent. People died. And all the animals
either escaped or were let out.'

'The troop.'

'About a dozen smart, vicious monkeys, yes. But also
dogs and cats . . . and nine of the prisoners.'

'And they're still loose?'

'Three of the prisoners were killed in the attempt to
recapture them. The military police enlisted our help.
That's when most of the cops in the department were
contaminated. But the other six and all the animals . . .
they were never found.'

The man-size barn door opened, and Toby stepped
into the threshold. 'Daddy?' Shuffling as much as
walking, he came to his father and hugged him fiercely.
He grinned at me. 'Hello, Christopher.'

'Hi, Toby.'

'Hi, Orson,' the boy said, letting go of his father and
dropping to his knees to greet the dog.

Orson liked Toby. He allowed himself to be petted.

'Come visit,' Toby said.

To Manuel, I said, 'There's a whole new troop now.
Not violent like the first. Or at least . . . not violent

yet. All tagged with transponders and set loose on purpose. Why?'

'To find the first troop and report their whereabouts. They're so elusive that all other attempts to locate them have failed. It's a desperation plan, an attempt to do *something* before the first troop breeds too large. But this isn't working, either. It's just creating another problem.'

'And not only because of Father Eliot.'

Manuel stared at me for a long moment. 'You've learned a lot, haven't you?'

'Not enough. And too much.'

'You're right – Father Tom isn't the problem. Some have sought him out. Others chew the transponders out of each other. This new troop . . . they're not violent but they're plenty smart and they've become disobedient. They want their freedom. At any cost.'

Hugging Orson, Toby repeated his invitation to me: 'Come visit, Christopher.'

Before I could respond, Manuel said, 'It's almost dawn, Toby. Chris has to be going home.'

I looked toward the eastern horizon, but if the night sky was beginning to turn gray in that direction, the fog prevented me from seeing the change.

'We've been friends for quite a few years,' Manuel said. 'Seems like I owed you some pieces of the explanation. You've always been good to Toby. But you know enough now. I've done what's right for an old friend. Maybe I've done too much. You go on home now.' Without my noticing, he had moved his right hand to the gun in his holster. He patted the weapon. 'We won't be watching any Jackie Chan movies anymore, you and me.'

He was telling me not to come back. I wouldn't

have tried to maintain our friendship, but I might have returned to see Toby from time to time. Not now.

I called Orson to my side, and Toby reluctantly let him go.

'Maybe one more thing,' Manuel said as I gripped the handlebars of my bike. 'The benign animals who've been enhanced – the cats, the dogs, the new monkeys – they know their origins. Your mother . . . well, maybe you could say she's a legend to them . . . their maker . . . almost like their god. They know who you are, and they revere you. None of them would ever hurt you. But the original troop and most of the people who've been altered . . . even if on some level they like what they're becoming, they still hate your mother because of what they've lost. And they hate you for obvious reasons. Sooner or later, they're going to act on that. Against you. Against people close to you.'

I nodded. I was already acting on that assumption. 'And you can't protect me?'

He didn't reply. He put his arm around his son. In this new Moonlight Bay, family might still matter for a while, but already the concept of community was slipping away.

'Can't or won't protect me?' I wondered. Without waiting through another silence, I said, 'You never told me who Carl Scorso is,' referring to the bald man with the earring, who had apparently taken my father's body to an autopsy room in some secure facility still operative beneath a far corner of Fort Wyvern.

'He's one of the original prisoners who signed on for the experiments. The genetic damage related to his previous sociopathic behavior has been identified and edited out. He's not a dangerous man anymore. He's one of their few successes.'

I stared at him but couldn't read his true thoughts. 'He killed a transient and tore the guy's eyes out.'

'No. The troop killed the transient. Scorso just found the body along the road and brought it to Sandy Kirk for disposal. It happens now and then. Hitchhikers, drifters . . . there's always been lots of them moving up and down the California coast. These days, some of them don't get farther than Moonlight Bay.'

'And you live with that, too.'

'I do what I'm told,' he said coldly.

Toby put his arms around his father as if to protect him, giving me a look of dismay because of the way that I'd challenged his dad.

Manuel said, 'We do what we're told. That's the way it is here, these days, Chris. Decisions have been made at a very high level to let this business play out quietly. A very high level. Just suppose the President of the United States himself was something of a science buff, and suppose that he saw a chance to make history by putting the funds behind genetic engineering the way Roosevelt and Truman funded the Manhattan Project, the way that Kennedy funded the effort to put a man on the moon, and suppose he and everyone around him are now determined to cover this up.'

'Is that what's happened?'

'No one at the top wants to risk the public's wrath. Maybe they're not just afraid of being booted out of office. Maybe they're afraid of being tried for crimes against humanity. Afraid of being torn apart by angry mobs. I mean . . . soldiers from Wyvern and their families, who might've been contaminated – they're all over the country now. How many have they passed it to? Could be panic in the streets. An international movement to quarantine the whole U.S. And for no good reason. Because the powers-that-be think the whole thing might run its course without a major effect, peak soon and then just peter out.'

'Is there a chance of that?'

'Maybe.'

'I don't think there's a chance of that.'

He shrugged and with one hand smoothed Toby's hair, which was spiky and disarranged from the strap on the goggles that he'd been wearing. 'Not all the people with symptoms of change are like Lewis Stevenson. What's happening to them has infinite variety. And some who go through a bad phase . . . they get over it. They're in flux. This isn't an event, like an earthquake or a tornado. This is a process. If it had ever gotten to be necessary, I would've dealt with Lewis myself.'

Admitting nothing, I said, 'Maybe it was more necessary than you realized.'

'Can't have just everybody making those judgment calls. There's got to be order, stability.'

'But there is none.'

'There's me,' he said.

'Is it possible you're infected and don't know it?'

'No. Not possible.'

'Is it possible you're changing and don't realize it?'

'No.'

'Becoming?'

'No.'

'You scare the hell out of me, Manuel.'

The owl hooted again.

A faint but welcome breeze stirred like a ladle through the soupy fog.

'Go home,' Manuel said. 'It'll be light soon.'

'Who ordered Angela Ferryman killed?'

'Go home.'

'Who?'

'No one.'

'I think she was murdered because she was going to try to go public. She had nothing to lose, she told me. She was afraid of what she was . . . becoming.'

'The troop killed her.'

'Who controls the troop?'

'No one. We can't even *find* the fuckers.'

I thought I knew one place where they hung out: the drainage culvert in the hills, where I'd found the collection of skulls. But I wasn't going to share this information with Manuel, because at this point I couldn't be sure who were my most dangerous enemies: the troop – or Manuel and the other cops.

'If no one sent them after her, why'd they do it?'

'They have their own agenda. Maybe sometimes it matches ours. They don't want the world to know about this, either. Their future isn't in undoing what's been done. Their future is the new world coming. So if somehow they learned Angela's plans, they'd deal with her. There's no mastermind behind this, Chris. There're all these factions – the benign animals, the malevolent ones, the scientists at Wyvern, people who've been changed for the worse, people who've been changed for the better. Lots of competing factions. Chaos. And the chaos will get worse before it gets better. Now go home. Drop this. Drop it before someone targets you like they targeted Angela.'

'Is that a threat?'

He didn't reply.

As I started away, walking the bicycle across the

backyard, Toby said, 'Christopher Snow. Snow for Christmas. Christmas and Santa. Santa and sleigh. Sleigh on snow. Snow for Christmas. Christopher Snow.' He laughed with innocent delight, entertained by this awkward word game, and he was clearly pleased by my surprise.

The Toby Ramirez I had known would not have been capable of even such a simple word-association game as this one.

To Manuel, I said, 'They've begun to pay for your cooperation, haven't they?'

His fierce pride in Toby's exhibition of this new verbal skill was so touching and so deeply sad that I could not look at him.

'In spite of all that he didn't have, he was always happy,' I said of Toby. 'He found a purpose, fulfillment. Now what if they can take him far enough that he's dissatisfied with what he is . . . but then they can't take him all the way to normal?'

'They will,' Manuel said with a measure of conviction for which there could be no justification. 'They will.'

'The same people who've created this nightmare?'

'It's not got only a dark side.'

I thought of the pitiful wails of the visitor in the rectory attic, the melancholy quality of its changeling voice, the terrible yearning in its desperate attempts to convey meaning in a caterwaul. I thought of Orson on that summer night, despairing under the stars.

'God help you, Toby,' I said, because he was my friend, too. 'God bless you.'

'God had His chance,' Manuel said. 'From now on, we'll make our own luck.'

I had to get away from there, and not solely because

dawn was soon to arrive. I walked the bike across the backyard – and didn't realize that I'd broken into a run until I was past the house and in the street.

When I glanced back at the Nantucket-style residence, it looked different from the way that it had always been before. Smaller than I remembered. Huddled. Forbidding.

In the east, a silver-gray paleness was forming high above the world, either sunrise seeping in or Judgment coming.

In twelve hours I had lost my father, the friendship of Manuel and Toby, many illusions, and much innocence. I was overcome by the terrifying feeling that more and perhaps worse losses lay ahead.

Orson and I fled to Sasha's house.

31

Sasha's house is owned by KBAY and is a perk of her position as general manager of the station. It's a small two-story Victorian with elaborate millwork enhancing the faces of the dormers, all the gableboards, the eaves, the window and door surrounds, and the porch railings.

The house would be a jewel-box if it weren't painted the station colors. The walls are canary yellow. The shutters and porch railings are coral pink. All the other millwork is the precise shade of Key-lime pie. The result is as though a flock of Jimmy Buffet fans, high on Margaritas and piña coladas, painted the place during a long party weekend.

Sasha doesn't mind the flamboyant exterior. As she notes, she lives within the house, not outside where she can see it.

The deep back porch is enclosed with glass; and with the help of an electric space heater in cooler months, Sasha has transformed it into an herb greenhouse. On tables and benches and sturdy metal racks stand hundreds of terra-cotta pots and plastic trays in which she cultivates tarragon and thyme, angelica and arrowroot, chervil and cardamom and coriander and chicory, spearmint and sweet cicely, ginseng, hyssop, balm and basil, marjoram and mint and mullein, dill, fennel, rosemary, camomile, tansy. She uses these in her cooking, to make wonderful, subtly scented potpourris, and to brew health teas that challenge the gag reflex far less than you would expect.

I don't bother to carry a key of my own. A spare is tucked into a terra-cotta pot shaped like a toad, under the yellowish leaves of a rue plant. As the deadly dawn brightened to a paler gray in the east and the world prepared to murder dreams, I let myself into the shelter of Sasha's home.

In the kitchen, I immediately switched on the radio. Sasha was winding through the last half hour of her show, giving a weather report at the moment. We were still in the wet season, and a storm was coming in from the northwest. We would have rain shortly after nightfall.

If she had predicted that we were due for a hundred-foot tidal wave and volcanic eruptions with major rivers of lava, I would have listened with pleasure. When I heard her smooth, slightly throaty radio voice, a big stupid smile came over my face, and even on this morning near the end of the world, I couldn't help but be simultaneously soothed and aroused.

As the day brightened beyond the windows, Orson padded directly to the pair of hard-plastic bowls that stood on a rubber mat in one corner. His name is painted on each: Wherever he goes, whether to Bobby's cottage or to Sasha's, he is family.

As a puppy, my dog was given a series of names, but he didn't care to respond to any of them on a regular basis. After noticing how intently the mutt focused on old Orson Welles movies when we ran them on video – and especially to the appearance of Welles himself in any scene – we jokingly renamed him after the actor-director. He has ever since answered to this moniker.

When he found both bowls empty, Orson picked up one of them in his mouth and brought it to me. I filled it with water and returned it to the rubber mat, which prevented it from sliding on the white ceramic-tile floor.

He snatched up the second bowl and looked beseechingly at me. As is true of virtually any dog, Orson's eyes and face are better designed for a beseeching look than are the expressive features of the most talented actor who ever trod the boards.

Aboard the *Nostromo*, at the dining table with Roosevelt and Orson and Mungojerrie, I had recalled those well-executed but jokey paintings of dogs playing poker, which seem perennially popular – and it had occurred to me that my subconscious had been trying to tell me something important by so vividly resurrecting this image from my memory. Now I understood. Each of the dogs in those paintings represents a familiar human type, and each is obviously as smart as any human being. On the *Nostromo*, because of the game that Orson and the cat had played with each other, 'mocking their stereotypes,' I had realized that some of these animals out of Wyvern might be far smarter than I had previously thought – so smart that I wasn't yet ready to face the awesome truth. If they could hold cards and talk, they might win their share of poker hands; they might even take me to the cleaners.

'It's a little early,' I said, taking the food dish from Orson. 'But you did have a very active night.'

After shaking a serving of his favorite dry dog food

from the box into his bowl, I circled the kitchen, closing the Levelor blinds against the growing threat of the day. As I was shutting the last of them, I thought that I heard a door close softly elsewhere in the house.

I froze, listening.

'Something?' I whispered.

Orson looked up from his bowl, sniffed the air, cocked his head, then chuffed and once more turned his attention to his food.

The three-hundred-ring circus of my mind.

At the sink I washed my hands and splashed some cold water in my face.

Sasha keeps an immaculate kitchen, gleaming and sweet-smelling, but it's cluttered. She's a superb cook, and clusters of exotic appliances take up at least half the counter space. So many pots, pans, ladles, and utensils dangle from overhead racks that you feel as if you're spelunking through a cavern where every inch of the ceiling is hung with stalactites.

I moved through her house, closing blinds, feeling the vibrant spirit of her in every corner. She is so *alive* that she leaves an aura behind her that lingers long after she has gone.

Her home has no interior-design theme, no harmony in the flow of furniture and artwork. Rather, each room is a testament to one of her consuming passions. She is a woman of many passions.

All meals are taken at a large kitchen table, because the dining room is dedicated to her music. Along one wall is an electronic keyboard, a full-scale synthesizer with which she could compose for an orchestra if she wished, and adjacent to this is her composition table with music stand and a stack of pages with blank musical staffs awaiting her pencil. In the center of the room is a drum set. In a corner stands a high-quality cello with a low, cellist's stool. In another corner, beside a music stand, a saxophone hangs on a brass sax rack. There are two guitars as well, one acoustic and one electric.

The living room isn't about appearances but about books – another of her passions. The walls are lined with bookshelves, which overflow with hardcovers and paperbacks. The furniture is not trendy, neither stylish nor styleless: neutral-tone chairs and sofas selected for the comfort they provide, for the fact that they're perfect for sitting and talking or for spending long hours with a book.

On the second floor, the first room from the head of the stairs features an exercise bicycle, a rowing machine, a set of hand weights from two to twenty pounds, calibrated in two-pound increments, and exercise mats. This is her homeopathic-medicine room, as well, where she keeps scores of bottles of vitamins and minerals, and where she practices yoga. When she uses the Exercycle, she won't get off until she's streaming sweat and has churned up at least thirty miles on the odometer. She stays on the rowing machine until she's crossed Lake Tahoe in her mind, keeping a steady rhythm by singing tunes by Sarah McLachlan or Juliana Hatfield or Meredith Brooks or Sasha Goodall, and when she does stomach crunches and leg lifts, the padded mats under her seem as if they will start smoking before she's half done. When she's finished exercising, she's always more energetic than when she began, flushed and buoyant. And when she concludes a session of meditation in various yoga positions, the intensity of her *relaxation* seems powerful enough to blow out the walls of the room.

God, I love her.

As I stepped from the exercise room into the upstairs hall, I was stricken once more by that premonition of impending loss. I began to shake so badly that I had to lean against the wall until the episode passed.

Nothing could happen to her in daylight, not on the ten-minute drive from the broadcast studios on Signal Hill through the heart of town. The night is when the troop seems to roam. By day they go to ground somewhere, perhaps in the storm drains under the town or even in the hills where I'd found the collection of skulls. And the *people* who can no longer be trusted, the changelings like Lewis Stevenson, seem more in control of themselves under the sun than under the moon. As with the animal men in *The Island of Dr. Moreau*, the wildness in them will not be as easily suppressed at night. With the dusk, they lose a measure of self-control; a sense of adventure springs up in them, and they dare things that they never dream about by day. Surely nothing could happen to Sasha now that dawn was upon us; for perhaps the first time in my life, I felt relief at the rising of the sun.

Finally I came to her bedroom. Here you will find no musical instruments, not a single book, no pots or trays of herbs, no bottles of vitamins, no exercise equipment. The bed is simple, with a plain headboard, no footboard, and it is covered with a thin white chenille spread. There's nothing whatsoever remarkable about the dresser, the nightstands, or the lamps. The walls are pale yellow, the very shade of morning sunlight in a cloud; no artwork interrupts their smooth planes. The room might seem stark to some, but when Sasha's present, this space is as elaborately decorated as any baroque drawing room in a French castle, as nurturingly serene as any meditation point in a Zen garden. She never sleeps fitfully but always as deep and still as a stone at the bottom of the sea, so you find yourself reaching out to touch her, to feel the warmth of her skin or the throb of her pulse, to quiet the sudden fear for her that grips you from time to time. As with so many things, she has a passion for sleep. She has a passion for passion, too, and when she makes love to you, the room ceases to exist, and you're in a timeless time and a placeless place, where there's only Sasha, only the light and the heat of her, the glorious light of her that blazes but doesn't burn.

As I passed the foot of the bed, heading toward the first of three windows to close the blinds, I saw an object on the chenille spread. It was small, irregular, and highly polished: a fragment of hand-painted, glazed china. Half a smiling mouth, a curve of cheek, one blue eye. A shard from the face of the Christopher Snow doll that had shattered against the wall in Angela Ferryman's house just before the lights had gone out and the smoke had poured into the stairwell from above and below.

At least one of the troop had been here during the night.

Shaking again but with fury rather than fear this time, I ripped the pistol out of my jacket and set out to search the house, from the attic down, every room, every closet, every cupboard door, every smallest space in which one of these hateful creatures might be able to conceal itself. I wasn't stealthy and cautious. Cursing, making threats that I had every intention of fulfilling, I tore open doors, slammed drawers shut, poked under furniture with a broom handle. In general I created such a racket that Orson sprinted to my side with the expectation of finding me in a battle for my life – then followed me at a cautious distance, as if he feared that, in my current state of agitation, I might shoot myself in the foot and him in the paw if he stayed too close.

None of the troop was in the house.

When I concluded the search, I had the urge to fill a pail with strong ammonia water and sponge off every surface that the intruder – or intruders – might have touched: walls, floor, stair treads and railings, furniture. Not because I believed that they'd left behind any microorganisms that could infect us. Rather, because I found them to be unclean in a profoundly spiritual sense, as though they had come not out of laboratories at Wyvern but out of a vent in the earth from which also rose sulfur fumes, a terrible light, and the distant cries of the damned.

Instead of going for the ammonia, I used the kitchen phone to call the direct booth line at KBAY. Before I keyed in the last number, I realized that Sasha was off the air and already on her way home. I hung up and keyed in her mobile number.

'Hey, Snowman,' she said.

'Where are you?'

'Five minutes away.'

'Are your doors locked?'

'What?'

'For Christ's sake, are your doors locked?'

She hesitated. Then: 'They are now.'

'Don't stop for anyone. Not anyone. Not for a friend, not even for a cop. Especially not for a cop.'

'What if I accidentally run down a little old lady?'

'She won't be a little old lady. She'll only look like one.'

'You've suddenly gotten spooky, Snowman.'

'Not me. The rest of the world. Listen, I want you to stay on the phone until you're in the driveway.'

'Explorer to control tower: The fog's pulling back already. You don't need to talk me in.'

'I'm not talking you in. You're talking me *down*. I'm in a state here.'

'I sorta noticed.'

'I need to hear your voice. All the way. All the way home, your voice.'

'Smooth as the bay,' she said, trying to get me to lighten up.

I kept her on the phone until she drove her truck into the carport and switched off the engine.

Sun or no sun, regardless of the effects of cumulative damage, I wanted to go outside and meet her as she opened the driver's door. I wanted to be at her side with the Glock in my hand as she walked across the house to the rear porch, which was the entrance that she always used.

An hour seemed to pass before I heard her footsteps on the back porch, as she walked between the tables of potted herbs.

When she swung open the door, I was standing in the wide blade of morning light that slashed into the kitchen. I pulled her into my arms, slammed the door behind her and held her so tightly that for a moment neither of us could breathe. I kissed her then, and she was warm and real, real and glorious, glorious and alive.

No matter how tightly I held her, however, no matter how sweet her kisses, I was still haunted by that presentiment of worse losses to come.

Six

THE DAY AND THE NIGHT

32

With all that had happened during the previous night and with all that loomed in the night to come, I didn't imagine that we would make love. Sasha couldn't imagine *not* making love. Even though she didn't know the reason for my terror, the sight of me so fearful and shaken so completely by the thought of losing her was an aphrodisiac that put her in a mood not to be refused.

Orson, ever a gentleman, remained downstairs in the kitchen. We went upstairs to the bedroom and from there into the timeless time and placeless place where Sasha is the only energy, the only form of matter, the only force in the universe. So bright.

Afterward, in a mood that made even the most apocalyptic news seem tolerable, I told her about my night from sundown until dawn, about the millennium monkeys and Stevenson, about how Moonlight Bay was now a Pandora's box swarming with myriad evils.

If she thought that I was way insane, she hid her judgment well. When I told her of the taunting by the troop, which Orson and I had endured after leaving Bobby's house, she broke out in gooseflesh and had to pull on a robe. As she gradually realized fully how dire our situation was, that we had no one to whom we could turn and nowhere to run even if we were allowed to leave town, that we might already be tainted by this Wyvern plague, with effects to come that we could not even imagine, she pulled the collar of the robe tighter around her neck.

If she was repulsed by what I'd done to Stevenson, she managed to suppress her emotions with remarkable success, because when I was finished, when I had told her about even the fragment of the doll's face that I'd found on her bed, she slipped out of her robe and, although still stippled with gooseflesh, brought me into her light again.

This time, when we made love, we were quieter than before, moved more slowly, more gently than we had the first time. Although tender before, the motion and the act were more tender now. We clung to each other with love and need but also with desperation, because a new and poignant appreciation of our isolation was upon us. Strangely, though we shared a sense of being two condemned people with an executioner's clock ticking relentlessly, our fusion was sweeter than it had been previously.

Or maybe that isn't strange at all. Perhaps extreme danger strips us of all pretenses, all ambitions, all confusions, focusing us more intensely than we are otherwise ever focused, so that we remember what we otherwise spend most of our lives forgetting: that our nature and purpose is, more than anything else, to love and to make love, to take joy from the beauty of the world, to live with an awareness that the future is not as real a place for any one of us as are the present and the past.

If the world as we knew it was this minute being

flushed away, then my writing and Sasha's songwriting didn't matter. To paraphrase Bogart to Bergman: In this crazy future tumbling like an avalanche straight at us, the ambitions of two people didn't amount to a hill of beans. All that mattered was friendship, love, and surf. The wizards of Wyvern had given me and Sasha an existence as reduced to the essentials as was Bobby Halloway's.

Friendship, love, and surf. Get them while they're hot. Get them before they're gone. Get them while you're still human enough to know how precious they are.

For a while we lay in silence, holding each other, waiting for time to start flowing again. Or maybe hoping that it never would.

Then Sasha said, 'Let's cook.'

'I think we just did.'

'I mean omelets.'

'Mmmmmm. All those delicious egg whites,' I said, ridiculing her tendency to carry the concept of a healthy diet to extremes.

'I'll use the whole eggs today.'

'Now I *know* it's the end of the world.'

'Cooked in butter.'

'With cheese?'

'Somebody's got to keep the cows in business.'

'Butter, cheese, egg yolks. So you've decided on suicide.'

We were doing cool, but we weren't *being* cool.

We both knew it, too.

We kept at it anyway, because to do otherwise would be to admit how scared we were.

≈   ≈   ≈

The omelets were exceptionally good. So were the fried potatoes and the heavily buttered English muffins.

As Sasha and I ate by candlelight, Orson circled the kitchen table, mewling plaintively and making starving-child-of-the-ghetto eyes at us when we looked down at him.

'You already ate everything I put in your bowl,' I told him.

He chuffed as if astonished that I would make such a claim, and he resumed mewling pitiably at Sasha as though trying to assure her that I was lying, that no food whatsoever had yet been provided for him. He rolled onto his back, wriggled, and pawed at the air in an all-out assault of merciless cuteness, trying to earn a nibble. He stood on his hind feet and turned in a circle. He was shameless.

With one foot, I pushed a third chair away from the table and said, 'Okay, sit up here.'

Immediately he leaped onto the chair and sat at eager attention, regarding me intently.

I said, 'Ms. Goodall here has bought a fully radical, way insane story from me, without any proof except a few months of diary entries by an obviously disturbed priest. She probably did this because she is critically sex crazy and needs a man, and I'm the only one that'll have her.'

Sasha threw a corner of buttered toast at me. It landed on the table in front of Orson.

He darted for it.

'No way, bro!' I said.

He stopped with his mouth open and his teeth bared, an inch from the scrap of toast. Instead of eating the morsel, he sniffed it with obvious pleasure.

'If you help me prove to Ms. Goodall that what I've

told her about the Wyvern project is true, I'll share some of my omelet and potatoes with you.'

'Chris, his heart,' Sasha worried, backsliding into her Grace Granola persona.

'He doesn't have a heart,' I said. 'He's all stomach.'

Orson looked at me reproachfully, as if to say that it wasn't fair to engage in put-down humor when he was unable to participate.

To the dog I said, 'When someone nods his head, that means *yes*. When he shakes his head side to side, that means *no*. You understand that, don't you?'

Orson stared at me, panting and grinning stupidly.

'Maybe you don't trust Roosevelt Frost,' I said, 'but you have to trust this lady here. You don't have a choice, because she and I are going to be together from now on, under the same roof, for the rest of our lives.'

Orson turned his attention to Sasha.

'Aren't we?' I asked her. 'The rest of our lives?'

She smiled. 'I love you, Snowman.'

'I love you, Ms. Goodall.'

Looking at Orson, she said, 'From now on, pooch, it's not the two of you anymore. It's the three of us.'

Orson blinked at me, blinked at Sasha, stared with unblinking desire at the bite of toast on the table in front of him.

'Now,' I said, 'do you understand about nods and shakes?'

After a hesitation, Orson nodded.

Sasha gasped.

'Do you think she's nice?' I asked.

Orson nodded.

'Do you like her?'

Another nod.

A giddy delight swept through me. Sasha's face was shining with the same elation.

My mother, who destroyed the world, had also helped to bring marvels and wonders into it.

I had wanted Orson's cooperation not only to confirm my story but to lift our spirits and give us reason to hope that there might be life after Wyvern. Even if humanity was now faced with dangerous new adversaries like the members of the original troop that escaped the labs, even if we were swept by a mysterious plague of gene-jumping from species to species, even if few or any of us survived the coming years without fundamental changes of an intellectual, emotional, and even physical nature – perhaps there was nevertheless some chance that when we, the current champions of the evolutionary game, stumbled and fell out of the race and passed away, there would be worthy heirs who might do better with the world than we did.

Cold comfort is better than none.

'Do you think Sasha's pretty?' I asked the dog.

Orson studied her thoughtfully for long seconds. Then he turned to me and nodded.

'That could have been a little quicker,' Sasha complained.

'Because he took his time, checked you out good, you know he's being sincere,' I assured her.

'I think you're pretty, too,' Sasha told him.

Orson wagged his tail across the back of his chair.

'I'm a lucky guy, aren't I, bro?' I asked him.

He nodded vigorously.

'And I'm a lucky girl,' she said.

Orson turned to her and shook his head: *No.*

'Hey,' I said.

The dog actually winked at me, grinning and making that soft wheezing sound that I swear is laughter.

'He can't even talk,' I said, 'but he can do put-down humor.'

We weren't just doing cool now. We were being cool.

If you're genuinely cool, you'll get through anything. That's one of the primary tenets of Bobby Halloway's philosophy, and from my current vantage point, post-Wyvern, I have to say that Philosopher Bob offers a more effective guide to a happy life than all of his big-browed competitors from Aristotle to Kierkegaard to Thomas More to Schelling – to Jacopo Zabarella, who believed in the primacy of logic, order, method. Logic, order, method. All important, sure. But can all of life be analyzed and understood with only those tools? Not that I'm about to claim to have met Big Foot or to be able to channel dead spirits or to be the reincarnation of Kahuna, but when I see where diligent attention to logic, order, and method have at last brought us, to this genetic storm . . . Well, I think I'd be happier catching some epic waves.

For Sasha, apocalypse was no cause for insomnia. As always, she slept deeply.

Although exhausted, I dozed fitfully. The bedroom door was locked, and a chair was wedged under the knob. Orson was sleeping on the floor, but he would be a good early-warning system if anyone entered the house. The Glock was on my nightstand, and Sasha's Smith & Wesson .38 Chiefs Special was on her nightstand. Yet I repeatedly woke with a start, sure that someone had crashed into the bedroom, and I didn't feel safe.

My dreams didn't soothe me. In one of them, I was a drifter, walking alongside a desert highway under a full moon, thumbing a ride without success. In my right hand was a suitcase exactly like my father's. It couldn't have been heavier if it had been filled with bricks. Finally, I put it down, opened it, and recoiled as Lewis Stevenson rose out of it like a cobra from a basket, golden light shimmering in his eyes, and I knew that if something as strange as the dead chief could be in my suitcase, something even stranger could be in me, whereupon I felt the top of my head unzipping – and woke up.

An hour before sundown, I telephoned Bobby from Sasha's kitchen.

'How's the weather out there at monkey central?' I asked.

'Storm coming in later. Big thunderheads far out to sea.'

'Did you get some sleep?'

'After the jokesters left.'

'When was that?'

'After I turned the tables and started mooning *them*.'

'They were intimidated,' I said.

'Damn right. I've got the bigger ass, and they know it.'

'You have a lot of ammunition for that shotgun?'

'A few boxes.'

'We'll bring more.'

'Sasha's not on the air tonight?'

'Not Saturdays,' I said. 'Maybe not weeknights any-more, either.'

'Sounds like news.'

'We're an item. Listen, do you have a fire extin-guisher out there?'

'Now you're bragging, bro. The two of you aren't *that* hot together.'

'We'll bring a couple of extinguishers. These dudes have a thing for fire.'

'You really think it'll get that real?'

'Totally.'

≈ ≈ ≈

Immediately after sunset, while I waited in the Explorer, Sasha went into Thor's Guns to buy ammunition for the shotgun, the Glock, and her Chiefs Special. The order was so large and heavy that Thor Heissen himself carried it out to the truck for her and loaded it in back.

He came to the passenger window to say hello. He is a tall fat man with a face pitted by acne scars, and his left eye is glass. He's not one of the world's best-looking guys, but he's a former L.A. cop who quit on principle, not because of scandal, an active deacon at his church and founder of – and largest contributor to – the orphanage associated with it.

'Heard about your dad, Chris.'

'At least he's not suffering anymore,' I said – and wondered just what had been different about his can-cer that made the people at Wyvern want to do an autopsy on him.

'Sometimes, it's a blessing,' Thor said. 'Just being allowed to slip away when it's your time. Lots of folks will miss him, though. He was a fine man.'

'Thanks, Mr. Heissen.'

'What're you kids up to, anyway? Gonna start a war?'

'Exactly,' I said as Sasha twisted her key in the ignition and raced the engine.

'Sasha says you're gonna go shoot clams.'

'That's not environmentally correct, is it?'

He laughed as we pulled away.

~ ~ ~

In the backyard of my house, Sasha swept a flashlight beam across the craters that had been clawed out of the grass by Orson the previous night, before I'd taken him with me to Angela Ferryman's.

'What's he have buried here?' she asked. 'The whole skeleton of a *T. rex*?'

'Last night,' I said, 'I thought all the digging was just a grief reaction to Dad's death, a way for Orson to work off negative energy.'

'Grief reaction?' she said, frowning.

She'd seen how smart Orson was, but she still didn't have a full grasp on the complexity of his inner life or on its similarity to our own. Whatever techniques were used to enhance the intelligence of these animals, it had involved the insertion of some human genetic material into their DNA. When Sasha finally got a handle on that, she would have to sit down for a while; maybe for a week.

'Since then,' I said, 'it's occurred to me that he was searching for something that he knew I needed to have.'

I knelt on the grass beside Orson. 'Now, bro, I know you were in a lot of distress last night, grieving over

Dad. You were rattled, couldn't quite remember where to dig. He's been gone a day now, and it's a little easier to accept, isn't it?'

Orson whined thinly.

'So give it another try,' I said.

He didn't hesitate, didn't debate where to start, but went to one hole and worked to enlarge it. In five minutes, his claws clinked against something.

Sasha directed the flashlight on a dirt-caked Mason jar, and I worked it the rest of the way out of the ground.

Inside was a roll of yellow pages from a legal tablet, held together by a rubber band.

I unrolled them, held the first page to the light, and at once recognized my father's handwriting. I read only the first paragraph: *If you're reading this, Chris, I am dead and Orson has led you to the jar in the yard, because only he knows of its existence. And that's where we should begin. Let me tell you about your dog . . .*

'Bingo,' I said.

Rolling up the papers and returning them to the jar, I glanced at the sky. No moon. No stars. The scudding clouds were low and black, touched here and there by a sour-yellow glow from the rising lights of Moonlight Bay.

'We can read these later,' I said. 'Let's move. Bobby's alone out there.'

33

As Sasha opened the tailgate of the Explorer, shrieking
gulls wheeled low overhead, tumbling inland toward
safer roosts, frightened by a wind that shattered the
sea and flung the wet fragments across the point of
the horn.

With the box from Thor's Gun Shop in my arms, I
watched the white wings dwindle across the turbulent
black sky.

The fog was long gone. Under the lowering clouds,
the night was crystalline.

Around us on the peninsula, the sparse shore grass
thrashed. Tall sand devils whirled off the tops of the
dunes, like pale spirits spun up from graves.

I wondered if more than the wind had harried the
seagulls from their shelter.

'They're not here yet,' Bobby assured me as he
took the two pizza-shop boxes from the back of the
Explorer. 'It's early for them.'

'Monkeys are usually eating at this hour,' I said.
'Then a little dancing.'

'Maybe they won't even come at all tonight,' Sasha
hoped.

'They'll come,' I said.

'Yeah. They'll come,' Bobby agreed.

Bobby went inside with our dinner. Orson stayed close by his side, not out of fear that the murderous troop might be among the dunes even now but, in his role as food cop, to guard against the unfair distribution of the pizza.

Sasha removed two plastic shopping bags from the Explorer. They contained the fire extinguishers that she'd purchased at Crown Hardware.

She closed the tailgate and used the remote on her key chain to lock the doors. Since Bobby's Jeep occupied his one-car garage, we were leaving the Explorer in front of the cottage.

When Sasha turned to me, the wind made a glorious banner of her lustrous mahogany hair, and her skin glowed softly, as if the moon had managed to press one exquisite beam through the clotted clouds to caress her face. She seemed larger than life, an elemental spirit, wind goddess drawing the storm to her.

'What?' she said, unable to interpret my stare.

'You're so beautiful. Like a wind goddess drawing the storm to you.'

'You're so full of shit,' she said, but she smiled.

'It's one of my most charming qualities.'

A sand devil did a dervish dance around us, spitting grit in our faces, and we hurried into the house.

Bobby was waiting inside, where the lights were dialed down to a comfortable murk. He locked the front door behind us.

Looking around at the large panes of glass, Sasha said, 'I sure wish we could nail some plywood over these.'

'This is my house,' Bobby said. 'I'm not going to board up the windows, hunker down, and live like a prisoner just because of some damn monkeys.'

To Sasha, I said, 'As long as I've known him, this amazing dude hasn't been intimidated by monkeys.'

'Never,' Bobby agreed. 'And I'm not starting now.'

'Let's at least draw the blinds,' Sasha said.

I shook my head. 'Bad idea. That'll just make them suspicious. If they can watch us, and if we don't appear to be lying in wait for them, they'll be less cautious.'

Sasha took the two fire extinguishers from their boxes and clipped the plastic pre-sale guards from the triggers. They were ten-pound, marine-type models, easy to handle. She put one in a corner of the kitchen where it couldn't be seen from the windows, and tucked the second beside one of the sofas in the living room.

While Sasha dealt with the extinguishers, Bobby and I sat in the candlelit kitchen, boxes of ammunition in our laps, working below table level in case the monkey mafia showed up while we were at work. Sasha had purchased three extra magazines for the Glock and three speedloaders for her revolver, and we snapped cartridges into them.

'After I left here last night,' I said, 'I visited Roosevelt Frost.'

Bobby looked at me from under his eyebrows. 'He and Orson have a broly chat?'

'Roosevelt tried. Orson wasn't having any of it. But there was this cat named Mungojerrie.'

'Of course,' he said drily.

'The cat said the people at Wyvern wanted me to walk away from this, just move on.'

'You talk to the cat personally?'

'No. Roosevelt passed the message to me.'

'Of course.'

'According to the cat, I was going to get a warning.

If I didn't stop Nancying this, they'd kill my friends one by one until I did.'

'They'll blow *me* away to warn you off?'

'Their idea, not mine.'

'They can't just kill you? They think they need kryptonite?'

'They revere me, Roosevelt says.'

'Well, who doesn't?' Even after the monkeys, he remained dubious about this issue of anthropomorphizing animal behavior. But he sure had cranked down the volume of his sarcasm.

'Right after I left the *Nostromo*,' I said, 'I was warned just like the cat said I would be.'

I told Bobby about Lewis Stevenson, and he said, 'He was going to kill Orson?'

From his guard post where he stared up at the pizza boxes on the counter, Orson whined as if to confirm my account.

'So,' Bobby said, 'you shot the sheriff.'

'He was the chief of police.'

'You shot the sheriff,' Bobby insisted.

A lot of years ago, he had been a radical Eric Clapton junkie, so I knew why he liked it better this way. 'All right. I shot the sheriff – but I did not shoot the deputy.'

'I can't let you out of my sight.'

He finished with the speedloaders and tucked them into the dump pouch that Sasha had also purchased.

'Bitchin' shirt,' I said.

Bobby was wearing a rare long-sleeve Hawaiian shirt featuring a spectacular, colorful mural of a tropical festival: oranges, reds, and greens.

He said, 'Kamehameha Garment Company, from about 1950.'

Having dealt with the fire extinguishers, Sasha came into the kitchen and switched on one of the two ovens to warm up the pizza.

To Bobby, I said, 'Then I set the patrol car on fire to destroy the evidence.'

'What's on the pizza?' he asked Sasha.

'Pepperoni on one, sausage and onions on the other.'

'Bobby's wearing a used shirt,' I told her.

'Antique,' Bobby amended.

'Anyway, after I blew up the patrol car, I went over to St. Bernadette's and let myself in.'

'Breaking and entering?'

'Unlocked window.'

'So it's just criminal trespass,' he said.

As I finished loading the spare magazines for the Glock, I said, 'Used shirt, antique shirt – seems like the same thing to me.'

'One's cheap,' Sasha explained, 'and the other isn't.'

'One's art,' Bobby said. He held out the leather holder with the speedloaders. 'Here's your dump pouch.'

Sasha took it from him and snapped it onto her belt.

I said, 'Father Tom's sister was an associate of my mother's.'

Bobby said, 'Mad-scientist-blow-up-the-world type?'

'No explosives are involved. But, yeah, and now she's infected.'

'Infected.' He grimaced. 'Do we really have to get into this?'

'Yeah. But it's way complex. Genetics.'

'Big-brain stuff. Boring.'

'Not this time.'

Far out to sea, bright arteries of lightning pulsed in the sky and a low throb of thunder followed.

Sasha had also purchased a cartridge belt designed for duck hunters and skeet shooters, and Bobby began to stuff shotgun shells into the leather loops.

'Father Tom's infected, too,' I said, putting one of the spare 9mm magazines in my shirt pocket.

'Are you infected?' Bobby asked.

'Maybe. My mom had to be. And Dad was.'

'How's it passed?'

'Bodily fluids,' I said, standing the other two magazines behind a fat red candle on the table, where they could not be seen from the windows. 'And maybe other ways.'

Bobby looked at Sasha, who was transferring the pizzas to baking sheets.

She shrugged and said, 'If Chris is, then I am.'

'We've been holding hands for over a year,' I told Bobby.

'You want to heat your own pizza?' Sasha asked him.

'Nah. Too much trouble. Go ahead and infect me.'

I closed the box of ammo and put it on the floor. My pistol was still in my jacket, which hung on the back of my chair.

As Sasha continued preparing the pizzas, I said, 'Orson might not be infected, exactly. I mean, he might be more like a carrier or something.'

Passing a shotgun shell between his fingers and across his knuckles, like a magician rolling a coin, Bobby said, 'So when does the pus and puking start?'

'It's not a disease in that sense. It's more a process.'

Lightning flared again. Beautiful. And too brief to do any damage to me.

'Process,' Bobby mused.

'You're not actually sick. Just . . . changed.'

Sliding the pizzas into the oven to reheat them, Sasha said, 'So who owned the shirt before you did?'

Bobby said, 'Back in the fifties? Who knows?'

'Were dinosaurs alive then?' I wondered.

'Not many,' Bobby said.

Sasha said, 'What's it made of?'

'Rayon.'

'Looks in perfect condition.'

'You don't abuse a shirt like this,' Bobby said solemnly, 'you treasure it.'

At the refrigerator, I plucked out bottles of Corona for everyone but Orson. Because of his body weight, the mutt can usually handle one beer without getting sloppy, but this night he needed to keep a totally clear head. The rest of us actually needed the brew; calming our nerves a little would increase our effectiveness.

As I stood beside the sink, popping the caps off the beers, lightning tore at the sky again, unsuccessfully trying to rip rain out of the clouds, and in the flash I saw three hunched figures racing from one dune to another.

'They're here,' I said, bringing the beers to the table.

'They always need a while to get up their nerve,' Bobby said.

'I hope they give us time for dinner.'

'I'm starved,' Sasha agreed.

'Okay, so what're the basic symptoms of this not-disease, this process?' Bobby asked. 'Do we end up looking like we have gnarly oak fungus?'

'Some may degenerate psychologically like Stevenson,' I said. 'Some may change physically, too, in minor ways. Maybe in major ways, for all I know. But it sounds as if each case is different. Maybe some people aren't affected, or not so you'd notice, and then others really *change*.'

As Sasha fingered the sleeve of Bobby's shirt, admiring it, he said, 'The pattern's a Eugene Savage mural called *Island Feast*.'

'The buttons are fully stylin',' she said, in the mood now.

'Totally stylin',' Bobby agreed, rubbing his thumb over one of the yellow-brown, striated buttons, smiling with the pride of a passionate collector and with pleasure at the sensuous texture. 'Polished coconut shell.'

Sasha got a stack of paper napkins from a drawer and brought them to the table.

The air was thick and damp. You could feel the skin of the storm swelling like a balloon. It would burst soon.

After taking a swallow of the icy Corona, I said to Bobby, 'Okay, bro, before I tell you the rest of it, Orson has a little demonstration for you.'

'I've got all the Tupperware I need.'

I called Orson to my side. 'There are some throw pillows on the living-room sofas. One was a gift from me to Bobby. Would you go get it for him, please?'

Orson padded out of the room.

'What's going on?' Bobby wondered.

Sitting down with her beer, Sasha grinned and said, 'Just wait.' Her .38 Chiefs Special was on the table. She unfolded a paper napkin and covered the weapon with it. 'Just wait.'

Every year, Bobby and I exchange gifts at Christmas. One gift each. Because we both have everything we need, value and usefulness are not criteria when we shop. The idea is to give the tackiest items that can be found for sale. This has been a hallowed tradition since we were twelve. In Bobby's bedroom are shelves on which he keeps the collection of tasteless gifts that I've given to him; the only one he finds insufficiently tacky to warrant space on those shelves is the pillow.

Orson returned to the kitchen with this inadequately tacky item in his mouth, and Bobby accepted it, trying to look unimpressed with the dog's feat.

The twelve-by-eight-inch pillow featured a needle-point sampler on the front. It was among items that had been manufactured by – and sold to raise funds for – a popular television evangelist. Inside an elaborate border were eight words in scrollwork stitching: JESUS EATS SINNERS AND SPITS OUT SAVED SOULS.

'You didn't find this tacky?' Sasha asked disbelievingly.

'Tacky, yes,' Bobby said, strapping the loaded ammo belt around his waist without getting up from his chair. 'But not tacky enough.'

'We have awesomely high standards,' I said.

The year after I gave Bobby the pillow, I presented him with a ceramic sculpture of Elvis Presley. Elvis is depicted in one of his glitziest white-silk-and-sequins Vegas stage outfits while sitting on the toilet where he died; his hands are clasped in prayer, his eyes are raised to Heaven, and there's a halo around his head.

In this Yuletide competition, Bobby is at a disadvantage because he insists on actually going into gift shops in search of the perfect trash. Because of my XP, I am restricted to mail order, where one can find enough catalogues of exquisitely tacky merchandise to fill all the shelves in the Library of Congress.

Turning the pillow over in his hands, frowning at Orson, Bobby said, 'Neat trick.'

'No trick,' I said. 'There were evidently a lot of

different experiments going on at Wyvern. One of them dealt with enhancing the intelligence of both humans and animals.'

'Bogus.'

'Truth.'

'Insane.'

'Entirely.'

I instructed Orson to take the pillow back where he'd found it, then to go to the bedroom, nudge open the sliding door, and return with one of the black dress loafers that Bobby had bought when he'd discovered that he had only thongs, sandals, and athletic shoes to wear to my mother's memorial service.

The kitchen was redolent with the aroma of pizza, and the dog gazed longingly at the oven.

'You'll get your share,' I assured him. 'Now scoot.'

As Orson started out of the kitchen, Bobby said, 'Wait.'

Orson regarded him expectantly.

'Not just a shoe. And not just a loafer. The loafer for my left foot.'

Chuffing as if to say that this complication was insignificant, Orson proceeded on his errand.

Out over the Pacific, a blazing staircase of lightning connected the heavens to the sea, as if signaling the descent of archangels. The subsequent crash of thunder rattled the windows and reverberated in the cottage walls.

Along this temperate coast, our storms are rarely accompanied by pyrotechnics of this kind. Apparently we were scheduled for a major hammering.

I put a can of red-pepper flakes on the table, then paper plates and the insulated serving pads on which Sasha placed the pizzas.

'Mungojerrie,' said Bobby.

'It's a name from a book of poems about cats.'

'Seems pretentious.'

'It's cute,' Sasha disagreed.

'Fluffy,' Bobby said. 'Now that's a name for a cat.'

The wind rose, rattling a vent cap on the roof and whistling in the eaves. I couldn't be sure, but I thought that I heard, in the distance, the loon-like cries of the troop.

Bobby reached down with one hand to reposition the shotgun, which was on the floor beside his chair.

'Fluffy or Boots,' he said. 'Those are solid cat names.'

With a knife and fork, Sasha cut a slice of pepperoni pizza into bite-size pieces and set it aside to cool for Orson.

The dog returned from the bedroom with one loafer in his mouth. He presented it to Bobby. It was for the left foot.

Bobby carried the shoe to the flip-top trash can and disposed of it. 'It's not the tooth marks or the dog drool,' he assured Orson. 'I don't plan ever to wear dress shoes again, anyway.'

I remembered the envelope from Thor's Gun Shop that had been on my bed when I'd found the Glock there the night before. It had been slightly damp and stippled with curious indentations. Saliva. Tooth marks. Orson was the person who had put my father's pistol where I would be sure to find it.

Bobby returned to the table and sat staring at the dog.

'So?' I asked.

'What?'

'You know what.'

'I need to say it?'

'Yeah.'

Bobby sighed. 'I feel as if one honking huge mondo crashed through my head and just about sucked my brain out in the backwash.'

'You're a hit,' I told Orson.

Sasha had been fanning one hand over the dog's share of pizza to ensure that the cheese wouldn't be hot enough to stick to the roof of his mouth and burn him. Now she put the plate on the floor.

Orson banged his tail against table and chair legs as he set about proving that high intelligence does not necessarily correlate with good table manners.

'Silky,' Bobby said. 'Simple name. A cat name. Silky.'

As we ate pizza and drank beer, the three flickering candles provided barely enough light for me to scan the pages of yellow lined tablet paper on which my father had written a concise account of the activities at Wyvern, the unanticipated developments that had spiraled into catastrophe, and the extent of my mother's involvement. Although Dad wasn't a scientist and could only recount – largely in layman's terms – what my mother had told him, there was a wealth of information in the document that he had left for me.

'"A little delivery boy,"' I said. 'That's what Lewis Stevenson said to me last night when I asked what had changed him from the man he'd once been. "A little delivery boy that wouldn't die." He was talking about a retrovirus. Apparently, my mother theorized a new kind of retrovirus . . . with the selectivity of a retrotransposon.'

When I looked up from Dad's pages, Sasha and Bobby were staring at me blank-eyed.

He said, 'Orson probably knows what you're talking about, bro, but I dropped out of college.'

'I'm a deejay,' Sasha said.

'And a good one,' Bobby said.

'Thank you.'

'Though you play too much Chris Isaak,' he added.

This time lightning didn't step down the sky but dropped straight and fast, like a blazing express elevator carrying a load of high explosives, which detonated when it slammed into the earth. The entire peninsula seemed to leap, and the house shook, and rain like a shower of blast debris rattled across the roof.

Glancing at the windows, Sasha said, 'Maybe they won't like the rain. Maybe they'll stay away.'

I reached into the pocket of the jacket hanging on my chair and drew the Glock. I placed it on the table where I could get at it more quickly, and I used Sasha's trick with the paper napkin to conceal it.

'Mostly in clinical trials, scientists have been treating lots of illnesses – AIDS, cancer, inherited diseases – with various gene therapies. The idea is, if the patient has certain defective genes or maybe lacks certain genes altogether, you replace the bad genes with working copies or add the missing genes that will make his cells better at fighting disease. There've been encouraging results. A growing number of modest successes. And failures, too, unpleasant surprises.'

Bobby said, 'There's always a Godzilla. Tokyo's humming along, all happy and prosperous one minute – and the next minute, you've got giant lizard feet stamping everything flat.'

'The problem is getting the healthy genes into the patient. Mostly they use crippled viruses to carry the genes into the cells. Most of these are retroviruses.'

'Crippled?' Bobby asked.

'It means they can't reproduce. That way they're no

threat to the body. Once they carry the human gene into the cell, they have the ability to neatly splice it into the cell's chromosomes.'

'Delivery boys,' Bobby said.

'And once they do their job,' Sasha said, 'they're supposed to die?'

'Sometimes they don't go easily,' I said. 'They can cause inflammation or serious immune responses that destroy the viruses *and* the cells into which they delivered genes. So some researchers have been studying ways to modify retroviruses by making them more like retrotransposons, which are bits of the body's own DNA that can already copy and slot themselves into chromosomes.'

'Here comes Godzilla,' Bobby told Sasha.

She said, 'Snowman, how do you know all this crap? You didn't get it by looking at those pages for two minutes.'

'You tend to find the driest research papers interesting when you know they could save your life,' I said. 'If anyone can find a way to replace my defective genes with working copies, my body will be able to produce the enzymes that repair the ultraviolet damage to my DNA.'

Bobby said, 'Then you wouldn't be the Nightcrawler anymore.'

'Goodbye freakhood,' I agreed.

Above the noisy drumming of the rain on the roof came the patter of something running across the back porch.

We looked toward the sound in time to see a large rhesus leap up from the porch floor onto the windowsill over the kitchen sink. Its fur was wet and matted, which made it look scrawnier than it would have appeared when dry. It balanced adroitly on that narrow ledge and pinched a vertical mullion in one small hand. Peering in at us with what appeared to be only ordinary monkey curiosity, the creature looked quite benign – except for its baleful eyes.

'They'll probably get annoyed quicker if we pretty much ignore them,' Bobby said.

'The more annoyed they are,' Sasha added, 'the more careless they might get.'

Biting into another slice of the sausage and onion pizza, tapping one finger against the stack of yellow pages on the table, I said, 'Just scanning, I see this paragraph where my dad explains as much as he understood about this new theory of my mother's. For the project at Wyvern, she developed this revolutionary new approach to engineering retroviruses so they could more safely be used to ferry genes into the patient's cells.'

'I definitely hear giant lizard feet,' Bobby said. 'Boom, boom, boom, boom.'

At the window, the monkey shrieked at us.

I glanced at the nearer window, beside the table, but nothing was peering in there.

Orson stood on his hind legs with his forepaws on the table and theatrically expressed an interest in more pizza, lavishing all of his charm on Sasha.

'You know how kids try to play one parent against the other,' I warned her.

'I'm more like his sister-in-law,' she said. 'Anyway, this could be his last meal. Ours, too.'

I sighed. 'All right. But if we aren't killed, then we're setting a lousy precedent.'

A second monkey leaped onto the windowsill. They were both shrieking and baring their teeth at us.

Sasha selected the narrowest of the remaining slices of pizza, cut it into pieces, and placed it on the dog's plate on the floor.

Orson glanced worriedly at the goblins at the window, but even the primates of doom couldn't spoil his appetite. He turned his attention to his dinner.

One of the monkeys began to slap a hand rhythmically against the windowpane, shrieking louder than ever.

Its teeth looked larger and sharper than those of a rhesus ought to have been, plenty large enough and sharp enough to help it fulfill the demanding role of a predator. Maybe this was a physical trait engineered into it by the playful weapons-research boys at Wyvern. In my mind's eye, I saw Angela's torn throat.

'This might be meant to distract us,' Sasha suggested.

'They can't get into the house anywhere else without breaking glass,' Bobby said. 'We'll hear them.'

'Over this racket and the rain?' she wondered.

'We'll hear them.'

'I don't think we should split up in different rooms unless we're absolutely driven to it,' I said. 'They're smart enough to know about dividing to conquer.'

Again, I squinted through the window near which the table was placed, but no monkeys were on that section of porch, and nothing but the rain and the wind moved through the dark dunes beyond the railing.

Over the sink, one of the monkeys had managed to turn its back and still cling to the window. It was squealing as if with laughter as it mooned us, pressing its bare, furless, ugly butt to the glass.

'So,' Bobby asked me, 'what happened after you let yourself into the rectory?'

Sensing time running out, I succinctly summarized the events in the attic, at Wyvern, and at the Ramirez house.

'Manuel, a pod person,' Bobby said, shaking his head sadly.

'Ugh,' Sasha said, but she wasn't commenting on Manuel.

At the window, the male monkey facing us was urinating copiously on the glass.

'Well, this is new,' Bobby observed.

On the porch beyond the sink windows, more monkeys started popping into the air like kernels of corn bursting off a hot oiled pan, tumbling up into sight and then dropping away. They were all squealing and shrieking, and there seemed to be scores of them, though it was surely the same half dozen springing-spinning-popping repeatedly into view.

I finished the last of my beer.

Being cool was getting harder minute by minute. Perhaps even *doing* cool required energy and more concentration than I possessed.

'Orson,' I said, 'it wouldn't be a bad idea if you sauntered around the house.'

He understood and set out immediately to police the perimeter.

Before he was out of the kitchen, I said, 'No heroics. If you see anything wrong, bark your head off and come running straight back here.'

He padded out of sight.

Immediately, I regretted having sent him, even though I knew it was the right thing to do.

The first monkey had emptied its bladder, and now the second one had turned to face the kitchen and had begun to loose his own stream. Others were scampering along the handrail outside and swinging from the porch-roof rafters.

Bobby was sitting directly opposite the window that was adjacent to the table. He searched that comparatively calm part of the night with suspicion equal to mine.

The lightning seemed to have passed, but volleys of thunder still boomed across the sea. This cannonade excited the troop.

'I hear the new Brad Pitt movie is really hot,' Bobby said.

Sasha said, 'Haven't seen it.'

'I always wait for video,' I reminded him.

Something tried the door to the back porch. The knob rattled and squeaked, but the lock was securely engaged.

The two monkeys at the sink windows dropped away. Two more sprang up from the porch to take their places, and both began to urinate on the glass.

Bobby said, 'I'm not cleaning this up.'

'Well, *I'm* not cleaning it up,' Sasha declared.

'Maybe they'll get their aggression and anger out this way and then just leave,' I said.

Bobby and Sasha appeared to have studied withering sarcastic expressions at the same school.

'Or maybe not,' I reconsidered.

From out of the night, a stone about the size of a cherry pit struck one of the windows, and the peeing monkeys dropped away to escape from the line of fire. More small stones quickly followed the first, rattling like hail.

No stones were flung at the nearest window.

Bobby plucked the shotgun from the floor and placed it across his lap.

When the barrage was at its peak, it abruptly ended.

The frenzied monkeys were screaming more fiercely now. Their escalating cries were shrill, eerie, and seemed to have supernatural effect, feeding back into the night with such demonic energy that rain pounded the cottage harder than ever. Merciless hammers of thunder cracked the shell of the night, and once again bright tines of lightning dug at the meat of the sky.

A stone, larger than any in the previous assault, rebounded off one of the sink windows: *snap*. A second of approximately the same size immediately followed, thrown with greater force than the first.

Fortunately their hands were too small to allow them to hold and properly operate pistols or revolvers; and with their relatively low body weight, they would be kicked head over heels by the recoil. These creatures were surely smart enough to understand the purpose and operation of handguns, but at least the horde of geniuses in the Wyvern labs hadn't chosen to work with gorillas. Although, if the idea occurred to them, they would no doubt immediately seek funding for that enterprise and would not only provide the gorillas with firearms training but instruct them, as well, in the fine points of nuclear-weapons design.

Two more stones snapped against the targeted window glass.

I touched the cell phone clipped to my belt. There ought to be someone we could call for help. Not the police, not the FBI. If the former responded, the friendly officers on the Moonlight Bay force would probably provide cover fire for the monkeys. Even if we could get through to the nearest office of the FBI and could sound more credible than all the callers reporting abduction by flying saucers, we would be talking to the enemy; Manuel Ramirez said the decision to let this nightmare play itself out had been made at 'a very high level,' and I believed him.

With a concession of responsibility unmatched by generations before ours, we have entrusted our lives and futures to professionals and experts who convince us that we have too little knowledge or wit to make any decisions of importance about the management of society. This is the consequence of our gullibility and laziness. Apocalypse with primates.

A still larger stone struck the window. The pane cracked but didn't shatter.

I picked up the two spare 9mm magazines on the table and tucked one into each of my jean pockets.

Sasha slipped one hand under the rumpled napkin that concealed the Chiefs Special.

I followed her lead and got a grip on the hidden Glock.

We looked at each other. A tide of fear washed through her eyes, and I was sure that she saw the same dark currents in mine.

I tried to smile reassuringly, but my face felt as though it would crack like hard plaster. 'Gonna be fine. A deejay, a surf rebel, and the Elephant Man – the perfect team to save the world.'

'If possible,' Bobby said, 'don't immediately waste the first one or two that come in. Let a few inside. Delay as long as you can. Let them feel confident. Sucker the little geeks. Then let me open on them first, teach them respect. With the shotgun, I don't even have to aim.'

'Yes, sir, General Bob,' I said.

Two, three, four stones – about as hefty as peach pits – struck the windows. The second large pane cracked, and a subsidiary fissure opened off that line, like lightning branching.

I was experiencing a physiological rearrangement that would have fascinated any physician. My stomach had squeezed up through my chest and was pressing insistently at the base of my throat, while my pounding heart had dropped down into the space formerly occupied by my stomach.

Half a dozen more substantial stones, whaled harder than before, battered the two large windows, and both panes shattered inward. With a burst of brittle music, glass rained into the stainless-steel sink, across the granite counters, onto the floor. A few shards sprayed as far as the dinette, and I shut my eyes briefly as sharp fragments clinked onto the table top and plopped into the remaining slices of cold pizza.

When I opened my eyes an instant later, two shrieking monkeys, each as large as the one that Angela had described, were already at the window again. Wary of the broken glass and of us, the pair swung inside, onto the granite counter. Wind churned in around them, plucking at their rain-matted fur.

One of them looked toward the broom closet, where the shotgun was usually locked away. Since their arrival, they hadn't seen any of us approach that cupboard, and they couldn't possibly spot the 12-gauge balanced on Bobby's knees, under the table.

Bobby glanced at them but was more interested in the window opposite him, across the table.

Hunched and agile, the two creatures already in the room moved along the counter in opposite directions from the sink. In the dimly lighted kitchen, their malevolent yellow eyes were as bright as the flames leaping on the points of the candle wicks.

The intruder to the left encountered a toaster and angrily swept it to the floor. Sparks spurted from the wall receptacle when the plug tore out of the socket.

I remembered Angela's account of the rhesus bombarding her with apples hard enough to split her lip. Bobby maintained an uncluttered kitchen, but if these beasts opened cabinet doors and started firing glasses and dishes at us, they could do serious damage even if we did enjoy an advantage in firepower. A dinner plate, spinning like a Frisbee, catching you across the bridge of the nose, might be nearly as effective as a bullet.

Two more dire-eyed creatures sprang up from the porch floor into the frame of the shattered window. They bared their teeth at us and hissed.

The paper napkin over Sasha's gun hand trembled visibly – and not because it was caught by a draft from the window.

In spite of the shrieking-chattering-hissing of the intruders, in spite of the bluster of the March wind at the broken windows and the rolling thunder and the drumming rain, I thought that I heard Bobby singing under his breath. He was largely ignoring the monkeys on the far side of the kitchen, focusing intently on the window that remained intact, across the table from him – and his lips were moving.

Perhaps emboldened by our lack of response, perhaps believing us to be immobilized by fear, the two increasingly agitated creatures in the broken-out windows now swung inside and moved in opposite directions along the counter, forming pairs with each of the first two intruders.

Either Bobby began to sing louder or stark terror sharpened my hearing, because suddenly I could recognize the song that he was singing. 'Daydream Believer.' It was golden-oldie teen pop, first recorded by the Monkees.

Sasha must have heard it, too, because she said, 'A blast from the past.'

Two *more* members of the troop climbed into the windows above the sink, clinging to the frames, hellfire in their eyes, squealing monkey-hate at us.

The four already in the room were shrieking louder than ever, bouncing up and down on the counters, shaking their fists in the air, baring their teeth and spitting at us.

They were smart but not smart enough. Their rage was rapidly clouding their judgment.

'Wipeout,' Bobby said.

Here we go.

Instead of scooting backward in his chair to clear the table, he swung sideways in it, rose fluidly to his feet, and brought up the shotgun as if he'd had both military training and ballet lessons. Flame spouted from the muzzle, and the first deafening blast caught the two latest arrivals at the windows, blowing them backward onto the porch, as though they were only a child's stuffed toys, and the second round chopped down the pair on the counter to the left of the sink.

My ears were ringing as though I were inside a tolling cathedral bell, and although the roar of the gunfire in this confined space was loud enough to be disorienting, I was on my feet before the 12-gauge boomed the second time, as was Sasha, who turned away from the table and squeezed off a round toward the remaining pair of intruders just as Bobby dealt with numbers three and four.

As they fired and the kitchen shook with the blasts,

the nearest window exploded at me. Air surfing on a cascade of glass, a screaming rhesus landed on the table in our midst, knocking over two of the three candles and extinguishing one of them, spraying rain off its coat, sending a pan of pizza spinning to the floor.

I brought up the Glock, but the latest arrival flung itself onto Sasha's back. If I shot it, the slug would pass straight through the damn thing and probably kill her, too.

By the time I kicked a chair out of the way and got around the table, Sasha was screaming, and the squealing monkey on her back was trying to tear out handfuls of her hair. Reflexively, she'd dropped her .38 to reach blindly behind herself for the rhesus. It snapped at her hands, teeth audibly cracking together on empty air. Her body was bent backward over the table, and her assailant was trying to pull her head back farther still, to expose her throat.

Acutely aware of the presentiment of loss that had troubled me earlier, certain that Sasha was the one who would be taken from me, I dropped the Glock on the table and seized the creature from behind, getting my right hand around its neck, using my left to clutch the fur and skin between its shoulder blades. I twisted that handful of fur and skin so fiercely that the beast screamed in pain. It wouldn't let go of Sasha, however, and as I struggled to tear it away from her, it tried to pull her hair out by the roots.

Bobby pumped another round into the chamber and squeezed off a third shot, the cottage walls seemed to shake as if an earthquake had rumbled under us, and I figured that was the end of the final pair of intruders, but I heard Bobby cursing and knew more trouble had come our way.

Revealed more by their blazing yellow eyes than by the guttering flames of the remaining two candles, another pair of monkeys, total kamikazes, had sprung into the windows above the sink.

And Bobby was reloading.

In another part of the cottage, Orson barked loudly. I didn't know if he was racing toward us to join the fray or whether he was calling for help.

I heard myself cursing with uncharacteristic vividness and snarling with animal ferocity as I shifted my grip on the rhesus, getting both hands around its neck. I choked it, choked it until finally it had no choice but to let go of her.

The monkey weighed only about twenty-five pounds, less than one-sixth as much as I weighed, but it was all bone and muscle and seething hatred. Screaming thinly and spitting even as it struggled for breath, the thing tried to tuck its head down to bite at the hands encircling its throat. It wrenched, wriggled, kicked, flailed, and I can't imagine that an eel could have been harder to hold on to, but my fury at what the little fucker had tried to do to Sasha was so great that my hands were like iron, and at last I felt its neck snap. Then it was just a limp, dead thing, and I dropped it on the floor.

Gagging with disgust, gasping for breath, I picked up my Glock as Sasha, having recovered her Chiefs Special, stepped to the broken window near the table and opened fire at the night beyond.

While reloading, apparently having lost track of the last two monkeys in spite of their glowing eyes, Bobby had gone to the light switch by the door. Now he cranked up the rheostat far enough to make me squint.

One of the little bastards was standing on a counter beside the cooktop. It had extracted the smallest of the knives from the wall rack, and before any of us could open fire, it threw the blade at Bobby.

I don't know whether the troop had been busy learning simple military arts or whether the monkey was lucky. The knife tumbled through the air and sank into Bobby's right shoulder.

He dropped the shotgun.

I fired two rounds at the knife thrower, and it pitched backward onto the cooktop burners, dead.

The remaining monkey might have once heard that old saw about discretion being the better part of valor, because he curled his tail up against his back and fled over the sink and out the window. I got two shots off, but both missed.

At the other window, with surprisingly steady nerves and nimble fingers, Sasha fumbled a speedloader from the dump pouch on her belt and slipped it into the .38. She twisted the speedloader, neatly filling all chambers at once, dropped it on the floor, and snapped the cylinder shut.

I wondered what school of broadcasting offered would-be disc jockeys courses on weaponry and grace under fire. Of all the people in Moonlight Bay, Sasha had been the only one remaining who seemed genuinely to be only what she *appeared* to be. Now I suspected that she had a secret or two of her own.

She began squeezing off shots into the night once more. I don't know if she had any targets in view or whether she was just laying down a suppressing fire to discourage whatever remained of the troop.

Ejecting the half-empty magazine from the Glock, slamming in a full one, I went to Bobby as he pulled

the knife out of his shoulder. The blade appeared to
have penetrated only an inch or two, but there was a
spreading bloodstain on his shirt.

'How bad?' I asked.

'*Damn!*'

'Can you hold on?'

'This was my best shirt!'

Maybe he would be all right.

Toward the front of the house, Orson's barking
continued – but it was punctuated now with squeals
of terror.

I tucked the Glock under my belt, against the small
of my back, picked up Bobby's shotgun, which was
fully loaded, and ran toward the barking.

The lights were on but dimmed down in the living
room, as we had left them. I dialed them up a little.

One of the big windows had been shattered. Hooting
wind drove rain under the porch roof and into the
living room.

Four screaming monkeys were perched on the backs
of chairs and on the arms of sofas. When the lights
brightened, they turned their heads toward me and
hissed as one.

Bobby had estimated that the troop was composed
of eight or ten individuals, but it was obviously a lot
larger than that. I'd already seen twelve or fourteen,
and in spite of the fact that they were more than half
crazed with rage and hatred, I didn't think they were
so reckless – or stupid – that they would sacrifice most
of their community in a single assault like this.

They'd been loose for two to three years. Plenty of
time to breed.

Orson was on the floor, surrounded by this quartet
of goblins, which now began to shriek at him again.

He was turning worriedly in a circle, trying to watch all of them at once.

One of the troop was at such a distance and angle that I didn't have to worry that any stray buckshot would catch the dog. Without hesitation, I blew away the creature on which I had a clear line of fire, and the resulting spray of buckshot and monkey guts would cost Bobby maybe five thousand bucks in redecorating costs.

Squealing, the remaining three intruders bounded from one piece of furniture to another, heading toward the windows. I brought down another one, but the third round in the shotgun only peppered a teak-paneled wall and cost Bobby another five or ten grand.

I pitched the shotgun aside, reached to the small of my back, drew the Glock from under my belt, started after the two monkeys that were fleeing through the broken window onto the front porch – and was nearly lifted off my feet when someone grabbed me from behind. A beefy arm swung around my throat, instantly choking off my air supply, and a hand seized the Glock, tearing it away from me.

The next thing I knew, I *was* off my feet, lifted and tossed as though I were a child. I crashed into a coffee table, which collapsed under me.

Flat on my back in the ruins of the furniture, I looked up and saw Carl Scorso looming over me, even more gigantic from this angle than he actually was. The bald head. The earring. Though I'd dialed up the lights, the room was still sufficiently shadowy that I could see the animal shine in his eyes.

He was the troop leader. I had no doubt about that. He was wearing athletic shoes and jeans and a flannel shirt, and there was a watch on his wrist, and if he were put in a police lineup with four gorillas, no one would have the least difficulty identifying him as the sole human being. Yet in spite of the clothes and the human form, he radiated the savage aura of something subhuman, not merely because of the eyeshine but because his features were twisted into an expression that mirrored no human emotion I could identify. Though clothed, he might as well have been naked; though clean-shaven from his neck to the crown of his head, he might as well have been as hairy as an ape. If he lived two lives, it was clear that he was more attuned to the one that he lived at night, with the troop, than to the one that he lived by day, among those who were not changelings like him.

He held the Glock at arm's length, executioner style, aiming it at my face.

Orson flew at him, snarling, but Scorso was the quicker of the two. He landed a solid kick against the dog's head, and Orson went down and stayed down, without even a yelp or a twitch of his legs.

My heart dropped like a stone in a well.

Scorso swung the Glock toward me again and fired a round into my face. Or that was how it seemed for an instant. But a split second before he pulled the trigger, Sasha shot him in the back from the far end of the room, and the *crack* I heard was the report of her Chiefs Special.

Scorso jerked from the impact of the slug, pulling the Glock off-target. The teak floor beside my head splintered as the bullet tore through it.

Wounded but less fazed than most of us would have been once shot in the back, Scorso swung around, pumping out rounds from the Glock as he turned.

Sasha dropped and rolled backward out of the room,

and Scorso emptied the pistol at the place where she had stood. He kept trying to pull the trigger even after the magazine was empty.

I could see rich, dark blood spreading across the back of his flannel shirt.

Finally he threw down the Glock, turned toward me, appeared to contemplate whether to stomp my face or to tear my eyes from my head, leaving me blinded and dying. Opting for neither pleasure, he headed toward the broken-out window through which the last two monkeys had escaped.

He was just stepping out of the house onto the porch, when Sasha reappeared and, incredibly, pursued him.

I shouted at her to stop, but she looked so wild that I wouldn't have been surprised to see that dreadful light in her eyes, too. She was across the living room and onto the front porch while I was still getting up from the splintered remains of the coffee table.

Outside, the Chiefs Special cracked, cracked again, and then a third time.

Although, after the events of the past few minutes, it seemed reasonable to assume that Sasha could take care of herself, I wanted to go after her and drag her back. Even if she finished Scorso, the night was probably home to more monkeys than even a first-rate disc jockey could handle – and the night was their domain, not hers.

A fourth shot boomed. A fifth.

I hesitated because Orson lay limp, so dreadfully still that I couldn't see his black flank rising and falling with his breathing. He was either dead or unconscious. If unconscious, he might need help quickly. He had been kicked in the head. Even if he were alive, there was the danger of brain damage.

I realized I was crying. I bit back my grief, blinked back my tears. As I always do.

Bobby was crossing the living room toward me, one hand clamped to the stab wound in his shoulder.

'Help Orson,' I said.

I refused to believe that nothing could help him now, because maybe to think such a terrible thing would be to ensure that it be true.

Pia Klick would understand that concept.

Maybe Bobby would understand it now, too.

Dodging furniture and dead monkeys, crunching glass underfoot, I ran to the window. Silvery whips of cold, windblown rain lashed past the jagged fragments of glass still prickling from the frame. I crossed the porch, leaped down the steps, and raced into the heart of the downpour, toward Sasha, where she stood thirty feet away in the dunes.

Carl Scorso lay facedown in the sand.

Soaked and shivering, she stood over him, twisting her third and last speedloader into the revolver. I suspected that she had hit him with most if not all the rounds that I'd heard, but she seemed to feel that she might need a few more.

Indeed, Scorso twitched and worked both out-flung hands in the sand, as if he were burrowing into cover, like a crab.

With a shudder of horror, she leaned down and fired one last round, this time into the back of his skull.

When she turned to me, she was crying. Making no attempt to repress her tears.

I was tearless now. I told myself that one of us had to hold it together.

'Hey,' I said gently.

She came into my arms.

'Hey,' she whispered against my throat.

I held her.

The rain was coming down in such torrents that I couldn't see the lights of town, three-quarters of a mile to the east. Moonlight Bay might have been dissolved by this flood out of Heaven, washed away as if it had been only an elaborate sand sculpture of a town.

But it was back there, all right. Waiting for this storm to pass, and for another storm after this one, and others until the end of all days. There was no escaping Moonlight Bay. Not for us. Not ever. It was, quite literally, in our blood.

'What happens to us now?' she asked, still holding fast to me.

'Life.'

'It's all screwed up.'

'It always was.'

'They're still out there.'

'Maybe they'll leave us alone – for a while.'

'Where do we go from here, Snowman?'

'Back to the house. Get a beer.'

She was still shivering, and not because of the rain. 'And after that? We can't drink beer forever.'

'Big surf coming in tomorrow.'

'It's going to be that easy?'

'Got to catch those epic waves while you can get them.'

We walked back to the cottage, where we found Orson and Bobby sitting on the wide front-porch steps. There was just room enough for us to sit down beside them.

Neither of my brothers was in the best mood of his life.

Bobby felt that he needed only Neosporin and a bandage. 'It's a shallow wound, thin as a paper cut, and hardly more than half an inch from top to bottom.'

'Sorry about the shirt,' Sasha said.

'Thanks.'

Whimpering, Orson got up, wobbled down the steps into the rain, and puked in the sand. It was a night for regurgitation.

I couldn't take my eyes off him. I was trembling with dread.

'Maybe we should take him to a vet,' Sasha said.

I shook my head. No vet.

I would not cry. I do not cry. How bitter do you risk becoming by swallowing too many tears?

When I could speak, I said, 'I wouldn't trust any vet in town. They're probably part of it, co-opted. If they realize what he is, that he's one of the animals from Wyvern, they might take him away from me, back to the labs.'

Orson stood with his face turned up to the rain, as if he found it refreshing.

'They'll be back,' Bobby said, meaning the troop.

'Not tonight,' I said. 'And maybe not for a way long time.'

'But sooner or later.'

'Yeah.'

'And who else?' Sasha wondered. 'What else?'

'It's chaos out there,' I said, remembering what Manuel had told me. 'A radical new world. Who the hell knows what's in it – or what's being born right now?'

In spite of all that we had seen and all that we had

learned about the Wyvern project, perhaps it was not until this moment on the porch steps that we believed in our bones that we were living near the end of civilization, on the brink of Armageddon. Like the drums of Judgment, the hard and ceaseless rain beat on the world. This night was like no other night on earth, and it couldn't have felt more alien if the clouds had parted to reveal three moons instead of one and a sky full of unfamiliar stars.

Orson lapped puddled rainwater off the lowest porch step. Then he climbed to my side with more confidence than he had shown when he had descended.

Hesitantly, using the nod-for-*yes*-shake-for-*no* code, I tested him for concussion or worse. He was okay.

'Jesus,' Bobby said with relief. I'd never heard him as shaken as this.

I went inside and got four beers and the bowl on which Bobby had painted the word *Rosebud*. I returned to the porch.

'A couple of Pia's paintings took some buckshot,' I said.

'We'll blame it on Orson,' Bobby said.

'Nothing,' Sasha said, 'is more dangerous than a dog with a shotgun.'

We sat in silence a while, listening to the rain and breathing the delicious, fresh-scrubbed air.

I could see Scorso's body out there in the sand. Now Sasha was a killer just like me.

Bobby said, 'This sure is live.'

'Totally,' I said.

'Way radical.'

'Insanely,' Sasha said.

Orson chuffed.

34

That night we wrapped the dead monkeys in sheets. We wrapped Scorso's body in a sheet, too. I kept expecting him to sit up and reach out for me, trailing his cotton windings, as though he were a mummy from one of those long-ago movies filmed in an era when people were more spooked by the supernatural than the real world allows them to be these days. Then we loaded them into the back of the Explorer.

Bobby had a stack of plastic drop cloths in the garage, left over from the most recent visit by the painters, who periodically hand-oiled the teak paneling. We used them and a staple gun to seal the broken windows as best we could.

At two o'clock in the morning, Sasha drove all four of us to the northeast end of town and up the long driveway, past the graceful California pepper trees that waited like a line of mourners weeping in the storm, past the concrete *Pietà*. We stopped under the portico, before the massive Georgian house.

No lights were on. I don't know if Sandy Kirk was sleeping or not home.

We unloaded the sheet-wrapped corpses and piled them at his front door.

As we drove away, Bobby said, 'Remember when

we came up here as kids – to watch Sandy's dad at work?'

'Yeah.'

'Imagine if one night we'd found something like that on his doorstep.'

'Cool.'

There were days of cleanup and repairs to be undertaken at Bobby's place, but we weren't ready to bend to that task. We went to Sasha's house and passed the rest of the night in her kitchen, clearing our heads with more beer and going through my father's account of the origins of our new world, our new life.

My mother had dreamed up a revolutionary new approach to the engineering of retroviruses for the purpose of ferrying genes into the cells of patients – or experimental subjects. In the secret facility at Wyvern, a world-class team of big brows had realized her vision. These new microbe delivery boys were more spectacularly successful and selective than anyone had hoped.

'Then comes Godzilla,' as Bobby said.

The new retroviruses, though crippled, proved to be so clever that they were able not merely to deliver their package of genetic material but to select a package from the patient's – or lab animal's – DNA to replace what they had delivered. Thus they became a two-way messenger, carrying genetic material in *and* out of the body.

They also proved capable of capturing other viruses naturally present in a subject's body, selecting from those organisms' traits, and remaking themselves. They mutated more radically and faster than any microbe had ever mutated before. Wildly, they mutated, becoming something new within hours. They had also become able to reproduce in spite of having been crippled.

Before anyone at Wyvern grasped what was happening, Mom's new bugs were ferrying as much genetic material out of the experimental animals as into them – and transferring that material not only among the different animals but among the scientists and other workers in the labs. Contamination is not solely by contact with bodily fluids. Even skin contact is sufficient to effect the transfer of these bugs if you have even the tiniest wound or sore: a paper cut, a nick from shaving.

In the years ahead, as each of us is contaminated, he or she will take on a load of new DNA different from the one that anybody else receives. The effect will be singular in every case. Some of us will not change appreciably at all, because we will receive so many bits and pieces from so many sources that there will be no *focused* cumulative effect. As our cells die, the inserted material might or might not appear in the new cells that replace them. But some of us may become psychological or even physical monsters.

To paraphrase James Joyce: It will darkle, tinct-tint, all this our funanimal world. Darkle with strange variety.

We know not if the change will accelerate, the effects become more widely visible, the secret be exposed by the sheer momentum of the retrovirus's work – or whether it will be a process that remains subtle for decades or centuries. We can only wait. And see.

Dad seemed to think the problem didn't arise entirely

because of a flaw in the theory. He believed the people at Wyvern – who tested my mother's theories and developed them until actual organisms could be produced – were more at fault than she, because they deviated from her vision in ways that may have seemed subtle at the time but proved calamitous in the end.

However you look at it, my mom destroyed the world as we know it – but, for all of that, she's still my mom. On one level, she did what she did for love, out of the hope that my life could be saved. I love her as much as ever – and marvel that she was able to hide her terror and anguish from me during the last years of her life, after she realized what kind of new world was coming.

My father was less than half-convinced that she killed herself, but in his notes, he admits the possibility. He felt that murder was more likely. Although the plague had spread too far – too fast – to be contained, Mom finally had wanted to go public with the story. Maybe she was silenced. Whether she killed herself or tried to stand up to the military and government doesn't matter; she's gone in either case.

Now that I understand my mother better, I know where I get the strength – or the obsessive will – to repress my own emotions when I find them too hard to deal with. I'm going to try to change that about myself. I don't see why I shouldn't be able to do it. After all, that's what the world is now about: change. Relentless change.

∽ ∽ ∽

Although some hate me for being my mother's son, I'm permitted to live. Even my father wasn't sure why I should be granted this dispensation – considering the savage nature of some of my enemies. He suspected, however, that my mother used fragments of my genetic material to engineer this apocalyptic retrovirus; perhaps, therefore, the key to undoing or at least limiting the scope of the calamity will eventually be found in my genes. My blood is drawn each month not, as I've been told, for reasons related to my XP but for study at Wyvern. Perhaps I am a walking laboratory: containing the potential for immunity to this plague – or containing a clue as to the ultimate destruction and terror it will cause. As long as I keep the secret of Moonlight Bay and live by the rules of the infected, I will most likely remain alive and free. On the other hand, if I attempt to tell the world, I will no doubt live out my days in a dark room in some subterranean chamber under the fields and hills of Fort Wyvern.

Indeed, Dad was afraid that they would take me, anyway, sooner or later, to imprison me and thus ensure a continuing supply of blood samples. I'll have to deal with that threat if and when it comes.

≈ ≈ ≈

Sunday morning and early afternoon, as the storm passed over Moonlight Bay, we slept – and of the four of us, only Sasha didn't wake from a nightmare.

After four hours in the sack, I went down to Sasha's kitchen and sat with the blinds drawn. For a while, in the dim light, I studied the words *Mystery Train* on my cap, wondering how they related to my mother's work. Although I couldn't guess their significance, I felt that Moonlight Bay isn't merely on a roller-coaster ride to

Hell, as Stevenson had claimed. We're on a journey to a mysterious destination that we can't entirely envision: maybe something wondrous – or maybe something far worse than the tortures of Hell.

Later, using a pen and tablet, I wrote by candlelight. I intend to record all that happens in the days that remain to me.

I don't expect ever to see this work published. Those who wish the truth of Wyvern to remain unrevealed will never permit me to spread the word. Anyway, Stevenson was right: It's too late to save the world. In fact, that's the same message Bobby's been giving me throughout most of our long friendship.

Although I don't write for publication anymore, it's important to have a record of this catastrophe. The world as we know it should not pass away without the explanation of its passing preserved for the future. We are an arrogant species, full of terrible potential, but we also have a great capacity for love, friendship, generosity, kindness, faith, hope, and joy. How we perished by our own hand may be more important than how we came into existence in the first place – which is a mystery that we will now never solve.

I might diligently record all that happens in Moonlight Bay and, by extension, in the rest of the world as the contamination spreads – but record it to no avail, because there might one day be no one left to read my words or no one capable of reading them. I'll take my chances. If I were a betting man, I'd bet that some species will arise from the chaos to replace us, to be masters of the earth as we were. Indeed, if I were a betting man, I'd put my money on the dogs.

~ ~ ~

Sunday night, the sky was as deep as the face of God, and the stars were as pure as tears. The four of us went to the beach. Fourteen-foot, fully macking, glassy monoliths pumped ceaselessly out of far Tahiti. It was epic. It was so *live*.

Author's Note

Moonlight Bay's radio station, KBAY, is entirely a fictional enterprise. The real KBAY is located in San Jose, California, and none of the employees of the Moonlight Bay station is based on any past or present employee of the Santa Jose station. These call letters were borrowed here for one reason: They're cool.

In chapter seventeen, Christopher Snow quotes a line from a poem by Louise Glück. The title of the poem is 'Lullaby,' and it appears in Ms. Glück's wonderful and moving *Ararat*.

Christopher Snow, Bobby Halloway, Sasha Goodall, and Orson are real. I have spent many months with them. I like their company, and I intend to spend a lot more time with them in the years to come.

—DK

Praise for FEAR NOTHING:

'This is a moral fable for the turn of the millennium, an engagingly written, hugely entertaining parable for our times. Just what I expected' *The Times*

'Fast and furious – like a hospital trolley on a toboggan run' *Mail on Sunday*

'Readers will be riveted to the narrative' *Publishers Weekly*

'Plausibly chilling . . . Koontz at his best' *Express on Sunday*

Praise for Dean Koontz:

'Tumbling, hallucinogenic prose . . . "Serious" writers might do well to examine his technique' *New York Times*

'Koontz has bridged the commercial gap between the occultism of Stephen King and the scientism of Michael Crichton' *Publishers Weekly*

'Masterfully styled, serious entertainment. These are Koontz's great years' *Kirkus Reviews*

'Koontz keeps up a breakneck pace, and provides spectacular set-pieces' *Locus*